Ephraim Clark was raised in the United States. After he obtained his undergraduate degree at the University of Notre Dame, his wanderlust itinerary took him from Latin America to the UK and Europe, where he earned his way as a karate instructor, nightclub bouncer, pop singer, and recording artist. He has post graduate degrees from the University of Madrid and the University of Paris, where he obtained his PhD in Financial Economics Summa cum Laude. As a full professor in finance, he has authored or coauthored nine books and over one hundred papers in top academic and professional journals. *Cult Stalker* is his second spy thriller. His first, *Requiem for Betrayal*, is an Amazon Best Seller and was a finalist in the Thriller category for the National Indie Excellence Awards. Visit www.ephraimauthor.com for more information and to join Ephraim Clark's reading club.

Also by Ephraim Clark

Requiem for Betrayal (2023)

CULT STALKER

EPHRAIM CLARK

GLASSSPIDERPUBLISHING

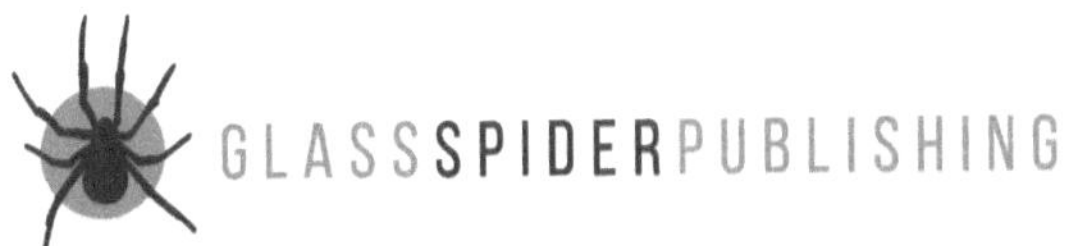

To my little sweetheart Maria.

Acknowledgments

I want to thank my wife, Maria, for all her patience and support; my little sister, Chrissie; my friends Konstantino Kassimatis and David Bernthal, for their many helpful suggestions on the text and plots; and Vince Font for his great editing.

Prologue: The Prophecy

There were four of them—four handmaidens. They were solemn and silent, their movements slow and deliberate, gestures befitting the sacred ceremony. They bathed her and washed her hair. Special attention was paid to her hands and feet. The Prophet was particularly attentive to hands and feet. Her hands and feet were cleansed, massaged, and anointed with the holy oil. Each nail was painted pearl-white. Her thick, auburn hair was brushed carefully to the side and placed delicately to tumble over her right shoulder. There would be no makeup. There would be no clothes. There would be no sandals or shoes. She would offer herself exposed, defenseless, and pure.

Through the bars in her cell, she could see the red ball of the sun setting on the sea. It drenched the beach in a fiery mist that sparkled in the sand. She loved this sight, her faithful evening companion ever since she was chosen for the Prophecy's highest honor. Tonight, she would receive that honor. It was a lifetime honor with a lifetime commitment. Tonight, she would be consecrated into the Prophet's personal harem. She hunched her shoulders and shivered at the thought.

The harem was the Prophecy's inner sanctum. It was located in a separate compound surrounded by a brick wall twelve feet high topped by concertina wire. Only the Prophet, the Prophecy's small circle of high priests, and their accomplices were allowed inside. Only the Prophet, the Prophecy's small circle of high priests, and their accomplices were allowed to exit. Once inside, the harem's honored members would dedicate their bodies, their souls, and their lives to God and the Prophet.

Her body was prepared. It was time to prepare her soul. She was ready for her communion. She knelt before her prayer post and folded her hands. The handmaidens chanted soft litanies to the Prophet and His Majesty. The Prophecy's Priest of Priests approached. In his hand was the sacred white pill that would transport her for the next twenty-four hours to a parallel reality, a reality of vivid colors and soothing sounds, a world of mystery and revelation. When she emerged, she would be a new person in a new life in selfless service to God and the Prophet.

She closed her eyes and opened her lips to receive the "Holy Communion." The Priest of Priests placed the lozenge on the extended tongue, raised his arms toward the heavens, and whispered, "Go to God." She bowed her head, buried her face in her hands. With the subtlest movements of tongue and teeth, she surreptitiously expelled the lozenge into her hands folded over her face.

This was the crucial moment when all could be lost. Discovery meant death—slow death, agonizing death, death meant to torture, death meant to punish, death meant to deter any and all who would defy the Prophet and his holy cult, the Prophecy. She placed her folded hands under her chin and rose solemnly to her feet. Head bowed, she turned and shuffled to the single bed in the corner of her cell. She lay down on her back with her arms at her sides, the lozenge held by the thumb in the palm of her hand. The eyes of the Priest of Priests followed her every move. She closed her eyes and pretended to embark on the voyage fueled by the explosive drug in the sacred white pill.

They left her alone and locked the door behind them. The countdown had begun. She had only a few precious minutes before they would return. Her heart was pounding. Her limbs were paralyzed, and she was choking with terror. She struggled to control the panic coursing through her trembling body and exploding in her brain. Her life depended on it. Heretics were executed in a sadistic month-long ritual of mutilation and torture. The slightest sound would bring her minders back to investigate.

She shifted her weight and arched her back in a contortion she hoped would resemble a drug-fueled reaction—if anyone was watching. She reached under the thin mattress of her bed and recovered the syringe and hypodermic needle she'd managed to conceal. She had been hiding it over the two weeks of her "purification" period in the cell. It was filled with the drug administered for purification or as a punishment for misbehavior. The drug was powerful. A single drop caused intense pain and a paralyzing death-like experience. A full dose was enough to kill a medium-sized man. She had decided after her first injection that she would never again misbehave.

She attached one end of a short string to a hair clip and the other end to the syringe on the hypodermic needle. She then used the clip to fasten the apparatus on the underside of the thick lock of hair flowing down her right shoulder. It would be invisible—at least she fervently hoped it would. She prayed it would.

They came for her and led her through the throng of chanting worshippers to the magnificent altar in the Prophecy's cathedral. Menacing shadows swayed over the flames of the ceremonial candles lining the walls. The air, heavy with incense and anticipation, electrified the atmosphere. Excited the congregation. Intensified the trance. Step by step to the cadence of a hundred chanting souls she shuffled toward her destiny. She showed no emotion. She offered no resistance. She forced herself into a beatific state of submission. One false step—one slight hesitation, one off-key glance—and it would be the beginning of the hell that would end her life.

The ceremony was solemn and elaborate. The Prophet looked on as the Priest of Priests anointed her naked body, exposed, defenseless, and pure. The Prophet suddenly rose from his throne. Caught off guard by the unexpected move, she blinked. The Priest of Priests stiffened and stared. He had felt it. Did he see it? He was a man of exceptional intuition. She didn't move. She couldn't move. She was paralyzed by fear. The Priest of Priests moved closer, but he wasn't sure. He raised his hand.

The Prophet's impatience saved her. He stepped forward and took her hand. The chanting ceased. The Priest of Priests stepped back. The Prophet blessed his subjects, turned, and led the newly anointed addition to his harem into his private chamber.

There would be five days of celebration. The Prophet would be the first. She would pass each successive day with a different high priest. The order was designated by their rank. At the end of the fifth day, she would be consigned to the harem.

She could not wait five days. She could not wait one day. She had to act now.

The doors closed onto the Prophet's private chamber. It was spacious and opulent. There was a canopied bed in the middle of the room. Crystal bed tables on ornate bronze stands bracketed the bed. The ceiling was mirrored. At the foot of the bed, four steps led to a round, sunken bath the size of a small swimming pool. A large bathroom of pearl-white marble opened up behind the bed.

The only other furniture stood in the far corner. It was comprised of a glass table on crossed glass legs adorned with two ebony black chairs.

On first inspection, she didn't see any entrance or exit other than the one leading to the altar. This was bad news because there was always someone watching the altar. She was confident, however, that there had to be another exit. Someone as crafty as the Prophet would never allow himself to be cornered in this room like a stupid rat.

The Prophet led her gently to the bed and had her lie down. He circled the bed and admired his prey. The hands, the breasts, the waist, the pubis. Everything was perfect. He stopped at the feet and stared. She counted ten Mississippis. Something was amiss. The Prophet's legendary sixth sense. Was he suspicious? She willed back the urge to sneak a quick peek. Discovery meant detention and a long, slow death.

The Prophet studied the perfect body. He took the right foot in his hand and began to examine it. He ran his forefinger around the elegant outline. Replaced it gently on the bed. He took up the left foot and examined it. His fingers caressed the suntanned toes and perfectly manicured, pearl-white toenails. He closed his eyes and let his tunic fall to the floor.

The first thing she noticed was his scrawny legs. They didn't go with the rest of his body. His torso was wide-shouldered with muscular pecs and abs. His beard was thick, black, and well-trimmed. His hair was long and thick and wavy. When he smiled through his sensuous lips, his white teeth sparkled in the overhead light and his eyes gleamed green. It was the eyes that had first attracted her. She thought they were inspiring. Now the only thing they inspired was fear and hate.

He was excited. She knew from the first time she met him he

was interested. She was flattered. That was her first mistake. Her second mistake was to cultivate that interest. Her third mistake was when she eavesdropped on an explosive conversation between the Prophet and a mysterious, peculiar-looking middle-aged female FBI agent. She couldn't believe it! They were discussing how much money they were making from prostitution, drug dealing, and human trafficking. How their political cover was in jeopardy. Which clients they would have to sacrifice. And who would be the "fall guy" to justify the protection they were getting from the FBI. In fact, overhearing the conversation wasn't really a mistake. It was bad luck—bad luck she heard the conversation, and bad luck the conversation was so explosive. The mistake was that she let herself get caught.

The Prophet pulled her to her knees, then lay down beside her and had her straddle him. "Now you will ride the beast."

She started to ride. What he called "the beast" was surprisingly tame at first. She knew that a tame beast was not what she needed. She needed to drive the beast wild, and she was ready to use everything in her playbook to make sure this happened.

The beast began to respond. He came to life and started to react. The Prophet closed his eyes. She reached into her hair and pulled out the syringe.

He opened his eyes when she began her thrust. He was too slow. She hit the plunger when the needle hit his neck. He thrust forward and tried to scream. She covered his mouth. The drug washed through his body, which was paralyzed by intense pain, as he passed through the portal of his experience with death.

Strangely enough, the wild beast lived on, which caused her some difficulty when she tried to dismount. This worried her a little, but she didn't have time to dwell on it. She had to find the secret exit, if there was one, and put as much distance between herself and the Prophecy as she could.

She grabbed the Prophet's tunic and stepped into it. Too big. She hiked it up and tied it at the waist, giving her legs the freedom of movement she would need when she started to run. His sandals were a better fit. A quick reconnoiter of the room told her the secret exit must be in the back where the bathroom was located. She heard voices and movement coming from the cathedral. She froze. The voices drifted away. False alarm.

She raced to the bathroom. There was nothing, just the toilet and a ceiling-to-floor medicine closet. Panic was pounding. She was hyperventilating. She had to stay cool. She had to think.

A shadow fell across the door. Startled, she whipped around. There in the doorway stood the Prophet, buck naked with his arms outstretched, his eyes riveted on her sandaled feet. He reached for her. She dodged. He clutched her shoulder. She twisted free and seized the metal hand mirror from the washbasin. He lurched forward on unsteady legs. She pivoted right and took a full swing back to the left. The metal mirror crashed against the side of his head. He stumbled. She swung back to the right and caught the back of his head. He crumbled face-first onto the marble floor. A thin line of bright-red blood oozed through his hair and trickled down his neck.

Too noisy. Someone outside the room was calling to the Prophet. There was no time left. She returned to the medicine closet. Fumbled around. Found a hand grip. Pushed. Nothing happened. Pulled. Nothing. Jerked to the right. There was a click. Pulled. Felt something give way. Pulled again, harder. The bottom half of the medicine closet wall swung open. She fell to her knees and there, through the small doorway, she saw the highway that ran behind the compound.

She slipped outside, closed the door carefully behind her, and dashed for the highway. The compound was a long way from no-where, and escape routes were few. The most obvious to her were also obvious to her pursuers. Remaining on the road was not an option. She ran for the mountains and started to climb.

1: The Dilemma

Brad James sat in a café on the Place d'Italie. This would be the next-to-last control point. He scanned the street.

First came a young couple with a walkie-talkie on a motor scooter. They dismounted and stared up the Boulevard de l'Hôpital. Next came a dark Renault with two middle-aged men inside. One held a walkie-talkie. It double parked in the alleyway next to Brad's café.

A well-dressed, middle-aged woman stationed herself on the corner of the Boulevard Vincent Auriol. She also held a walkie-talkie. A scruffy-looking Mediterranean twenty-something dude with a walkie-talkie came down and stopped at the corner of the Avenue d'Italie. All eyes were on the Boulevard de l'Hôpital.

Brad spotted him. He came off the Boulevard de l'Hôpital and headed around the Place. Gary Richards was the CIA station chief. He was six feet five inches tall and two hundred and twenty-five pounds heavy with wide shoulders, huge hands, enormous feet, and a mop of bright-red hair. He looked like a jock, he walked like a jock, and he *was* a jock—all-state basketball in high school and first-string forward for the University of Dayton in college.

Brad identified at least four other surveillants trailing along behind Gary. As he came by the café, Brad gave him the still-being-followed signal.

Gary headed down the Avenue d'Italie. The couple cranked up the motor scooter and drove down the Avenue d'Italie ahead of him. The Renault didn't move. The surveillants on foot scurried around changing position, those in front dropping back and those in back getting ahead.

Brad was in a hurry to get to the last control point at Denfert-Rochereau ahead of Gary.

It happened in a flash. The woman was old, limping out of the bank with a wooden cane. Brad was moving too fast. It was a glancing blow, but it took her down. He stopped, helped her to her feet. She was shaken up, but apparently not hurt.

"My purse. My purse." She was crying. "I cashed my check. My pension was in my purse."

"I'm so sorry." Brad lifted her onto her feet, scooped up her purse, and guided her to a terrace table at the café. The recovery of her purse and pension calmed her down. She was trembling. He sat with her to make sure she was okay. She stopped shaking. "How do you feel?"

"I'm fine, fine. No broken bones. Don't worry, young man, all is well. It's the excitement."

He ordered her a tea with milk and glanced at his watch. Way behind time. He had to move it, but he was not about to leave until he was sure she was okay. She squeezed his hand. Graced him with a grandmotherly smile. "I'm fine now. Thank you so much for your kindness." Brad paid the waiter, gave her a goodbye hug, and hustled off to Denfert-Rochereau.

Gary slipped into a high-rise two blocks down from Place d'Italie. He took the elevator to the fifth floor, exited, and hurried down the stairs to the underground parking area.

A young man in a leather jacket waved from the driver's seat in a dark Peugeot parked by the exit. Gary crawled into the backseat, lay down as best he could, and covered himself with a blanket. After a roundabout drive through the Latin Quarter, Gary slipped out of the car at the corner of Raspail and Montparnasse where he entered the Metro Vavin.

Brad was just in time to catch Gary as he exited the metro at Denfert-Rochereau. A full head taller than anybody else with his bright-red hair gleaming in the sun, he was hard to miss. Brad took the opposite side of the street and walked toward him, checking for surveillance.

Gary passed by and took a seat at the café terrace across from the entrance to the *Catacombes*. After five long minutes, there was no movement. No surveillance. Brad stepped forward and nodded. The meeting was on.

They had been working together since 1969 when Brad rolled into Paris, fresh from a master's degree from the University of Madrid, on his vintage, vertical, single 220cc Indian Arrow. He still had the fine, not-quite-effeminate features that went well with the six-foot-two-inch frame and one hundred seventy-six pounds of long, rangy muscles rippling beneath his tight T-shirts. When he wasn't in the recording studio, hosting his dinner show at the Barbary Coast Saloon, or working out at the dojo, Brad was part-time undercover on special ops for the CIA.

This meeting at a café was out of the ordinary. They did their regular meetings at the Barbary Coast Saloon where Gary was a regular customer. Otherwise, for more in-depth discussions, they met at designated safe houses. All this cloak-and-dagger stuff flagged Brad's curiosity.

Gary was more distracted than usual, casting around, picking at a fingernail. "Thanks for coming on such short notice. Sorry about all the interference. The French are on a full-court press. There's usually only a five-man team on me that drops off after half an hour."

Brad was impressed by the manpower the French had employed to tail Gary. "Must have been at least twenty or thirty surveillants. I made fifteen of them myself and saw at least five others peel off when they got in too close. They had cars and bikes and walkie-talkies. It took two hours and the old garage trick to get free."

"They're on their home turf, Brad. They have all the manpower they need. We put up some manpower ourselves, including you and the chauffeur, not to mention two hours of me stomping around town trying to ditch their manpower."

"Okay. What's up?"

Gary's smile faded. He folded his hands under his chin. "We've got a five-alarm election alert."

That was a heavy-duty problem description. Gary wasn't addicted to overkill. "Is that why the surveillance was so heavy?"

"Yes, it is." Gary stroked his chin, expressionless. "You know President Pompidou died?"

"Of course."

"Well, it looks like the Left has a strong chance of winning the election to replace him. A victory by the Left would be a diplomatic catastrophe. It would upset the balance of power in Europe. We are not doing our part over here to stop that from happening. Watergate is killing us. It has crowded everything else off the table. The administration and Washington are focused on Nixon and the break-in coverup. They have no time for anything else. We're basically on our own over here, flying blind. The embassy is in turmoil."

Brad had read the press, but he figured it was just a bunch of journalists conjuring up self-serving narratives. He couldn't see the French switching into the Soviet camp. "Got a hard time believing the Left really stands a chance."

"I wish, Brad. I wish. France is vulnerable. Take a look at the headline."

There it was in black and white in the *Herald Tribune. Oil Crisis Causes Recession: Record Unemployment and Inflation.*

Gary went on. "France's 'social contract' is under attack, and the Left sees their chance. The Socialist Party, the French Communist Party, and the Movement of Left Radicals agreed on a *Programme Commun* in 1972. They know the word 'communism' scares off the voting public, so they decided to rally around the Socialist Party leader, François Mitterand. Mitterrand is a credible candidate. He succeeded in forcing a second ballot in 1965 against de Gaulle."

"So they've really got a chance."

"For the first time since the war, they have an excellent chance. It doesn't help that there is total confusion in the *majorité présidentielle.* They have no natural candidate. The prime minister, Pierre Messmer, said he'd run if he was the only candidate of the majority. That didn't happen, and he withdrew. Read the next-to-last paragraph in the article."

Four other men have declared their willingness to run: former Gaullist prime minister, Jacques Chaban-Delmas; the chairman of the French National Assembly, Edgar Faure; the former Craftsmen and Shopkeepers minister representing the ultra-conservative wing of the Gaulist Party, Jean Royer; and finally, the economy minister and leader of the Independent Republicans, Valery Giscard d'Estaing.

"We hope that Faure and Royer will withdraw and leave the real competition on the Right to Chaban-Delmas and Giscard d'Estaing. You can imagine all the urgent intelligence gathering and analysis going on," Gary said.

Brad deadpanned him. "So you want me to sort this all out for you?"

"Very funny. I don't think even you could do it. I *am* going to ask you to help, though. Something urgent has come up, something that could really upset the applecart." Gary cocked his head, leaned in, and lowered his voice. "Several months ago, I received an intel briefing on a potential nexus of terrorists, drug cartels, and religious cults. The California desk of the FBI broke up a drug-dealing cult last year. Most of the members died in a mass suicide. According to testimony from the few stragglers that managed to escape, besides drug dealing, the cult was into providing logistical support and safe spaces for terrorist groups."

He sat back and took a breath. Brad lit up a Gitane but didn't react.

"So, anyway," Gary continued, "the Company red-flagged it to me because the rumor was that the hierarchy of the cult escaped and set up shop in France. Yesterday, I received urgent intel on an imminent terrorist attack in Paris. One and one makes two. We're taking it seriously. Can you imagine how a terrorist attack could upset the election? We can't let that happen. I wanted to run it by you."

"Why not just turn this over to the French? They have the resources."

"You're right. Maybe I should turn it over to the French. But, as far as we know, everybody involved is American. American terrorists interfering in the French elections is a surefire diplomatic snafu and surefire fodder for Leftist propaganda. Until we know more about the who and the what, we have to play it close to the vest. This is top secret. That's why I'm coming to you. Just so you know, this has been cleared at the highest level." Gary let Brad think that over while he signaled the waiter and ordered.

"This mission includes some troublesome complications," Gary rolled on. "The agent I assigned to the case who reported the terrorist intel was arrested on drug charges before I could meet with her to get the details. Cops picked her up, raided her apartment. Found needles, all kinds of drugs, and drug paraphernalia spread all over the place. It's serious. She's in *detention provisoire*—provisional custody. That means the French and the DEA are going to be all over this. They'll be focusing on the drug angle. They will be getting in our way, your way. Here's the monkey wrench. You could be forced to testify if the DEA or the French get enough proof to prosecute somebody."

Brad's eyes flashed through several cycles of potential scenarios, all of them bad. "Public testimony is not part of my deal. I've got too much on the line—my record contract, my dinner show, my life in France. I'll be at the mercy of politicians, lawyers, and bureaucrats. Not to mention the risk of reprisals."

"That's true, but no man is an island. You're a part of society. Think it over."

"What is this DEA, anyway?"

"The Drug Enforcement Administration. They merged the Bureau of Narcotics and Dangerous Drugs and the Office of Drug Abuse Law Enforcement last July. It's a new agency. It has no clearly defined territory, and it's invading our turf. There's a DEA official for Paris, and he's in charge of everything involving drugs. *Everything.* So, in spite of my arguments to the contrary, he was notified when they busted my agent. The guy's an eager beaver and a loose cannon. He is not on our team. We can't let him know anything about what's going on, especially that the person they arrested is working for me."

"Hey, Gary, isn't the DEA an ally?"

"It's supposed to be, Brad, but beware of how you choose your allies. They can turn out to be your worst enemies. The French say, *'L'habit ne fait pas le moine'*—wearing monk clothes doesn't make you a monk. In other words, bad people can disguise themselves. They hide in religious institutions like the Salvation Army, secular institutions like the Boy Scouts, and government institutions like the FBI or, in our case, the DEA. It happens all the time. And when bad people take over good institutions, the good institutions can do a lot of harm."

"Can't argue with that. So, who's your agent who got arrested?"

Gary looked down and flicked an imaginary crumb off his sleeve. "Her name is Jeanie Jones. I think you know her."

Brad snapped to attention. "That's a shocker. Never would have guessed she was working for the Company. She comes by the Barbary all the time. She doesn't drink alcohol and doesn't do drugs—at least that's what she always said."

"I can confirm she neither drinks nor does drugs. I have the blood tests to prove it."

The waiter came over, and they ordered more espressos. Brad dug into his white leather pouch and pulled out his Gitanes sans filtre and a silver Zippo. He lit up and took a deep drag, then let the smoke filter slowly between his lips while he thought over what Gary had just told him.

Gary pointed his finger. "This is important. I think the drug charges might be related to the deaths of three American Children of God cult members she was close to who perished in suspicious, drug-related circumstances."

Brad was having trouble digesting the info. "I don't get it."

"Jeanie had contacts in the music business. You know that. She managed the Children of God choir. Three members of this choir were also part of the Children of God hierarchy. As they got to know and trust her, their tongues loosened up. They became a fountain of information on what their cult was up to. Then, suddenly, it ended. All three died from drug overdoses over a six-week period. The circumstances were suspicious, to say the least. One on a deserted riverbank. Another in a raunchy hotel room registered in a fake name. The third was in the toilets of a strip club in Pigalle. All three were important members of the Children of God. All three had been members of another sect in California before coming to France. They all died from the same unique drug cocktail. Medical expert says a cocktail like that would cause intense physical pain and mental anguish. The postmortem facial expressions confirm that. 'Hideous' was the word he used. Taken together, these deaths look like serial executions. I'm afraid the cult found out they were dealing info to my agent and assassinated them. If that's true, her life is in danger as well."

Brad finished off his coffee. "Okay, what's the bottom line?"

"The bottom line is that we have three suspicious deaths and an agent arrested on a drug charge. Plus, we have a terrorist threat linked to an American cult coming down the pike in the middle of the French presidential election. Finally, we have what is potentially the most serious problem of all." Gary hesitated for dramatic effect. Closed his eyes. Nodded his head. "Jeanie Jones."

Now it was Brad's turn to be incredulous. "What do you mean, Jeanie Jones? She's the inside man."

Gary nodded, looked around. Dropped his voice and leaned forward. Brad was surprised by the dark pouches under his eyes and the heavy lines from the sides of his nose to the corners of his mouth. He looked tired and worried. "Jeanie Jones died in a car accident ten years ago."

Brad's body didn't move, but his mind was dancing a gig. "So, Jeanie Jones is not Jeanie Jones. Man! How'd you miss that one?"

"Preliminary background check came in clean. She was a perfect fit. Right age. Right look. Right sex. Law degree and experience in law enforcement. We were in a world of need. There was no real confidential information involved. She passed the lie detector test, and Langley gave me the green light. Standard procedure. The deep background check looked like a mere formality. Her cover was almost perfect."

"When did you find out?"

"Yesterday, the day she got arrested."

"Now I understand the big hurry. So, who is she?"

"We don't know. We're working on it. That's what makes your investigation all the more urgent, as well as all the more complicated. We don't have much time." Gary summoned up his most erstwhile expression, eyes open wide, sucking air through his teeth. "Can I count on you, Brad?"

Brad rocked back and forth, deep in thought. "I dunno. For me, it's a 'no.' The whole thing stinks to high heaven. Jesus freaks, serial murders, drugs, the DEA and potential public testimony, unverified intel from an unidentified agent. It looks like a perfect concoction for a colossal clusterfuck. I'm also tied up on a case with Latorre Legal on a missing person."

It was Gary's turn to be surprised. "Who is it?"

"An all-American girl. Pretty, popular, good student, outstanding athlete, outdoor enthusiast. Name is Sally Ann Hastings. Had a major life crisis, joined a hippie cult in California, and dropped off the radar a couple of years ago. Cut off all contact with her family and friends back home. It looks like she changed her name and got a new identity. Last sighted in Paris. Big reward if we find her."

Gary tapped his knuckles lightly on the table. "Okay, I understand. Take some time to think it over. But not too much. This is urgent. I really need your help on this. One last thing. I have to warn you. You already have a problem with the DEA."

27

2: The Warning

B rad leaned back and shook his head. "What do you mean the DEA has fingered me as a person of interest in Jeanie Jones's drug affair?"

This was a giant irritation. Connections like this endangered his ongoing situation in France. He one hundred percent did not want to get involved with the DEA.

"The DEA guy went through the information the French gave us," Gary told him. "He noticed you were identified as a fellow American she knew well and that, like her, you were in the music business. Asked me if I knew you. What could I say?"

"You didn't rat me out?"

"He has no idea you're on the payroll. Jeanie, either, for that matter. He's just interested in Jeanie's involvement in cults and drugs. That's why he wanted to talk to you."

"We weren't close friends, you know."

Gary was apologetic. "I know. I told you that the DEA would be getting in our way. It's a new agency attempting to get some traction. We will have to live with it for the moment. Anyway, I told him to come by. I have to at least pretend to cooperate. He should be here in fifteen or twenty minutes. His name is Brandon Butler."

Brad closed his eyes to think it over. "You know what has me worried? If Brandon Butler fingered me on info from the French, the French must have fingered me as well. In the worst-case scenario, the French will have their eye on me. Gary, I don't see myself anywhere near the Jeanie case."

"Calm down. Brandon's under pressure from the home office to get results, establish the DEA's authority. The French frown on drugs in general, and especially on Americans involved in drugs. You'll have to be careful and play it by ear. Let's see what he says."

"Do you see any link between Jeanie Jones's arrest and the terrorist threat?"

"As far as I'm concerned, the raid, the bust, the *detention provisoire*—it's all suspicious. Jeanie was definitely not involved with drugs. Like I said, I've got the blood tests to prove it. Does it have something to do with the terror threat? I don't know. In any case, Jeanie's intel on the terrorist threat coincides with the info from the FBI. Terror is our immediate concern. By the way, this info is top secret. Nobody can know. Nobody at all. Especially not Brandon Butler."

"Tell me more about Brandon."

"Let's just say he's a former FBI man with all the FBI baggage. You know what I mean. He's a political animal from J. Edgar's gigantic political machine. We know these guys and we're very, very wary."

The waiter came with the espressos. As usual, when he was under pressure, Gary took two cubes of sugar from his saucer. He put one into his cup. The other he dipped into the coffee and ate like candy. Brad took his coffee down in one gulp. He took a long look around the room. A beautifully tailored navy-blue cashmere sports coat on a medium-sized man standing at the end of the bar caught his eye. The fitted gray worsted pants, black, soft leather loafers, and carefully coiffed black hair completed the American-style picture.

"Does Brandon have slicked-back, black hair and dresses like a movie star?"

"Yeah, don't tell me you know him?"

"No, but I think he's standing over at the far end of the bar. Don't turn around. Let's see what he's up to."

"Okay. He's early. I don't like that. Remember, Brandon is not on our team. He stays out of the loop. This is top priority."

When Brad checked out the bar again, Brandon had disappeared. Finally, Brad spotted him coming down the Avenue du Général Leclerc. He must have slipped out of the café and circled back.

In he came. He pretended to look around for Gary. Pretended to find him. With an ostentatious sweep of his hands, he slicked his hair back. Came over. "Running late. Sorry. Had some slow connections in the metro."

Brad filed that away for future reference. Gary played it cool. "Brandon, meet Brad."

"Nice to meet you, Brad."

"My pleasure."

Brandon not only dressed like a movie star. He looked like one. Thick, black hair slicked straight back. Big brown eyes, thin nose, white teeth, strong jaw. He was a young version of Tyrone Power, but just a little too short. They shook hands and Brandon took over. No preamble. Straight to the point. "So, Brad, Gary tells me you're friendly with Jeanie Jones."

His voice was strong and deep. He leaned back in his chair and peered down his nose. He held the pose just long enough for the desired effect, then leaned forward and allowed himself a condescending smile. Brad didn't move. His expression didn't change. Brandon was oozing confidence, completely convinced of his charisma, authority, and charm. Undeterred by Brad's failure to react, he cocked his head and raised his eyebrows in a silent question. Still no reaction from Brad. An uncomfortable silence. Brad was having trouble appreciating Brandon's style, even if he was an officer of an important government agency.

Brad opted for a charm offensive. Might as well have an open mind and give the guy a chance. "Before we get into that, Brandon, let's get you a seat and something to drink. Gary tells me you were an FBI man."

"Yeah, worked out of San Francisco. Narcotics division."

"Sounds exciting. How did you end up at the DEA?"

The waiter came over. *"Monsieur?"*

Brandon didn't miss a beat. In fluent but heavily accented French, he ordered. "I'll have an espresso with a drop of milk, please." To Gary and Brad, *"Voulez-vous autre chose?"* Both declined. Then back to Brad. "It's a long story. In a nutshell, when the DEA was created, they needed experienced agents with the right background. I had the experience and the background. Was ready to travel. Got a raise and a good promotion to go along with it." His smile was beautiful. He was really strutting his stuff.

Brad nodded his head. "Smart move."

"So here I am in Paris, Brad, and I need your help." He slicked his hair back as he spoke.

Brad was smiling, but he was feeling very negative. Brandon was his own worst enemy. The words, the tone, the delivery, the condescending smile. It all just rubbed Brad the wrong way—in spades, diamonds, hearts, and clubs. "Can't imagine what a guy like me could do for somebody like you."

Brandon's smile faded. He leaned toward Brad. He was intense. His eyebrows were arching. His dark eyes locked into Brad's. "Brad, I need your cooperation, and I am asking you officially to cooperate with me on this. You do know you could be in real trouble if I thought you were less than forthcoming."

Brandon was really overdoing it. He had absolutely no authority in France. He knew it. Gary knew it. Brad knew it. It would be easy to humiliate Brandon and challenge him directly. Brad contemplated the handsome face of this conceited creature seated in front of him. He was tempted to make a smart remark but reconsidered. Nothing to be gained from confrontation. Anyway, the guy was a government agent, and bullying was not Brad's thing. He opted for subtlety and some undercover humor. He sat back and feigned shock. Lightened up the situation.

"Thanks for cluing me in, Brandon. Heavy stuff. No problem. Count me in. I'm always ready and willing to help out the FBI."

It worked. Brandon blinked and cleared his throat. "It's the DEA, Brad, not the FBI. I am DEA station chief, and I would really appreciate your help. You did know Jeanie, didn't you?"

For the umpteenth time, Brandon took his head in his hands and slicked back his hair. Brad recognized it as a self-conscious nervous tic that got more irritating every time he did it.

"Yeah, I knew her. But she wasn't somebody I hung out with. She was like an *empresario*. You know, like a talent manager. She'd bring some of her clients by to sing in my show. We'd sometimes cross paths at the radio stations, television shows, and recording studios."

Brandon was warming up. "Look, Brad, Jeanie was known to be close to three Americans who died from an overdose in the Paris region over the last few months. Now she's been arrested for possession. Could be a coincidence, but I doubt it. I think there's a link. I think you can help us out here, and I'd appreciate it if you would. Okay?"

Brad looked him in the eye and tapped the table. "You can count on me."

Brandon was not satisfied, but he could see that was all he would get for the moment. "Thanks, Brad. I'm sorry, but I have another appointment. I know where to find you if anything comes up. If you think of anything, you can get a hold of me through Gary. We've got to get to the bottom of what's going on with Jeanie."

"No problem, Brandon. Drop by my show some night if you want to get in touch. See ya."

Brandon hesitated a short second, then turned back. There was a touch of triumph in his tone. "By the way, I'm going to identify you to the French as a person of interest. They'll be in touch."

Brad sucked it in and prepared for the worst.

3: Gangbangers and the Vigilante

PARIS, GARE SAINT-LAZARE, APRIL 1974

The Gare Saint-Lazare metro station is popular with buskers. It's in an affluent part of Paris, it's always crowded, and the acoustics are good. A mediocre musician singing a few well-known songs can make a hundred francs in an hour on a good day. An excellent musician can draw a crowd and make much more in twenty minutes. The girl on the guitar was good, but it was the singer that drew the crowd. His voice was round and full. It soared on the high notes.

Brad was in luck. He recognized the singer as the frontman for the Children of God choir, the cult that Gary was on about. The guy had just finished a rendition of "Suspicious Minds" worthy of Elvis himself. The girl stayed in the background. Entranced, she swayed and she played, chin in the air, eyes on the ceiling. The guy stood leaning slightly forward with one foot in front of the other in a modest Elvis pose. His eye contact with the crowd was like a magnet drawing them in. Most people in the audience threw a few francs into the black beret positioned on the floor in front of the two buskers. Some threw in bills. They did four songs before the crowd broke up, leaving close to a hundred francs in the black beret that served as a cash register.

Brad chipped in a fiver and was about to move on to his recording session when he spotted a couple of raunchy-looking street toughs eyeing the black beret with all the money. A quick check of the station revealed a third guy hanging out by the exit on lookout duty. Tough Number One was between twenty and twenty-five. His hair was short and black and wiry. His body was long and lean and sinewy. Tough Number Two was a taller and heavier version of Tough Number One. Rolling their torsos from side to side, they ghetto-swaggered over to the two buskers.

Brad backed off to the side. He had plenty of time to get to the Studio Davout.

Tough Number One went for the female. She was putting the guitar back in the case. He patted the guitar and smiled through a row of brown teeth. "You play good." He had a thick jive accent from the suburbs of Paris.

Taken by surprise and suddenly on her guard, the girl's smile failed her. "Thanks." She pulled the guitar away and retreated to where her partner was counting the money. The young singer felt the danger. He saw Tough Number Two's concupiscent fixation on the money in his hand. He quickly stuffed it in his pocket.

Tough Number One made a big show of ogling the girl's bust line highlighted by the almost transparent, white cotton dress. Still sneering, he switched his attention to the singer. "You didn't get permission to sing here."

The singer frowned and adopted a concerned expression. "We didn't know that was necessary."

Tough Number Two moved in closer to the singer. The singer's expression didn't change. His eyes were clear blue and open wide, like he was having a vision. Tough Number One's sneer turned sarcastic. "Not an excuse." The singer showed no sign of being intimidated. He looked thoughtfully at Tough Number One, nodded his head, and produced a broad, beatific smile. Brad noticed the singer was a nice-looking young man, five-ten, maybe six feet tall, a hundred and sixty-five to a hundred and seventy pounds. He had a short, light-brown beard, the same color as his medium-length hair. The beard hid most of a nasty-looking scar on the left side of his square jaw.

The girl picked up her guitar case. Her eyes were brown, round, and open wide, like she, too, was having a vision. Contrary to the singer, her smile was more like a painful grimace than a friendly social message. "Come on, Zebulon, we have to go."

Tough Number One grabbed her arm. "Hold it, *chérie*. First, you got some bills to pay." He smirked at the singer. "Zebulon. That's a Jew name."

The girl jerked her arm away and stepped back. She was close to tears. The singer's beatific expression didn't change. He spoke softly. "Zebulon is a biblical name."

"Well, Zebulon from the Bible, you're gonna have to pay for your permit."

Zebulon touched the scar on his jaw, his expression changed only by some tightness in the eyes. He remained silent.

"That'll be a hundred francs."

Zebulon tensed up. His eyes clouded over. He was blinking fast, wrestling with his predicament. The tough guys moved in closer. Zebulon looked to the left, then to the right, shook his head, made his decision, and relaxed. He reached into his pocket and pulled out a handful of notes and coins that he handed over to Tough Number One. Tough Number One made a show of counting the cash. Rush hour was over, but there was still a steady stream of commuters passing through the station. Few, if any, noticed the shakedown drama going on in the corner. Tough Number One was enjoying it.

Zebulon signaled to the girl and they turned to leave. Tough Number Two moved to cut off their escape route. He had thick, bushy eyebrows flaked with dandruff and black, hooded eyes. He was a study in cruelty just itching for a reason to demolish Zebulon. Zebulon's expression didn't change, but his left eye began twitching.

"Sorry, Zebulon from the Bible, the fine is a hundred francs, not ninety-nine. You'll have to put up a guarantee for the shortfall." He made a big show of looking around for something that could serve as a guarantee and pretended to discover the girl's guitar. He pursed his lips and nodded his head approvingly. "Hey, what about this? This could be worth something. It really could. Okay, we'll just take this guitar as a guarantee."

The girl winced and gripped the guitar with both hands to her chest. Her guitar was an expensive Gibson worth at least ten thousand francs. For the first time, Zebulon let his expression slip. Brad could feel his fury. The corner of his mouth started to twitch. He bowed his head and clasped his hands. When he looked up, he was still in control, barely. "Wait a minute. That guitar's worth a lot of money. We can't let you have that." His voice was pitched a little higher and thinner. He was excited and struggling to keep himself under control.

Tough Number One reached slowly into the inside pocket of his black leather jacket and produced a switchblade. He held it in front of Zebulon's thin nose and flipped it open. "You wanna argue about it?"

By this time, the group had moved from the station's main hallway into an infrequently used exit that opened onto a side street.

Zebulon saw the writing on the wall. He didn't like the text, but he was going to have to accept it. His shoulders fell and he stared at his sandaled feet. He turned to the girl. "Give him the guitar, Sarah."

She had read the same words on the same wall. With tears in her eyes, she handed the guitar over to Tough Number Two.

The whole scene hadn't lasted more than three minutes. Brad knew he should mind his own business. Not his problem. Good Samaritans are never appreciated, and they always cause problems. For themselves. Still, there was something in his psychological DNA, some kind of a mind-blowing congenital defect that made it impossible for him to ignore situations like this. It had cost him dearly in high school and college and should have cured him. It didn't. It only made him cynical and rebellious and ever more determined to insulate himself from the nefarious effects of human nature and the power structures that exploited it. Of course, he was too realistic to entertain the childish notion of withdrawal from mainstream society. Mainstream society offered too many things he loved like wine, women, and song, and too many things he needed like doctors, food, and shelter. His solution was to develop the physical and mental potential from the good hand he was dealt at birth. He had decided to dance around the edges of mainstream society, close enough to benefit from the advantages, but far enough to avoid the disadvantages. Stay independent and detached. Sometimes, this philosophy was simply impossible. He just could not mind his own business and let these raunchy sewer shits get away with bullying and robbing these two peace-and-love Jesus-freak buskers.

He verified that the lookout, Tough Number Three, was still in position at the other end of the hallway, and made his move. Two steps forward left him blocking the entrance to the exit. "Excuse me, gentlemen. We have a problem."

Tough Number One froze in place and studied the floor in front of him for five long seconds, irritation oozing from his pores. He nodded his head knowingly and turned slowly toward the source of this annoying interference. He flashed his switchblade. "Butt out, buddy." It was a hiss.

Brad kept a respectable distance between himself and the two toughs. "Can't do it. You're gonna have to return their money and the guitar."

Tough Number One was an experienced street fighter. Hesitation was not an option. He struck with a slash to the arm and tried to follow it with a headbutt. Brad caught the slashing wrist in his right hand and used Number One's forward momentum to propel him toward the corner of the exit wall. With his left hand, he gripped the elbow and smashed Number One's forearm against the edge of the wall.

The middle of the forearm, held by the wrist and elbow, powered by the momentum of Number One's body and Brad's weight, snapped like a dry twig. Because of the tearing of the muscles and ligaments, it made a mushy sound when it snapped. Number One fainted before he could scream.

Number Two bull-charged. Brad sidestepped and pushed him forward toward the exit steps. Before Number Two could regain his balance, Brad grabbed his wiry hair and smashed his face against the edge of a step. His body went limp. Brad smashed it again as a bonus and a guarantee that he was out. You can never be too careful.

Zebulon and Sarah stood there. Sarah was terrified. Zebulon was relieved.

Brad stepped into the hallway and saw Number Three on his way to see what was happening. At the exit, he saw his broken buddies slumped on the steps. Brad stepped behind him to shut off a retreat down the hallway, but the guy was not thinking of retreating. He pulled a knife and went for Brad.

Brad was faster. A front kick took the guy down. His knife slid across the floor. Brad stomped his ankle, roundhoused him to the ribs, grabbed him by the collar, and bum-rushed him headfirst into the wall. There was a loud crack when his skull encountered the tiled wall. Tough Number Three dropped chin-first onto the cement floor. Sarah wisely scooped up the knife. Zebulon helped Brad drag the guy to the steps.

Zebulon and Sarah had seen enough. They were aching to leave. Brad asked them to wait. "We have some unfinished business."

The three toughs came to their senses. They were sprawled out on the cold metro steps, bruised, bleeding, badly hurt, and suffering. Several commuters had come by the exit, but when they smelled trouble, they scurried off. There were no cameras, so Brad felt secure for at least the next few minutes.

"You gentlemen are trespassing. The fine for that is one hundred francs. There is a two-hundred franc fine for misrepresenting yourselves. The fine for attempted guitar robbery is seventy francs, and there is a three-hundred-franc penalty for pissing me off. Empty your pockets, gentlemen."

Tough Number One was hurt. He was beaten. But his rage was stronger than his smarts. "Fuck you, asshole. You can't do that."

Brad didn't argue. He gently took Number One by his broken arm and began to study it. Seconds ticked by. Number One began to perspire. The loudspeaker announced delays on line number three. Brad pursed his lips and nodded his head like he had come to a difficult decision. He gave the tortured limb a sharp shake. Once. Pain trumped rage. Number One screamed. Beads of sweat dripped from his upper lip. He began to moan. Brad smacked him in the head. "Not negotiable. Empty your pockets."

They obeyed. Some small change, three wallets, and eight hundred francs. It looked like their metro activities of theft and extortion were a lucrative pursuit. Brad returned ninety-nine francs to Zebulon and pocketed the rest along with the identity papers of the gangbangers.

"I have your identity cards, telephone numbers, and the addresses of your friends and relatives. I know where to find you. These buskers are my friends. Please remember that and respect them. And please don't make me come looking for you. Do you understand what I'm saying?"

The toughs were in bad shape. They needed a doctor. They were in a hurry to get away. They understood.

Brad turned to Zebulon. "No need to mention this episode to anybody."

"Thanks, man. I don't know what we would've done if we lost the guitar. What's your name?"

"My name is Brad, Brad James."

"Nice to meet you, Brad. I'm Zebulon, and this is Sarah. You're American."

"Yeah, from South Carolina. How about you?"

"I'm from Chicago, and Sarah's from California. We're Children of God. I think these three dudes followed us from our compound in the 14th arrondissement. They were hanging around there yesterday, and they were there when we left to go busking this morning."

Brad feigned surprise. "You're from a choir, *Les Enfants de Dieu*. I knew I'd seen you before. You guys had a hit last year. What are you doing busking in the metro?"

"We're 'fishing for souls.' This is how we meet people who might convert to the Children of God."

"A recruitment tool! Does it work?"

"Yeah, we're pretty successful. It's not an easy sell trying to get somebody to donate all their possessions as well as their lives to God."

Correction, thought Brad, *to God's intermediary, the leader of the sect.* He gestured toward the three wounded toughs on the stairs. "You said these guys followed you?"

"I think they did."

"Any reason why they would target you personally, or the Children of God in general?"

"No, but many of our brothers and sisters have reported being robbed and harassed over the last few weeks. It's nothing new."

"I think you'll be safe from now on."

"Thanks, Brad. You're welcome any time over at the compound. If I can ever do anything…"

"Hey, don't mention it, Zeb. My pleasure. I'll see you over at the compound. You too, Sarah."

They thanked him and scurried off. Brad turned back to the tough guys. They were in bad shape. Number One's forearm was shattered, and there was a bone sticking out of the skin. Number Two's nose was smashed into mush, and his eyes were already swollen closed. Brad thought he might also have a skull fracture. He was barely conscious. Number Three probably had a concussion and possibly a skull fracture as well. He was groggy but conscious.

"Remember that I know how to find you guys."

On his way back from the recording studio, Brad was still thinking about the metro encounter as he crossed the street and headed for his apartment building. The university faculty next door was closed for the evening, but there was a black Citroën DS parked in the driveway. Two dark-suited figures with thin mustaches exited the car as Brad passed by. "Monsieur James, Brad James?"

Full alert. Brad stopped to face the two men. They looked like cops. They smelled like cops. And they acted like cops. They brandished their badges. They were cops. "*Oui*, that's me."

"Please come with us. We have some questions to ask you."

The smaller of the two produced a set of handcuffs. Brad felt a rush of adrenaline. This was definitely not a routine control. He could think of many reasons why they might want to interrogate him—all of them bad. He extended his hands and felt the cold metal of the cuffs close around his wrists.

4: Person of Interest

Brad had been in the police station sitting in a small room on an uncomfortable wooden chair for the last forty-five minutes. Standard interrogation technique: Make the suspect wait and worry. Make him eager to talk.

Three uniformed national policemen banged open the door. One carried an old-fashioned typewriter. Another carried a sheaf of paper. The third, the oldest of the three and ostensibly the boss, carried a simple manila folder. He pulled up a wooden chair, an exact replica of the uncomfortable seat Brad occupied, and sat down. The other two men set up the typewriter and positioned themselves on either side of the boss. He nodded his head, and they sat down on their uncomfortable wooden chairs.

Brad was sitting face-to-face with three specimens of the French bureaucracy who are never seen or mentioned in US movies or TV talk shows. They were big, strong, no-nonsense professionals. The boss was about forty-five years old. The other two were in their middle twenties. There was nothing hostile or aggressive in their demeanor, but their authority dominated the atmosphere. For a long moment, the boss, the one the other two called Chef, shuffled through the papers in his folder. From time to time, he looked up and studied Brad. Finally, he broke the silence and asked Brad his name. When Brad answered, "Brad James," Cop Number One on Chef's left began to type.

The next twenty minutes were filled with background questions. Where were you born? What date? Where do you live? How long have you lived there? Each question and answer was diligently typed by the young cop on the typewriter. This part of the interview took an inordinate amount of time due to the young cop's frequent typing mistakes that had to be whited out and typed over. It was nerve-racking and increased the tension in the room. Brad figured all this was just part of the staging and interrogation technique. Whatever it was, it was working, and Brad's throat was getting dry. He still had no idea why he was being interrogated. Whatever it was, it was not your run-of-the-mill identity check, and he knew he had to be wary.

Brad decided to shake up the rhythm. "Excuse me, Chef, can I have some water, please?"

Chef didn't look up. "Get him a glass of water."

Brad decided to push it. See if he could get a reaction. "I could use a coffee, too."

Chef's body stopped and stiffened for a count of three Mississippi's that seemed like thirty minutes. He slowly raised his head and peered over the rims of his reading glasses. "This is a police station, not a coffee shop, Monsieur James."

This was the kind of reaction Brad was hoping for. It would give him the opportunity to make the relationship a little more personal. "I'm running on empty, Chef. Didn't anticipate a late date with three national policemen. A hot, black coffee with one lump of sugar would go a long way to improving my disposition."

Chef wrestled with that one for less than a second and made his decision. "Let's all of us take a break and have a coffee."

Brad sensed a mood change. When Cop Number Two came back with the steaming beverages, Chef was smiling. His face was big, and it was strong. Square jaw, straight nose over thin lips, and a graying crewcut receding at the temples. Big shoulders, big pecs, big stomach. Brad figured he was a good athlete going soft on desk duty. His men clearly respected him.

"So, Monsieur James, where do you work out?"

"What makes you think I work out, Chef?"

"You can only get those knuckles by hitting the *makiwara* thousands of times over many months."

"That's for sure. I'm over at la Montagne Sainte-Geneviève."

"That's Henri Pley's place. First dojo in France. Is Maître Kasé still there?"

"No, he's got his own dojo down in the 14th on Rue Daguerre."

"I'd like to get back into a regular workout routine over at la Montagne, but this job and these two guys"—he head-motioned toward his assistants—"keep me tied up until all hours of the night."

His two subordinates beamed at Chef's left-handed compliment.

"Okay, let's get back to work," Chef said. Once they were all seated, he got straight to the point. "Do you know a young lady by the name of Jean Jones?"

Just as Gary had predicted, the Jeanie Jones drug affair would be an issue for Brad. Thanks to DEA Brandon, it was happening sooner than anyone expected. "I do."

"How do you know her?"

"She comes into the Barbary Coast Saloon where I work. I run a dinner show there. She's involved in the music business somehow and comes in 'looking for talent,' she says."

"Do you know her well?"

"Not at all. Just enough to say hello and chat a bit. We're both American and more or less in the music business. She's okay."

"You know that she has been arrested and placed in *detention provisoire?*"

"Yeah, I heard about that. It's a big story in the American community. All the embassy people are gossiping about it. She was always bragging about being a teetotaler and anti-drugs. So it was a surprise."

There was a knock at the door, and another uniformed cop looked in and motioned to Chef. They went off together. After a few minutes, Chef came back in and excused himself. "Sorry, Mr. James. I have a few more questions." Cop Number One resumed his hesitant typing. "When was the last time you saw Mademoiselle Jones?"

"She came by the Barbary last week and I talked to her for a few minutes. That's it."

"Has she ever mentioned anything about drug overdoses by any of the artists she manages?

"No."

"Are you aware that three artists she manages in the Children of God choir died from overdoses?"

"No, I've got nothing on that."

"So you have nothing to do with the deaths?"

"Of course not."

"You are sure she was just a casual business acquaintance? No *hanky-panky* as you Americans say?"

"No, no, nothing like that. Why did you bring me all the way over here to ask me about someone I hardly know?"

"What do you know about the drug trade?"

"I know the guys who sell them in the saloon, but you know them too. Actually, not much of that goes on in the club. I'm not into drugs myself. I'm more beer and wine. So the short answer is, 'Not much.'"

"As you said, she was anti-drugs. Yet, her apartment was filled with drugs and drug paraphernalia. She frequents drug users and abusers. We find that suspicious."

"Where do I come in?"

"She mentions your name frequently in her diary, and, well, we found this in her belongings." Chef pushed a wrinkled sheet of A4 paper across to Brad. Written in neat American script with blue ballpoint ink, Brad read *Brad James/COG/urgent.*

That was a wicked curveball. Brad swung and missed. Couldn't figure it out. His mind was racing. "I have no idea. Maybe she wanted to schedule a gig. Mind if I smoke?"

Cop Number One stopped typing. Chef squinted his annoyance over his reading glasses. "Go ahead."

Brad offered his Gitanes around. Chef hesitated, then pulled one from the proffered pack and tamped it down. The two subordinates followed suit. This was a good sign. Brad screwed his Gitane between his lips, then lit the cops up. He held his Zippo three inches from the end of his cigarette and looked Chef in the eye. "Absolutely no idea what she's talkin' about, Chef." Then he lit his cigarette and snapped the lighter shut.

Chef took a big drag on his *clope*, blew out a full blast of pure white smoke, and made a big show of rubbing out his cigarette in the ashtray. "What about sex trafficking?"

"Sex trafficking?" This was a whole new ball game. Brad was totally blindsided by that one. "I've got nothing on that whatsoever. Nothing at all."

"Mr. James, you have been identified by your own embassy as

a person of interest in this inquiry. We have done some investigating on our own. Your acquaintances and past activities have brought you across my screen more than once. This is one time too many. Nevertheless, I have decided not to detain you, as I had planned, but that could change at any moment. Think carefully about your situation and get back to me with everything you know. Preferably, before I come back looking for you."

The meeting with Chef focused Brad's mind. First of all, his worst fears had become reality. The French considered him a major suspect in a case of serial murders, drug dealing, and sex trafficking. So he was already compromised by Jeanie, the Children of God, and the terrorist trainwreck coming down the tracks.

That pissed him off. To Brad, sex trafficking was worse than drug dealing. It was even worse than murder. Chef's unfounded insinuation really pissed him off. He was in deep trouble, and the entire situation totally pissed him off. Worst of all, he wasn't sure what to do.

5: Hare Krishna

COURBEVOIE, FRANCE, APRIL 1974

You don't see many pink 1957 Ford Thunderbird convertibles in Paris. You never see one in Courbevoie. So when the pink 1957 Ford Thunderbird convertible pulled into the driveway of the Pavillon des Indes at 140 Boulevard Saint-Denis in Courbevoie, it was an instant attention-getter. Four robed males nineteen or twenty years old kneeling on the lawn next to the building stopped their chanting and got to their feet. Their heads were entirely shaved except for a short ponytail at the back of the crown. Two robed females no older than seventeen or eighteen appeared from the other side of the building. They were also draped in long, flowing robes, but their hair was long and straight. They waited. They watched. Softly, they resumed their chant and moved forward in a slow shuffle toward the pink convertible.

"Hare, Hare Krishna. Hare, Hare Krishna."

From his spot in the shotgun seat, Brad looked at his companion, Charles "Chuck" Hall, and made a face. Chuck shrugged his shoulders. It was kind of eerie, but there was no sign of hostility.

They were here for Latorre Legal and Sally Ann Hastings. Brad's cousin, Tom Clark, was running the Hare Krishna compound here in Courbevoie. This was the logical place to start. They could try and get some useful inside background info on the COG while they were at it. Like any industry, these cults keep an eye on one another.

Now, however, Brad was starting to question whether coming over here was such a good idea. By the time he got out of the car, the first six Krishnas had been joined by four more, two males and two females. It was unpleasant. Eerie. They were all chanting, "Hare, Hare Krishna," doing the walking-dead shuffle and bearing down on Brad.

He met them head-on. He went toward the largest of the six males, brushed his dark blond forelock off his left eye, and said, "Excuse me. I'm looking for Tom Clark. I think he's the boss of your outfit."

The big guy stared for a long moment at the knuckles of callus and bone that stood out half an inch on the back of Brad's hands. "Damodar Pandita, Hare Krishna."

Brad answered, "Hare Krishna, Damodar Pandita. I'm looking for Tom Clark. He's supposed to be around here."

"Damodar Pandita."

"Damodar Pandita. Can you tell him his cousin is here?"

By this time, Chuck was out of the car flashing his friendliest smile and talking with the four girls. He was five feet nine inches tall and two hundred twenty pounds of pure muscle. His strong, dimpled chin, high cheekbones, and crooked nose made him look like an imperfect version of Napoleon Solo's *Man from U.N.C.L.E.* He was also the driver of the pink Thunderbird convertible and had the girls' attention.

Before Chuck could launch his charm offensive, a short, thin man exited the Pavillon and called out, "Hare Krishna, Brad, Damodar Pandita."

Brad recognized his cousin despite the shaved head and the ponytail. "Hare Krishna, Tom, Damodar Pandita."

Tom shook his head and smiled. "Damodar Pandita's my name, Brad. When we consecrate ourselves to Krishna, we take a new name. My new name is Damodar Pandita."

The ice was broken. Brad couldn't stop laughing. "Man, that's a good one. I thought it was some kind of sophisticated Indian greeting. Sorry about that, Damodar. Let me introduce you to Chuck, my sidekick."

Chuck grabbed Damodar's outstretched hand. "Nice to meet you, Damodar."

"Nice to meet you, Chuck. Let's go inside and get some refreshments. How about a hot cup of tea?"

"Yeah, thanks, Dammy. Sounds like a winner."

Damodar winced at the "Dammy" but said nothing. Chuck noticed the Krishna disciples were crowding closer and closer around the pink vehicle and decided to lock it up before going inside. Damodar stopped him. "Don't worry about your car, Chuck. It's safe." He waved his hand, and the disciples backed off. "These disciples are at the first stage of their spiritual journey and are still impressed by worldly goods. They've never seen a car like that, and neither have I. It's really a work of art."

Chuck was pleased. "Thanks, Dammy. Only twenty thousand ever made, and only ten of 'em were pink. A hot young bachelor from the embassy brought it over from the States, fell in love, and got married. The oil crisis and a first child made the car too expensive and impractical. I graciously volunteered to take it off his hands, and here I am, slam, bam, thank you, ma'am. Runs like a charm."

"There was a time when I would have killed for a car like that, Chuck. Fortunately for you, that time for me has passed."

Chuck chuckled. Dammy was a man after his own heart.

Brad had a flashback of Tom racing hotrods on the backroads of Missouri. He was actually pretty good, but acute laziness and an outsized appetite for violence, sex, and drugs got the better of him and he flamed out. Here he was five years later, reinvented as Damodar Pandita, a guru honcho in a Hindu toga dedicated to the worship of an obscure Indian god named "Harry"—spelled "Hare" Krishna. Well, he'd always liked Tom, Damodar, in spite of his worthlessness. Tom had charisma. He also had a nose for intrigue. If anything was going on in the cult community, Tom would know about it. Best to start slow and work up to the hard questions.

"Tom, Damodar, tell me how in God's name you got involved with Hare Krishna in Paris, of all places."

Damodar's features relaxed, and his eyes began to shine beneath the overhead lights reflecting off his bald brow. Brad detected a hint of condescension in his enigmatic smile, and that annoyed him in spite of himself. There was also a spot of cupidity that put Brad on his guard. "I found God, Brad. I found peace and love. I found my place in the world. I found that the spirit is everything. Material things have no meaning. Hare Krishna."

Coming from a guy who could party for two weeks straight and never lose his hard-on, Brad was respectfully skeptical. Time would tell on that score.

"My disciples and I take care of this pavilion. It's a big job. Tell me, Brad, what you're doing in Paris and how you found me here."

"Came here in sixty-nine after a master's degree in Madrid. Got a job in a nightclub as a bouncer. Started singing and got involved in the Parisian music scene. Hey! Got a new record comin' out in May. Anyway, your mom told my mom where to find you, and my mom has been harassing me to come say hello."

"So you're here on a family mission?"

"Not really."

Brad looked around the room. It was open and empty except for the three of them and smelled of incense or perfume. It was beautiful. The walls were composed of wooden panels carved into intricate designs. The ceiling was a mosaic of carved wooden panels and colorful paintings. The tables and chairs were made of elaborately carved wood. It was slightly overwhelming, and Chuck was visibly uncomfortable.

Brad sipped his tea while he observed his cousin's moving lips and studied his calm composure. "You counting, Damodar?"

"No, praying. I say the Hare Krishna prayer ten thousand times every day."

Brad figured that for a definite time-consumer. "Look, Damodar, I know you're a busy man. We can catch up on the past another time. I really came here to ask you to help me out."

"Of course. If I can, I will. No problem."

The problem at hand was to find info on the disappearance of Sally Ann Hastings. He went into his white leather pouch and pulled out a picture of a pretty, smiling young woman about twenty years old. "This is Sally Ann Hastings. She was last seen somewhere in Paris a few months ago."

"You know her?"

"No, her parents contacted Latorre Legal to see if we can find her."

Damodar sat back in his chair and frowned. "Why do you think I would know her?"

Brad sensed some resistance. "Her father says she's into all this hippie culture and spiritual awareness, no disrespect intended."

"None taken."

"I figured this would be right down your alley and a good place to start."

Damodar studied the picture carefully. He was wringing his hands and blinking rapidly just like he used to do before he got into a fight. He seemed to come to a decision, and just as he put the picture down, one of his disciples came in. The spell was broken. Damodar smiled and patted Brad on the shoulder. "Sorry, cuz, can't help you. I don't think I've ever seen this girl before. Hare Krishna."

"Maybe you can give me a tip on where to look."

Damodar thought it over and said, "You ever hear of the Children of God?"

"Of course, we're all children of God, but I suppose you're referring to something else."

"It's a cult down in the 14th arrondissement. They attract a lot of American expats. In France, they're known as *Les Enfants de Dieu*."

Brad knew Damodar was holding back on him and wondered why. He doubted it was some kind of *omerta* bond among the different cults. Maybe something happened to Sally while she was with the Krishnas. Or maybe she was involved in something he wanted to stay out of. He'd worry about that later. Now was a good time to see if he knew anything about Jeanie and the Children of God.

"I've heard of them," Brad said. "A friend of mine, Jeanie Jones, works with them sometimes. Do you know her?"

Damodar took a sip of the dark tea and closed his eyes. "Yeah, Jeanie. I know her. She used to come around here a lot. Haven't seen her for a while. I heard she's hanging out with the Children of God now. How's she doing?"

"Fine, as far as I know. I haven't seen her for a while either. The Children of God are a big deal in France. Know anybody over there?"

"Yeah. Been there a few times. Our disciples were being harassed in the metro. I found out their disciples were being harassed as well, even worse than us. Went over there and met with one of the honchos, a guy called Benjamin. He told me the gangbangers would follow his disciples until they had scrounged a few hundred francs. Then they'd go in and rip 'em off. Sometimes they'd beat the guys up. He told me the gangbangers concentrated on the buskers. Those are the ones racking up the most money. Every morning, the Children of God choir breaks up into groups of two or three. They go to the big metro transfer stations like Montparnasse and Saint-Lazare where they play and sing. I told my guys to stay away from those stations and the Children of God to avoid the gangbangers preying on them. Since then, the attacks on us have dropped off a little."

Brad filed that away as important. "Have you been back to the COG since then?"

"Couple of times. Got a cold reception. Not much contact. I hear they have some new blood over there that's changing the system."

Back in the car, Chuck was quiet, concentrating on the road ahead. "Nothing personal, Brad, but that cousin of yours is an off-key high C."

"You got that right. He's a worthless shitbird, always has been and probably always will be. But he has charm. I think he did recognize Sally Ann, but she moved on and he didn't want to get involved. Didn't have much to say about Jeanie except she was hanging out with the Children of God. We already knew that."

"Where does that leave us?"

"He told me the COG was having problems with muggers in the metro. I think we can use that to—" The sharp blast of a semi-double diesel's horn crashed through their conversation. Brad just had time to glimpse the driver's angry face as the truck flashed by. "Goddamn it, man. What are you doing?"

"Cool your jets, captain. That guy was in our lane. I just wanted to give him a little scare. Everything's under control."

"That guy was in a ten-ton truck that would wipe us off the face of the earth if he hit us. Who's scaring who?"

"My little Bird can dance around him all day and never even come close to getting a scratch. So what about the metro?"

"I was down there the other day. Had a run-in with three gang-bangers trying to rip off a couple of buskers from the COG. Jeanie manages their choir."

"I've never seen Jeanie. What does she look like?"

"She's pretty. Long, wavy, auburn hair. Short, turned-up nose. Brown eyes, beautiful body she makes no effort to promote. Wears mostly long, formless shirts and skirts. Saw her once all dolled up at the *Maison-de-la-Radio*, the government radio and television center. She was a knockout. Could have been a serious target if she wasn't so disinterested. On a stingy day, I'd give her an eight and a half or a nine. In high school, I'd have given her a ten."

"You didn't know she was working for the Company?"

"Had no idea. Gary's the station chief. He only tells us what we need to know."

The pink Bird pulled up to Brad's building at number 90 Rue d'Assas. "You doin' the dinner show at the Barbary tonight?"

"Yeah. I'll see you tomorrow."

6: Gangbanger Ambush

Brad was still wrestling with what he should do about Chef's warning. Playing it cool and hoping for the best was a non-starter. He would be less visible but less effective if he sniffed around on his own. He'd have more resources and access to information if he accepted Gary's proposition. He would also be more visible and vulnerable. He decided to start on his own over at the COG compound.

The Children of God compound was fronted by a white, ten-foot wall topped off with concertina wire. The only opening to the outside was a small cast-iron door painted black. There were two cameras on the fence above the door—one aimed at the street and the other aimed at the entrance. Reminded Brad of a fortress or a prison.

Brad hesitated before hitting the button on the intercom and decided to walk around the neighborhood before announcing himself. The COG was central to the investigation. The problem was finding a credible pretext for coming around. His encounter with Zebulon and Sarah in the metro gave him the perfect pretext.

Nevertheless, he still had not formulated a clear strategy on what to do once he made contact with God's children.

He remembered that Zebulon mentioned the gangbangers had followed him from the compound. There was a café across the street with a nice terrace. Brad took a table at the back of the terrace and settled in to get a feel for the area.

The sun was up, and there was a cool breeze just strong enough to keep it comfortable. Only three other tables were taken. There was an old couple at one of them having an early lunch or a late breakfast. The other two tables were taken by young men, three at each table. They were dressed in jeans and leather jackets, or jeans and sweatshirts. Their eyes were glued to the entrance of the Children of God compound.

Brad lit up a Gitane and ordered a double espresso when the waitress came over. She was bouncy and cute with a teasing little smile.

The door to the compound opened and three young hippie types came out, two boys and a girl. The men at both tables came to attention. The heavyset guy at one of the tables made a hand signal, and the three guys at the other table got up and went after the hippies.

That was what Brad suspected. These guys were gangbangers. He wanted to be ready for the next group of hippies to come out. He signaled the waitress. She came over, and Brad paid with a good tip. She gave him a wink and swished off just in time for another group of hippies coming out of the compound. There were four of them, three boys and a girl.

The heavyset guy got up along with his sidekicks and went after the hippies. Brad followed behind. The hippies seemed oblivious. They were talking and laughing. At the Porte d'Orléans, they split up. The hippie girl and one of the hippie boys went toward the

Parc Montsouris. Another boy headed right down the Boulevard des Maréchaux. The third boy went into the metro.

This seemed to cause some confusion in the ranks of the gang-bangers. Finally, they split up as well, each one taking a different target. Brad decided to stay with the couple heading for the Parc Montsouris.

He checked to make sure there was no surveillance behind him. That's when he spotted the two hippies coming out of the café on the corner. They were not dressed like typical hippies. No flowing love clothes and sandals. They were wearing jeans and sneakers. But with the long hair, beads, and beards, there was no doubt that hippies they were.

They fell in behind the gangbanger following their two hippie brethren from the compound. It was a procession. The two Children of God, followed by the gangbanger, followed by the two disguised hippies from the café at the Porte d'Orléans, followed by Brad.

At the Parc Montsouris, the hippie couple chose a small path and slowed their pace. Brad was so far back that he could barely see them. He was focused on their brethren, who picked up their pace and started closing the distance on the gangbanger.

They went around a bend, and Brad lost them for a few seconds. He heard some shouts and some grunts. Coming around the bend, he saw a body stretched out motionless on the ground and the two hippies from the café legging it off in the opposite direction. The guy on the ground was the gangbanger, and he was not moving.

Brad cut to a path on the right to get a better look. Two young men Brad had never seen before approached the gangbanger's immobile body from the opposite direction. They were in their early thirties, well-built, and dressed in fashionable bell-bottom jeans with colorful shirts open to the navel. They each took an armpit and lifted the body upright. They carried it in the drunk-man's-drag to a white Renault parked in front of the exit to the park.

Brad followed at a discreet distance and watched as the two men loaded the body into the backseat of the Renault. Then they jumped into the front seat and roared off.

Brad noted the license plate number. It ended in 78. The last two digits indicated the department where the car was registered, which meant these guys lived in Les Yvelines, just outside of Paris.

Brad found an operational telephone cabin and called Chuck's office. He gave Chuck the license plate number and asked Chuck if he could find out who owned the car and where that person lived.

"I can do it," Chuck said, "but it will take some time and a carton of Marlboros."

"Make it two cartons and get it by this afternoon. I'll meet you at your office at four. Ten-four and out."

That little scene was a game-changer. Something way beyond a simple metro feud between the buskers and the gangbangers was going on here. He had just witnessed a pre-meditated murder in broad daylight. It was a professional hit job with body disposal included.

Chef fingering him as a person of interest in something like this was a serious problem. He was completely innocent, but there was no way to prove the contrary.

On the other hand, by helping out the buskers in the metro, he may have inadvertently put himself on the firing line. No good deed ever goes unpunished. Chef obviously believed he was involved.

He hesitated to engage and actually get involved. If he did, it would mean a lot of egg-breaking and omelet-making. But, then again, the only way to get his life back on track was to meet this thing head-on.

Brad's next stop was his meeting with Gary. He had made up his mind to accept Gary's proposition. He'd worry about the consequences later.

7: The Bounty Hunter

If you're looking to avoid people, Grand Teton National Park in Wyoming is the place to go. With approximately 550,000 inhabitants, Wyoming is the least populous state in the entire USA, and the Grand Teton Range has a density of less than one inhabitant per square mile. When she escaped from the Prophecy, that's where she went. And that's where she met a gnarled old bounty hunter who took her under his wing, gave her a new identity, and taught her a new profession—a profession adapted to her intelligence, her looks, and her physical prowess.

She was now a bounty hunter. The new identity came from a young look-alike whose life had been cut short by a drunk driver. The old bounty hunter taught her how to shoot, how to fight, and how to use a knife. Her natural strength and athletic ability made her a fast learner.

He taught her the ins and the outs of the laws on fugitives and how to track them through the city and in the wild. He soon discovered she had a knack for the profession. She could anticipate fugitives' reactions and was creative in trapping them. After several months of working together, he could see there was no more he could teach her. She began to hunt on her own, and her partner was happy to begin his retirement.

Her dresser was adorned with two photos. The first was with the two other women who had qualified in the pentathlon for the 1968 Olympic team. They were smiling and flashing the "V" sign. The second was taken a month later. She was alone on crutches, her right leg in a cast up to the hip. There were tears in her eyes. She was recovering from the most depressing setback she could ever have imagined. For ten long years, she had devoted her life to sport. Everything revolved around her training—how much and when she worked out, how much and what she ate, how much and when she slept, her weight, her heart rate, her friends, her enemies, everything. A moment of distraction, a slip on the track, a crash into the hurdle. A blown-out knee. A silly accident that ended her career. At nineteen years old, it looked like the end of her world. The beginning of the Prophecy. Well, that was all over. She had a new life now.

A surprise visit by a group of the Prophet's high priests brought an abrupt end to her new life in Grand Teton. Returning from a mission, she found the old bounty hunter beaten beyond recognition and left to die on the dirt floor of his barn. He managed to warn her before he gave out, "I got one of those varmints. There's two left."

A timely warning. Her horse skittered and reared. She rolled to the right. Two blasts from her double-barreled twelve gauge. One blew the intruder's shin off at the knee. The other blew out his guts.

She rolled back to the left. Just in time. Dirt kicked up behind her. Small caliber. She kept rolling. Drew her pistol and got off two shots. Missed their mark, but she was behind a bale of hay.

Couldn't locate the shooter. This one, she wanted alive.

He was trapped. Only one way out. She and her bale of hay were between him and the exit. She had plenty of ammo. There were three horses left in the barn. They were nervous. A few blasts from her twelve gauge made them panicky. She could hear the shooter dodging around in the restricted space of the stall he shared with a big, spooked palomino.

She crept up on the stall. "Throw out your gun and come out with your hands behind your head."

The shooter decided to shoot instead. The palomino began to kick and paw. The shooter went down. The palomino was trampling him.

She needed him alive. She flipped the latch and threw open the door. The palomino charged out. The shooter lay immobile in the dirt. Playing possum.

She'd seen this act too many times. Wasn't fooled. Didn't hanker to see it again. She shot from the hip. The bullet blasted the shoulder bone of the shooter's gun arm. The shooter screamed and rolled over.

It was more than she could ever have hoped for, or even imagined. Here before her, writhing around in the dirt, screaming and moaning, was the high priest. Sammy, the Prophet's purifier. It was he who administered punishments at the Prophecy. It was he who delighted in inflicting pain and humiliation on his fellow believers. It was he who had personally administered her purification.

She grimaced as she remembered Sammy mixing her "purification cocktail." His eyes shined as he described the intimate details of each ingredient and the gut-wrenching agony it would inflict. His vivid descriptions, as ghastly as they were, were nothing compared to the reality of the cocktail's effects. Her eyes burst, her brain exploded, muscles cramped, heart raced, suffocating, freezing, burning, seizures, vomiting, coughing, frothing at the mouth. Few survived the purification. She was one of the few, and this was bad news for Sammy.

He was small and stringy and scroungy. His head was narrow. His face was long. His eyes, nose, and mouth crammed oddly together in the center of his face gave him a curious, unworldly look. His thin lips were usually constricted in a predatory smile. Today, they were open and twisted and squirming around.

"So, Sammy, we meet again."

Her voice seemed to breathe new life into Sammy's wounded body. "Didn't think we'd find you? Thought you could get away?"

"How did you find me, Sammy?"

"Wouldn't you like to know, sister?"

Hands on her hips, she frowned at Sammy. He glared back, but his defiance was losing its edge. She looked down, started to speak, thought better of it, turned, and marched to the back of the barn. She returned with a thick leather pouch and a wire rat-trap containing one big, brown rat running around frantically, seeking an escape route.

She put the pouch over Sammy's head with the drawstrings tight around his throat. Using her Bowie knife, she cut a small opening in the top of the pouch just large enough for a big, brown rat to slip through. The rat was shrieking his high-pitched terror cry. Sammy was screaming and cursing.

"Sammy, I have some questions—"

Sammy cut her off. "You will regret this, bitch."

"Thank you for making this easy for me. Last chance. I want to know how you found me, and who else knows."

She ignored Sammy's stream of profanities. Using a pair of blacksmith's tongs, she extracted the rat from the cage and inserted him into the pouch covering Sammy's head.

A machine stapler closed the hole. There was a delay of two, maybe three Mississippis. When Sammy realized who his new pouch partner was, his head began to jerk left, right, up, and down. Then his whole body. A long stream of profanities punctuated by shrieks and screams.

He peed in his pants and started to beg.

"You know the questions, Sammy. Give me the answers."

He wasn't eloquent, but he was detailed and he was fast. It was a race against the rat. The rat was hungry and scared, and it was chewing its way out. "Credit card. You used your credit card. FBI traced it to Wyoming. Nobody knows. Nobody knows this place. Even your friend. Even she doesn't know." Sammy screamed. His body shook. "He's eating me! He's eating me!"

The rat was winning the race.

Suddenly, she was very much afraid. "What about my friend?"

Sammy was screaming now. "We asked her. She knows nothing. We're sure."

"So, you hurt her?"

"No, no, not me. The Feds. They did it. The Feds did it! The Feds are the ones who killed her!"

She flinched, but she took the punch. She would grieve later, in private. Her lifelong friend, partner, and confidant was gone. All because she let herself get involved with a bunch of sadistic perverts.

"Last question, Sammy. Where is the Prophet?"

She could see the rat had positioned itself on Sammy's face. Sammy was jerking up and down, banging his head against the hitching post in a futile attempt to shake the rat loose. He was shrieking and wailing. Made it difficult to understand what he was trying to say. "Europe! He's going to Europe. He's in Europe!"

"Where in Europe?"

Sammy's head jerked left to right. He was moaning. Now the rat was squealing. "France. Paris. Going to Paris. No one has seen him since the day the Prophecy purified itself. Help! Help me! Help me!" His agony was boundless.

She had all the information she needed. The Prophet was still alive. The one and only time she used her credit card with her real name on it while she was cleaning out her accounts, they traced her to Wyoming and used an old picture to find her here in no-man's-land.

Their arm was longer than even she had imagined. The resources of the FBI were at the Prophet's disposal. As for the assertion that nobody else knew she was living at this particular address, she had no doubt this was true. She was listed nowhere. Of course, if these two miserable misfits could find her, it would be child's play for someone with any professional experience to do the same.

They couldn't possibly know her new name of someone long deceased. She had no official existence under her new name. Her bounty hunting was done in the name of her mentor. Still, she had to accept the fact that her life here was over.

Sammy was having an unpleasant time. The rat had found a delicious route out of the pouch through Sammy's head. She had all the information she was going to get from Sammy. It was time to put him out of his misery.

She pulled the pouch off his head. The rat jumped out of Sammy's throat and ran off to the barn. Sammy wasn't moving. His face was half gone. No nose. No cheeks. No eyes. Just blood, teeth, and ragged strands of flesh. The rat had won the race. She put a compassionate bullet in Sammy's brain just to make sure.

Back in the house, she stepped over the Prophet's priest, who her mentor had terminated. She left him where he lay, went into the bedroom, packed her knapsack, and erased any lingering evidence of her presence.

Out in the barn, she wiped down the twelve gauge and fixed it in her mentor's hands. It would take a genius to figure out what had happened here. By then, she'd be long gone. To France. To do what she did best. She was going to hunt them down, one by one, each and every one of them.

8: Latorre Legal

Back in his sixth-floor office on the Champs-Elysées, Chuck stared out through the glass terrace doors. The far side of the street below was bathed in soft shadows cast by the streetlamps shining through the branches of the trees lining the sidewalk. Pedestrian traffic was relatively thin on that side of the Champs-Elysées. There wasn't much to do there at this time of the night outside of the dimly lit terraces of a few restaurants and cafés. His side of the avenue was a different story. The lights were brighter, the shops were open. A river of strolling humanity flowed back and forth through a festival of buskers, street performers, souvenir hawkers, restaurants, and sidewalk cafés.

The avenue was alive. The atmosphere was electric. Chuck felt it and shivered. He didn't turn on the light. He liked to do his thinking cloaked in the shadows. Made him feel secure. In four short years, he had gone from fierce Vietnam warrior to the head of a paralegal firm catering to an American expatriate clientèle. His offices occupied the whole sixth floor at number 78 on the most famous boulevard in the world.

Some of it was luck. Some of it was bluff. Most of it was hard work. The luck was meeting the director of HEC, France's most prestigious business school. The bluff was convincing him he had the academic background to qualify for entry. In fact, Chuck knew the director was not fooled by the Army achievement documents he submitted. The director was impressed with his experience, background, and personality. The three hundred confirmed kills were the clincher. The hard work was going to school in a foreign language. It helped that many of the books and articles were written in English. Nevertheless, for two-and-a-half years Chuck burned the midnight oil and studied on weekends and holidays.

His big break came when he met Big John Latorre at an embassy cookout. Big John had a thriving paralegal business called Latorre Legal. He was a former Marine with a reputation as a fierce warrior and skilled businessman. He had been in Paris since the end of the Korean War. The two of them hit it off like peanut butter and jelly. Big John offered Chuck a job as his assistant. Six months later, Chuck was promoted to president and Big John retired. Chuck took over and never looked back. The business was thriving, and Chuck was having the time of his life.

He and Brad had decided they could piggyback on the Sally Ann Hastings disappearance as cover for their investigation into the terror plot. Anything relating to Jeanie would be relevant.

The more he thought about it, the more he was convinced he had met Jeanie Jones a few months back. He was at the police station at Orly Airport for an American teenager from Britain who was stopped in transit on her way to Lebanon. She had no money and no passport. She claimed the man she was traveling with had her money and her passport. The man could not be located, and the French authorities arrested her. They contacted the embassy. The embassy contacted her parents and put them in touch with Latorre Legal. Chuck handled the paperwork with the embassy and the interface with the French bureaucracy. It turned out the girl was a member of an obscure religious sect in London that was probably a front for a human trafficking ring. When she got arrested, she was just one short flight away from disappearing into their netherworld.

Chuck organized her return to the US. When he went to collect her at the commissariat, she was being interviewed by a young woman who claimed she was sent by the embassy. Chuck was suspicious. In the short conversation he had with her, all his survival senses went on full alert. The way she moved. Her awareness. Her confidence. Her nosiness. He had pegged her for a journalist or the moral equivalent of a tree hugger. This woman was Jeanie Jones. He was sure.

Meanwhile, he dug into his files to see what his researchers had found out about the Children of God—*Les Enfants de Dieu*, as they were called in France. They were better known in France as a singing group than a religious cult. The lead singer was called Zebulon, an American. They had a hit song in 1973 called "*Redeviens un Bébé*" (become a baby again). Their new 45, "*Liberté*," was moving steadily up the charts. They had a big compound over in the 14th arrondissement. This afternoon, the director of the Children of God compound in Paris contacted Latorre Legal with a curious proposal. He wanted Latorre Legal to represent the Children of God for the details of a new recording contract.

9: Danger

Jeanie had been incommunicado for almost a week now, not even a lawyer. She had no idea what her rights were in France. Outside of the guards and her daily interrogation sessions, no one had spoken to her since she was placed in solitary confinement—*detention provisoire* they called it. All the questioning revolved around drugs, over and over in revolving scenarios of the good cop/bad cop routine.

"Who is your supplier?"

"I don't do drugs."

"Why do you have drugs in your apartment?"

"I have no drugs in my apartment."

"We found a whole assortment of drugs in your apartment in plain sight."

"Someone else put them there."

They were starting to believe her when she said she didn't take drugs herself. Their focus shifted to using drugs on others.

"Did you know the three young men who overdosed?"

"Yes. They were members of the Children of God choir. I manage this group."

"Can you explain why they overdosed on the same unusual mixture of drugs found in your apartment?"

"No."

And that was what worried her. She did not do drugs and she did not store drugs in her home. Those drugs had to have come from someone else.

The bad cop always closed out the session. She believed him when he said, "You know that many bad things can happen to someone who refuses to cooperate."

Jeanie lay back on the small cot fixed to the wall in the corner of her cell and tried to concentrate. She found it terribly difficult to get her thoughts together, although it was quiet enough in there. The problem was the lack of ventilation and the pungent odor emanating from the rudimentary toilet in the opposite corner of the tiny cell. There was also some pungency in her own person that made the problem worse. She hadn't had a shower since they brought her in.

As hard as it was to concentrate, Jeanie had to analyze her situation. Now was the moment to put everything together. She came off the cot, straightened her dress, and hand-combed her long, wavy hair. It was four short steps from one end of the gray cell to the other. She started pacing back and forth, gathering her thoughts.

There were two explanations for the drug cocktail found in her apartment. The frame-up hypothesis didn't hold water. If someone had gotten wind of her cult investigation and was trying to shut her down, getting her arrested wouldn't keep her quiet. In fact, the opposite was true. The more likely explanation was the drugs were there to kill her. The two suspects seen fleeing from her apartment confirmed it for her. Most probably it was related to the terrorist plot. She had spent a lot of time with her informant and grown close to her. That might have raised enough suspicion to warrant her elimination.

Jeanie went back to the cot, stretched out on her back, and did fifty sit-ups. When she finished, she had a good idea of the situation she was facing. She was a seasoned pro. She knew she could count only on herself. This was part of the deal. Help from the embassy was out of the question. Her life was in danger, maybe even here in a French prison. Those French politicians who would benefit from a successful terrorist attack would protect their interests.

She stopped her pacing in front of the small wash basin, leaned forward, and took a long look at herself in the mirror. No makeup. No creams. Incipient insomnia from the lumpy cot. She was still holding up pretty well. They had nothing on her and would eventually have to release her. Until then, the food was bad and her social life was pretty dull, but despite the bad cop's veiled threat, she hoped she was safe here.

Heavy footsteps on the concrete hallway snapped her back to reality. At this time of day, not routine. It wasn't time to eat or interrogate. There were two of them. More than one person at this time of day was totally not routine. Definitely alarming.

The coordinated military cadence of the echoing footsteps conjured up images of jackboots and Gestapo agents. Maybe she wasn't so safe in French custody after all. If this was the case, she was determined to go down fighting.

She padded around the naked cell, desperate for a weapon. Came up with a toilet brush. It was dirty and disgusting, but it was metal and would do some serious damage if she started smacking people with it. She held it out of sight close to her leg. It was dripping on her pants into her shoe. She bit it back and held her ground as the footsteps echoed down the hall. At the corner, they suddenly stopped. Some whispering. She was ready. They were on the move again. Came around the corner. There were two of them.

It was the two guards she knew. This was the first time they came together. But she knew them. She relaxed. They were going to take her to the interrogation room.

The guards had some curious looks for the toilet brush she was brandishing, but they didn't say anything. She replaced it in the dish, extended her arms, and allowed herself to be cuffed and ushered down the hall.

This was not the route to the interrogation room. She was alarmed. After a few twists and turns, they arrived at a brown wooden door. She had never been here before. She was on full alert.

The guard knocked, and the door opened. There were three men seated in front of a small metal table. Two of them were cops smoking and drinking coffee. The third was a small, thin male with wild eyes and a shaved head. He was smiling benevolently. Jeanie started to panic.

10: The House in Louveciennes

LOUVECIENNES, APRIL 1974

It was a forty-five-minute drive to Louveciennes in Chuck's pink Thunderbird. He got the address of the license plate from his friend at 4 p.m. He and Brad left Paris at 4:30 to beat the traffic. It was now 5:30, and they were driving around Louveciennes looking for the Rue de Montbuisson. The car Brad had seen at the Parc Montsouris was registered at number 6.

Louveciennes is a beautiful little town. It has castles built in the 17th and 18th centuries as well as an ancient aqueduct. It was popular with impressionist painters of the past like Renoir, Pissarro, Sisley, and Monet. Many famous scientists, authors, composers, and musicians lived and died in Louveciennes.

All that history still didn't make it any easier to find where they were going. It was a maze of narrow, winding residential lanes barely wide enough for one car. Many, if not most, had no street signs. Most buildings had no numbers. Brad knew the suburbs were difficult and had counted on doing a thorough area reconnaissance, but his patience was wearing thin.

Chuck was undeterred. "No problem. Let me handle this." He spotted a pedestrian coming around the corner, stopped, and exited the car. "Excuse me, sir, I'm looking for the house where Anaïs Nin used to live."

The man in his early sixties had rosy-red cheeks and long white hair. He didn't smile, but he was obviously amused. He pointed a gnarled finger at the three-story house right beside the pink Thunderbird. "That's it."

"That's it?"

"*Oui.* That's it."

"*Merci beaucoup.*"

Chuck got back into the car. "Number 6 is just down the street."

Brad said nothing. About fifty meters down the road, on the corner of another obscure lane they would later learn was Rue Louis Forest, stood an iron gate and a white brick wall protecting a large three-story residence on a full acre of land. The number 6 in bronze was fixed to the gate.

Chuck made a sweeping *voilà* motion with his right hand. "This is it, daddy-o."

They drove slowly past the property all the way to the Rue Saint-Michel where they found a café. They parked and took a table inside. "Okay, Chuck. Explain to me what went on back there."

"As Sherlock once said, 'Elementary, my dear James.' I knew Anaïs Nin had lived at number 2 bis, Rue de Montbuisson. That meant number 6 couldn't be far away."

"Who is Anaïs Nin, and how did you know about her?"

"Anaïs Nin was a popular Cuban novelist born in Neuilly who lived in Louveciennes from 1930 to 1936 at 2 bis, Rue de Montbuisson. Her career as an author started in this town. I knew about her because I'm a great detective, man, like Dick Tracy."

Brad squinted back at Chuck and waited for the punch line. There was no way the Charles "Chuck" Hall sitting next to him had dug up this obscure nugget of literary history on his own. Chuck squinted back at him, grinning and gooning.

When a punch line was not forthcoming, Brad caved and asked the question, "Okay, Dick, besides your detective genius, where did you get the info?"

"From your university friend with a PhD in French history, John Hommeheureux. I knew Louveciennes was a historical suburb that would be complicated to navigate. He was the logical go-to source for ideas on how to find my way around there. He checked his books for landmarks near 6 Rue de Montbuisson and gave me the tip on Anaïs Nin. It served as a way to ask for directions to where we were going without giving the address and without raising suspicions about why we were going there. Suburbanites around here are suspicious. We can use Anaïs Nin as cover if anybody notices us snooping around and gets curious."

Brad was impressed. Chuck never stopped surprising him.

"He also told me we should try and fit in and not draw attention to ourselves."

"Then that explains why you decided to take a one-of-a-kind pink convertible Thunderbird to scout out the area. Fly under the radar."

"Not to worry. Anybody who saw us would only remember the car. From here on in, we take the Indian. Your motorcycle is less conspicuous."

Brad thought it over. "We're already here and we've scouted out the area. We've got a few more hours of daylight and dusk. People are coming back from work. Good time to get a close look at the property and see who's in there. Did you bring the camera and the box for taking clandestine pictures?"

"Yeah. Everything's all set. Got a new roll of film, thirty-six frames. It's all in the box and ready to shoot. Got some infrared, too, in case we want to shoot some night scenes."

"Let's tourist-walk down the lane. Start clicking when we get to the edge of the property. We'll hang a left at the corner and photograph that side of the property as well. By the way, what did you decide to do about representing the Children of God? Are you gonna take them on?"

"Haven't decided yet. Depends on what my lawyer says. Their status in France is as a nonprofit corporation under the law of 1901. Could cause us some problems. I'll let you know."

It took about fifteen minutes to walk down Montbuisson to number 6. Chuck started snapping pictures ten meters from the edge of the property. There wasn't much to see, just the top of the house and the white brick wall. When they got to the end of the property on the corner of Rue Louis Forest, they stopped to rest and Chuck got a few good pictures of the house and driveway that were visible through the bars of the cast-iron gate.

On the Louis Forest side of the property, the white cinderblock fence extended only about twenty yards. After that, the property was bounded by a thick line of underbrush and trees. Brad looked around and saw there were no houses or anything on the other side of the lane. Just more underbrush and trees. There was nobody around, and nobody to see them. He decided to go for it. He signaled Chuck, and they both slipped into the underbrush bordering the property at number 6.

From their vantage point in the underbrush, they could see the driveway and the side and back of the house. Three vehicles were parked in front of the garage behind the house. There was the white Renault Brad had seen at Parc Montsouris, a van painted in colorful psychedelic patterns with German plates, and, to Brad's surprise and Chuck's delight, a brand-new bright-yellow Jaguar E-type with UK plates.

"This is a pretty good vantage point," Brad said. "Let's stick around and see what goes on in there. Their automotive diversity intrigues me. Write down the numbers on the van and the Jag. We can find out who their visitors are."

As the sun went down, lights started popping on and off in the house. There seemed to be at least four and maybe six different people in the building. The two young males Brad had seen in the Parc Montsouris came out and went into the garage. While they were in there, Brad and Chuck saw shadowy outlines of at least three other people moving around inside the main building.

After the two young men went back into the house, things seemed to calm down. Two other young men, not much different from the first two, came outside, smoked a cigarette, and went back inside.

Chuck took some photos. The lights went out. No more movement. Brad and Chuck were about to leave when the back door to the house flew open and the yard lit up. A man they hadn't seen before dragged a young girl out onto the lawn. From where Brad and Chuck sat, she looked like she couldn't be over sixteen years old. She had long, blond hair parted down the middle and wore one of those long, flowing hippie gowns. The man was in his thirties. He was wide-shouldered with a heavily muscled upper body on narrow hips and short legs. He sported a thick, black, well-trimmed beard. His hair was long and thick and wavy. From what they could see of his face, he was a good-looking guy. Chuck snapped a few more photos.

The guy was pissed off, and the girl was terrified. He slapped her around the head a few times and left her on the ground sobbing and pleading. He went into the garage and came back out with a small tray. He placed the tray on the fender of the Renault and came up with what looked like a syringe.

When the girl saw it, she tried to crawl away. He plunged the syringe into her neck. She began to tremble. Quivering, quaking shivering, shaking. Thrashing. Cramping. Screaming. Faster. Harder. An uncontrollable fit. Then, nothing. She was out like a light.

The man bent toward the girl's inert body. Stopped. Cocked his head. Carefully surveyed the perimeter of the property. Looked back down at the girl, grabbed her arm, and dragged her back into the house.

After that disgusting scene, Brad and Chuck figured they'd had enough for tonight and were about to leave when the back door to the house opened again. There was some movement in the doorway, but it was too shadowy to make out what was going on. Suddenly, two mammoth Doberman Pinschers leaped into the light, barking and drooling. They were heading straight for Brad and Chuck. Only a thin leather leash held them back, and the guy holding the leash was also holding a .32 caliber pistol. They'd have to make a run for it. Outrunning the dogs was improbable. Outrunning a .32 caliber bullet was impossible. They were goners if the guy could shoot.

The dogs were straining at the leash, pulling the leash-holder along behind them. Chuck pulled his knife. Brad grabbed his arm. "Wait. Look at that."

Halfway between them and the dogs sat a big, fat jackrabbit. That's what the dogs were going for. The rabbit broke its cover and began to run for its life. The dogs tried to follow, but the guy with the leash held them back. They continued barking, snorting, and straining with all their attention on that wonderful, jumping jackrabbit. Brad and Chuck were off the hook, for the moment. Once the dogs forgot about the rabbit, they would sniff out another target.

A voice from the house boomed. "See anything?"

"Naw. It was just a rabbit."

"You sure? I had a feeling."

"Just a fucking rabbit, okay?"

The guy took the dogs back into the house. Brad and Chuck crept quietly out of the bushes back onto the lane. They brushed off their clothes and headed back toward their car parked by the café.

Chuck was incredulous. "There's no way the guy in the house could have seen or heard us."

"He was sure enough to send out a search party. If it wasn't for Bugs Bunny, we were dead meat. I know you've never tangled with a Doberman."

"How do you know?"

"Because if you had, you wouldn't be here to talk about it."

Chuck stopped and looked around. His sixth sense had kicked into action "I think we got trouble."

"Where?"

"In the doorway by the car. Take the left. I'll take the right."

They split up. Moved forward. Shadows shifted in the doorway. A long shadow from the streetlight fell across the sidewalk. Brad from the left, Chuck from the right, they slid forward, ready for action.

Brad jerked to a halt. Chuck slowed down, hands on his hips. False alert. The shadow belonged to a small seventeen or eighteen-something dude in a tight black leather jacket with a turned-up collar, tight boot-cut blue jeans, red cowboy boots, and slicked-back brown hair. He was pointing to the pink Thunderbird. "These your wheels?" His voice was a soprano. His accent was thick, and he talked out the side of his mouth like a crafty old cowboy in a B-grade western.

Chuck's arms were at his sides, his features relaxed, but he wanted to smile. "Yeah, they're mine."

"Groovy." Outdated vocabulary. He seemed like a friendly little fellow, but Brad still checked for bumps or bulges that could signal a weapon. "I'm Country. My real moniker's Jean-Michel. Everybody's hankerin' to call me Country, you know, because of my cowboy style."

"What are you doing out here, Country? Everything's closed up tight."

"Ridin' herd, makin' sure everything's safe. I do this every night before I rustle up some grub. Gotta keep the neighborhood safe. For the womenfolk. You know."

"Have you ever seen anything?"

"Oh, yeah. Mostly whippersnappers breakin' into cars or throwin' rocks. Once I saw a purty female woman get hit by a car."

"What do you do when you see something?"

"I call John Law. They know me. You gents Americans?"

"Yep."

"I love the States. Gonna go live there when I get outta school."

Brad started thinking this charming, innocuous young vigilante-wannabe might come in handy. "Listen, Country, we've gotta get a move on, but we'll probably be coming around here often. Got some friends in the area. French suburbs aren't as safe as the city. Maybe we can check with you to make sure the coast is clear."

Country smiled ear to ear. "Cool. Here's my brand." He pulled out a card with his telephone number and address typed on it. This boy was dying to do good deeds.

"Thanks, Country. I'll be in touch."

Brad and Chuck jumped into the car and vroomed off. Country looked on wistfully as the pink Thunderbird disappeared around the bend.

11: Safe Haven

Jeanie took stock of her immediate situation. How had Benjamin managed to find out where she was being held incommunicado? She also was not buying his cock-and-bull story that as the *empresario* for the COG choir, she should benefit from the COG's legal department. Nevertheless, he handled all the legal work and had her out of there in less than an hour.

Those considerations notwithstanding, her situation was a significant improvement over what it was one hour before. She was now free from her *detention provisoire*. When she saw wild-eyed Benjamin with the cops in the interrogation room, she was sure it would end badly.

Benjamin was a "shepherd" over at the compound of the Children of God. She knew him well, and she recognized him as an ambitious, scheming, nasty little scumbag.

He was aiming for big things in the Children of God organization that Jeanie's investigation revealed had more than four thousand "disciples" in over a hundred and fifty colonies all over the world.

Most colonies only had about twenty disciples. Paris was the largest colony with over seventy-five disciples. More were arriving from the US every day. They believed the prediction by cult leader, David Berg, otherwise known as Moses, that a comet was going to destroy the USA.

Jeanie recognized this as the classic cult con game of the Jesus Revolution. Recruit credulous and vulnerable disciples. Relieve them of their worldly possessions. Brainwash them into total submission. Exploit them sexually and work them like slaves. When the scam risks being exposed and/or the profit evaporates, create a cataclysmic event as a pretext for a mass suicide that will eliminate the victims. The shepherds go onto greener pastures and fatter sheep.

Jeanie saw two twists to this scenario. The first was that the disciples were being warned to flee the cataclysm. Rather than using the cataclysm to motivate mass suicide, it looked like Moses was using it to drive his disciples overseas away from the US. The second twist was that the Children of God was changing its morality policy to support prostitution, drug trafficking, and pedophilia.

The new policy was being encouraged and enforced by a group of newcomers, aggressive surfer types from California. They came at an opportune moment just when the cult was under attack in the metro and on the streets by a bunch of gangbangers.

They stepped in to assure the protection of the other disciples. Their success had gained them a strong voice in how the cult was being run. They were encouraging aggressive "flirty fishing" by the females and drug sales by the males. She wondered how long the French police and reigning mafia would allow activities like that to go on.

Jeanie also thought there was more to it than petty crime and cult politics. These new California surfers were professional enforcers. They were intimidating and inspired fear in the hearts of the cult members. However, it was the terrorist angle that worried her. She really could not see any symbiotic benefit between the COG and the terrorist plot, but she was convinced her info was one hundred percent accurate. There had to be a link.

Her immediate problem was where she was going to sleep. Benjamin had offered her protection at the compound. She rejected it out of hand. That was the last place she wanted to end up.

Her apartment was a no-go, as well. It was a former crime scene and she would be uncomfortable. She wouldn't be safe there anyway. Her best bet was to disappear for a while and get the lay of the land. She decided to go to the safe house near the Porte de Champerret, where she regularly met with Gary.

When she left Benjamin, she pretended to head for her apartment. If anyone was following her, they would probably assume she was going home and start to relax their vigilance.

There was a taxi stand two blocks away from her apartment. She was relieved to see there were a couple of taxis waiting there for a fare.

She jumped in and gave the driver an address on the Champs-Elysées. She left the taxi at George V and went into the metro. She changed at Etoile and changed again at Villiers. She took line 3 to Louise Michel, then walked back to the Porte Champerret. She couldn't be sure she had not been followed. The metro and the streets were too crowded. She had a feeling. Just to make extra sure, she walked around the block before entering the building on the Rue Vernier where Gary had his safe house.

When she got into the apartment, she immediately called the emergency number and sat back to wait.

An hour and ten minutes later, she heard a knock at the door. She didn't move. That was the protocol. You could never be sure it wasn't a salesman or a neighbor. Seconds ticked by. Nothing.

She considered her options. There was a service entrance at the back of the apartment that led to the garage. She was headed to the service entrance when she heard the keys jangling in the lock. She stopped and started to relax. The door opened. It wasn't Gary.

12: Children of God

It was only 10 a.m., early enough that Zebulon and Sarah would still be around, even if they were planning on busking in the metro that day. He hesitated before the white ten-foot wall topped off with concertina wire, then stepped up to the small black cast-iron door. He hit the intercom and smiled at the camera aimed at the entrance.

Brad heard some rustling around behind the door, but nothing happened. He hit the intercom a second time and smiled again at the camera. There was some more rustling around. Then silence. The door opened, and Brad was face-to-face with a beautiful blond Amazon. Six feet tall. Dressed in a transparent, flowing ankle-length gown. Built like something Michaelangelo could only dream about. Smiling through gleaming white teeth. Brad lost his concentration. Her soft voice brought him back to reality. "Good morning, God bless. Can I help you?"

Brad figured he had a few Mississippis to spare, so he took his time to admire before he answered. "I'm Brad James, here to see Zebulon."

"I am Leila. Praise be to God. Please come in."

She preceded him up the walk to the main house and left him in a large, austere room devoid of any and all decoration. There were two wooden chairs and a wooden table. Brad chose a chair and sat down. It was creepy. He was alone, but he could feel he was being observed.

He cast around as discreetly as possible in search of potential peepholes or hidden cameras. He spotted a few. What the hell! They wouldn't see anything different than if they came at him in person. He made a big show of reaching into his white leather pouch, pulling out his Gitanes and his Zippo. With his left hand, he slipped a Gitane sans filtre out of the pack and placed it delicately between his lips. With his right hand, he cranked up the Zippo and used it to ignite the white cylinder of delicious black tobacco. He took a deep drag, held it for three Mississippis, and blew out a solid stream of pungent white smoke.

It produced the desired effect. The statuesque blond Amazon rushed into the room. "Brother Brad, we prefer that our guests refrain from smoking."

"So sorry, Sister Leila. I didn't see a sign."

That confirmed it. He was being observed.

It was a long wait. Too long. He could have smoked three Gitanes by the time he heard the noise in the hallway and the door opening. In walked Zebulon, smiling the smile. Surprise, surprise! He was followed by two hippie/guard types, the same two hippie/guards from the Parc Montsouris and the house at number 6, Rue de Montbuisson, Louveciennes. Zebulon introduced them as Joseph and Michael.

Zebulon took a seat across the table from Brad. He seemed relaxed, but the muscle twitching under his left eye suggested otherwise. Hippie soldiers Mike and Joe stood expressionless behind Zebulon. Zebulon sat silently with a laconic smile on his face. Brad sensed the hostility emanating from Mike and Joe. He sensed Zebulon's distress. It was an uncomfortable situation. Brad decided to wait it out.

He studied the two hippie soldiers. Good-looking, surfer-type specimens—tall, suntanned, and well-muscled; one blond, the other dark. Their demeanor and their presence were a message of negativity. Brad didn't like the message or the messengers. In fact, there were many things Brad didn't like about these two guys. The thing he disliked most was their arrogant belligerence. They were challenging him, and he was dying to take up the challenge.

A few years ago, he might have done it with a wisecrack or a rude gesture. He wouldn't do it today. It had cost him dearly in the past. He had learned long ago it was better to control his stupid personality defect that made defiance his default mode when he felt challenged.

Zebulon broke the silence. "Hey, Brad, what's up? What did you want to see me about?"

Brad had a number of questions he wanted to ask, but the presence of these two babysitters complicated the discussion. Brad decided to jump right in. "I came to see you about my friend, Jeanie Jones."

The name Jeanie Jones didn't get a reaction from Zebulon, but the two babysitters came to attention. "Yeah, Jeanie. What about her?"

"She missed an important meeting with me last night, and I have to see her. She hasn't been around here, has she?"

"I haven't seen her in a while, but Benjamin is the one who usually deals with her. She has been very successful in getting us on television."

"Any way I can get to talk with Benjamin?"

"I doubt it. He's one of the chief shepherds. Really busy. French elections and stuff." He hesitated and looked back at Joe. Joe nodded. Zebulon continued. "Maybe he can get free. Let me see."

Zebulon got up and left the room. Mike and Joe stayed standing right where they were, still arrogant, still menacing. Five minutes later, Zebulon was back. He was accompanied by a scrawny young thirty-something. The posture was slightly stooped, like an aging accountant. The head was shaved. The lips were thin, and the nose was pointed. It was the eyes. Big, round, clear blue rays blazed from deep within the dark sockets on either side of his nose. These were ambitious eyes—greedy, cruel, and malevolent. He stuck out his hand. "Brad, I'm Benjamin. So nice to meet you."

His wild eyes held Brad's attention. One word came to Brad's mind—actually, two words: pure evil. "My pleasure."

They shook hands. Brad checked. He still had all his fingers.

"Brother Zebulon tells me you're looking for Miss Jean Jones. May I inquire as to why?"

"She missed an appointment with me last night. I know she does a lot of business here, so, I thought I'd give it a try."

"You can put your mind at ease. I saw her yesterday over at the Rue de la Santé near the Hôpital Cochin. I can assure you that she is just fine."

"That's a relief. She wasn't hurt, was she?"

"No. Not at all. Just fine. She was visiting the prison. She was on her way home when we parted. By the way, please let me thank you for your timely intervention in the metro."

"No problem, Benjamin. My pleasure."

Visiting the prison! That was a euphemism. Sounded to Brad like she was now free. He'd better get in touch with Gary.

"I better get going, then. Thanks for the hospitality."

"Brad, please come any time you want. The Children of God could be your home."

"I appreciate that, Benjamin."

Mike and Joe crowded him a little too closely as they ushered him out. Benjamin was stroking his chin when they came back. "This guy will have to be dealt with. Transmit my message."

13: Sandbagged

Only two people were supposed to come through the safe house door: Jeanie Jones herself, and Gary Richards, Paris CIA station chief.

The sight of one of the handsomest men she had ever seen standing in the open doorway sent her into shock. She blinked to clear her vision. Thick black hair slicked straight back. Thin nose, white teeth, strong jaw. He was a shorter version of a young Tyrone Power. She didn't know whether to run for it or go on the attack.

He didn't seem to recognize her. There was no anger in his somber eyes, and he was smiling benevolently. "Don't be afraid. Gary sent me."

He entered the room and closed the door. She stepped back, looking for something she could use as a weapon.

"We got your emergency message. Gary's out of the office. He asked me to come and handle the situation."

That was not the agreed protocol. The agreed protocol was only Gary would have access to the emergency signal and the safe house. This guy's smooth good looks did nothing to calm her wariness. "Who are you?"

"My name is Brandon Butler. I work with Gary."

"Gary is station chief. You work for Gary?"

He slicked his hair back. "No. I am the DEA station chief. We work together."

"Never heard of the DEA."

"The Drug Enforcement Administration. They merged the Bureau of Narcotics and Dangerous Drugs and the Office of Drug Abuse Law Enforcement last July. Calm down, have a seat, and we can discuss the emergency."

Jeanie's alarm system was going full blast. She needed time to get a grip on the situation. Something was crooked. "Okay," she said. "Have a seat. I'll get us something to drink, and we can talk this over. Beer, wine, coffee, tea?"

"A coffee, please." Brandon was a gentleman.

Jeanie slipped into the kitchen. She didn't smoke and she didn't drink and she didn't take recreational drugs. She did take drugs to make her sleep and she always had them with her. One pill would knock her out for eight hours. She dropped five little pills into Brandon's coffee.

"Sugar?" she called.

"Two cubes."

Jeanie brought the beverages to the table and served Brandon. If the pills had any taste, the two sugars would take care of it.

Brandon slugged back his coffee in two gulps. He leaned forward and beamed out his most engaging smile. "I really needed that. I was running on empty."

He peered deep into Jeanie's eyes for a long second. Then dropped his eyes. When he looked back up, his expression was serious, concerned. Compassion was oozing from his pores.

"Okay, Jeanie, tell me what's up."

Jeanie squeezed out a worried frown and pursed her lips. "The French police put me in jail."

"We know that. They found drugs and drug paraphernalia in your apartment."

Jeanie fixed Brandon and studied his features, looking for an effect. She thought she detected some cloudiness in his eyes. "Those weren't my things. I don't take drugs. I have no idea how they got there, none whatsoever."

Brandon sat up a little straighter and wiped his forehead with his handkerchief. He leaned forward and adopted a severe expression. "The French are convinced you do. Why did they let you go?"

Jeanie didn't like the way this conversation was going. He was asking the wrong questions in the wrong way. "I don't know. They returned my things and told me to be available in case they wanted to talk to me."

"And just like that, they let you go, huh?" Brandon rubbed his eyes and broke into a jaw-snapping yawn. "Excuse me, got a sleepy spell. Got any more of that coffee?"

Jeanie went back into the kitchen and poured the last of the coffee into Brandon's cup. She added two lumps of sugar and two more pills for good luck. Stirred. Stopped. Went into her purse for two more pills and dropped them into the cup just to make sure.

Back in the sitting room, Brandon gulped down the coffee. Jeanie excused herself and slipped into the bathroom. When she came out, Brandon was slumped in his chair, four sails to the wind, stacking up the Z's.

She called the emergency number again, hurriedly changed her clothes, and went down the service stairway to the garage. She hesitated at the ground floor and listened.

It sounded like two people were going up the stairs. They

stopped at her floor and rang the bell. It wasn't the right ring. So, it wasn't Gary.

Now she was really on high alert. She continued on down to the garage exit on the side street and headed for the fallback destination.

14: Rude Awakening

The safe house was ransacked. A total mess. Brandon was sitting up in a sleepy stupor, trying to get a grip on consciousness. Gary was standing there, hands on his hips, surveying the scene. He was seriously griped off. "What happened here? What the hell are you doing here?"

Brandon was bumbling and mumbling. "That bitch. She drugged me."

Gary grabbed Brandon and pulled him up by his lapels. Nose to nose, Gary whispered, "Tell me, goddamn it, what the hell you are doing here?"

Brandon was slow and ropey, but he knew he was just one answer away from some serious time in the hospital. "You were out. The emergency signal came in. It was Jeanie. I had to make a call."

"You had to make nothing. The signal came to my office. For me. Only me. This house is a secret CIA asset. You have no authority and no permission. Zilch. Nada. Nothing. You shouldn't even know this place exists."

Brandon grabbed his head with both hands and slicked his hair back. "Okay, okay. I might have exceeded my remit. But Jeanie is part of my remit. Your assistant got the emergency signal. She knew we were working together. She asked me if I knew where you were. I convinced her you had cleared me to take care of emergencies. When I got here, Jeanie was waiting. She made me a coffee, and the next thing I remember is you shaking me awake. She drugged me."

"I congratulate Jeanie for that. Good work. She knew you weren't supposed to be here. And my assistant can thank you for losing her bonus and promotion, maybe even her job. She blew away Jeanie's cover and a safe house. The next question is who ransacked the apartment and why. The most important question is what happened to Jeanie."

Gary finished his inspection of the house. Nothing seemed to be missing, but it was compromised. It was possible that whoever ransacked the house also kidnapped Jeanie, but Gary didn't think so. There would be no reason to ransack the house if they already had Jeanie. Brandon's unauthorized appearance may have precipitated Jeanie's departure and saved her from those who ended up ransacking the apartment. That left the fallback plan. It would take Gary a lot of time and effort to get there. He was starting from a compromised safe house, so he would have to be sure he didn't bring any fleas along with him.

"Get outta here, Brandon. I'll deal with you back at the embassy."

Brandon slinked out of the apartment and Gary got on the phone to Chuck. He gave Chuck four appointments at four different places at precise times. Chuck understood Gary was requiring countersurveillance at these "appointments" and indicated he would handle it.

Gary set off. He took the metro at Porte de Champerret, got

off at Saint-Lazare, and went into the Printemps, a big department store. He climbed the stairs to the top floor, where Chuck was browsing around.

Two hippie types Chuck thought he recognized followed Gary out of the stairway. They lurked around, keeping their eyes on Gary. Gary worked his way down to the third floor, seemingly shopping but actually trying to expose any surveillance on him. When he slipped into the elevator on the third floor, the two hippies were taken by surprise. It was too late to get into the elevator with him, so they rushed for the stairway. Chuck watched them dash down the stairs, then headed for the next control point at the metro Pyramides.

Gary took the elevator to the basement, where he accessed the metro at Havre Caumartin. He changed at the Opéra and exited the metro two stations later at Pyramides, where he jumped into a taxi.

Chuck was there, observing the crowd. The hippies he had spotted in the Printemps must have lost Gary when he slipped into the elevator. There was nothing to suggest Gary was being followed when he jumped into the taxi. Gary was clean at the next two observation points as well.

Chuck gave Gary the all-clear sign, and Gary went to find Jeanie at the Hotel Intercontinental.

THE US EMBASSY, LATER IN THE DAY
Once Brandon got away from the safe house, he made a beeline for the embassy to get his version of the events back to Washington before Gary made his own report and destroyed Brandon's career.

He was disgusted with himself for forcing his way into Gary's operation. It was a beginner's blunder, one he would never repeat.

Gary would have ended up by cluing him in on what was going down, anyway.

Most of all, he felt humiliated Jeanie Jones had outmaneuvered him. A rookie, female beginner. She could have killed him. He could still feel the effects of the sleeping pills she fed him. He slept through the ransacking of the safe house. It was Gary who woke him from his drug-induced slumber, completely oblivious to the chaos that had been wreaked all around him. He had been totally at the mercy of the ransackers.

His report was a masterpiece of smoke, mirrors, and spin. Without explicitly stating any provable falsehoods, the report presented him as having saved the operation in general and Jeanie in particular from catastrophe. In his report, a deep undercover asset warned him of an impending attack on a Company employee at an embassy safe house. When he intercepted the emergency signal in Gary's absence—an absence he mentioned repeatedly in his report—he decided he would put his career at stake and go to the rescue. Fortunately, he arrived before the bad guys and was able to warn Jeanie. Unfortunately, he didn't have time to convince her of his honorable intentions, and she drugged him senseless.

He hit the button and transmitted his report to Washington. His future depended on his ability to convince Washington that Gary was mismanaging the whole affair.

15: Hostile Takeover

Chuck found Brad working out at the dojo at Montagne-Sainte-Geneviève and filled him in on the emergency. Their meeting was scheduled at Brad's apartment on the Rue d'Assas, right next to the Université de Paris II.

Brad hurried over and parked his Indian in front of his building where he could see it from his terrace on the second floor. That motorcycle was his pride and joy. He'd purchased it for a song in Madrid right after he came over from the States over six years ago. It was nothing but a rusted heap of metal that took him over a full-time month of sweat, tears, elbow grease, and many thousands of *pesetas* to get restored. Since then, it had been his constant companion.

Inside his apartment, he pulled down the shades and checked the wooden dresser drawer with the secret compartment where he kept sensitive documents and his Beretta 950. The Beretta was a well-crafted tool that had come in handy on more than one occasion. He wiped it down gently with the felt cloth wrapping, then closed the compartment.

From the terrace, he surveyed the street below. Bicycles,

Solexes, scooters, and motorcycles were parked everywhere. The uni itself was nothing but a seven-story building with amphitheaters, classrooms, offices, and a restaurant on the top floor. Chuck had arrived, and his pink Thunderbird parked out front was the star of the show with the students who were milling around the entrance to the uni. Chuck showboated a little, then broke off and strode into Brad's building.

Chuck filled Brad in on the little he knew about the emergency. Jeanie had been released, a safe house had been compromised and ransacked, and Jeanie was on the run from some unknown aggressors. Gary would be there shortly to give them the details.

Brad was interested in the countersurveillance Chuck had provided for Gary. He was intrigued Chuck had recognized the two hippies following Gary as two of the guys they had seen at the house in Louveciennes. "You sure it was them?"

"Positive. They're the religious enforcers ridin' herd on the hippies. Gary managed to ditch them somewhere along the line."

"These guys are all over the place. Besides the Printemps and Louveciennes, they scooped up the body at the Parc Montsouris and stood guard at the Children of God compound while I met with Zebulon, the singer. Their names are Michael and Joseph. Zebulon was afraid of them."

Brad sat back and lit up a Gitane sans filtre. Chuck pulled out a brown pipe, fumbled around with a tobacco pouch, and stuffed the tobacco into the pipe bowl. The bowl was big and round. The stem was curved and had a yellow plastic mouthpiece. Chuck chomped down on the mouthpiece, started puffing, and lit up the tobacco. Stupidly, he tried to inhale a lungful of the pungent smoke. He was immediately seized by a spasm of violent coughing.

Brad was smiling, but he was more amazed than amused. "You look like an accomplished educator. Or even worse, like an aspiring intellectual. All you need is a pair of brown corduroy pants, a baggy jacket, and some wire-rimmed grandma glasses. They'll hire you as a university professor with tenure thrown in. Might even get invited to discuss books, politics, and the meaning of life on TV. Forget the pipe, man. It's too ridiculous, even for you."

Chuck finally stopped coughing. "Hey, croon daddy, the French girls prefer the mind, not the body."

"Feel safe, then, because you've got neither. Has Gary seen your pipe?"

"Naw, just bought it."

The knock came. It was Gary. His usually impeccable appearance was looking worse for the wear. His face was drawn, and he was standing slightly stooped. His concern featured in the hollow eyes and tight lips.

"Hi, guys. I could use a coffee. What a day! It looks like Mitterrand's going to win the election. We can't get involved directly, but everybody is anxious, buzzing around contacting, analyzing, cajoling, worrying. And you know? Before they do anything, they come to me for information."

Brad motioned toward the kitchen. "Serve yourself. The coffee's hot, and the sugar's on the shelf."

Gary came back with a mug of steaming coffee and four lumps of sugar. He plopped two in the mug and stirred. The third lump he dipped into the coffee and ate like candy. He held the fourth lump between his thumb and forefinger for all to see. "I deserve this." He dipped it into his coffee, then gobbled it up.

That seemed to relax him. Brad turned on the radio to add some background noise to the street noise coming in from the terrace on the off chance somebody was trying to listen in. "Baby Sugar Love" by the Rubettes came blasting out of the box. Brad loved it. Gary frowned. He was more Kris Kristofferson than this be-bop-a-lula-bubble-gum stuff. At the end of the day, background music was background music, and it was Brad's digs.

"What's up, Gary?"

"Jeanie's out of jail. The honcho from the Children of God, a guy called Benjamin, managed to spring her. Looks like he has some kind of political influence. Anyway, the cops had nothing, no fingerprints on the drug paraphernalia, no evidence of personal use, no motive for rubbing out the COG shepherds. They had to release her. Jeanie told me Benjamin wanted to take her to their compound, but she refused. She used her head, followed our protocol, and went to the safe house instead. This is where it gets interesting. I was out of the office when the emergency signal came in. Brandon interacted with my assistant and went in my place."

"Is that regular procedure?"

"Absolutely not. Brandon used his considerable charm to circumvent procedure." He shook his head disgustedly.

Brad noticed the furrowed brow and the deep lines at the corners of his eyes. Suddenly, his face lit up. "I'll handle Brandon and my assistant in due time. In any case, Brandon showed up at the safe house instead of me. Jeanie was suspicious and afraid. She drugged Brandon and slipped away while he was unconscious."

"Drugged him? Oh, man! How'd she do it?" Brad was laughing.

"With pills for her sleeping disorder. She hit him with ten times the recommended dosage in his coffee. It really took him out. Could have killed him. When I woke him up, he looked like he was coming off a long night in the barrel. He was wasted."

There was some cheering coming from the students outside. Brad went to take a look. Students were taking pictures of themselves using Chuck's Thunderbird as a backdrop.

The students were all in an uproar with the oncoming elections just around the corner. They were organizing demonstrations and anticipating battles with the students from the uni (university) at Paris-Panthéon. The Assas fac next door was a Rightist stronghold. Paris-Panthéon was a Leftist stronghold. Bad blood between them. They often squared off with iron bars, baseball bats, brass knuckles, and bricks.

Somebody had used a roll of toilet paper to write *"mort à la gauche,"* death to the Left, on the hood of the car. Chuck had a conniption fit. He wanted to run down there and massacre a mass of those worthless students. If the Leftists saw that message, they would destroy his pride and joy.

Brad held him back. "Cool your jets, man. They're our friends. They know you. They're just using your car to take pictures. They'll clean off the toilet paper once they get their pics." He whistled and yelled down to the students. "Go easy on the merchandise and clean off the car when you're finished."

"No problem. We're taking good care of it."

That satisfied Chuck. "Okay, Gary. What happened after Jeanie drugged Brandon?"

"Like I said, she slipped out the back service stairway. On her way out, she heard two people go up the stairs and ring at the safe house."

"Did she see what they looked like?"

"No, she only heard them. She didn't stick around for any more info. She hightailed it out of there and went to plan B. By the time I got there, the safe house had been ransacked, probably by them."

"How did they know about the safe house? Did Brandon tip them off?"

"Doubt it. I think Benjamin had her followed when she left la Santé."

"Why would he do that?"

"Jeanie told me a group of new jock-style, alpha macho-male

types was gaining influence in the Children of God. They were pushing to force the female members to prostitute themselves as a means of recruiting new members and influencing 'decision-makers' in France on drug policy. 'Flirty fishing,' they called it. They're also sending some of the girls to COG compounds in other countries. Jeanie says they're being trafficked."

"Hey," Brad interrupted, "that's interesting. Chef, the French cop, asked me about sex trafficking when he was interrogating me."

"Yeah," Gary rambled on, "sex trafficking doesn't surprise me. These are really bad dudes. They also want the guys to sell drugs. Nothing really sensational here, though. Prostitution, blackmail, human trafficking, and drug dealing. Just run-of-the-mill, conventional bad stuff. Many of these sects end up resorting to such things in order to survive and provide their masters with a sumptuous lifestyle."

"Doesn't sound like anything that would warrant all this frame-up, incarceration, ransack-a-safe-house stuff that's going on," Brad said.

"You're right on that. If it's just an internal power struggle within the family of the Children of God, we're not really worried about it. But, goddamn it, after debriefing Jeanie, I think it's something much worse."

"Cut to the chase, man."

Gary clasped his hands and gathered his thoughts. "The urgent message Jeanie had for me when she got busted was the Children of God have made a deal with a radical revolutionary cell operating in the Paris area. This cell is violent. It has killed and is willing to kill in the name of its ideology. The ideology is more or less the same as the Weathermen in the States or the Red Brigades in Italy. They want a revolution to free the world from *impérialisme*. Jeanie says the Children of God are cooperating with these terrorists to launch some kind of attack before the elections."

Chuck was still curious. "Why would the Children of God do that? What do they get out of it?"

Gary nodded. "Good question."

There was a long silence while everybody was thinking it over. Brad broke the silence. "The guys in the metro who attacked the two buskers from the COG were being paid by some mysterious person to attack them. The guy who got clobbered in the Parc Montsouris looked like he was one of the gangbangers being paid to target the COG disciples. The two guys I saw at the COG compound were the same two who cleared his body out of the Parc. If Jeanie's info about hijacking a religious cult is correct, it could be this revolutionary gang is organizing the attacks on the disciples to create a need for their protection. They infiltrate the cult by providing the protection that ends the attacks and basically take it over by force."

Chuck was impressed. "Crafty, fox daddy! Organize the attacks. Provide protection from the attacks you organized. Establish your power base by ending the attacks. Take over the organization."

Brad was on a roll. "We know the two macho alpha-type hippies from Louveciennes are involved with the COG, but there's no evidence any of them belong to any terrorist cell. What about the foreign license plates? Can you get your friend to help us, Chuck?"

"I'll check out the license plate numbers and get the information on the owners."

Brad had one more question for Gary. "Is Jeanie's informant on the terrorists reliable? She can lead us to the terrorists."

"The girl calls herself Salanha. She's about twenty-two or twenty-three. She dresses like a typical flower child, long hair, no makeup, long dresses and sandals. But that's where the similarity ends. Jeanie says she's very well-spoken and polite. She doesn't drink or take drugs and follows a strict health regimen that includes two hours of strength and cardio exercise every day. She lives in an apartment she sublets on the Boulevard Saint-Germain. Must cost a fortune."

Brad was impressed. "A far cry from your typical hippie."

"She has no obvious means of support, but she has no money problems. Her family is probably supporting her. She has flirted with a couple of cults in Paris, one of which was the COG. Jeanie says she was disappointed with the reality of life in a cult. That's why she took the apartment. But she's still interested in the COG. Here's the clincher. Her fiancé is a member of the terrorist cell linked to the COG. Jeanie says it was Salanha who introduced her boyfriend to the COG hierarchy."

"It's a no-brainer," Chuck said. "We just follow her when she goes to meet her boyfriend."

Gary shook his head. "That's the problem. She doesn't go to meet him. He comes to meet her. She says she has no idea if and when he comes. She says she has no idea where he lives or how to get in touch with him. He just pops around whenever the desire hits him. Claims it's for security."

Chuck whistled appreciatively through his teeth. "A situation almost too good to be true, eh? Anything else?"

"Just that she has a class three times a week at the Alliance Française over on Raspail. You could probably pick her up leaving for class some morning. Can't be too many young women fitting her description living in this building."

"Good. We'll check it out. Meanwhile, Chuck and I can go back to Louveciennes and add some electronic improvements to the house and garage. What do you think, Chuck?"

"I like it," Chuck said. "We have some new equipment at Latorre Legal I'm dying to use. One problem. What about those dogs?"

Brad just smiled. "I've got an idea. Let me handle it."

Gary finished off his coffee and stood up. "Okay, I'll leave it with you two. I've got to get Jeanie set up in some new digs. Too dangerous for her to go back to her apartment. She's our main source of info for the moment. I don't want to lose her." He bowed his head. "I'm afraid she's ready to disappear."

"Why."

"She used the safe-house phone to make two calls. One was to her bank. The other was to a travel agency."

16: The Bug

It was 7:03 and the sun was setting. In another thirty-five minutes, it would be totally dark. Brad parked his motorcycle on the Rue Saint-Michel down the street from the café. Chuck dismounted with his toolkit and electronic eavesdroppers. Brad had his white leather pouch and a rucksack. They were dressed in dark suits and ties to fit right in with the up-and-coming young professionals who infested the area. By the time it got dark, these residential streets would be all but deserted, and they didn't want to attract any undue attention.

Their plan was straightforward. They would walk down Rue de Montbuisson to number 6, turn left on Rue Louis Forest, slip into the strip of woods bordering the property, and sit down and wait until the lights went off in the house. They would then proceed to install the electronic voice-activated eavesdroppers Chuck had acquired in the garage and, if possible, in the house. The devices were small and very expensive with a battery life of two to three weeks.

The most delicate phase of the operation involved neutralizing the two Doberman watchdogs. This would have to be done without riling up the dogs. Brad reached into his rucksack and pulled out a plastic bag. "See this bag?"

"Yep. What's in it? Smells like hamburger."

"It *is* hamburger. Hamburger augmented with acepromazine and telazol, dog sedatives. Got a buddy in veterinary medicine school. He got the drugs for me. Says a couple of these delicious meatballs should make the dogs so sleepy they can't move. The disclaimer is that sometimes there are exceptions, and you get the opposite effect."

"How do you plan to deliver the payload?"

"The kennel where they keep the dogs at night isn't far from the street. I plan on lobbing the meatballs into it from the edge of the woods."

"Good luck with that, Willie Mays. What if those dogs don't like hamburger?"

"All dogs like hamburger. The drugs are supposed to act fast and last several hours. I figure we have about twenty minutes to install one device in the garage and one in the kitchen, if we can get in."

They slipped into the woods close enough to watch the house but far enough away that they wouldn't attract the dogs' attention. The downstairs lights went off at 10 p.m. By 11, the house was completely dark. In the driveway were the same three vehicles as before along with a shiny red Ferrari sports car with Italian plates. At 11:30 Brad said, "Let's go."

They used the wooded strip as cover to approach the house. When they were in position, Brad opened the bag of hamburger and began to make his first meatball. The dogs didn't give him a chance. Their olfactory organs were operating overtime. They began to growl, bark, and whine.

A light went on upstairs. Brad stuck the hamburger back in the sack and retreated to their former position. "I'm going to have to make the meatballs away from the dogs and keep it in the bag so they can't smell it until I throw it to them. Somebody on the second floor is already on the alert."

When Brad got back into position with his drug-laced meatballs, the dogs were restless. He launched the first three quarter-pound meatballs perfectly. The dogs scarfed them up before he got the fourth one out of the bag.

The light on the second floor went on again. Brad melted back into the underbrush with Chuck. They waited and watched. Fifteen minutes went by. The light on the second floor went off, but the dogs' behavior didn't change. They were milling around, waiting for the next meatball delivery. Brad launched the fourth meatball into the kennel. Each dog got a piece of it.

Another fifteen minutes and the dogs were sprawled out in the kennel, apparently sufficiently sedated. Brad signaled to Chuck it was time to move.

Chuck's jungle sixth sense kicked in. "Wait."

There was a shadow moving on the street at the corner, and it was holding a shotgun. It was one of the hippie soldiers, and he was moving their way. There was nowhere to hide from somebody who was really looking. This guy was really looking. There was also nowhere to run. They would have to fight. Their only chance was to ambush him before he knew they were there. If the ambush succeeded, they would be safe, but their operation would be over. If the ambush failed, it would be the end of their existence.

Chuck began to advance stealthily through the trees toward the oncoming hippie soldier. He drew his knife. Coiled to spring.

The hippie stopped, peered into the shadows. Started to move. Stopped dead in his tracks.

A bloodcurdling wail exploded from the kennel. The hippie jerked himself upright, cocked his ear, whipped around, and dashed through the underbrush toward the sound. Brad and Chuck took advantage of the distraction to hightail it off down Rue Louis Forest, where they found a vantage point at the end of the property.

"Sounded like a Doberman was having a bad trip."

"Second that."

The hippie's ministrations calmed the wailing Doberman, but now the other dog was agitated, growling and snorting and snarling. This canine security system was shutting down. Lights went on all over the house. Three guys came out onto the patio—the second macho hippie, the good-looking, well-dressed bossman, and a short, stocky Mediterranean type, probably the owner of the red Italian sports car.

The bossman was holding a pistol. "We got visitors?"

"No, I think the dogs are sick. What did they have to eat?"

"Regular dog food and some leftovers from the kitchen."

"Well, that must be it. I've told you not to feed them leftovers. They are goddamned dogs and should only eat dog food."

"Yeah, well I'm gonna check it out."

He went to the tree line and walked to the fence at the end of the property. Brad and Chuck were out of sight down the street. Bossman poked around in the bushes. Looked around in the thin strip of woods. Turned around and walked back to the patio.

"Got any medicine for the dogs?"

"No, they'll be okay."

Chuck saw his chance. He took advantage of the darkness outside the ring of light from the patio where the four guys were standing. They had checked it out. Their guard was down. This was how Chuck had sent many a gook to the happy hunting grounds. He scurried onto the property to the back of the garage. The door was unlocked. Chuck slipped in.

The back of the garage was filled with junk. Bedsteads, pots and pans, some tools, books, old clothes. The usual. However, on the right wall of the garage just behind the main door, there was a desk covered with assorted documents both typed and handwritten. Maps of Europe, the United States, and the UK were pasted on the wall above the desk. The deep shelves to the right of the desk were stocked with a wide range of handguns, rifles, shotguns, machine guns, and ammunition to go along with the firearms. The bottom shelves contained what looked like explosive devices. It was a small arsenal.

Chuck was deciding on where to hide the listening device when he heard heavy footsteps approaching. He shrank to the back of the garage and squatted down. The good-looking bossman came in with the Mediterranean dude. The Mediterranean dude was decked out in what looked like a white silk designer suit that fit so elegantly it had to be custom-made. His mauve silk shirt was open to the navel, exposing an elliptical gold medallion hanging from a thick gold chain. He had a Jesus Christ mustache and beard, and his hair was cut like Jesus in Michaelangelo's *Last Supper*. Except for the fact his hair was a little too dark and his nose a little too long, he could have been a candidate for crucifixion back in the day.

Bossman pointed to a map on the wall. "Luigi, I have marked the locations of the new clients you have found us with the green pins. We can go over the details on each one before you leave."

Luigi extended his arms in supplication and shook his head. "Not Luigi, *amico mio*. Il Messia, I am Il Messia. The world knows me as Il Messia. You are known as Lazarus. I call you Lazarus, not Jimmy."

Lazarus launched a beautiful, beaming smile. His green eyes gleamed in the yellow light of the lantern. "Il Messia, *perdonami*. We are so close. Sometimes I forget. I have the wines you wanted locked away in the back of the garage. Want to take a look?"

A short hesitation. "Yes, I would like that."

Chuck was in the back of the garage. He cast around for a place to hide. Nowhere. Anyway, he couldn't move without being heard. He placed his kit bag carefully beside him and pulled out his knife for the third time this evening. This was going to be a bloody affair. He hoped it would also be silent.

Lazarus started toward the back of the garage when Il Messia put a hand on his shoulder. "Hold it. Maybe better to take a look later, *amico mio*. I have a devoted disciple waiting upstairs to share an anti-capitalist experience with me. Not good to keep her waiting."

Bossman reluctantly agreed. The two men left and closed the door. Chuck breathed a sincere sigh of relief. He proceeded to fix the listening device on the wall behind a beam near the desk and scooted out the back of the garage to the safety of the wooded strip.

Brad was there. "Got some interesting info, Brad."

17: The Gangbangers from Department 93

"We've been through this a hundred times, Chuck. We know the people at number 6 Montbuisson are up to no good. The bug you installed should give us some inside info on what exactly they're up to."

"My contact at police headquarters got me the info on the Renault. It's on a long-term lease to an American from California, thirty years old. Name is Michael Bishop. He's been in France since early 1973. Bishop is also the guy who rents the house in Louveciennes."

"Any info on what he does?"

Chuck laughed. "He's got a student resident card to study French. He's applied for permanent residency."

"Anything else?"

"My contact's workin' on it. He has to be super careful. French police frown on unauthorized collaboration with foreigners. These elections coming up are making them more sensitive than ever."

Brad got up and walked out onto the terrace. Sunny and cloudless with a soft south-easterly breeze. The uni down below was deserted. The students were out demonstrating. Mayday is Labor Day everywhere in the world outside the US. Everything is closed except the essential services like restaurants, hotels, and cafés, and the Communist Party comrades are out selling bouquets of lily of the valley at exorbitant prices. That means everybody is free to demonstrate, and every Mayday, that is exactly what many Frenchmen and women do. Because of the upcoming elections and the surging power of the Leftists, today the demonstrations would be on steroids.

"What do you think they're doing with the Children of God?" Brad asked.

"These are probably the ones Jeanie says are trying to take over the cult."

"Yeah, it looks that way, but I don't see these guys as underground terrorists. They're too open. They buy cars and rent apartments in their real names. They aren't even French. They stand out like the bearded lady. There's no real attempt at subterfuge. They have flashy sports cars parked in plain sight of the street."

"Maybe they're the frontmen for the underground."

"Could be! But what's the motive? There has to be more to it than that."

Chuck slugged back the rest of his beer and looked at his watch. It was getting late, and Brad knew Chuck always stopped by his office for a few hours before he went out on the town.

"You busy tonight, Chuck?"

"There are a few gorgeous French females lusting after my mind and my body, but I suppose I could convince them to wait a few hours. What did you have in mind?"

"I think the secret lies in their relationship with the

gangbangers. Let's find the gangbangers and talk to them."

"Sounds like a loser to me. We don't know how to find them, and even if we did, how would we get them to talk to us?"

Brad went to his pouch and pulled out an envelope with some documents in it. "You see these documents? They belong to the guys I dueled with in the metro. Photo, age, and address. We could pay them a visit. Find out how their relationship with the Children of God is going."

"You surprise me, snoop daddy. What department do they live in?"

"Ninety-three."

"Ninety-three!" Chuck was dubious. "Ninety-three is the most dangerous department in the whole country. It's crawling with ba-dass Arabs and Blacks. It's a goddamn war zone. We would stand out like ears on the headless horseman."

BONDY, DEPARTMENT 93, LATE EVENING MAY 1, 1974
By the time Brad got to Bondy in department 93, it was a full moon, a star-studded sky, and sixty-five degrees. Just too beautiful to be wasted in this crummy Parisian suburb. He parked his Indian on a quiet side street a kilometer away. Chuck would come in from the other side. Brad traded his helmet for a baseball cap, shrugged into an oversized hoodie, and set off on foot for Tough Number One's address. He felt almost naked without his pouch but had to leave it at home. It would attract too much attention.

He had already scouted out the area, passing by several times trying to get the lay of the land. Just as Chuck had predicted, the place was crawling with groups of young Arabs and Blacks bop-ping around and hanging out, looking for a victim or some other kind of unsavory excitement. Loners drew attention, especially lon-ers foreign to the area. All three of the toughs he had confronted in the metro lived in the same high-rise, so Brad decided the café on the corner was his best bet to spot one of them.

Strangely enough, no one paid any attention when he entered the café and went to a table on the terrace where he ordered a *demi*. If not an open challenge, he was expecting at least some hostile stares. The place was really rocking, so to speak. The females were squealing and laughing. The guys were strutting around boasting and high-fiving. The attire was diverse. The guys' getups were pretty tame: sneakers, hoodies, and jeans, just like Brad. The girls' getups were wild. Some were in colorful short skirts and high-heeled boots; some were in sneakers and jeans; some were in hijabs and veils and sneakers; some in hijabs and veils and spike-heeled shoes; and some combined all the elements. The music was that Oriental, whiney string stuff with a beat. Everybody was animated in gesture, in word, and in deed.

After about thirty minutes, Brad was starting to feel like those ears on the headless horseman. Nothing specific, just a feeling. He decided to call it a night, paid, and headed down the street. He'd have to find another way to access Tough Number One.

"Hey, man. Nice boots."

The voice came from nowhere. Brad stopped, surprised, on his guard. He stepped back toward the cars parked on the street. With his back protected, he peered into the doorway where the voice was.

A Black dude stepped into the circle of light emanating from the only functioning streetlamp. Then another one, another one, another one, another one. There were five of them in all. They weren't smiling. Neither was Brad.

18: The Discussion

"I said, 'nice boots.'"

The voice belonged to the biggest and blackest of the five. He was six feet ten inches tall, a fierce-looking mountain of muscle from the top of his shaved head to the tips of his oversized black Army boots. His forearm was bigger than Brad's thigh. The other four dudes came in various sizes, hairdos, and sartorial selections.

They had two things in common: They were mean-looking mothers, and they were all in good shape.

They began to form a semicircle around Brad.

Running was not an option. Brad was fast, but his endurance was limited by all the Gitanes sans filtres he consumed every day. Negotiation was obviously not an option, either. Confrontation was the only thing left.

The odds were bad, five to one. The Blacks all had blades of one kind or another. Brad had his Beretta with eight bullets in it. The Beretta would have to be a last resort, however. Gunshots would draw a crowd, and he was an outsider.

Brad's experience told him that if he took out the two baddest, the other three would back off. Big Black was obviously the baddest, and the guy to his left moved like he was pretty bad, as well. So, Big Black would be target number one. The guy to his left would be number two.

Big Black was strong but slow. Brad's plan was to draw Big Black in close and take him out with a side kick to the knee. He would use his forward motion to go after Black Number Two. His attack would depend on how Black Number Two reacted to Brad's assault on Big Black. Everything depended on speed, accuracy, and timing.

Brad's adversaries were organized and ready to pounce. He let his training transport him to combat mode, the zone, a world of slow motion and kinetic calm. He stared down Big Black in the middle of the semicircle, challenging him with raised eyebrows and a curled lip to transmit a clear signal of his disdain.

"These boots *are* nice. Thanks for the compliment."

"Hand 'em over."

"They're yours if you can take 'em, fat boy."

"Fat boy" was the touch Brad figured would infuriate Big Black. Make him lose his cool. He wasn't wrong. Nobody challenged Big Black. The last guy who tried it won a one-way ticket to the paraplegic ward in the Hôpital Cochin.

Big Black waved back his flunkies. He made a big show of moving slowly forward while flexing his outsized biceps, shoulders, and pecs. At the two-meter mark, he lunged forward and planted his right foot as he slashed at Brad with the knife in his right hand.

Brad slipped to the left, raised his right knee, and placed a perfectly executed side kick to the outside of Big Black's right knee. Bullseye. With the crunch of tearing cartilage and breaking bone, Big Black crashed to the ground writhing and moaning and clutching his knee.

Brad let his follow-through propel him forward to engage Black Number Two, who had dodged to his left rather than advancing or retreating. He was out of Brad's reach, with Big Black's writhing body separating the two of them.

A third Black came at Brad from the left, straight razor at the fore. Brad just managed to whip around and block the attack. He used Black Number Three's momentum to propel him into Black Number Two, who was rushing in from the right. They collided and tumbled to the ground.

Black Number Three jumped to his feet, his razor dripping blood. Black Number Two stayed down, holding his throat. It started as a thin red line. Then blood began to trickle between Number Two's fingers. The thin red line opened, and a red river of blood gushed from Number Two's severed carotid. Number Three's attack had missed Brad but scored a bullseye on his crime buddy.

The three remaining Blacks continued to threaten and curse, but they stayed far from Brad's reach. He was considering his options when a semiautomatic with a silencer on the end of it emerged from the bushes. On the other end of the semiautomatic stood Tough Number One from the metro, the very person Brad was looking for.

"You move, motherfucker, you're dead."

Brad didn't move. Tough Number One pointed at the two downed Blacks. Black Number Three went to check out Black Number Two. He was a goner. Another Black went over to help Big Black to his feet. The last Black stood beside Tough Number One and his semiautomatic, who were doing the talking.

"Been waitin' for this. Spotted you before you walked into the café, white boy. Big mistake. This is my turf. First, I'm gonna break your arms. Then I'm gonna break your legs. Then I'm gonna kick your head in. You see this arm?"

It was the one Brad had smashed up in the metro. It was in a heavy plaster cast from the shoulder to the fingers.

"This arm is fucked up forever. I'm a goddam invalid. Because of you. My best friend's brain is fucked up. He'll never be normal again. Because of you. My cousin's face is fucked up, and he's blind in one eye. Because of you."

What could Brad say? Tough Number One was speaking the truth. Brad had treated them badly. No sense in debating the point. Of course, they'd gotten exactly what they deserved, and Brad had no remorse whatsoever. On the contrary! Teaching these scumbags a lesson had made his day. Brad wisely decided to keep that to himself. Belaboring the point would be unhelpful in the present circumstances.

Tough Number One motioned to Brad. "See that door? Start walkin' toward it." It looked like the entrance to a cellar or an underground garage. "We'll have some privacy there."

Brad knew his options were few and none and getting scarcer all the time. Either he got away or he was sentenced to death—a painful death. His only chance was to disarm Tough Number One, but Number One was wary and was staying out of Brad's range. It wouldn't be long before the other neighborhood tough guys came over to join the fun, and the game would be all over.

Brad still had his Beretta. This was one of those proverbial rock-and-hard-place situations. If he used the gun, the whole neighborhood would come alive, and he didn't have enough ammo to wipe out half the town's population. On the other hand, if he didn't use it, he was dead meat anyway. End of story.

As he turned toward the door, he let his hand slip into his pocket. His fingers curled around the handle of his Beretta. Tough Number One caught the move. "Get your hands in the air."

In the split second Brad was deciding to dodge and draw, he heard a pop. The Black guy next to Tough Number One dropped to the ground holding his thigh. Tough Number One whipped around and came face-to-silencer with a .38 caliber protruding from Chuck's right hand. Tough Number One froze. Brad pulled his pistol.

Chuck snatched the semiautomatic. "This might come in handy for me. You'll have to tell me how you get your ammo for it." He handed it to Brad. "Okay, tough guy, start walking straight ahead. Move it, Brad. I've got a car parked around the corner."

Tough Number One understood that any resistance would spell the end of his ongoing existence. He didn't resist. His buddies were less perceptive. They realized what was happening and began to scream and yell, building up their courage to rush the two outsiders. Brad squeezed off a short leg-level burst with the semi. Two Blacks went down screaming and holding their shins. The others ran back and started to regroup.

Chuck and Tough Number One were almost to the corner where the car was parked. By now, there were at least fifteen men in the group bearing down on Brad. Five of them broke off into the street in an effort to outflank him.

Brad squeezed off another waist-high burst. Two of the five went down. The other three dove for cover. The main group hung back and started to spread out.

One of them had found a gun and began firing away. Brad finally made it to Chuck's car. Chuck had used a company car instead of his scooter or his pink T-Bird. He jumped into the car and cranked it up. Brad pushed Number One into the back and jumped in after him.

The gang was closing in, but it was too late. Chuck popped the clutch, laid some rubber, and tore down the street.

Number One was trying to look defiant, but his heart was not in it. His arm was crippled. He had just been humiliated in front of all his buddies, and he was the prisoner of a guy he had tried to kill just minutes before. How much worse could it get?

Brad felt sorry for him in a way, but not sorry enough not to smack the plaster cast on his arm to let him know he was in deep shit.

"I need some answers," Brad said. "I don't have much time. If I don't believe you, I'm going to smash that plaster cast to smithereens and beat your arm to a pulp with this hammer. Do I have your full attention?"

"Yeah."

"Question number one: Are you still preying on the Children of God?"

Number One's face clouded. "Whaddaya mean 'preying'?"

"Attacking."

"Oh. Thought you meant like church. No."

"Why?"

"The hoodie dude told us to stop."

Brad took Number One's bad arm in his hands and lifted it gently. Number One started to squirm. A bead of perspiration formed on his forehead and rolled down his nose. "A hoodie dude? You're telling me that some foreign hoodie dude told you to stop and just like an obedient child, you stopped?"

"No, no, it wasn't like that. He was paying us to roll those guys. Then he told us to stop, but it was good business and we continued."

Number One was fighting for his life.

"He found out about it. He knew everything that goes on in the metro. Then our guys started getting attacked by guys like you. Bigger than you. Worse than you. Well, maybe not worse, but bigger.

Couple of my buddies just disappeared. He called again and told me the Children of God were off-limits, just like you did. He also told me my buddies would never be coming back. We decided to leave the Children of God alone."

"Why do you say he knew everything that goes on in the metro?"

"We couldn't cheat him. If we claimed more attacks than what we really did, he knew it. He penalized us for cheating. Sometimes we would take out some of those Krishna guys and try to claim credit for it. He knew the attacks were on the Krishnas and not the Children of God. He knew the exact times and places of the attacks as well as the items we robbed. The guy was magic."

Brad watched the buildings flash by. Sounded like the truth. Fit in with Brad's analysis.

The foreign hoodie dude knew about every attack because he was in cahoots with the victims' superiors. His knowledge of the attacks on the Krishnas suggested he was in cahoots with that hierarchy, as well.

He pulled a Gitane sans filtre out of the pack in his jacket pocket. Lit up with his Zippo. Tough Number One was eyeing the cigarette with unvarnished desire.

"Smoke?"

"Merci."

Brad lit him up.

"How 'bout you, Chuck? Smoke?"

"No thanks. What're we gonna do with this guy? Gonna have to kill him?"

Brad turned to Tough Number One. Number One's face was all twisted up. Perspiration flowed freely down his cheeks. "I don't know. Are we gonna have to kill you?"

"No. No way, man. No way. I'm with you guys. I can help you

find the guy with the hoodie."

"Why would you do that?"

"To stay alive, man. Besides, the hoodie guy really pissed us off. Disrespected us. We want his ass. We're already trying to hunt him down."

"How do I know I can trust you?"

"My word, man. You got my word. My word is my bond. Here's my number. Call me. Don't come into the neighborhood. They'll remember you."

Brad didn't really believe that once out of the car he would keep his word, bond or no bond. Warning Brad away from the neighborhood was a sign he was sincere, at least in the heat of the moment.

It was also likely he hated the foreign hoodie more than he hated Brad. The attacks had been orchestrated, then terminated. That's all Brad needed to know, and anyway, he had no intention of killing the guy.

"Okay. It's a deal. I'm gonna drop you off at a metro station. Got a ticket?"

"No."

"Here's one I won't need. I have a personal chauffeur in the front seat."

"Thanks, man. Thanks." He exited the car, stopped, hesitated, then turned to Brad. His voice was filled with admiration. "Hey, you know Kong's never lost a fight in his whole life."

"Who's Kong?"

"The big Black. See ya." He was gone down the stairs.

Brad climbed into the front seat with Chuck. Chuck was dubious. "You don't trust that creep, do you?"

"I believe what he told us is true. Confirms what you said the other day. The attacks on the Children of God were orchestrated by the same people who are pretending to protect them. Sounds like they might be involved with the Krishnas as well. I think we should pay another visit to Damodar."

"Me, too."

19: Brandon Wins a Round?

Gary Richards went to the coffee machine he had set up on a small table in the corner of his spacious office and poured himself a long one. It was one of the perks of his position as CIA station chief. The machine was surrounded by ample supplies of sugar cubes and ground Costa Rican arabica. He was a coffee aficionado and knew Costa Rican arabica, grown high in the mountains and prepared in a five-step washing procedure, was the best coffee in the world—even better than premium Ethiopian arabica.

Today, his machine had been working overtime ever since he'd come in. His thought process improved when it was accompanied by a sugar jolt bathed in buckets of the Costa Rican brew.

It was getting close to the meeting time he had set up with Brandon Butler, and he had a bad feeling. From his bird's-eye view of the Place de la Concorde, another perk of his position, he could see that traffic was already heavy with cars, trucks, and taxis swirling around the monument. The sun shining through the thick exhaust fumes produced a surrealistic shimmering effect that made Gary rub his eyes. The branches of the trees in the park across the street swayed to the rhythm of the heavy, humid breeze blowing up the Champs-Elysées. He smelled trouble on the way.

When the knock came, Gary was ready. "Come in."

In walked a beaming Brandon Butler. He was decked out in a perfectly fitted dark silk suit that had to have cost two months of his salary. His black brogues were shined to perfection. He was shaved and perfumed, and not one strand of his thick, wavy hair was out of place.

"Gary. I'm so happy you made time to see me. I was anxious to discuss yesterday's events. I've been thinking. We were really lucky to have avoided a potential catastrophe. If I hadn't twisted protocol a bit, those hoodlums would certainly have gotten to Jeanie."

Gary folded his hands and closed his eyes. Twisted protocol a bit! Brandon Butler was peddling a far-fetched fairy tale. When he broke the rules, he committed a mortal sin. An agent was outed, a safe house was burned, and his own identity was compromised. Most humiliatingly, he'd allowed himself to be drugged and slept through it all. But there he was, taking a victory lap for a clusterfuck created by his own incompetence. These FBI guys were incredible—pure political animals. They spent more time message managing and spinning events to fit their narrative than they did fitting their narrative to the job they were supposed to be doing. It worked. Anyone who didn't have to deal with them directly believed they were all clones of Elliot Ness.

Gary reminded himself that Brandon was no longer with the FBI. He was DEA. Didn't change anything. His conclusion was the same as wise old William Shakespeare's: A sewer by any other name still smells like a sewer.

There was no longer any doubt in Gary's mind. Brandon had to go. Unfortunately, Gary had just been advised that the director of the DEA had commended Brandon for his timely intervention in saving Jeanie and was pressuring the CIA to include him in all aspects of the Jeanie affair. His boss at Langley informed him that political pressure from above made it impossible to refuse the request. That was going to complicate Gary's life for the immediate future, at least until he figured out how to get Brandon out of his hair.

"Have a seat, Brandon. Coffee?"

Brandon flashed a radiant smile. "After yesterday, I'm trying to stay away from coffee. I'm still feeling the effects."

Cute reply. Gary had to admit Brandon had charm. That made him even more dangerous. "You cost me a safe house and an agent yesterday. You also compromised yourself. If we're going to work together, we'll have to have an understanding. I make the rules. You obey them."

Brandon was apologetic. Normally, this would be the moment Brandon would revert to his slick-hair tic. Not today. He was oozing confidence. "Yeah, Gary, I know I was a little too zealous." There was just enough self-deprecation to make him believable. "I want to get to work on this case. I'm gonna need all the information on Jeanie. I'll have to talk to her as well. Where is she?"

Gary's face froze. He closed his eyes and took a deep breath. He could only marvel at the shameless chutzpah. Brandon was turning yesterday's fiasco into a personal triumph and using it to take over the whole operation. Gary could see Brandon felt empowered. He dipped a sugar cube into his cup of Costa Rican arabica and popped it into his mouth. Where was this coming from? All this interest and zeal in an operation only marginally related to Brandon's remit, for what? Gary's long experience and knowledge of human nature and the FBI were telling him there was more to it than professional pride and personal ambition. Brandon Butler was going to be a major problem.

"All in due time," Gary said, "all in due time. Jeanie's on the run for the moment. You'll be the first to know when she gets in touch."

"It's a good idea if I get into this case ASAP. Orders from above, you know. Why don't you just give me the file and let me go through it?"

That was a non-starter. The file was filled with all kinds of info only marginally related to Jeanie's incarceration. With information like that, Gary would never get Brandon and the DEA/FBI off his back. Difficult to refuse, though. Very, very difficult, given the current bureaucratic status quo. That was when it happened. That was when Gary had a "eureka" moment.

"There are some confidential things in there, Brandon. Let me clean it up, and I'll have Marilyn get back to you."

Marilyn was his secretary. She was a mousy little feminist complaining machine, and she was head over heels in love with beautiful Brandon. Brandon knew it and would take advantage of it. Gary decided he would, too.

Brandon was relentless. "I'd like to have the whole file. Like I said, orders from above, you know."

Gary straightened in his chair. Folded his hands on his chest. His eyes narrowed. His voice was soft. The tone conclusive. "Not possible, Brandon, but I'll give you more than enough."

Brandon was outwardly fuming and slicking back his hair. Gary was gloating inside.

When Brandon had gone, Gary retrieved the file from his safe. He proceeded to divide the file into three piles: pile one, for innocuous information; pile two, for information that seemed to be important but was either false or misleading; and pile three, for information that was important, accurate, and had to remain confidential.

He took pile three and locked it in his safe. He took his pen to paper and wrote furiously for fifteen minutes. When he finished, he put the handwritten notes with the documents in pile two and filed them away in an envelope marked *Confidential.* Pile one he left on his desk. Then he called in Marilyn.

"Here's a file for Brandon Butler." He handed her the file. "I had to take out some sensitive information. I'm keeping that info here for easy reference." He showed her the envelope marked *Confidential* and put it in the top desk drawer.

Marilyn had a sour look on her face. She knew Gary had put in to have her transferred, and she had salt stuck in her craw. "Is that all?"

"That's it. Thank you, Marilyn."

Gary sat back in his chair, put his feet on the desk, and treated himself to another Costa Rican arabica-flavored sugar cube. God is great!

Brandon would see immediately that the file was incomplete. His first stop would be Marilyn. He wondered how long it would take Marilyn to give Brandon a look at the documents in the envelope filed away in the top drawer of his desk. He figured it wouldn't be long. Love conquers all.

20: Looking for Leads

Chuck had never seen her before, but he recognized her immediately when she exited her building on Boulevard Saint-Germain. Young and fresh, about twenty-two years old, long hair, no makeup, long flowing dress, and sandals. She had even braided a pair of lily of the valleys into her hair. A typical flower child except for one thing. She had a feline-fluid prowl in her step, like a jungle cat—powerful and balanced, exceedingly sexy, exceedingly physical.

It was 9:30. She went down Saint-Germain and turned left onto Raspail headed—Chuck assumed—to the Alliance Française at number 101. Since he was pretty sure of where she was going, he decided he could hang back on the other side of the street.

Suddenly, someone yelled her name. She stumbled. Wheeled around. A motorcycle with two riders on it skidded to a stop. The passenger jumped off the bike and rushed toward her. She stood frozen on the spot.

Chuck scooted across the street to the median, ready to intervene. The driver was revving the engine. The girl retreated. Covered her chest with her arms. The passenger reached out. Ripped off his helmet. Called her name. She shrieked, dropped her books, and fell into his arms. The driver of the motorcycle popped the clutch and disappeared down Raspail.

Their lips met in a spontaneous expression of unguarded passion, right there in the middle of the sidewalk at 9:37 a.m. on the Boulevard Raspail. Chuck was impressed. An original, unconventional greeting. Some Gallic overkill, but it had panache. On a sunny spring morning in the most romantic city in the world, it fit right in. Like in a movie.

Unfortunately, when Chuck got a look at the swashbuckling romantic, he was disappointed. The guy was thin and sallow and scroungy, one of those supercilious, brooding, self-absorbed cool cats. Chuck disliked him immediately.

The girl had other feelings. She took her swashbuckler's hand and padded back the way she had come. When they disappeared into her building, Chuck decided to break off. He was betting they would be up there for a while. Anyway, he had a picture of the guy, the girl, and the motorcycle with the license plate number in plain view.

COURBEVOIE, FRANCE MAY 2, 1974

Brad pulled his Indian into the driveway of the Pavillon des Indes. The group of Krishna males poking around in the grass beside the Pavillon didn't look up when he dismounted and headed for the entrance.

Damodar, alias Tom, met him at the doorstep. "Cousin Brad. What's up?"

"Besides the sky, not much. Just came by to say hello and see if you had any news on Sally Ann Hastings."

"Come on in and take a load off your mind. Nothing new on Sally Ann. Why?"

Brad settled into one of the comfortable arm chairs by the doorway. "I dunno. Just had the feeling you held back on me the last time I was here."

"Held back? Whaddaya mean?"

"Look, Damodar, this is important. This girl means a big reward for Latorre Legal if we find her. She was here. She was cute. You noticed her. Being a Hare Krishna doesn't change a man's nature. You wouldn't let her get away without a fight."

The corners of Damodar's lips spread into a sheepish smile. "Yeah, you're right. She was here. A really impressive young woman. Pretty and sexy. Very mature. Athletic. Spent a lot of time working out. She had this way of looking at people. Sizing them up. I thought she was dangerous. Never knew her real name. But she doesn't look much like the picture you showed me. Fell for a French loser. He was coming around causing trouble. So I banned him, and she left."

"What kind of trouble?"

"Criticizing Krishna. Our lifestyle. Our hairdos. Our passivity. Preaching about revolution. Got so bad I almost lost my Krishna karma and kicked his ass."

"I went over to the Children of God's place in the 14th. She's not there."

"I know. The guy caused trouble there, too."

"What does the boyfriend look like?"

"Not bad looking. Thin, a little taller than me. Scroungy around the edges. One of these inner-conflicted bad boys raging against the unjust world and the bad hand he's been dealt. He has this self-satisfied look on his face. You know, like all-knowing, adolescent disdain. Extremely obnoxious."

"That's a pretty detailed description. Can I smoke?"

"Not a problem."

Brad lit up a Gitane sans filtre and took a few short drags. He couldn't help but notice that Damodar was keeping the Pavillon des Indes spic and span. He was about to take off when Damodar chimed in. "What did you think of the Children of God's compound?"

"Strange. Creepy."

"Yeah. That's what I thought, too."

"I witnessed an attack on two Children of God buskers in the metro at Saint-Lazare."

"Looks like that's all over now. I'm hearing that the Children got some protectors. The word is these protectors are so vicious that the muggers won't go near anybody who could be even remotely related to a Child of God. My guys are benefiting from this."

"So you do stay in contact with the COG?"

"Yeah, we touch base from time to time."

"Okay, thanks for the company, Damodar. I've gotta move it. See you soon."

21: Chef

The old Apache medicine man said it better than many a Western philosopher: "Better to be safe than sorry." Following this advice had saved Brad many a bad moment. That's why he had started parking his Indian Arrow at random spots one or two hundred yards from his building. It gave him time and space to check out the area for any suspicious activity. Today was one of his lucky days. Parked across from Brad's building in a dark blue Renault station wagon sat Chef with his two wingmen. Brad stopped to think it over. He hadn't done anything to attract Chef's attention. Maybe Chef was just there on a simple reconnaissance mission. Fat chance of that! Better find out what he wanted.

He came up behind the car and gave the roof three big, booming bangs. The three men in the car burst out of their seats like a house afire, eyes popping, arms flapping, heads whipping right and left. They were ready for war.

There stood Brad, smiling from ear to ear. "Hi, Chef. Hi, guys. Long time no see."

His cheery greeting overpowered their desire to beat him senseless. Chef climbed out of the car. His movements were slow and labored. He had aged ten years in the two weeks since Brad had last seen him. His tight lips and squinting eyes betrayed his battle to control his churning emotions. "Mr. James, so nice to run into you." His two wingmen were still pumping adrenaline, but they were all smiles. They were big, strong country boys.

"To what do I owe this pleasant surprise, Chef?"

"Have you seen Jean Jones?"

"Last I heard she was in jail."

"Well, she got released. She didn't go home, and we can't find her."

"You thought maybe she was here, is that it?"

"Yep. Is she here?"

"Nope."

"Do you know where she is?"

"Nope." This was true. Brad had no idea where Gary had put her up.

"This is very important. Are you sure she's not here?"

"Positive. Come on up and have a coffee. It's not as good as the stuff at the commissariat, but it's pure arabica."

Chef looked down at his police boots. He was tempted. He hesitated. He could see his men needed a break. "Okay, I'll call your bluff. Just to make sure."

Brad brewed a batch of coffee and the four of them sat back to relax and enjoy, but not before they had inspected every nook and cranny of Brad's apartment. Brad offered a round of Gitanes sans filtre. Nobody declined. They puffed away in silence, long enough for the room to cloud up in smoke. Brad went over and opened the terrace doors. The blast of fresh air was a relief.

"Chef. You look tired."

"I am tired. Jean Jones and all the hippies and druggies are making it impossible for me to get any exercise. Or any sleep. Look, we can't stay for long. Shouldn't even be up here. I want to talk to Mademoiselle Jones. She got away before I got permission to see her. I know she has information that can help my investigation. Tell her when you see her."

"What makes you think I'll see her?"

Chef raised his eyebrows and lowered his chin in the French facial expression for "Don't try to bullshit me."

"Okay, I'll tell her, but I can't guarantee she'll go see you."

"Do your best. It's in everyone's interest. Let me just say there is more to this than the three dead hippies. Much more. The pressure from above is killing me."

After Chef and his men's departure, Brad sat back and took a deep drag on his Gitane. Something big must have happened for them to come to Brad for help. Brad had to find out why. Chef didn't give anything away. Two cups of pure arabica later he thought he might have it figured out. Now, he had to make sure.

22: Il Messia

Lazarus stood immobile before the five men seated around the table. His white designer T-shirt was taut on the wide shoulders and rippling muscles of his pecs and abs. His long, thick, wavy hair combed straight back from his forehead gleamed in the rays of the overhead light. When he smiled, his teeth sparkled and his eyes glowed green. There was an evil edge to the power and authority emanating from his persona.

The man immediately to his left was Il Messia. Every strand of his Jesus Christ hairdo, beard, and mustache was perfectly coiffed. He wore a red silk shirt open to the navel with an elliptical gold medallion hanging from a thick, shiny chain around his neck. His dark eyes were penetrating, constantly in motion, shifting, searching, wary. The ten-inch hunting knife in the underarm body holster was almost invisible beneath his shirt. He sat there relaxed, unsmiling, waiting for Lazarus to speak.

To the right of Lazarus sat Michael and Joseph, the high priest's hippy enforcers responsible for operations. They had been with Lazarus since the infancy of the Prophecy when Lazarus was known as the Prophet. They were true believers in Lazarus and his powers, and they were ruthless in following his orders.

The fifth young man at the table sat directly across from Lazarus. His fashionably long, light-brown hair was pulled back into a short ponytail. He wore a white button-down shirt. The sleeves of a pink cotton sweater thrown over his shoulders were crossed over his chest. His socks matched the pink of the sweater. In his circle of society, the sweater on the shoulders and the matching socks were *de rigeur*, even in the height of summer. He stretched out in his chair and positioned one hand on his hip. The thumb and forefinger of his other hand stroked his chin. There was a hint of condescension in the semi-smirk on his thin lips and the way he drew back his head and looked down at the others through the rimless glasses perched on the end of his nose.

Lazarus had never liked Thibault, this supercilious BCBG—*bon chic bon genre*—preppy product of the French branch of the European Business School. Thibault was forced on him by Thibault's father, who wanted to give his son a start in business. Thibault's father controlled more than fifty percent of the cocaine and hash sold in France. He controlled one hundred percent of the cocaine and hash Lazarus sold in France. This was the influence that landed Thibault the job of organizing Lazarus's drug delivery and human trafficking.

Lazarus took his seat. "Thibault, let me start with you." His voice was cold like a sharp icicle. "I know all merchandise deliveries have been completed and paid for this month. No problem. Good job."

Thibault nodded his head, obviously pleased with himself.

Lazarus continued, even colder this time. "I am interested in the state of our human exports."

Thibault tilted his head, smiled, and looked confidently down at the table. "We have delivered four units, two women and two babies, and received payment in full. I have decided the maritime route is the safest and most secure. I have also decided to relax the financial conditions—"

"Excuse me?" Lazarus rose from his seat. Slowly, his expression of indifference morphed into a chilling mask of intense malevolence. His presence expanded. It was overwhelming. It filled the garage. Squeezed out the air.

Thibault looked down. He pushed back his glasses. Scratched his nose. Wiped his lips. He began to tremble. It started in his feet. Rumbled through his legs, his chest, his hands. When he was finally able to swallow and speak, his voice was husky and halting. "I mean, I decided to ask you about the maritime route and relaxing the financial conditions for our best customers."

Thibault looked down and began to examine his hands. Lazarus continued to study this insolent creature the father had imposed on him. After a long ten-count, he sat back down. His voice was hard. "Il Messia will personally take delivery of this shipment. It will be for the truck that goes out on the 10th. I may have one more delivery before the election run-off, if there is one. Once the election is settled, we will go into full production." He waved his hand. "You can go now."

Thibault's relief was palpable. He stuttered out a few thank-yous and goodbyes. It was still difficult for him to swallow. Michael escorted him out to the street, where he headed off to his car.

Lazarus turned to Il Messia. His voice was warm and soothing. "I need a favor, old friend."

Il Messia turned his dark eyes on Lazarus. He waited.

"Joseph, tell Il Messia what you know."

Joseph pushed back his chair and stood up. He was all business. "Our project with the Children of God is proceeding according to plan. The metro operation worked perfectly. Benjamin, the head shepherd, turned to us to protect his disciples from the attacks we had organized. We terminated the attacks, and now Benjamin depends on us for security. We had a few problems with the gang we recruited to carry out the attacks. It was lucrative for them, and they didn't go quietly. We convinced them it was in their best interest to stand down."

"So everything is under control?" Il Messia did not see where this information concerned him.

"More or less. We have a few loose ends. Some of the disciples are not convinced that using sacramental drugs and the bodies of our female disciples as tools to spread God's Word is consistent with Jesus's teachings. No problem. We can convert these doubters or weed them out over time. The main problem is we have lost the three disciples positioned to take over the compound."

Il Messia took a sip of his Petrus, savored it, and leaned forward. "Give me the details."

"Overdosed."

"All three? Same drug?"

"All three, yeah, like a serial killer, one in a hotel room, one on the riverbank, and one in a strip club toilet. There was a woman involved every time, a very pretty woman. Descriptions vary, but it's probably the same one."

Il Messia nodded his head. "Do your men do 'flirty fishing'?" Joseph stiffened. Il Messia smiled. "I mean are your disciples supposed to go off to take drugs and fornicate?"

Joseph didn't like where this was going. He pointed his finger at Il Messia and growled, "What do you mean by that?"

Lazarus decided to intervene. He knew Joseph's temper. He also knew Il Messia was the most dangerous knife fighter he'd ever known. It was said his hands moved faster than the eye could see.

Lazarus looked at Joseph. "Just stick to the facts."

Il Messia was still smiling benignly. "Just give me the facts, please."

Joseph shook it off and continued. "As I said, we have lost three men over the last few weeks. They had been with us since the days in California. They were experienced. They were reliable. They were positioned to take over the Children of God's operations in Paris."

Il Messia ran his fingers through his hair, stretched his shoulders, and cracked his knuckles. He poured himself another shot of Petrus and took his time savoring a generous sip of the crimson liquid.

Joseph licked his lips and drummed the table with his fingers. Lazarus let the scene drag on. The finger drumming accelerated.

Il Messia savored a second sip and smacked his lips. "*Amici*, dear *amici*, it has been a long day. So if there is nothing else, I shall go to my room and have a serious theological discussion with one of my faithful disciples. She must be wondering where I am."

The finger drumming came to an abrupt stop. Joseph fixed Il Messia in a death stare. "I'm not finished." His voice had an edge.

"*Alora*, please get to the point, dear friend, my disciple is waiting."

Joseph started to move. This dago pimp needed a lesson. Lazarus gave Joseph a friendly pat on the hand and leaned forward. "What Joseph wants to say is that we need your help."

"What can I do?"

"Find out who's responsible for the murders. It has to be somebody with inside knowledge of the Children of God. Our action against the French state could be imperiled. Benjamin says it's the agent who represents his singing group, an American woman named Jeanie something."

"Do you want me to perform my famous magic trick?"

"What kind of magic trick?"

"Make her disappear."

Lazarus had to smile. "No. If it's her, we have to know where she's coming from, what's her game, who's behind it."

"What about Benjamin? Could be him."

"No, it's not him. He needs us. If we go down, he goes down. Joseph will give you all the info Benjamin gave him on Jeanie, and you can take it from there."

Il Messia leaned back in his chair. He lifted his wineglass toward the light from the table lamp and studied the last of his crimson Petrus. His eyes were shining. "I understand, *amico mio*. I understand that this is too important to be left to the inexperienced."

Joseph pushed back his chair. Lazarus grabbed Joseph's arm and saved his life again. He held Joseph and spoke softly to Il Messia. "Your experience will be appreciated."

Il Messia stood up with a theatrical flourish and spread his arms. "I will find Miss Jeanie for you. I am sure I will be able to convince her to confide in me. My intuition tells me it will be a pleasurable experience."

Lazarus sat alone at the table. It was littered with dirty ashtrays, glasses, and bottles. He turned to the Petrus. The bottle was empty. Il Messia had seen to that. He reached for a cigarette from the pack of Marlboros on the table, fingered the brown filter, but didn't light up.

Something was bothering him. It wasn't Thibault. Thibault's father would see to it he didn't screw up. It wasn't the growing friction between Joseph and Il Messia. That was a simple cultural conflict that would eventually burn itself out. Meanwhile, Lazarus would see to it that Joseph stood down.

It wasn't the loss of the three disciples. He had many more in reserve. It wasn't the setback in the takeover of the Children of God. That was only temporary, and in the medium term, not a problem. Benjamin had proven himself to be a willing accomplice.

His intuition was calling up images of dark forces of death and destruction circling his empire, threatening his life. His intuition had saved him from many a potential catastrophe. It had failed him only once. That one failure had almost cost him his life. It ended up costing him the Prophecy. He swore vengeance. His intuition was telling him the time had come.

23: The London Connection

Brandon could understand Richard Burton's and Elizabeth Taylor's attachment to this place. It had atmosphere, tradition, and class. From his sixth-floor balcony on Park Lane, Hyde Park stretched out before him like a giant canvas panorama in luscious greens, browns, and blues. The Dorchester was without the slightest doubt an excellent hotel choice for his stay in London. The sky was clear, the sherry was delicious, the service was efficient and discreet, and most of all, he was free to pursue the Jeanie Jones investigation far away from Gary Richards's prying eyes.

At the end of the day, it was thanks to Gary he was here. The big, fat dossier Gary gave him on the matter was obviously just a decoy. It was full of documents, descriptions, names, and places, but was devoid of any information with any relevance to Jeanie and the investigation. Brandon understood that immediately. His fifteen years with the Bureau made him an expert in administrative obfuscation. Gary probably thought he had sidelined Brandon for a while. Wrong. It just made him more determined. Gary didn't realize how important this investigation was for him.

A small sip of sherry brought a smile to his face. He closed his eyes and relived the scene. A private lunch in a café on the Rue de Rivoli, some serious heart-to-heart conversation, intense eye contact, and a few well-timed pats on the hand, and the deed was done. Gary's secretary volunteered to supply him with the inside information he needed. By the end of the day, she had photocopied the secret file locked away in Gary's desk drawer. Only she and Gary had a key. By the end of the evening, Brandon had hit the jackpot: a UK license plate number for an E-Type Jaguar with a handwritten note by Gary that this was "top priority."

Brandon knew that following normal administrative channels meant Gary would have to wait a minimum of a week before he got any feedback on the license plate number. Going straight to London and pushing it personally meant he had the information two hours after he arrived at the embassy. The car belonged to a James MacDonald, who lived in a third-floor apartment in Hampstead.

From there on, it was child's play. Brandon used the workman's button to buzz into the building. The first two locks on the door to the apartment went down in less than thirty seconds each. The FBI spared no expense when it trained its agents for breaking and entering. The third lock was more problematic but finally gave way after another five minutes. He got a scare when the neighbor down the hall came out to see what was going on. She was one of those old busybodies who populated every apartment building in the world. He found it strange that she just looked at him and said hello. He said hello and hustled into the apartment.

The initial search turned up nothing. The apartment was clean. Too clean! There was nothing more personal than bills and receipts for water, gas and electricity, a few books, and a map of the London underground. He was ready to despair when he looked in the bathroom wastebasket and scored a mother lode. It was an envelope addressed to James MacDonald. Underneath the address, written in pencil, was the acronym COG, the name Benjamin, a telephone number, and an address in the 14th arrondissement in Paris. Brandon copied the information, replaced the envelope, and exited the apartment. He was careful to relock the locks he'd picked.

Brandon had an early flight back to Paris. Until then, he decided to relax and enjoy. It was time for tea at five, a Dorchester tradition in the restaurant the Promenade he was looking forward to.

PARIS EMBASSY, SATURDAY, MAY 4

Gary could not stop congratulating himself. He had cleverly managed to send Brother Brandon off on a wild goose chase. The security traps he had set on his drawer and the "secret" file had both been breached. His secretary had been true to herself and Gary's expectations. Brandon had taken the bait and swallowed it. Now he was digesting it. He was off to London on urgent business, or so said his secretary.

Gary sat back and sipped his freshly brewed pure Costa Rican arabica. Through his triple-glazed, reinforced picture window he could see but not hear the motorcycles, cars, and trucks swarming around the Place de la Concorde—horns blaring, drivers waving wildly, cursing and screaming. It conjured up pleasurable images of Brother Brandon running around London trying desperately to figure out how that license plate number fit in with Jeanie Jones and her investigation.

Gary scratched his ear and winked at his reflection in the window. "Nice play, Gary," he chuckled and pointed his finger. "Bang. I gotcha."

24: Shanghaied

"**G**ood night, ladies and gentlemen. Enjoy the rest of the evening." Brad waved to the roomful of diners, flashed the V sign, and left the stage to a big round of applause.

Lydie Bastien signaled him from the back of the room. She was the boss, and it looked like she had something important to tell him. It never ceased to amaze him that this fifty-something, overweight woman with penciled-in eyebrows and a loose-fitting black wig had once been a mysterious, irresistible double agent who had almost single-handedly wiped out the French resistance during WWII. She was the French Mata Hari to those impressed by her exploits. She was the *diabolique de Caluire* to those revolted by her treachery. To Brad, she was a curious study in intelligence, mystery, and charm.

"We have a special reservation for tomorrow night," she told Brad. "Some people from the embassy. Do you think you can get some of your artists in for an early show? Robert Hermann already agreed."

As the pianist, Robert Hermann was a key element in the show.

"Then I don't think that will be a problem."

"Thank you, Brad."

"My pleasure."

Off he went. On his way over to the bar, he spotted a twenty-something young woman waving to him. He had noticed she was animated and responsive during the show. She had a nice face, no makeup, wire-rimmed glasses—unquestionably American.

"Hi, what's up?"

"I loved your show."

"Thanks. Enjoyed doing it."

"That song 'If You Don't Like Johnny Hallyday, You Can Kiss My Ass' is great. You should make records."

Her enthusiasm was contagious, and he loved flattery. He also was not above a little self-promotion. "Got one coming out next month. Mind if I join you?"

"I was hoping you would. My name is Judy." She was really nice with an infectious personality. He liked to hang around with girls like Judy, and they loved to hang around with him. Since his high school days, he had been surrounded by what could loosely be described as adoring fans. Besides being charismatic and teen-idol good-looking, he was also a genuine gentleman. And here was where Brad encountered one of life's great mysteries. The nice, wholesome girls, as beautiful as they might be, held absolutely no sex appeal for him.

He was transported back to Alice, his old childhood sweetheart. She was the epitome of the nice, girl-next-door, goody-two-shoes, American-apple-pie beauty with big blue eyes and long blond hair. Their romance ended in the ninth grade when Brad's testosterone told him she was more like a beloved sister than a hot date. He dumped her unceremoniously, but their love affair turned into mutual respect and deep friendship. He surprised himself with renewed romantic interest when they reconnected in Paris three years ago. It was only belatedly that he realized his renewed romantic interest was fueled by Alice's developing sexual awareness. His failure to realize it sooner had cost Alice her life and Brad the only true love he had ever known. Hard to get over. Impossible to forget.

"A penny for your thoughts."

Brad snapped back to the present. He and Judy had been hitting it off for over an hour. It was enjoyable but going nowhere. He was trying to think up an escape line that wouldn't hurt her feelings when she grabbed his hand. "Wait, Brad, my friend just came in." Judy stood up and waved toward the bar. "I want you to meet her."

Her friend glided over to the table and stood there, left leg cocked in a pair of tight jeans, left hand on her hip, a half-smoked Marlboro in her right hand and a provocative smile on her face. Light-brown, medium-long hair hung over her left shoulder à la Veronica Lake, with arched eyebrows, slightly darker than her hair, and black, oval eyes somewhere between demure and smoldering.

"Brad," Judy said, "I want you to meet Brandy. Brandy, this is Brad."

Brad forgot about his urgent obligation and invited Brandy to sit down. She nodded and slipped into a chair with her back to the bar. Judy declined and excused herself, pretexting an early morning appointment. That left Brad and Brandy head-to-head.

Brandy wasn't a nice-personality person like Judy, but she did have a nice personality once you got past the sexual posturing. And once you stopped thinking about how good she looked. They had gone through all the usual foreplay. What are you doing in Paris? Where did you go to school? What sports did you play? What music do you like? Your favorite films, etc.

Brandy had finished one of those elite women's universities in the North, Brawn Mawr or something like that up in Philadelphia. She was traveling around Europe before going back to graduate school; she did ballet; she loved classical music, and her favorite movie was *And God Created Woman* by Roger Vadim.

She checked all the boxes, but somehow, graduate school, ballet, classical music, and Roger Vadim did not coalesce with her sultry body language or her semi-detached conversation style. Brad was hearing whispers of warnings from the depths of his past starting to echo through the canyons of his plans for the present. That's when Brandy rubbed it all out with a fastball straight down the middle.

"I thought you might have room for me at your place tonight."

Brad took the pitch looking. "You mean you don't have a place to stay?" He was uncharacteristically slow on the draw.

Brandy didn't move. She didn't smile. She didn't frown. She just looked and waited. Brad came to his senses. "I mean, of course you can. No problem." He took a long swig of his beer, pulled out a Gitane sans filtre, popped open his Zippo, and fired up. He held Brandy's gaze and blew out four perfect smoke rings. His mojo was back. "Maybe we better get going."

Off they went. Two handsome, well-groomed, muscular young men followed them as they left the Barbary Coast Saloon and headed for Brad's digs at number 90 Rue d'Assas.

*　　　　*　　　　*

Brad struggled to open his eyes. His brain was exploding. He was blind. He struggled to move his arms. They were paralyzed. There were voices. His legs were paralyzed. There was movement to his left. He swallowed. It hurt. Bad. He tried to turn his head. It moved. It hurt. Bad. What was happening?

The voices penetrated the fog in his brain. "Lover boy's back online."

Before he could translate that remark, his head was jerked to the right by a vicious slap to the left jaw. Another slap to the right ear jerked his head back to the left. A few more of these back-and-forths returned him to reality.

He was blindfolded, hogtied to a chair, and being smacked around by at least two assholes with hands. Impossible to remember how he got into this unfortunate situation. The last thing he remembered was sharing a bottle of rosé wine with beautiful Brandy. That's when the lights went out. She must have slipped him a mickey and called in her buddies after he went missing in action.

The question now was what these guys wanted. It couldn't be money, because they weren't asking for any, and he clearly was not rolling in dough. They might just be perverts. If that was the case, he was in trouble. They couldn't be rogue cops because they were speaking perfect American English. The good news was they kept him blindfolded, which signaled they were not intending to kill him. Meanwhile, Brad decided to try not to piss these guys off, to get in the zone, and wait for his chance.

He took a few more blows to the head, which was making it increasingly difficult for him to stay in the zone. His body was still aching, but now it was because of the constricted blood flow to his arms and legs and the beating he was taking rather than from the drug dose administered by Brandy.

Suddenly, everything went quiet. Brad felt someone approach and position themselves just in front of him. The voice was soft and firm, the voice of a mature man. Surprisingly, it was also cultured.

"Mr. James. I have some questions, but very little time to obtain answers. For our mutual benefit, I would be extremely grateful for your cooperation. Understand?"

Brad wanted a few Mississippis to think about this deal. A punch to the gut ended that plan, in spite of his six-pack abs. He managed to squeeze out a grudging, "Yeah."

"You do know Jeanie Jones?"

"Yeah."

"Where is she?"

"Dunno." Brad waited for another blow, but nothing happened.

"How well do you know her?"

Everybody wanted to know something about Jeanie Jones. "She's the agent for a few musicians around Paris. She comes around the Barbary Coast Saloon trying to get them gigs in my dinner show. I see her around the radio stations and recording studios as well. That's it."

"That's it?"

"Yeah, that's it."

Another punch to the gut took the rest of Brad's oxygen, and he almost went out.

"If you don't know her well, why is the embassy relying on you to find her?"

Brad was gasping. "I told them the same thing I told you."

From somewhere behind the man with the soft voice came the voice of another mature, young man. This voice was harsher and less cultured. "Cut the crap, man. Let's flip to the conclusion. He's just jaggin' us around."

"Okay. Start with his ear. This will make him understand the profound importance of our questions and our determination to obtain satisfactory replies."

Brad heard the second man approach. Felt his presence at his side, his Coca-Cola flavored ketchup breath on his cheek. He heard the snap of the switchblade opening. "Since you're right-handed, I'll just take your left ear for a souvenir." Stand-up comedy was not this guy's strong suit. He took Brad's ear between his thumb and forefinger and held it delicately.

Brad braced himself for what was going to be a very long and painful experience. He tried to concentrate on the background music coming out of the radio. It was "Bad, Bad Leroy Brown" by Jim Croce. No help at all.

He felt the knife begin to slice into his ear, and a little stream of blood dripped down his cheek.

"Sure you got nothin' to say before I collect my souvenir?"

*   *   *

Chuck was excited. The tape from the listening device he'd placed in the garage over at Louveciennes was dynamite, and it was urgent.

When he arrived at the Barbary, he saw Brad was experiencing an intense moment of emotion with a foxy-looking female. While deciding whether to interrupt his buddy with the info or wait him out, he spotted two dudes over in the corner taking an inordinate amount of interest in Brad's ongoing seduction offensive. They were mature, well-muscled, and nice-looking, but there was something off-key about their appearance. Chuck decided to wait and watch.

It wasn't long before Brad and his foxy friend got up and headed for the exit. It wasn't ten seconds later that the two off-key muscle dudes got up and followed them out. Chuck did the same.

Out on the street, Chuck saw that Brad and his friend were headed down Jules-Chaplain toward Brad's apartment a few blocks away on the Rue d'Assas. Dudes one and two were following a safe distance behind. They were also checking for countersurveillance.

Chuck decided to cut one street over and head them off at the Place. From there, he would be able to watch Brad all the way down to the Rue d'Assas with no risk of being spotted.

He was just getting set up when Brad and his girlfriend came by. The dudes followed on their heels a few seconds later but started to hang back the closer they got to the Rue d'Assas. Chuck deduced from their behavior that this was only a surveillance mission and Brad was in no imminent danger.

Brad and his friend were almost out of sight when they turned right onto the Rue d'Assas, followed way back by the dudes. Chuck hustled down to the Rue d'Assas, crossed the street, and took up a position on the steps of an apartment building behind a Peugeot station wagon parked on the curb. He had a clear view of Brad's building through the windows of the Peugeot, but he was basically invisible to anybody around Brad's building.

Dudes one and two stationed themselves on the steps of the uni next to number 90. Chuck prepared himself for a long, boring wait. He was pleasantly disappointed.

Brad's foxy friend exited the building no more than thirty minutes later. She left the entrance door open, then moved warily toward the sidewalk. She stopped at the gate, took a long, careful one-hundred-and-eighty street recon, and sniffed the air like a hunted beast. She relaxed when dudes one and two hit the sidewalk and gave her a signal. She pointed to the open door and flashed two fingers. Chuck figured she was signaling the floor of Brad's apartment. Then she was gone, and the dudes were heading into number 90. They closed the door behind them.

Chuck strode straight to number 90. He had the keys and went right in. He took the stairs but did not turn on the lights. When he got to Brad's flat, the door was closed. There was some scuffling around, some grunting and huffing, and some muffled conversation. Then everything went quiet for a few minutes.

Now the question was whether he should wait a while to see what the two dudes were up to or break in immediately. Waiting would put Brad in danger. Immediate intervention would probably ignite a violent reaction from the two muscle dudes and queer any chance of a reasonable exchange of information.

The decision was made for him when he put his ear to the door and heard, "Start with his ear." Time to intervene.

Chuck slipped the key into the lock and opened it slowly. Silent. Swift. Surprise. He was three steps into the room before the dudes realized they had company. Two more steps, and he was on Dude Number One.

Number One was a pro, and he reacted like a pro with a right hook to the head. Chuck blocked it with his fighting blade, which glanced off One's forearm and tore off half of his bicep. He went down holding his arm. Chuck kicked him in the head as he whipped around to face Number Two.

Number Two had had time to prepare, and his knife was out. He circled to his right, shifting it from hand to hand like they do in the movies. Chuck faked right, faked left. Number Two wasn't fooled. Suddenly, he faked forward with his right hand.

Chuck saw it coming and slid inside. He drove his blade into number two's armpit up through the shoulder. Two's switchblade dropped to the floor. He lurched toward the open door. Number One had already managed to get out of the apartment onto the landing.

Chuck was going for the kill when the hall lights came on and the upstairs neighbor called down, asking if there was a problem. Witnesses were bad. The fight was over. The two dudes scuttled away in silence. Their silence was testimony to their professionalism; their wounds were exceedingly worthy of excruciating pain. Chuck got the door closed before the neighbor could get downstairs. He knocked. "Mr. James. Are you okay?"

Chuck did a stand-up imitation of Brad's voice. "No problem, Monsieur Grand. I just had a nightmare. *Bonne soirée.*"

He started to relax when Brad's baritone broke the silence. "Get me outta this goddamn chair."

It wasn't humorous, but Chuck couldn't stifle the urge to smile. He cut off Brad's blindfold and freed his arms and legs. Brad tried to get up but flopped back down in the chair. His circulation was only just coming back, and the needles and pins in his legs were overpowering.

Brad sat and rubbed his limbs, trying to restore the circulation. Chuck wanted to know what was going on.

"I don't know," Brad said. "I had a girl over. We were drinking some wine. Then the lights went out. When I came to, there were a couple of guys smacking me around and asking questions about Jeanie. Lucky for me you came by. They were going to start cutting me up. Part of my ear is gone already."

"Naw, it's just a little nick. When I heard them going for your ear, I decided to get involved."

"You mean you were outside listening?"

"Not for long. Look, not to question your innate sex appeal, but this whole thing was a setup. That sexy broad you brought up here was a plant. She was working with the two guys who roughed you up. They were in the Barbary watching you do your charm offensive. They followed you and waited outside your building. The girl came down thirty minutes later. She left the door open and signaled the two guys before disappearing back toward Montparnasse. When they went in, I followed 'em."

Brad went to the terrace and studied the street. No traffic. No pedestrians. Just a big, round moon and the sweet fragrance of spring wafting over from the Jardin du Luxembourg.

"Chuck, the setup was even more professional than that. It was the old bait-and-switch trick. They lured me over with another girl called Judy. When she saw I wasn't interested, she passed me over to her friend, Brandy, the fox I brought back here. I guess she drugged my drink when I went to the head."

"What were they after?"

"They wanted to know about Jeanie. Wanted to know where she was. I think they have some kind of a mole in the embassy. They know the embassy was asking me to help them find her."

"Looks like Jeanie's the person of interest in all this. I checked out our bug over at the house in Louveciennes. Wait till you hear! It was a bonanza."

The doorbell interrupted his monologue. They fell silent. It rang again, this time with more insistence.

Brad went for the Beretta stashed in his bedroom. Chuck drew his knife and went to the door. The ringing stopped. Someone was playing with the lock. Suddenly, the doorknob turned and the door flew open. Brad and Chuck froze in place.

25: New Team Member

Jeanie was clad in black from head to foot—snug black T-shirt over black bra, black leotard, black sneakers, black socks, black backpack. Brad couldn't help but admit this outfit highlighted the major-league figure it clung to. He also couldn't help but wonder what Jeanie Jones was doing picking his lock at 3 a.m. on an election day Sunday.

The Beretta Brad was holding made Jeanie take a step back. She took another step back when she saw Chuck with his bloodstained hunting knife in hand. She relaxed when she saw they were as surprised as she was.

Brad motioned for Jeanie to come inside and then stepped out onto the landing to check for other uninvited guests. He checked upstairs, then slipped down to the ground floor and spent two minutes scoping out the street. He checked the elevator. It was empty. Convinced the coast was clear, he padded back upstairs to his apartment on the second floor.

Chuck was checking the Colt .38 caliber six-shot he found in Jeanie's backpack. "You know how to use this?"

"I do."

The attitude was convincing. Chuck believed her. "You know how dangerous it is to carry one of these in France?"

"I do."

Again, he believed her. So did Brad. The question they both had was why she was breaking into Brad's apartment with a loaded gun in her backpack. Her answer was that she would explain.

Brad turned on the radio for some background noise. It was Elvis singing "You Don't Know Me." He opined that every red-blooded American man had been in the you-don't-know-me situation with a woman to one degree or another at some time or another. This was Brad's time. He definitely did not know Jeanie.

Jeanie melted into the black leather armchair facing the terrace. Her black attire against the black of the chair made her body disappear and gave the troubling illusion of her face floating around unattached. She spoke softly with the assurance of someone who had faced down danger more than once.

"I need help." She nodded toward Chuck. "I'm glad to see you, as well. We met at the commissariat a while back. A human trafficking affair. Maybe you remember."

Chuck did remember and gave an affirmative nod.

"Brad, you know I've been working with the Children of God's choir." It was a statement, not a question. "I've gotten to know the cult and its members pretty well. Most of the members are just your run-of-the-mill insecure youths seeking refuge in some kind of divine truth before they grow up and get on with their lives. Some are emotionally or psychologically impaired in one way or another, which makes it difficult for them to cope with reality. The procedures and rules of the cult give their lives structure and meaning. But others are psychopaths feasting on the weakness and insecurity of the first two groups. I found out that the psychopaths in the Children of God are planning to use their disciples for a terrorist event in the near future."

Chuck was smiling. Brad was more reflective. "Why don't you go straight to the authorities with your story?" Brad said.

"I have been to the embassy, and they are taking me seriously. But I think there's a traitor in there, and I'm not safe with them anymore."

This jibed with Brad's opinion on a mole. "Why?"

"I was holed up in a luxurious, one-hundred-and-twenty-square-meter apartment on the tenth floor of a brand-new high-rise overlooking the Seine. There was a doorman and an armed guard on the ground floor. I never went out, and no one came to see me. The bad guys still found out where I was."

"How do you know?

"I saw some disciples from the Children of God snooping around outside the building."

"What makes you think I can help you?" Brad asked.

Jeanie cocked her head and raised her right eyebrow, pretended to think for a short moment, then looked up. "Most recently, the Beretta you were holding when I came in. Otherwise, you took down a group of muggers in the metro who were trying to rob Zebulon and Sarah. Since then, all the muggings have stopped. Everybody in the compound thinks you're responsible for that."

"What do you think?"

"I think you might have had something to do with it, but not all of it. I also think you have somehow displeased the psychopaths running the cult. The chief psychopath at the compound is a nasty little creep named Benjamin. He is very, very interested in you, and not in a good way. My conclusion is that you're involved in this thing, and you're one of the white hats. That makes you an ally who can help me."

Brad went out onto the terrace and studied the street. There was still no traffic. Still no pedestrians. The big, round moon was almost gone, but the sweet fragrance of spring was still wafting over from the Jardin du Luxembourg. He was about to go back inside when he saw a cigarette burning in the window of a dark sedan parked across the street. He recognized the car.

He took his time lighting up a Gitane sans filtre and taking a few puffs while scoping out the scene. He sauntered back inside, changed gears, and whipped into action. "Let's clean up all this blood on the floor. Get that switchblade out of sight. We're gonna get raided. Where's your car, Chuck?"

"I parked over by the Barbary."

"The law says they can't come in before 6 a.m. That gives us two hours. I know these guys, and they know me. They're looking for you, Jeanie. Anything on you?"

Jeanie stood and did a graceful pirouette. There was no room for anything but her body in that outfit.

"How about your backpack?" Brad asked her.

"It's brand new, just out of the box before I came over."

"Maybe they're not looking for you, then. Maybe somebody tipped them off about the intruders. In any case, we've got to get you out of here."

That's when the doorbell rang.

A look through the peephole froze Brad's blood. It was Chef, standing there radiating displeasure. Brad took his time undoing the lock. "Hi, Chef, what's happenin'?"

Chef's eyes bored into Brad's good-natured greeting. The five seconds he stroked his chin with the thumb and forefinger of his left hand seemed like five minutes to Brad. Finally, he dropped his hand and let it rest on the handle of the sidearm on his hip.

"You alone?"

"Just me and Chuck."

Chuck stepped from behind the door. "I'm Chuck."

Chef gave Chuck the once-over. "You're the private eye, right?"

"At your service, Chef. What can I do for you?"

Chef didn't smile. He let his eyes wander around the room. "You can tell me what's going on around here."

Brad knew Chef couldn't legally come into his apartment before 6 a.m. He also knew Chef was not a "rules man." The guy was capable of coming in whenever he thought he had trapped a rat. Better to bluff. "Come on in. It's too late for coffee, but I've got some good wine."

Chef leaned forward, then stopped mid-move. "Not now. Got complaints from some residents about noise and strange people coming and going from your apartment. I recognized the address and came to see for myself."

"Yeah, sorry about that, Chef. Chuck was being an asshole and we started rasslin' around. All in fun. I noticed those strange people as well when I checked out some noise I heard on the landing. Go see Mister Grand in the apartment above me. Maybe he knows."

"He was one of the people who called to complain." Chef's eyes were searching relentlessly. He noticed the blood on the floor they hadn't had time to clean up. "What's that on the floor?"

Brad feigned surprise. "Accident. Knocked over some wine while we were horsin' around. I'm gonna have to clean it up before it stains."

Chef cracked a wry smile and shook his head. "Okay. I'll be in touch. *Bon soir.*"

From the terrace, Brad made sure Chef had, indeed, departed. Back in the living room, Brad interrupted Jeanie and Chuck's animated conversation. "Jeanie, clue me in on what's going on."

Jeanie took a deep breath that stretched the tissue of her T-shirt and accentuated her full breasts. "How about a glass of that wine you're bragging about. My throat says I need some refreshment."

Brad went for the glasses, and Chuck went for the wine. He poured all around, held up his glass, and said, "Chin, chin."

"Chin, chin," they said in unison. They drank, and Jeanie started to talk.

"I think you know I'm working for Gary."

"What makes you think that?" Brad asked.

"When I told you the embassy was hiding me, you weren't surprised, and you didn't ask me why."

"Okay, so you know we're on the same team."

"I do, and that's why I'm here. There's a problem with security in the embassy. This is the second time a safe house I've been hiding out in has been compromised. I need a safe place to stay."

Brad squinted out a concerned look, popped a Gitane sans filtre out of the pack on the end table, and held it thoughtfully between his thumb and forefinger. There was a long silence. He straightened up and nodded. "There's no way you can stay here. My place is starting to look like Grand Central Station at rush hour. You do need someplace safe to stay. You're obviously in some kind of danger. Gary gave us the basic outline of what you've been doing and what's been done to you."

Chuck came in almost on cue. He had been chomping at the bit to get his story out ever since he chased off the two guys beating up on Brad. "She's in trouble, Brad. They're going after her. The guy who calls himself Il Messia has been sent to bring her back dead or alive."

Jeanie's eyes opened wide. She snapped to attention. "What are you talking about?"

"No lie. Got it straight from the tape of the bug in the garage."

Brad was making faces, trying to signal Chuck to keep his information to himself. They still didn't know who Jeanie really was.

Too late! Jeanie sank her teeth into the info and started to chew. "What bug? Where? Who is this Il Messia, and who's sending him after me?"

The cat was out of the bag. Damage control was the only way forward. Brad was more worried about protecting classified information than he was about frightening Jeanie. She didn't come across as your typical feminine fright risk. On the contrary! But could she be trusted? She was almost certainly not on the team of the religious freaks in the black hats. Whether she was on his team in the white hats or not was another question.

Chuck realized his mistake and tried to change the subject. "Jeanie can stay in the little studio behind my office. Good location with the main access on the Champs-Elysées and the other through a garden on the Rue de Ponthieu behind the Champs. The only three people who know about it are us three. Even the French don't know about it. On paper, it's part of the office space. Big John transformed it secretly for occasions just like this."

Chuck was really throwing in his lot with Jeanie, but Jeanie was having none of it. She stood her ground with her hands on her hips. "What about this 'bug' and Il Messia? I need to know what's going on."

Brad backed off and took a long look at his Omega. "It's late. We've got to get a move on if we're gonna get you into the studio before sunrise. We'll fill you in on the details once you're safe. Here's what we do. Chuck, you go down to your car and start to head home. I'll check for surveillance from here. You check while you're driving. It's next to impossible to follow somebody discreetly at this time of the morning. I'll turn out the lights and go downstairs with Jeanie. She waits in the lobby and checks for surveillance. I take off on my bike. If the coast is clear, she heads to Montparnasse and grabs a taxi to the Champs-Elysées. She walks to the Rue de Ponthieu, where you meet her and take her to the studio."

"What if the coast's not clear?" Chuck said.

"Jeanie makes the necessary moves, gets clean, and meets you as planned."

Jeanie's face was set in stone. "We're not going anywhere until I get some answers about this 'bug' and Il Messia? I need to know what's going on."

Brad decided to give her the minimum. "We found out where some people of interest have their headquarters. The guy who runs the place is a good-looking American guy who calls himself Lazarus. Il Messia is an Italian guy who looks like a dark-haired version of Jesus and dresses like a color-blind pimp. He's Lazarus's henchman. We know there's a link with the Children of God, but we don't know exactly what it is."

"Are you going to tell me where this place is?"

"We'll take you there tomorrow."

26: Lazarus Rises

The E-Type was too flashy. Lazarus had reluctantly decided to take the Renault instead. It was much less comfortable than his E-Type, but it was discreet and efficient. He reviewed the situation over at the Children of God as he drove toward Paris. The disciples were steadfastly docile and credulous. They accepted his policy of flirty fishing and drug distribution in the name of recruiting converts to the service of God. This provided him with a reliable source of income to pay his expenses and finance his other activities.

The Children of God was the perfect framework for human trafficking. They had colonies located all around the world. These colonies recruited converts and sent the new disciples to the sect's central hub in Paris.

The frequent arrivals at the Paris compound of disciples from around the world with few or no social and familial ties provided Lazarus with a source of vulnerable victims. Once the victims had been identified, the role of the Paris compound in recycling the new arrivals to other colonies made it possible for Lazarus to subvert the process and redirect the unsuspecting disciples chosen to be victims directly into the hands of his paying customers.

Young women between the ages of eighteen and twenty-four constituted over sixty percent of the sect's new converts. Combined with the sect's open encouragement of unlimited sexual activity, young, pregnant women and young women with young children proliferated. Consequently, Lazarus had decided to specialize in babies and young women. It was a symbiotic relationship. The babies were sold for adoption, and the mothers were sold into the underworld of human slavery, never to be heard from again, and especially never to complain about the loss of their babies.

Everything seemed to be rocking along with only a few minor hiccups. In the short time since he'd been sent to Europe, he had managed to build the infrastructure for a lucrative business that was just coming online. Nevertheless, it was still impossible for him to shake the feeling that hostile forces were threatening his new operation.

He was an accomplished pro with a seasoned team and a balance sheet top-heavy with successes. His only failure, the failure that drove him to Europe, was the Prophecy. The Prophecy's fate revealed the delicate balance of his business model and its vulnerability to exposure, even with high-level political and legal cover. One indiscretion, one minor lapse in security, one determined succubus, a female demon, and his entire operation came crashing to the ground. His political patrons deserted him. His employers terminated him. He was lucky they did help him deliver the final solution for his disciples and provided him and his team with new identities, a new country, and a new job.

Lazarus was early for what he wanted to do. He parked the car on a quiet side street near the tomb of Guy de Maupassant and fished under the seat for a small plastic sachet. He laid two thin lines of coke on the dashboard and used a rolled hundred-franc note in his left nostril as a straw to suck up the line on the left. He lay back and took the hit. He transferred the straw to his right nostril and sniffed up the line on the right.

One lousy woman, a magnificently crafted work of beauty, sex, and physical force, and the inability of his political patrons and employers to find and neutralize her brought an end to his "California Dreamin' ". It had almost killed him as well.

The Prophecy was founded on the premise of a black hole. Anyone who came in and learned its secrets never came out—alive. Of course, no organization catering drugs and sex to outsiders, no matter how select the group of outsiders and no matter the level of political protection, can avoid the long arm of the law forever. Even before the escape of the treacherous succubus, the Prophecy was on the state's radar. The demise of the Prophecy was just a matter of time. Her escape only precipitated it.

Lazarus sat up and snorted into his handkerchief. The coke was starting to burn out his membranes. He'd have to switch to something else pretty soon. Meanwhile, he was going to check out the potential threats to his operation. The most obvious was Jeanie Jones. She had an insider's view of the Children of God's compound. Benjamin was supposed to have taken care of her, but she got away. The second threat was the stalker, the person terminating Lazarus's men in the Children of God compound. He knew the stalker would make a mistake. They always did. When he did, Lazarus would be there to make him regret the day he crawled out of his mother's womb. The third threat was the least likely to be important, but it was the one giving him the most food for thought.

It was the American guy who interacted with the gangbangers, recruited by Mike and Joe to terrorize the Children of God. This guy was also Jeanie's colleague and friend. He had been around the Children of God compound looking for her. Lazarus was wary of coincidences. He knew where to find this guy and decided that now was a good time to start.

He knew his drive past Jeanie Jones's apartment would be a waste of time. She was long gone. He did feel something when he drove past the high-rise where she was supposedly now staying. This was something that needed to be explored.

A drive down the Rue d'Assas where Jeanie's American friend lived finally produced the sensation he was seeking. The danger was there, and it was powerful.

There was too much at stake to ignore his intuition. His intuition was telling him his carefully laid plans were in danger. It was calling up images of dark forces of death and destruction circling his empire, threatening his life.

His intuition had saved him from many a potential catastrophe in the past. It had failed him only once. That one failure had ended up costing him the Prophecy and almost cost him his life. He swore vengeance. His intuition was telling him the time had come.

It was already almost 3 a.m. There was no ostensible surveillance around, and this reassured him.

He managed to find a parking space two blocks past number 90. He slid out of the car, closed the door quietly, and headed back toward the American's place.

A soft sound and a flickering shadow from a dark sedan parked across from number 90 stopped his progress at the corner of the Rue Vavin. He melted back into the darkness of a garage exit and waited. There was no traffic. No pedestrians. No birds and no bees. Only a peaceful silence bathed in the dim light of a disappearing moon and the cool, bosky aroma flooding out of the Jardin du Luxembourg.

The door to the sedan opened, and a brawny middle-aged man climbed out. He lumbered across the street and entered number

90. "French cop" was written all over the man's car, his clothes, and his haircut. Lazarus praised his intuition and cursed his luck. His intuition hadn't failed him. The goddamn American was in cahoots with the French cops.

27: Jeanie and Country

Chuck was at his massive mahogany desk littered with all kinds of papers, pens, and pencils. The only ornament was a photo of himself in full Marine dress taken during his days as a jarhead.

Brad sat by the window, staring down at the masses of humanity flowing up and down the sidewalk of the Champs-Elysées. Today was the first round of the French presidential elections. The atmosphere was electric. For the first time since the war, the Left had a strong chance to win. Brad could feel it, even from his perch up on the sixth floor. "Frogs are out in full force today."

"Yeah, lotta cute girls runnin' around down there." Chuck missed the point. He never strayed far from the essentials. "So, who were your friends from last night?"

Brad turned to face his buddy. When he spoke, he weighed each word. "They were American. That's for sure. I could tell by their accents. One of them even had ketchup and Coca-Cola breath. They were also cops or ex-cops. They used law enforcement lingo, but they were well-spoken. They were educated, like Brandon."

"So, tell me, croon daddy, why were these educated and well-spoken law enforcement officers trying to cut your ears off? You don't think they were Brandon's buddies?"

Brad did a sharp take. "I didn't even consider that as a possibility. He doesn't have those kinds of assets running around the embassy. And even if he did, Gary would know about it."

"Yeah. That's for sure. But he's like a jazz saxophone in a symphonic orchestra. Sounds like he's not playing from the same sheet of music. What about Jeanie?"

Jeanie's role in last night's adventures had been troubling Brad. She broke into his apartment and when she got caught, pleaded for help. Her story held water. It was her past that made Brad suspicious. "I don't know what to say. The more I see of her, the better I like her."

"Me too."

"You know the problem, Chuck." Brad furrowed his brow and nodded his head. "Jeanie Jones died ten years ago."

"Yeah. But then I would really like to know who the black-clad babe boppin' around in my studio is."

"Gary says he's still workin' on it. Like he told us, she just appeared one day in Paris. Been working for Gary ever since."

"You said you knew her from the Barbary?"

"Yeah. Like I said before, she came around the Barbary looking for 'talent.' Said she was a talent scout, an *empresario* as they say in France. She was already managing the Children of God choir. I don't how she swung that. She could hardly speak French when I first met her. Didn't pay much attention to her until Gary told me about her. That was a mistake. She's a number. Got a lot of presence, charisma. Not to mention a Marilyn Monroe body and an Elizabeth Taylor face."

Chuck took a sip of his coffee and thought it over. Brad was concentrating on the activity down on the street. Finally, Chuck broke the silence. "She knows what she's doin'. She made a complete check of the area before she went up to the studio. Moves like a big cat, unhurried, smooth, perfect balance. I didn't go up with her. Don't want anybody to know the Ponthieu exit communicates with my office."

"We're supposed to pick her up outside the metro Argentine in twenty minutes on our way to Louveciennes. Give Country a call and see if he's free."

LOUVECIENNES

Country turned up the collar on his black leather jacket and extended his hand. "I'm Country, ma'am. Pleased to meet'cha." His red cowboy boots were shined to perfection. Instead of his usual slicked-back Brylcreem hairdo, today he was sporting an impressive Elvis-style pompadour.

"So nice to meet you, Mister Country."

"Country. Just call me Country. That's what everybody calls me, you know, because of my cowboy style."

Jeanie had to smile at the sincerity and the naivety. "Okay, Country. What do you do?"

Country cocked his head and lowered his shoulder in the old John Wayne talkin'-to-a-beautiful-lady humility move. "Well, ma'am, I'm a first-year student at the European Business School. Also trainin' to be a private detective."

Chuck chirped in. "He's helping me on my investigation into a missing American girl, Sally Ann Hastings."

Jeanie flinched when she heard the name. It was imperceptible, but Brad saw it. Chuck saw it, too. Jeanie zeroed in on Country. "What do you do?"

"I keep my eye on that house down the road on Montbuisson. Lotta people in that house. Men and girls. Nice cars. Haven't seen anybody looks like Sally Ann, though. Hey, I did see something funny the other day. One of the guys from EBS—he's in third year, name of Thibault—was over there."

Now it was Brad's turn to flinch. Thibault was the dude on the tape responsible for trafficking. "What was he doing there?"

"Dunno. He was a-hankerin' to leave. Just said hello and moseyed off."

"How well do you know him?"

"Not too well. He comes along sometimes when I take my friends on a tour of the *égouts*—the sewers."

Now it was Brad's turn to be interested. "Sewers?"

Country was enjoying his moment of importance. "Many miles of sewers beneath Paris. Got 'em runnin' along under the streets. Got 'em runnin' wild in different directions all over the place. You get lost down there, you might never get out. Been mapping these sewers ever since I was a whippersnapper. It's my hobby. Know 'em better than anybody. The Germans used 'em when they were here. Got some big caverns down there, too. Students use 'em for parties. Lotsa rats and snakes and reptiles and bugs. You gotta be real careful." Country was on a roll.

Brad made a mental note to stay as far away from those sewers as possible. Rats, snakes, reptiles, and bugs were not his thing. From the way Jeanie was squinching up her face, it looked like she felt the same way.

"Okay, Country. We have to move out. I've got a show tonight."

Back in the car, Jeanie was quiet and thoughtful. This surprised Brad. She had seen the house at number 6 Rue Montbuisson, the garage, the cars, and the dogs. She had met Country. Brad thought she would be ripe with more questions than he could answer. Her silence put him on guard.

28: Salanha's Apartment

Jeanie glided down the Boulevard Saint-Germain and stopped at the corner of Raspail. The light was red. She waited, taking a slow, hundred-eighty-degree sweep of the area. *Jesus Christ!* It was an exclamation and a description. Brad had warned her, and there he was, slick and serene, Il Messia, sunning himself on the café terrace. Brad's description was right on the money. He was an unmistakable attention grabber.

The light changed. She crossed Raspail and headed toward Salanha's apartment building. This cutthroat Jesus-Christ-look-alike's presence near Salanha's residence was a bad omen. Salanha had contacted Jeanie earlier in the day for an urgent meeting. She said she knew where her boyfriend was living. Jeanie was ecstatic. The investigation was going nowhere fast. This info would break it wide open. Salanha's voice was trembling, and it sounded like she was on the verge of tears.

On the way to the meeting, Jeanie ran into some disciples from the Children of God compound. They told her Salanha had just returned there with Benjamin and two of the new disciples. This was an enormous surprise to Jeanie because Salanha had sworn she would never go back. She was especially adamant in her disapproval of the new disciples. So if Salanha had returned to the compound, she was in trouble. The investigation was in even worse trouble because Salanha was the only link to the terrorists. Jeanie was here to find out.

Black top, black leotard, black sneakers, black backpack, she moved like a panther, smooth, rolling strides, balanced and powerful. Jazzy Jesus's presence made her wary. She continued past Salanha's building and spent the better part of an hour and a half walking around the Latin Quarter, riding the metro and shopping in the Bon Marché, trying to flush out some surveillance. There was none. Now it was time to go back to Salanha's to find out what was going on.

She tapped the door code and slipped into the building. The entrance hall was dark and cool. The old-fashioned elevator with flapping wooden and glass doors stood at the back of the entrance hall next to the stairway. She eschewed the elevator and the stairway lights. No sense in publicizing her presence. She padded up the stairs to Salanha's apartment and knocked softly on the door. One, two. One, two, three. That was their simple code.

No response. She tried again, louder this time. Still no response. She pulled the keys out of her backpack and let herself in.

The blinds were drawn. It was dark. She lingered long enough in the vestibule for her eyes to adjust. Nothing seemed out of place. The mahogany coat rack was in the corner behind the door, and the green jade flower vase stood empty on the beige travertine-marble-topped hall table to the right of the door. There was no other object.

Ready to move, she sniffed the air. It was the unmistakable, nauseating stench of body odor mixed with deodorant. Brought her back to the days of the boys too lazy to take a post-training shower and too confident in their Mum roll-on. Somebody was in there, and it wasn't Salanha.

The vestibule was large, but not large enough for her to move freely in case of an attack. She fingered the Colt .38 six-shot from her backpack and adjusted the silencer. She waited.

There was some movement. Then silence. She squatted down in the corner behind the coat rack and waited. Waiting was a game where she excelled, her skills honed by many long hours hunting animals in the wild and criminals on the run.

The minutes dragged on. There were some hushed whispers, some heavy breathing, some shuffling around. Then silence.

Suddenly, the room exploded in a blaze of activity. Two dark shadows rushed through the entranceway. Jeanie managed to squeeze off three shots before the first shadow crashed down on her. It was Mister Body Odor. He wasn't moving.

Shadow Number Two stumbled over Body Odor and fell to the floor. He was moving, and he had a knife. Jeanie heard the swish as it sliced through Body Odor's arm when the falling shadow tried to regain his balance.

Jeanie's gun arm was trapped under Body Odor's inert torso. She wrenched herself free just in time to evade the shadow's knife thrust. She rolled right, away from the shadow, and raised the gun.

The shadow lunged. Jeanie fired. Twice. The first bullet took the shadow's right shoulder and flipped him to the left. The second bullet blasted away his left collarbone and knocked him to the floor.

Jeanie had one bullet left. She forward-rolled into the main room and came up on her feet ready to fire. Looked left. Nothing. Looked right. Nothing. Room empty. All clear.

Back in the vestibule, the shadow was starting to move. Another forward roll brought her back into the vestibule, where she landed on the shadow with all her force. She used the cross of the Colt to bash Shadow in the head. He went out like a candle in a crosswind.

She checked Body Odor. He was out as well. One of Jeanie's first three shots had found his heart. She went to her backpack and quickly reloaded. Then she searched the house for more adversaries. There were none. Back in the vestibule, she recovered the spent cartridges and stored them in her backpack.

Shadow was beginning to stir. She cracked open the blinds and dragged him into the light of the main room. She recognized him from the Prophecy as one of the Prophet's enforcers. He was conscious enough to realize the extreme fragility of his current status as a living organism. Jeanie highlighted this fragility with a kick to the head.

"I'm in a hurry. I need answers. You've got one chance. Where is Salanha?"

He hesitated. His brain was wrestling with his emotions. It was over quickly, and his brain won. Cooperation was his only chance. "They're shipping her off somewhere, some foreign country."

"What foreign country?"

His voice was weak, drifting off. "Don't know. Only Lazarus knows."

"Lazarus?"

"Yeah, Lazarus, the Prophet. You remember him."

So! He recognized her. His voice was a little stronger. He was trying to make a comeback. This confirmed what she already suspected. Lazarus and the Prophet were one and the same. "What are you and your smelly friend doing here?"

"Waitin' for you. Lazarus said you'd come." His voice trailed off again. The guy was starting to lose consciousness. A close look showed he was bleeding profusely from the wound to his collarbone. The bullet must have blasted away an artery.

"Me, personally? He named me personally?"

"Yeah, he called you Jeanie, or something like that."

Jeanie breathed a sigh of relief. The Prophet still didn't know who she was.

She could see Shadow's existence as a living organism was about to peter out. Judging from all the blood he'd lost, it was amazing he was still able to hang in there. Then he coughed. The blood stopped. His life was over.

She went into the bathroom and came back with a pile of towels, which she used to wipe up the puddles of blood forming on the tiled floor. No sense taking a chance it would leak out somewhere and alert the authorities to all the chaos and cadavers haunting the apartment.

Jeanie checked her watch. What seemed like a long couple of hours since she had entered the apartment was, in reality, only a little more than ten minutes. She thought of the Jesus look-alike she had spotted on the café terrace. The odds were heavy that he was working with these two bozos. Better to hurry. If this were the case, it probably wouldn't be long before he showed up to see what was going on.

She went into the bedroom. Salanha's diary was lying open on the dresser. Jeanie read the last entry and froze. This changed everything. Salanha, their only link to the terrorists, had been kidnapped by the terrorists and was being held in the COG compound.

She went to the door and listened. No sound. Nothing moving. She cracked it open and checked out the stairway. Empty. She slipped out and took the stairs three at a time to the ground floor. Came to a stop at the entry. Somebody was coming down the stairs. She exited the building and hustled down Saint-Germain toward the Assemblée Nationale.

As she passed the café, a Jesus in disguise vacated his table and began to trail along behind.

She crossed the bridge to the Place de la Concorde and made her way toward the US Embassy. Jesus had no trouble melting into the hundreds of tourists wandering around the Place. She cut into the park across from the embassy and paralleled the Champs-Elysées. Took the metro at Franklin Roosevelt and exited one stop later at Georges V.

Jesus lost her when she turned right off the Champs-Elysées onto the Rue de Berri.

29: Kidnapped

The spring air was warm. The sun was out and about, beaming down on the hustle and bustle of the Boulevard Montparnasse.

The terrace of La Rotonde was crammed with men and women taking their 4 p.m. coffee break. The impression of "business as usual" was exceedingly deceiving, however. There was only one subject of conversation, and it was intense.

François Mitterrand, the Socialist Party's (PS) presidential candidate, had garnered 43.25% of the ballots cast. In second place was Valéry Giscard d'Estaing, the candidate of the National Federation of the Independent Republicans (FNRI), with 32.6% of the votes. Far behind in third place, with 15.11%, was Chaban-Delmas, candidate of the Union of Democrats for the Republic (UDR).

Brad and Chuck agreed. France was upset. France was excited. France was ready for change. The prospect of fundamental political change had passed from an entertaining, hypothetical, intellectual game to a sobering, highly probable reality.

The French alliance of the Left, running on a collectivist initiative called the "Common Program," had soundly defeated the two top Rightist candidates and vaulted Mitterrand into the run-off election on May 19.

Chuck thought it over. "I'm trying to conjure up the consequences for our investigation."

"The consequences are we have to get our ass in gear," Brad said. "France is the main political pillar of the EEC, the European Economic Community. The EEC is the key to European peace and economic development. If the Left comes in and France goes rogue with its Common Program and aligns itself with the Communist Bloc, the world could become a very different, very dangerous place. France is volatile. Look at May 1968. One small event like a terrorist attack, a terrorist attack during a tense electoral period, could be the spark. The embassy is worried about this. We know there's something in the works over at the Children of God. We've got less than two weeks to figure out what it is and disarm it. I say we concentrate on the American girl with the terrorist boyfriend."

"Agreed. Let's get goin'."

Brad stood to leave. Chuck grabbed his arm.

"Hold it, amigo. Play it cool, and take a glance across the street. I think we got trouble."

Brad looked. His heart started to race. It was Jeanie. It was trouble. She should be hiding out in Chuck's studio, not running around Montparnasse. She gave the follow signal, turned, and walked nonchalantly down a side street away from the Boulevard Montparnasse.

Brad and Chuck went after her. To give them the time and opportunity to check for surveillance, she wandered around the streets behind the Boulevard Montparnasse until she got to la Rue du Départ. Brad gave Jeanie the all-clear signal and slipped into the Café Odessa. Chuck was right behind him. They took a table back behind the bar. Jeanie joined them five minutes later.

The Odessa was a popular rendezvous point for moviegoers early in the evening before the eight o'clock sessions. It was way too early for that crowd, so they had the place almost entirely to themselves. Jeanie's sudden appearance had Brad worried. She was outwardly calm but showed some slight irritation when he lit up a Gitane sans filtre.

Brad didn't waste any time. "You shouldn't be out and about. What're you doing here?"

Jeanie hesitated as the waiter came to take their order—espresso for Brad, beer for Chuck, and *jus d'orange* for Jeanie. Her calm expression changed to one of concern after the waiter traipsed off, and she recounted her escapade at Salanha's place earlier in the day. When she finished, all three of them were wearing concerned expressions. The yellow light beaming down from the gaudy chandelier hanging over their table highlighted the lines and wrinkles on their faces, accentuated their concern, and made them look older than they were.

Brad sat deep in thought, blowing smoke rings. The news couldn't be worse. The girl was in dire straits, and their investigation was off the tracks. She was the only live lead, and now she was gone. The whereabouts of the terrorist boyfriend would have gone a long way to ending the threat.

Chuck was the first to react. "So you left the two bodies there? Did you wipe everything down?"

"As much as I could. Probably didn't get everything. I've been over there many times. She and I are close."

Brad winced. If she left any prints, Chef would be sure to find them. Very bad news for Jeanie when Chef finally caught up with her.

The waiter came with the beverages, and Brad paid in advance.

He didn't want to be disturbed while he worked out the implications of what Jeanie was telling them. She had a feminine way of moving her hands when she spoke that made her seem kind of vulnerable. There was also a little catch in her voice that made Brad want to protect her. All this despite the fact she had just wiped out a pair of professional hatchet men and obviously needed no protection.

"One question, Jeanie. Who is Salanha?" Brad asked.

Jeanie's eyes widened, but she was focused and prepared for the question. "Before I came over here, I stopped by the apartment and left you a message in case I couldn't find you. Everything is there. Anyway, her real name is Sally Ann Hastings, the one you're looking for."

Now Brad understood why Jeanie had been so subdued after they left Louveciennes the other day.

Jeanie went on. "When she turned eighteen, she took some money she inherited from her grandparents and joined a cult in California. It was too close to home. She came to Paris. Wanted to escape her parents, be free, live her life. You know the story. She remade herself. Changed her name, her hair, her clothes, her makeup, everything. She did a good job, but if you look hard, you can see it's the same person."

"The picture we have isn't very good and was taken when she was barely a teenager. We missed that one."

"She tried the religious scene but found it too weird." Jeanie hit the stop button and looked down, searching for the right words. She absently ran her fingers across her neck while she thought. Brad and Chuck remained silent, waiting for the next chapter. It came with no urging. "One night at the Caveau de la Huchette, she met the antithesis of any boy she had ever known, an idealistic rebel, fragile and sensitive, socially timid and politically bold, determined to change the world. She fell in love. I think he did, too. They got together whenever he could free himself from 'saving the world.' That's it."

"That's it?"

"That's it until a few months ago when he hooked up with the bozos over at the Children of God and started planning some kind of attack on the French government. The bozos saw Salanha as a threat and wanted her to come back to the compound so they could keep an eye on her. She refused. When I heard she was back in the compound, I knew she was in trouble. My adventure at her place confirmed that."

Brad thought it over. "Any idea what they're planning?"

"Not really, but Salanha knows. That's why she decided to tip me off about her boyfriend's whereabouts. I saw her diary. She's in worse trouble than I thought. She heard them talking about selling her off somewhere as a slave."

30: The Penitence Suite

No one was smiling. Brad was deep in thought on the leather sofa by the window, blowing smoke rings at the ceiling. Jeanie was in the armchair sipping some kind of fruit concoction from a crystal glass she found in the studio behind the office. Chuck was at his desk, drinking a Stella and staring out the window. Their mood was more somber than the heavy air and cloudy sky out on the Champs-Elysées. Their options were not-so-good, bad, and worse.

Brad broke the silence. "Are you sure Salanha is at the compound?"

Jeanie didn't look up. "Positive."

"Where would they keep her? It's not likely they would want the disciples to be in touch with her."

"There's a couple of rooms down in the basement. They call it the Penitence Suite. It's a place where those who have 'sinned' go to meditate and repent. She's probably there. The Penitence Suite is heavily guarded."

Brad rubbed his left forearm, which was still sensitive from yesterday's workout and sparring over at Karate-Montagne. "Look,

Gary says that until this election is over, there's nothing he can do. It's too sensitive, even if we could prove it. Think of it. An American religious cult kidnapping other Americans on French soil to traffic them into slavery. It would be bad publicity all around, especially for the French, and especially when the political environment is so turbulent."

Jeanie's soft delivery and measured words could not disguise the intensity of the emotion in her quivering voice. "It will be worse publicity if they pull off the attack. Besides the fact that Sally's our last hope to shut down the attack, for her, it's a question of life, and life worse than death. We have to do something."

"Do you have any idea when they're planning to ship her out?" Chuck interrupted. "The tenth."

Brad jerked to attention. "Whaddya mean, the tenth? The tenth of this month? How do you know?"

"She's going out on the truck that leaves on the tenth, this Friday. It's on the tape. The Italian guy is taking personal delivery."

"That leaves us less than two days. There is no possible way for us to get into the compound and down to the basement without being seen. Their security is too tight, and they're armed to the teeth. We'd have to shoot our way in and shoot our way out, break down doors, climb walls, and do all the stuff they do in the movies, all the while protecting Salanha and avoiding the French police that would be waiting for us if we made it outside."

Jeanie was adamant. "I'll go in there alone if I have to." Her eyes were flashing, and her jaw was set.

Brad started to answer, stopped, and studied the burning ash on his cigarette. When he spoke, his voice resonated with subdued optimism. "No, I've got an idea. Let me run down to the European Business School over by the Opéra. I want to talk to Country."

Brad got to the European Business School at number 8 Rue de

la Paix just as the students were breaking for lunch. Country spotted Brad right away and "moseyed" on over. Brad pointed to the back of his Indian, and Country jumped on. Ten minutes later, they were in Chuck's office.

Country was decked out in his signature black leather jacket with a turned-up collar, boot-cut blue jeans, and red cowboy boots. His slicked-back brown hair was messed up from the breezy bike ride, but it didn't bother him a bit. He finger-brushed it back and said he was "chompin' at the bit."

When Brad outlined what he had in mind, Country leaned forward, looked down, and scratched the back of his head with his right forefinger. When he looked back up, Brad saw an astounding transformation. The young man standing before him had morphed from a lovable, cowboy wannabe into a confident whiz kid, ready to take charge and lead the way.

"We can get to that Jesus-lovin' compound through the sewers. Mighty dangerous place down there. Lotsa critters. Easy to get lost. But I know it. We can go down the manhole on the Rue de la Tombe Issoire. Usually locked. I can unlock it. From there, it'll take twenty minutes to the compound."

"How will you know where the compound is if we're twenty meters underground?"

"Been mappin' these sewers since I was knee-high to a grasshopper. Know 'em like the back of my hand." Country had mastered the lingo in the cowboy movies. He was a fountain of clichés from a bygone era. "*Electricité de France* has a basement-level service tunnel runnin' the length of the street that connects to all the buildings. Connects to the sewers. We come up from the sewer to the service tunnel. Just bricks and mortar separatin' us from gettin' in."

Brad was convinced this was their best shot. He caught Jeanie out of the corner of his eye. She was smiling at Country. "Do you think we can do it?" she asked.

Country put his hand on his heart. "Beggin' your pardon, ma'am, I'm a-countin' on it."

Brad turned to Chuck. Chuck's beatific expression showed he could already see himself, knife in hand, sneaking around these dark, dangerous sewer tunnels crawling with "lotsa critters."

That was enough for Brad. "Let's go for it,"

Country was pleased. "When the sun goes down tomorrow, we shall assemble."

31: Brandon Closes In

THE AMERICAN HOSPITAL IN NEUILLY, TUESDAY, MAY 7, 1974

Brandon shuffled out of the hospital and toward the taxi waiting at the curb. He turned slowly and looked back. The American Hospital in Neuilly was one of the best in the world. Also one of the most expensive. It had cost him an arm and a leg to get everything straightened out.

There would be no police report. He had paid in cash, and his two buddies had fake IDs, so for all practical purposes, there was no way to trace them or him. Both would mostly recover from their unfortunate hostile interrogation of Brad James. One would have limited use of his right arm for up to a year, and the other would never recover full use of his shoulder.

They were pissed off and swore they wanted revenge. Brandon doubted they wanted it bad enough to risk going up against the one-man demolition crew that had sent them to the hospital in the first place. They were not convincing, and, anyway, he advised against it. Stood to reason. If they couldn't take him down at full strength, how could they hope to succeed with only two valid arms between them?

Brandon couldn't imagine how one medium-sized man could have taken out his two former all-star colleagues single-handedly. They were trained agents with years of experience. They were the muscle in many an unofficial operation undertaken by the Bureau, and they were universally considered "the best." Okay, they were no longer with the Bureau, but they were still in the game, free-lancing and making a lot more money with a lot fewer constraints. Their skills had only improved, if anything.

A thin film of perspiration formed on Brandon's upper lip. The surge of adrenaline made him shiver. He closed his eyes and tried to concentrate. He was all alone now. The pressure on him was ramping up. Time was running out. There was no longer any doubt that Brad James was the key to Jeanie Jones, and Jeanie Jones was the key to his investigation. But he needed more information on what Gary was up to.

His charm campaign on Gary's secretary had produced a gold mine of information, information that Gary kept carefully and un-successfully locked away in his desk. He now knew a certain James MacDonald from London was an important element in Gary's in-vestigation. He also knew James MacDonald was linked to a cer-tain Benjamin and the Children of God. He had to smile when he looked back on how he had outsmarted Gary Richards, Mister CIA super spy.

Before he left London, Brandon had asked his vis-à-vis at the embassy for any information he could get on James MacDonald. So far, there was no feedback. On the other hand, the embassy in Paris had all the info on the Children of God he needed to put two and two together. The Children of God was a religious cult sus-pected of drug dealing and prostitution. This was the natural hab-itat of the Prophet, the object of his investigation, the man he was seeking and suspected of being in France.

Benjamin was the director, the chief shepherd of the cult. The cult had a popular singing group and close association with Jeanie Jones, who was the group's *empresario*. Benjamin had been instrumental in obtaining Jeanie's release from jail. Conclusion: Jeanie and Benjamin were working together through the Children of God, running the prostitution and dealing the drugs. Brandon recognized them as simple gophers who followed instructions and handled the day-to-day operations. Someone else was the mastermind with the contacts and the infrastructure to set the system up. Brandon was convinced this person was the Prophet.

Gary's confidential dossier fingered James MacDonald as a major person of interest in the investigation. Brandon suspected that James MacDonald and the Prophet were one and the same. The evidence was circumstantial, and there were holes in the story, but it would be easy to confirm one way or the other if he could just interrogate these two. All he needed was a description of James MacDonald. Then he would know. Meanwhile, he would have to try to identify James MacDonald on his own.

32: Along Came Jones

Gary's features were strained, but his eyes were shining. His mind was focused. The adrenaline was pumping. These were the days he lived for, the days that made all the long weeks of routine and drudgery worthwhile, like a sprinter in the US final of the hundred-yard dash. The reports were flowing across his desk. Langley was calling. The ambassador was continually requesting updates and soliciting advice.

The Left had won the first round and was well-placed to emerge victorious in the second. Rallies and demonstrations were planned. Rumors abounded. French security was on high alert, and his contacts were counting on his network for help in identifying and disabling any potential plots cooked up by foreign adversaries or, God forbid, foreign allies. He was running on Costa Rican arabica and sugar cubes. It couldn't get any better. And then the phone rang.

"Mister Richards?" It was a woman. The voice was not familiar. "Mister Gary Richards?" It was the voice of a middle-aged, demanding woman.

Gary's neck muscles tensed up. He leaned forward. He had a bad feeling. "Speaking."

"Mister Richards, I am Olivia Townsend Ritter-Jones. We have to speak."

Olivia Townsend Ritter-Jones! Everyone knew the name. Everyone recognized the face. Everyone wanted to avoid her. She had been around for as long as he could remember—as an FBI official, presidential consultant, political pundit, and television celebrity, among other things. For the last few years, she had been the White House legal consultant and liaison with the FBI. Her father had been a powerful senator from the great state of California. She aspired to follow in his footsteps, but the shoes were too big and her shoulders too narrow.

Gary jabbed, "What can I do for you, Miss Jones?"

She stepped right into it. "Ritter-Jones. Townsend Ritter-Jones."

Gary was a polished bureaucratic infighter. He dodged and danced out of range. "What can I do for you, Miss *Townsend Ritter-Jones?*"

"You can come to my office. I don't want to talk on the phone."

Gary sat back in his chair and relaxed. This might end up being easier than he thought. Miss Townsend Ritter-Jones was using a big Bowie knife for a job that called for a surgeon's scalpel. "Very sorry, Miss *Townsend Ritter-Jones*, I have a full schedule for today. I'll pass you to my secretary and see if she can work you in tomorrow or the day after."

"Today, Mister Richards, I must see you today. This is top priority." She was building up a head of steam, and Gary decided to throw a little coal into the furnace.

"At the moment, Miss *Townsend Ritter-Jones*, everything is top priority. I'm operating on a first-come, first-served basis. The list is long. Let me pass you to my secretary. You can outline to her what the issue is, she can brief me, and I'll have her get back to you as soon as possible."

The silence was ominous. Now Gary was grinnin' the grin. "Good day, Mister Richards." Click. The line went dead. That was too easy. He couldn't believe his luck.

He gave her four minutes, just enough time for her to contact the ambassador and for him to cook up another pot of coffee. Sugar cubes ingested and cup in hand, sure enough, the phone rang. He looked at his watch—four minutes and twenty seconds. She was running behind schedule.

It was the ambassador, requesting he go down to her office and meet with her. Gary was firm. He told the ambassador he was over-whelmed by current events and had no time for babysitting politicians. As a personal favor to the ambassador, however, he would agree to a ten-minute meeting in his own office. Otherwise, the ambassador would have to go to Gary's boss in Langley. Gary figured he would soon find out how badly she wanted to see him.

Very badly. Five minutes later, she was knocking on his door.

Gary took his time going over and opening up. Bigger than life, Townsend Ritter-Jones stood six feet tall if she stood an inch. Graying hair cut in what was called a "pageboy" framed her long, thin face, but only down to the earlobes. That left the bottom of her face sticking out and accentuated the tight, thin lips, the cleft chin, and wicked nose. Her long face, framed in the short pageboy and the way she carried herself, reminded him of Ed, the talking horse. Her skinny, narrow shoulders and big, bulky bottom re-minded him of a turkey.

She was dressed in a severe white blouse buttoned up to the neck, a long, gray hippie skirt, black brogans, and no makeup. The paleness of her skin clashed with her bushy, black eyebrows and dark, deep-set eyes. Her television image did not do justice to the image incarnate that reeked of menace and malevolence.

Gary's smile stretched from ear to ear. "Miss *Townsend Ritter-Jones*. How nice of you to drop by."

"Cut the Townsend Ritter-Jones crap, Richards. I get the point. Call me Olivia."

The sparring was over. Gary wasn't prepared for what came next.

Before he could extend an invitation, Olivia marched into the office and plopped herself down on the leather sofa. "We'll have to make this short, Richards. I have a telephone appointment with the president in thirty minutes. I need some answers, and I need them fast."

"Thanks for taking the time to drop by on such short notice. Please have a seat." Tongue in cheek. "What is it you need to know?"

"Are the Soviets having any success with their propaganda?"

"They are, and that's one of the reasons why the election is going to be so close."

"Don't be condescending. You know what I mean. Is there anything out of the ordinary I should know about? When I brief the president, my analysis and advice on what is going on need to be based on the latest and most relevant information. If I find that something was omitted, the president and I will be actively displeased."

That was a threat. Gary was an experienced bureaucratic infighter. It took a lot to impress him. He was impressed in spite of himself. "Of course, everything is hyperactive at the moment, but there is nothing we wouldn't normally expect in the given circumstances."

The COG, Jeanie, and the terrorists he would keep to himself. He was ready for some pointed follow-up questions that were not forthcoming. Instead, Olivia looked out the window and said,

"Yes, France is a strange country of individualistic, undisciplined citizens. Their politics is managed chaos. I understand they are now becoming enamored of religious cults."

This was an unforeseen change of pace. Olivia noticed Gary's baffled expression. She persevered. "There's an ongoing FBI investigation in the US on a suspected terrorist group. The leader of the group skipped town and came to France when he was called in for questioning. Our intelligence tells us he is now running the Children of God cult here in Paris. He goes by the name of Benjamin. Have you been following this?"

"This is the first I've heard about anything like that."

Olivia sat up to her full height. That weird-looking head and the narrow shoulders with her hands folded in front of her chin made her look like a praying mantis.

"Come, come, Richards," she said. "The president prizes cooperation between the FBI and the CIA. He is adamant that these agencies work hand in glove to ensure our country's security is guaranteed. You have undoubtedly been briefed."

"Not really." He knew Olivia was trying to steamroll him.

"Maybe I'm not surprised. Benjamin and his activities are the sole remit of the FBI. If you had any information on this dossier, you would have to turn it over to the FBI."

"Olivia, everyone in France knows the Children of God. They are one of the best-known singing groups in the whole country. I've probably seen Benjamin's name cross my desk, but nothing out of the ordinary, especially nothing about an FBI investigation."

Olivia thrust out her cleft chin and pursed her tight, thin lips. "A US terrorist is still a US terrorist, even if he changes his country of residence. Are you sure there is no evidence of contacts between the Children of God and terrorists?"

These were leading questions that Gary suspected Olivia

already knew the answers to. That should have been impossible because, outside of Brad and Chuck, he had discussed it with no one. Time to change the subject. "How about some coffee?"

"No, thank you."

"If you don't mind, I'll just join myself." He took enough time preparing the coffee to work out his strategy when Olivia threw him another curveball.

"How are you getting along with Brandon?" she asked.

"You know him?"

"Know him well. Worked for me in California when I was with the FBI. He is so handsome."

"He's with the DEA now."

"I suppose you work closely together."

"This we do."

"What are you currently working on?" Olivia was going out of bounds with these questions. She knew it. When Gary hesitated, she continued. "I was his mentor when I was in California. It's always so satisfying when one of your mentorees makes good."

"This is so true, Olivia. His office is right down the hall. He's often in."

Olivia was unfazed. She stuck out her chin and dug in. "It's so much more informative when it comes from someone else. Do you know what he's working on now?"

Gary straightened up and set his cup on his desk. He was going to shut down Olivia's nosy questions. There was a knock at the door. In walked Marilyn. "Langley calling, Gary."

"Thanks, Marilyn. I'll take it. Olivia, please excuse me."

"Oh, just pretend I'm not here. I have top security clearance."

Gary didn't let his annoyance infiltrate his reply. "I'm so sorry, Olivia, but Langley would skin me alive if I allowed you to stay."

Olivia did not appreciate being contradicted. Being evicted

from the office was akin to *lese majesté*. She scowled, huffed and puffed, struggled off the sofa. "You'll be hearing from me, Richards."

Langley agreed with Gary's analysis that Olivia Townsend Ritter-Jones was going to be a giant pain in the part of his body currently resting on the seat of his chair. Gary had two takeaways from the meeting with her.

The first was the FBI was using the pretext of a domestic terrorist link to horn in on CIA territory in Paris.

Since Olivia was the president's official liaison with the FBI, it looked like the operation at least had the president's *de facto* blessing. It also looked like Olivia was going to oversee the operation herself.

When she announced she expected Gary's complete cooperation, she meant that he was to turn over to her personally any and all information pertaining to the Children of God.

He played along with her but had no intention of cooperating. If he did that, his entire investigation would be in jeopardy, including the suspected terrorist attack. Langley agreed with him and ordered him to keep her at bay as long as he could.

The second takeaway was the surprise questions about Brandon.

Before the meeting, Gary would have bet that Brandon and Olivia would be allies, especially since they seemed to have worked closely together sometime in the not-so-distant past. Although couched in the language of getting an update on a former colleague's current situation, Olivia's questions suggested to Gary the opposite was true. The questions were full of suspicion and innuendo. It was almost as if she were afraid of Brandon.

Gary sat back, put his feet on the desk, and sipped some Costa Rican caffeine. Deep in thought, the corners of his eyes began to crinkle, his lips pursed, and finally, his face broke out into a full-fledged all-American smile.

He hit the intercom. "Marilyn, get in touch with Brandon. Tell him to share the information I gave him on the Children of God with Miss Olivia Townsend Ritter-Jones."

33: Sewer Rats

Country unlocked the manhole near the shopping center on the Rue d'Alésia. He, Brad, and Jeanie slipped inside and started a long descent down the shaft into the tunnel that ran under the Rue de la Tombe Issoire. They were dressed in black from head to toe. Country had supplied the helmets mounted with acetylene lamps as well as some battery-powered torches. Chuck was to stay with the car as the lookout. He fought against this job, to no avail. Country was the guide. Jeanie would be recognized immediately, as would Brad. That left Chuck. Since they had no idea how the operation would unfold once they penetrated the compound, Brad judged that having different options for exiting the sewers was worth one less man on the attack.

The first option was the manhole closest to the compound. Chuck would wait for them there, but if that option was compromised, Chuck's job was to warn them by hanging a length of thin rope from the cover down into the shaft. The rope would indicate that this exit was unsafe. Their second option was to navigate through the tunnels to the *Catacombes de Paris* at the Place Denfert-Rochereau. Country estimated it would take between forty-five minutes and an hour to get there through the sewers from the compound. Chuck would meet them there with the car.

By the time they hit the tunnel, they were somewhere between twenty and thirty meters underground. There was a loud *clunk* when Chuck replaced the manhole cover. They were instantaneously smothered in total blackness.

Brad's first reaction was to light up his electric torch. Country signaled him to extinguish it and listen. In the first few seconds, total blackness was complemented by total silence. The change came slowly, almost imperceptibly. A soft whoosh to the left. Something slithering to the right. A squeal. Little feet scratching. The place was teeming with invisible creatures. If Brad wasn't claustrophobic before, he was starting to come down with an acute case of the disease.

Country lit up his headlamp just in time. The noises ceased as suddenly as they had begun. "No need for you to light up. Mine'll do the trick. Savin' up the fuel. Might be needin' to use it later." He dug into his backpack and pulled out a hand-drawn map that he proceeded to study for a full five minutes.

Brad was not reassured. "You sure you know where we're going?"

"Just checkin' our escape route so I know where we're goin' when we get finished. Might not have much time to ponderate."

Brad was impressed. Country had a head on his shoulders.

Jeanie moved in close to Brad and took his hand. "He's right on that score. The Penitence Suite is always occupied, and it's always heavily guarded." She gave his hand a little squeeze. He liked it. Squeezed back.

For twenty minutes, they marched through a maze of tunnels, some straight and wide with signs indicating the street above, some narrow and winding with nothing but Country's map and sense of direction to guide them. Country stopped abruptly, put his finger to his lips, and extinguished his lamp. Total blackness, but no sound from the creatures lurking in the blackness.

Jeanie moved closer to Brad. He felt Country's hand on his shoulder pushing him to the right. He took Jeanie's hand and followed the pressure on his shoulder.

Country whispered, "We got company. There's somethin' else besides critters and varmints in this here tunnel."

"How close are we to the compound entry shaft?"

"Fifty meters as the crow flies."

Even with his mangled metaphors, Country was easy to understand. Brad could hear the movement now. Somebody was moving stealthily down the tunnel, and the movement was coming from where Country indicated the crow was flying.

Brad braced for the worst. The three of them held their breath and remained motionless as the movement made its way slowly toward their position.

Jeanie patted Brad's hand and slid forward, knife at the ready. She was about to brandish her torch and launch an attack when a light flared up around a bend ten or fifteen meters up the tunnel.

Then a deep male voice whispered, "See, I told you it was nothing but a rat. Nothing to be afraid of."

A feminine voice whispered back, "I still don't like it down here. Let's go back."

Their whispering continued as the couple headed back from where they had come. Country turned on his lamp when he heard them exit the sewer. His eyes widened when he saw Jeanie standing there, knife in hand, poised for battle. She gave him a thumbs-up and a smile, then sheathed her weapon.

Brad was less sanguine. The couple's exit point was also their exit point. Country noticed his quizzical squint and hustled to reassure him. "These here tunnels are powerful popular with high school and college kids hankerin' for adventure. Most of 'em stay on the main trails. I was gobsmacked to see a pair of tenderfoots this far south on a weeknight. Probably got no classes tomorrow."

They reconnoitered at the foot of the manhole shaft by the compound. Country reiterated that other people in a main tunnel like this one were not unusual. In the unlikely event they encountered any more sewer searchers, they shouldn't show any hostility. Just say, "Hello, where you headed, stranger?" He directed his remarks at Jeanie.

Country led the way up the shaft, rung by rung. Jeanie followed, and Brad brought up the rear. By the time they got to the platform at the level of the service tunnel, they were only about two meters below ground level. Brad was more than ready to take a little rest. It surprised him that Jeanie was seemingly unaffected by the long climb. In fact, she seemed invigorated. Her breathing was normal, and she had barely broken a sweat.

The door to the service tunnel was made of metal, and the lock looked like it was sophisticated enough to slow them down. Brad was preparing to go to work on the lock when Jeanie stepped up with an impressive set of tools she had pulled out of her backpack. She inserted one into the keyhole, jiggled it around, inserted another, did some more jiggling and turning, and the door cracked open.

Brad verified that the door could be opened from the inside without a key. Only then did he and Jeanie venture into the tunnel and close the door behind them. Country stayed outside to keep watch.

Once the door was closed, Jeanie drew her pistol and screwed on the silencer. She verified that the chamber was full and that all the moving parts were fully functioning. Brad had traded his white leather pouch for a black backpack. He went into it and pulled out his Beretta and a pair of nunchaks. He put the Beretta in his jacket pocket and stuck the nunchaks in his belt.

Brad led the way down the tunnel. It was made of concrete, narrow, and high enough for him to stand. The concrete had him worried. The pick in his backpack could handle brick, mortar, and cinder blocks with no problem. It wouldn't be enough for reinforced concrete.

He was relieved when he got to the station where the system connected to the compound. It was nothing but a break in the concrete wall about the size of a bedroom door. At eye level, there were several valves and a small instrument panel with gauges where all the wiring was concentrated. Otherwise, from top to bottom, it was the basement wall made of hollow clay builder's bricks and mortar. It would be child's play to make an opening large enough for them to slip through.

The mortar was old and fragile. Brad had no trouble removing the mortar and taking out nine bricks, which he stacked carefully in the tunnel. Through the opening, he could see a dimly lit corridor about nine feet wide and fifty to sixty yards long. The brick removal had been achieved with almost no noise. There was some muffled scratching to remove the mortar, and one brick broke. Other than that, nothing. Brad figured if anyone had heard anything, they would already have come snooping around. Nevertheless, the wise old Indian's admonition, "Better to be safe than sorry," was still relevant. It was time to wait and watch.

He and Jeanie lay head-to-head on the tunnel floor, peering through the opening. The soft fragrance of her lavender-blue perfume tickled his nostrils. "Dilly, dilly" echoed through his thoughts. After five minutes, he gave the signal. Jeanie slipped through the opening, gun first. Brad followed but left his weapons stashed in his clothes. He wanted his hands to be free.

Although Jeanie had never been down to the compound's basement before, she had been able to brief Brad on what she'd learned from talking to the disciples. The Penitence Suite was positioned at the back corner of the basement on the same side of the compound where the service tunnel was located. That put it to the right of where they had entered. It looked like they were on a main corridor spanning the entire width of the compound. Brad could make out at least three perpendicular corridors crisscrossing the one they were on.

Jeanie crept to the first corner. Checked right and left. Empty. She motioned Brad forward. He crept past her to the second corner. Checked right and left. Empty.

Brad gave the "go" sign. They paralleled each other down the separate corridors that ended in another long, dimly lit corridor spanning the width of the building. It was just as Jeanie had described. There were three main corridors going from one end of the compound to the other, and three or four narrower perpendicular corridors running from back to front.

Brad could see what looked like a jail cell to his right. There were iron bars and no lights. He figured this was the fabled Penitence Suite. Some muffled sounds of voices and laughter were coming from the other end of the corridor. This most probably was the reputed heavy surveillance team. It would have to be neutralized.

They stole down the corridor toward the source of the sound. Jeanie stayed to the left of the door, Brad to the right. They cocked their ears. Brad could make out three distinct male voices. He held up three fingers and Jeanie nodded "yes."

The plan was for Brad to bust in the door and for Jeanie to get the drop on them while Brad disarmed them and tied them up. It worked like a charm, except that instead of getting the drop on the guys, Jeanie fired off three bullseyes to the foreheads of the unsuspecting dudes sitting at a table playing cards and drinking beer.

They had no time to surrender, protest, or duck, and the only sounds were the *plop, plop, plop* of the three rounds and the *thud, thud, thud* of the three lifeless bodies hitting the concrete floor.

She rummaged around and found the keys to the Penitence Suite. Then she picked up the spent cartridges and checked if any bullets had exited the skulls. They hadn't. Her gun wasn't traceable, but you could never be too careful. She and Brad must have been talking to the same wise old Indian.

Brad was struggling to come to terms with what he had just witnessed. This was nonstandard operating procedure. Those guys didn't have a chance. But then again, they were no longer a threat and the operation was all the better for that.

They closed the door and hustled back to the jail cell. Jeanie could barely make out a human form cowering in the corner.

"Please…please."

It was Salanha. Sally Ann Hastings.

"Salanha, it's me, Jeanie."

Salanha began to sob. Jeanie tried to calm her down while Brad was working on the door. He fumbled around but finally came up with the right key and got it open.

Salanha fell into Jeanie's arms. She was half naked and moaning and sobbing uncontrollably. "We can't leave them. They took them upstairs. We can't leave them." Now she was shrieking.

Brad smelled disaster. "Let's get outta here."

Salanha continued to scream. Brad was trying to shut her down with his hand over her mouth. It wasn't working.

Jeanie dropped her with a right hook to the side of the head. "Pick her up. Let's go."

Brad did a double-take to make sure he hadn't imagined that. He hadn't. Jeanie was merciless. She was also effective. A few more Salanha screams and they would have been drowning in waves of COG gangbangers.

He scooped up Salanha and followed Jeanie back to the opening of the service tunnel. Jeanie stood guard while Brad dragged Salanha through the small opening and deposited her on the tunnel floor.

Jeanie was about to crawl into the service tunnel when a big, bald dude came lumbering around the corner. It took him a couple of Mississippis to work out what was going down. By the time he did, Jeanie was back on her feet. Her gun was aimed square at his flushed face. He decided to run and had a twenty-yard lead. Jeanie caught him at the forty and brought him down with a bullet to the back of the head.

Meanwhile, Brad had climbed back into the basement. It was a well-known fact that rats traveled in packs. He wasn't wrong. Rat Number Two came crashing out of a side corridor and smashed into Jeanie while she was recovering the spent cartridge. She lost her gun and was falling from a second blow to the shoulder when along came Brad. Number Two's attention turned to him. This was a whale of a dude. He was fast and he was strong. He charged.

Brad drove a powerful side kick into his solar plexus and slid to the right. The dude stumbled forward, gasping for breath. Brad caught him with a knee to the kidney and finished him off with an uppercut to the jaw. The dude was down and out.

He motioned toward Jeanie. "Let's go."

She had recovered her gun and was on her feet, rubbing her shoulder. One quick step brought her to the side of the inert body. In one smooth motion, she grabbed the chin with one hand and the back of the head with the other. She rotated her torso and twisted her arms. There was a squishing sound when the neck snapped. She let the body drop to the floor. Her voice was soft but firm and devoid of all emotion. "No witnesses."

Brad did dubious double-take number three.

Back in the service tunnel, Brad was just finishing replacing the bricks to cover up the opening. It might give them time for a little head start.

Salanha was coming to her senses under Jeanie's expert ministrations. Brad could hear voices in the basement and some kind of activity up on the ground level. Their presence was no longer a secret. By the time they got out of the tunnel and into the shaft, they saw the rope hanging from the manhole. It was too late. They would have to take the scenic route.

Country led the way back down the shaft into the sewers. Salanha was a little worse for the wear, but she was moving on her own, and at least she had stopped sobbing and screaming.

To Brad's relief, Country remained unexpectedly calm and collected. He said it was unlikely they could be followed in the sewers, and if they were, he could easily lose them. Jeanie was less sanguine. She said these guys were pros who made it a point to know every inch of their environment. They would know about the sewers.

Country said no one knew the sewers like he did. "Jeanie, ma'am, trust me. If they're a-tryin' to follow me, I'll bamboozle 'em so bad they're never gettin' back to the chuck wagon."

This was a claim he would get a chance to prove. About five minutes down the main sewer on the way to the *Catacombes*, they could hear the pious posse from the Children of God giving chase. Brad couldn't be sure, but it sounded like they had a dog. He had to smile. How appropriate! Dog was God spelled backward.

They did have a dog—or, more accurately, dogs. The growling and yelping echoed through the sewer tunnels. It was hard to tell how far back they were. Brad knew they weren't far.

Country led the way. His pace was brisk and steady, but not nearly as fast as Brad thought the situation warranted. "Got to pick up the pace, Country. They're gaining on us."

"Hold your horses, compadre. Gonna lose these bushwhackers."

They came to a fork in the trail where a narrow tunnel split off to the right. Country continued up the main trail for twenty meters, then backtracked and cut into the narrow tunnel to the right.

Brad pointed at Country. "What're you doing?"

Country gave him a wink. "Leavin' a trail for these bushwhackers to follow. They'll be thinkin' we were tryin' to throw 'em off the trail."

"We *are* trying to throw them off the trail."

"Gonna bamboozle 'em yonder." He pointed to a bend in the tunnel about twenty meters in. Around the bend, the tunnel opened onto a cavern carved into the limestone. It was at least thirty feet high and ninety feet in diameter. It was filled with dark water alive with the swirls and splashes of invisible creatures swimming around. "Plenty of critters and varmints in these here waters. Any dog that goes in likely won't come out barkin'."

There was a ridge running around the perimeter of the cavern. It was six to eight feet wide in most places, but in some places, it disappeared underwater for five or six feet. Brad saw there were at least four tunnels branching out of the cavern.

Country took Jeanie aside and whispered something. Jeanie nodded, and Country went over to Salanha. He took her hand and said, "Fancy comin' along with me, lovely lady?"

Salanha was still shell-shocked. She took his hand, and he led her to the ridge. They disappeared into the first tunnel for a few seconds, then reappeared and continued to the second tunnel, where they repeated the exercise. They did the same thing at the third and fourth tunnels.

There was a small problem going from the second to the third tunnel because there was a six-foot break in the ridge—not really a break; the ridge was just a few feet below the surface of the water. Country had convinced Salanha to get her feet wet with surprisingly little resistance. When they came out of the fourth tunnel, Country signaled for Jeanie and Brad to follow.

By this time, Country was far enough away that his acetylene lamp wasn't giving enough light. Brad and Jeanie fired up their own lamps. The yelps and growls of the dogs were loud enough to tell they were only minutes behind. Jeanie set off along the ridge. Brad followed.

At the break in the ridge, Brad passed with no problem. Jeanie stepped down. Slipped. Fell into the dark water. The water came alive. Jeanie screamed. Brad grabbed her wrist and pulled her out. She was shaking and she was wet, but she was safe.

"Thanks for that."

Brad just smiled.

Country led them off down the fourth tunnel. It was narrow and straight. Jeanie gave Country the thumbs-up. "Nice move back there. Like I told you, Salanha's scent is the only one they have. They'll have to explore every tunnel, and the dogs will probably lose the scent at the break in the ridge. The dogs will also have a hard time crossing without going in the water. You would be a difficult bounty, Country boy."

Country's smile was wider than the cavern they had just crossed, and his cheeks turned crimson. "Thanks a heap, ma'am. Much obliged." Jeanie was getting used to his strange vocabulary.

Country stepped up the pace. He took a torturous route through narrow tunnels, wide tunnels, straight tunnels, high tunnels, low tunnels, dry tunnels, and wet tunnels. They went sideways and in circles. Finally, Country stopped and said, "Led those bushwhackers on a wild goose chase. It's high time to skedaddle on down to the *Catacombes*."

It was a dead end. The only exit was the way they came in, and Brad was certain he could hear faint sounds of dogs barking in the background. "You hear what I hear, Country?"

"Hear it? We're gonna vamoose right outta here before them barkers come a-sniffin'."

Country pointed toward the end of the tunnel. It was made of the same sand and dirt covering the concrete floor. Brad didn't see it at first. It was a tiny tunnel bored into the wall about two and a half feet off the floor and two and a half feet in diameter. Brad did not like the look of this tunnel. It looked about as solid as a sand castle.

"This here sewer tunnel used to run into the *Catacombes*. Got sealed off many moons ago, 'cept for this little tunnel I dug." Country's satisfied expression was proof of pride in his tunneling prowess.

The barks were getting louder. Brad gave the signal. "Salanha goes first, then you, Jeanie. Me and Country'll go last." Jeanie hesitated, eyes squinting, features contracted. Brad shut her down. "Get into that hole with Salanha. You're the only one she trusts."

Jeanie raised her eyebrows, thought it over, and nodded. She turned to Salanha. "Come on, Sally. Let's crawl down the rabbit hole."

Salanha didn't resist. She turned and slithered into the tunnel. Jeanie followed. Brad was next, and Country brought up the rear.

To squeeze into the tunnel barely wide enough for his hips, Brad had to stretch his arms out in front of him and contract his shoulders. There was no structural support for this "tunnel." It was nothing but a hole dug straight into the sandy soil. Dirt from the top was raining down on him, a constant, terrifying reminder it could collapse at any moment. He didn't even want to think about what kind of a death that would be.

The limited movement in his outstretched arms made it extremely difficult for him to propel himself forward. Country had estimated the tunnel was about the length of a first down—ten yards. Brad figured it would be the longest ten yards of his life.

About five yards in, Brad's hand encountered Jeanie's foot. Bad sign. His considerable willpower was undergoing a serious challenge from the claustrophobia attack in the late stages of preparation deep in the depths of his subconscious. "Move it, Jeanie."

Then he heard Salanha. "Gonna die. Gonna die."

Jeanie was trying to calm her down. "Relax, Sally. Breathe slowly. One. Two. Three."

"I can't. I can't. I can't. Gonna die. Gonna die. Gonna die!" She was crying and moaning, and Brad knew she was paralyzed by fear. He could feel the soil shifting above him.

Country provided the final straw. "We gotta hightail it on outta here lickety-split. Sounds like a cave-in's a-comin'."

Brad drilled down into the depths of his psychological playbook. It was worth a try. He sucked in as much air as he could muster and shouted down the tunnel. "Snakes, snakes, snakes! Snakes in the tunnel!" He ended with a bloodcurdling, "Ahhhhhhhhh!"

Sudden silence. Mississippi one. Mississippi two. Mississippi three. Then, all at once, an ear-piercing scream. It was Salanha, a.k.a. Sally Ann Hastings, screaming like a banshee in a bear trap and crawling for her life. Just as Brad had hoped, she was more afraid of snakes than she was of the tunnel. Jeanie started to move, and Brad was right behind.

They landed on a stack of skulls piled neatly in an open stall. Other stalls ringed the room. Each one contained a different type of bone: forearms, thigh bones, tibias, and so on. In the center of the room stood what looked like a round stone fountain of some kind. Across the room was a black metal stairway leading to a circular gallery and the exit.

They regrouped behind the fountain. Salanha was trembling and crying. Jeanie had a faraway look in her eyes as if she were contemplating going back in. Brad was just happy to be out. Country was focused on the tunnel. "Thar she blows." Country had switched to whale-hunting lingo.

Country's strange use of English expressions coupled with a total absence of any movement or sound in the room left the other three staring at each other with puzzled looks on their faces. For five Mississippis. When it came, it came as a loud rumble, shuddering walls, and a thick cloud of dust, soil, and sand. The tunnel was no more.

It was one of those reality-check events that makes one face up to their own mortality. The fabled Fugawi tribe called it *uganu dail urntoo leevee weetat*, which loosely translated means "you are going to die; learn to live with it."

Brad himself was imagining what might have been and was thanking his lucky stars that it wasn't. He didn't know what the women were thinking. Salanha was comatose. Jeanie was checking her weapon, ostensibly unfazed. Country was in a hurry. "Gotta skedaddle. John Law's on the way."

They climbed the metal stairway to the service exit that opened from the inside onto a flight of concrete stairs leading to ground level. The landing was surrounded by a black metal fence. Jeanie went first. Brad and Country helped Salanha climb over, then followed.

Chuck was waiting at the curb. They jumped into the car and took off around the Place just as a *car de flics*—a police van—came careening around the other side, tires screeching and sirens blaring.

"Think they saw us?"

"Naw." Country was smiling and holding up a skull. "Gonna name him Billy, like Billy the Kid."

34: The Tip

It was lunchtime. The dojo was usually empty at this time of the afternoon, and today was no exception. Brad finished his workout with thirty minutes on the *makiwara*, the straw-padded punching post, then took a long shower while he thought over the events of the last forty-eight hours. All things considered, the sewer saga of Sally Ann Hastings had been highly successful and well worth the effort. The hierarchy over at the Children of God seemed to have somehow managed to cover up all the bodies Jeanie's visit had left behind. His team's presence in the *Catacombes* was covered up by the cave-in of the dirt tunnel. Their adversaries had no idea who they were or where they went, and, most importantly, Sally Ann Hastings was now safe and sound under the protection of the CIA. Chuck would cash in on that.

Sally Ann had had a bad couple of days. It started when her boyfriend "sacrificed" her to the noble cause of world revolution. He kept her locked in her bedroom until the henchmen from the Children of God got there, drugged her, and carted her off to the compound. She cried every time she remembered. "He knew they were selling me. He knew it. He told me. I loved him." So much for love *à la revolution-for-world-justice*! Then they put her in the Penitence Suite, where she was penned up with at least five other young women being groomed to be trafficked along with her. The grooming involved regular sessions of sexual abuse and torture. Sally Ann could not bring herself to talk about that. She could only tremble and sob when the subject came up. The saga ended with the rescue that featured mortal combat, five dead bodies, flight through dark, creature-infested sewers, and a claustrophobic crawl through a tunnel of terror.

In spite of all this, Sally Ann was a fountain of information. From her boyfriend, she learned he was preparing a spectacular attack on the French state that would occur sometime before the second round of the presidential elections. The shepherds of the Children of God were helping to organize the attack. Most importantly, contrary to what everyone believed, she did know where her boyfriend lived.

From the other young women imprisoned with her, she learned that tension was running high in the compound. Security was reinforced. Discipline was strict. No one was allowed out of the compound without a "babysitter." Over the last few days, ten new "babysitters" had integrated the compound. They called themselves disciples, but in reality, they were henchmen sent by the shepherds to enforce compliance in the compound. These were the guys responsible for grooming the current shipment of human cargo. Their presence only reinforced the nascent rumors of impending apocalyptic doom beginning to spread through the ranks of the Children of God.

Brad finished his shower and got dressed. He combed his hair, put on his jacket, and turned up his collar. He took a long, satisfied look in the full-length mirror. All set to move out, a soft draft of air and an almost imperceptible sound warned him of another presence in the dojo. The sound was too soft, too stealthy. He went on full alert.

The dressing room and showers were located behind a wooden screen at the end of the dojo. From here, the whole room was visible. There was a hardwood floor and ancient, undecorated stone walls on three sides. The fourth wall facing the courtyard consisted of four arched floor-to-ceiling windows that flooded the dojo with unfiltered sunlight. At the far end of the dojo, just after the *makiwara*, stood the narrow door that opened onto the spacious courtyard. There was nowhere to hide, and there was no one there. False alert. But the windows were all closed, so the draft of air he had felt could only have come from someone opening the door. Whoever had opened the door did it very quietly and then slipped away.

Still on full alert, Brad headed for the door. The dojo was located on the ground floor of a bourgeois residential building at the back of a huge cobblestone courtyard surrounded by shady chestnut trees. Before venturing into the courtyard, he went from window to window, scouring the area for signs of anything out of the ordinary. Satisfied that everything seemed normal, he exited the dojo, crossed the courtyard, and went into the street.

Out on the street, he stopped and took his time pulling his Zippo and a pack of Gauloises out of his white leather pouch. While he was lighting up, he took a good look around, but it was difficult to tell if there was anything suspicious going on. La Rue de la Montagne-Sainte-Geneviève was a small street, but it was a busy street. In the morning, it was bustling with shoppers out for their daily excursion to the butcher, the baker, and the candlestick maker. At midday, it was bustling with the lunchtime crowd looking for a restaurant. That's when he spotted Zebulon coming out of the café up the street.

It would be more precise to say they spotted each other. Zebulon was just as surprised as Brad. Brad sensed tension in Zebulon's forced smile and the way he was furtively looking around from right to left. Brad met him halfway. Zebulon shook his head to signal he did not want to acknowledge Brad. He passed him by without so much as a simple hello. Brad was astonished when Zebulon stopped, hit the entry buzzer at number 34, and entered the courtyard.

Brad followed him in. Zebulon was agitated. He was rubbing his hands together. Brad could see his fingernails were gnawed down to the nub. He grabbed Brad's arm. "God, am I glad to find you. I've come by every day this week. Today was my last chance."

"Calm down, Zeb. What's the problem? Still gettin' ripped off down in the metro?"

"No. No. No. Not that. I don't have much time. I'm busking in the metro Maubert-Mutualité at the bottom of the hill. I'm being watched. Can only get away to take a leak. I've come by here every day looking for you. Even today, but I didn't see you. I was just on my way back to the metro."

"I was in the locker room."

"Can't stay any longer. Gotta go. I just want to say that we need help. I think you can help us. You're the only one I know. Something bad is happening. Something big. We're afraid. I think it's happening on Sunday."

"What?"

"Don't know, exactly. I just know there are about twenty new 'watchdogs' bullying everybody in the compound. No one can leave without a watchdog. Two nights ago, there was some kind of an attack on the compound. The watchdogs were running wild all over the place. I also know my Children of God group will be at the ORTF—you know, the *Office de Radiodiffusion Television Française*, the big round building on the avenue du Président Kennedy—for a television show on Sunday. Benjamin is forcing me to accept four outsiders into the group. I've never even seen these guys before. They won't rehearse with us. They'll just show up on Sunday and go on stage with us. Lots of rumors. Lots of speculation about these guys. About what's going on in the compound. Lots of speculation about what happens after the show. The shepherds have programmed a big ceremony for Sunday night at the compound. Attendance required."

"Okay, Zeb. Stay cool. I think I can get this info to the right people. Just stay cool. Got it?"

"Got it. Got it. Gotta run. Thanks."

After Zebulon left, Brad tried to process the information. Four unknown guys from outside the Children of God group for a television show at the Maison de l'ORTF on Sunday. Big ceremony afterward. Attendance required. Brad had a good idea of what was going down. He hoped he was wrong.

35: The Sign

Lazarus gazed into the baby blue sky. He breathed in the lusty spring air and let the discordant melodies of the resurrecting earth transport him to a rare moment of pure happiness. "What a day for a daydream! One lovin' spoonful of this," he joked to himself, "is worth a million dollars. Well, maybe not a million, but at least five or ten." His religious instincts kicked in. "No sense in overpaying."

He needed to think. He did his best thinking racing along the autoroute in his E-Type Jaguar, top down, motor humming, wind blowing. No sooner said than done. He jumped into the driver's seat, cranked up the *machina*, hit the gate button, and roared out onto Montbuisson. A series of turns and controlled slides later, he was cruising along the autoroute.

He was just three days away from the final act of his miraculous resurrection. Lazarus, indeed! Everything had been carefully planned, and almost all the pieces were in place. Sunday was the big day. Il Messia would handle the last detail on Saturday when he delivered the five women currently waiting to be dispatched and take payment. The attack on the compound had made it necessary to move the women out of the compound to a place he was saving for another use. But so be it. As they say in France, *"C'est la vie."*

That attack had him worried. How could anyone have found out about the Penitence Suite? Fortunately, he had lost only one woman. When the attack came, the others were occupied elsewhere in the compound with his men. The woman he lost was the girlfriend of one of the revolutionaries. The revolutionaries couldn't possibly have done it. They were the ones who organized her kidnapping in the first place. It was someone else, maybe a rival gang, which meant there was a leak somewhere in his system. The leak had cost him five of his best men. It was ungodly. They were executed mafia-style, slaughtered like sheep. It was not the loss of his men, or the woman, that had him worried. It was the professional way the operation was planned and executed.

The leak did have him slightly worried, but he was not unduly surprised. There were close to ninety people in the compound. Keeping a secret from ninety people living together in close quarters is nothing short of impossible. Anyway, the invaders barely managed to get away and probably would not be coming back. He wished they would because he had prepared an interesting welcome for them if they did.

Overall, he felt fairly secure. No one knew he was here pulling the strings. He had made it a point to remain one step removed from direct involvement in the project. He had Michael and Joseph managing the takeover of the Paris colony of the Children of God. Benjamin was the intermediary for the revolutionaries. Thibault was responsible for the drug dealing, and Il Messia dealt directly with the human trafficking clients. Finally, three days ago, his sponsors sent the reinforcements he had been requesting—ten new men. They were the insurance policy he needed to guarantee that nothing and nobody got out of line between now and Sunday.

And yet there it was, nagging him mercilessly. His intuition would not let him relax. The leering image of bop-a-lula Brad James, flowing forelock, black leather jacket, turned-up collar, and snakeskin boots flashed across the windshield.

Be careful. A horn to the left blasted him out of his reverie. He jerked the steering wheel to the right. Too much. The wheels locked. He was sliding out of control.

A ten-wheel trailer truck blew past, honking away. Lazarus hit the brakes. Wrong move. The slide morphed into a spin. One, two, three. He was hanging on for dear life when the motor died and the car jerked to a stop.

He opened his eyes. Cars were whizzing past. He was in a roadside security zone facing in the right direction as if he had pulled off on purpose. Smoke and the stench of burning rubber were the only proof to the contrary. This was the sign he was waiting for. Brad James had almost cost him his life. Brad James would have to go.

Back in his quarters, he started laying his plans. Normally, in a delicate situation such as the present one, it would be preferable not to "rock the boat" as the saying goes, especially since Brad James was in contact with the French police. However, after Brad James almost wiped him out on the autoroute this afternoon, Lazarus was going to have to let his intuition override his logic. He would eliminate Brad James immediately, no questions asked.

Lazarus couldn't count on Il Messia. Il Messia was occupied with that Jeanie woman. He needed Michael and Joseph to stay engaged with the Children of God. The other survivors of his original group were all occupied with other aspects of Sunday's operation. That meant he would have to turn to the new guys. He figured two men would be enough to take care of that shitbird James, but given the delicacy of the ongoing situation, the unfamiliarity of the new soldiers with the terrain, and the necessity to ensure a swift, clean strike, six would be better.

CHAMPS-ELYSÉES, THURSDAY, MAY 9, 1974

Jeanie was up and about before sunrise. She traded her all-black night-prowler outfit for a pair of jeans and a matching jeans jacket over a white turtleneck and set out in search of her ride. She found it parked on the sidewalk on the Rue de Presbourg, the street that circles the Place de l'Etoile at the end of the Champs-Elysées. It was a light-green Honda 125 with white stripes on the gas tank. After checking there was plenty of gas in the tank, she picked the lock on the security chain, freed the wheel lock, and turned on the system. It only took three kicks to fire up the engine. She pulled the half-shell helmet out of her rucksack and tightened the strap. She was on her way to Louveciennes.

It was chilly at this time of the morning. Cleared her mind, made her feel alive, like in the old days on her way to her morning workout session. Today, she was on a mission. After the adventure in the sewers and long discussions with Sally Ann, Jeanie was sure the Prophet was behind the shenanigans going on over at the Children of God. Sally Ann had not seen anyone even remotely resembling the Prophet, but the modus operandi she described confirmed the picture she had already pieced together from the time she managed the Children of God's choir. It had "the Prophet" written all over it—religious mumbo-jumbo mixed with drug dealing, forced prostitution, and human trafficking. The new twist was terrorism. This was the detail giving her doubts. The Prophet played for profit, and Jeanie could see no profit in terrorism.

The secret recordings from the Rue de Montbuisson in Louveciennes featured a ringleader called Lazarus who sounded a lot like the Prophet. The low quality of the recording made it impossible for her to tell for sure. Otherwise, she had already identified three more "high priests" from the Prophecy. She would deal with them, just as she did with the first three, when she got the chance. For the moment, though, all her resources were focused on finding the Prophet. It looked like number 6 Rue de Montbuisson was the best place to start.

Jeanie parked her bike off the street so the license plate would not be visible. You could never tell. Knowing there would be people in the area who might recognize her, she had spent considerable effort making up her face. She went the ado route—big red lips, dark eyes, rosy cheeks. Her hair was done up in a cute little ponytail in the back, and bangs in the front. It changed her appearance. Made her look young and insouciant. A quick glance in the Honda's mirror confirmed it. She hardly recognized herself.

Her first pass by number 6 Rue de Montbuisson revealed only that there was nothing happening. The only distinctive element in the picture was the canary yellow E-Type Jag parked next to a white Renault in the driveway. At the end of the property, she took a left onto the Rue Louis Forest and continued on, circling back to where she had parked her "borrowed" motorcycle.

She had time to kill, and it was time for breakfast. She ordered a *grand café crème* and two croissants. Her problem was to find a way to stake out the property without being noticed. Chuck and Brad had used the cover of the foliage that lined the property on the Rue Louis Forest, but they had done their stakeouts in the evening or at night. That wasn't likely to work in full daylight. Too visible. The best she could do at the moment was to make a few passes on foot and hope she got lucky. She could come back tonight and do a more thorough job.

Her second pass started inauspiciously. The only change from hours earlier was a van painted in colorful psychedelic patterns with German plates. Otherwise, everything was the same. The E-Type Jag was still parked in the driveway, and the house was quiet. The birds were chirping, and the sky was blue.

At the end of the property, when she was turning left onto Louis Forest, she peered through the bars in the iron gate. She almost missed it. It was a man—a man with dark hair. There was something familiar about his demeanor. He stood there, immobile, like he was deep in thought. Suddenly, he turned toward the Jag and jumped into the driver's seat. The gate groaned and began to open before her. She slipped back behind the hedge as the car roared to life and surged forward onto Montbuisson. She got a good look at the driver as he flashed past. Familiar, for sure. There was no doubt in her mind. She had seen him clearly. The Prophet was back.

36: Stalk and Kill

The Studio Davout was constructed in the 1,200 m² of an old cinema built in 1946, called "Le Davout," on the Boulevard Davout in Paris's 20th arrondissement. Since its opening in 1965, it was considered the best in France. The Children of God choir had a recording session scheduled for the afternoon. Jeanie did not want to miss it. She was hunting. Her prey was the Prophecy and what was left of it. Some of them would be there. Her mission was to eradicate them.

This mission was not entirely at odds with Brad's mission of stopping the terrorist attack and neutralizing those associated with the terrorists. Only the priorities differed. Those who were associated with the terrorists were also the ones in the human trafficking trade. She shivered when she remembered how close she had come to being a victim. She closed her eyes and grieved for the fate of her beloved friend at the hands of the Prophecy's high priests and the FBI. Especially the FBI. The role of the FBI in all of this remained mysterious. What in God's name were they doing pussyfooting around with these cult creatures?

Her borrowed Honda 125 was parked down the street from the

studio. She stationed herself at a vantage point where she could observe the people flow in and out of the studio without exposing herself. Her new look contrasted with the plain-Jane look of the past, but anyone who knew her well—and the members of Children of God's choir knew her well—would recognize her if they got a good look. Her plan was to enter the studio once the session got underway. She figured the babysitters would get bored before they finished with the second take and go outside the recording booth to relax until everything was finished.

The choir arrived together on a bus. She gave them twenty minutes to set up before entering the studio. She checked the schedule posted at the entrance. They were in recording studio D, as she had anticipated. It was the largest one, and the choir counted thirty members. She hung out in the main hall, pretending to read some sheet music she had thought to bring with her. Nobody would bother her, and she was far enough away from the studio so she could slip out of sight if anyone from the choir who could recognize her came out.

It didn't take long for the two babysitters to emerge. She recognized them as remnants of the Prophecy. All to the good. At first, they hung around in front of the door, smoking and joking around. They were both about twenty-four or twenty-five years old. They both had long hair. One was blond. The other was dark. The blond guy was receding at the temples. She estimated the blond guy represented between one ninety-five and two hundred-ten pounds of pure muscle. His biceps bulged out of his T-shirt, and his pecs rippled when he moved his arms. The dark guy was a little shorter than the blond, probably five-eleven or six feet. He was also a little heavier but had less muscle definition.

They were horsing around, showing off, so obviously self-aware it was painful for her to watch. Finally, the blond grabbed his crotch and made a lewd gesture that he had to take a leak. To get to the men's room, he had to pass by Jeanie. As he passed, he made an ostentatious display of looking her over. She ignored him. Let him get around the corner, then got up and followed him to the toilets.

She hesitated in front of the men's room and extracted a syringe from her backpack, making sure it was loaded. It was a swinging door that swished when she opened it. The blond was at a urinal with his back to her. He did not turn around.

"Hey, asshole."

He didn't have time to react. The last thing he saw before the needle hit his neck and the drugs flooded into his body was the angelic face of a beautiful girl with a ponytail and bangs.

It took more than twenty seconds for the blond babysitter to fall, and another fifteen for his heart to give out. Jeanie waited at the door to confirm the kill. Confident he was dead and gone, she exited the men's room and went back to her vantage point where she could watch the dark babysitter. He was getting bored and kept looking at his watch. Finally, he went back into studio D for a few minutes. When he came back out, he checked his watch again. Then he headed for the men's room.

When he passed by, Jeanie trailed after him. He went into the men's room through the swinging doors and came up short when he saw his friend stretched out, motionless, on the floor. Unsure of what had happened, he rushed to his side.

"Hey, man. Wake up. Wake up, man. What's wrong?" He knelt down and began slapping his fallen friend's cheeks and calling his name.

Jeanie slipped up behind him. She was silent. She was fast. She bent down and deposited a syringe full of the Prophet's poison in Dark Babysitter's neck.

Dark Babysitter was less resilient than his blond partner. There was no count, no delay. He dropped immediately face-first onto the tile floor and twitched around for a few seconds.

Certain he was dead, Jeanie hurried to set the scene. She wiped the first syringe down and placed it in the blond babysitter's right hand. She was about to place the second syringe into Dark Babysitter's right hand when, suddenly, he rolled onto his back and sat straight up, eyes wild, screaming at the top of his lungs.

He lunged for Jeanie and seized the hand that held the syringe. She jerked back. He was too strong. She couldn't disengage. He jerked her toward him. She let herself go and rolled forward using his force and her weight to break his hold.

She landed on her feet and came back with a kick to the head. Too much. Too late. He was already dead.

The poison had done its job, but the noise had alerted the natives. She had no time to lose if she was going to get away without being seen. She strode out of the men's room and headed for the exit. The hall was filling up with people who came searching for the source of the bloodcurdling screams.

Jeanie left the building and headed for her Honda. There was a shout. "Hey, you. Stop!"

37: Big Game Hunting

Her bike was too far away to make a run for it. She stopped and confronted the voice behind her. "Are *you* talking to *me?*"

It was the studio manager. She knew him well. "Oh, hi, Jeanie. I didn't recognize you."

"What's going on in there?"

"Not sure. It looks like two guys got into a fight in the men's room. Sorry. I've gotta get back in there."

"Okay, see you."

Before she got on her bike, she looked around to make sure no one was noticing her. She didn't have to worry. Everybody was focused on the ruckus in the Studio Davout.

Jeanie caught the last rays of a beautiful gold-and-rose sunset as she tooled down the autoroute on her way to Louveciennes. By the time she got to Montbuisson in fifteen minutes, it would be almost 8 p.m., dark enough to do some serious detective work.

Before she left Paris, she had taken care to change license plates with another Honda 125 she found parked by the *Cité Universitaire*. The bike's owner would probably not even notice the change unless he got stopped by the cops. So she felt pretty safe on that score. Her only worry was getting stopped herself for some infraction and not being able to produce the bike's documents. Consequently, she was driving very carefully.

On her first pass at number 6, the lights were on all over the house. The Jag was back, and the psychedelic van was parked in the same place. She cut down Louis Forest and stopped at the next intersection to think over her strategy. She had to calm herself down. The Prophet was there, just within her reach. She wanted him so badly she could taste it, and therein lay the dilemma. If she acted hastily without proper preparation, she was very likely to fail. On the other hand, if she waited too long, the opportunity might be lost, never to reappear.

Destiny delivered the decision. As she debated with herself, the psychedelic van roared past, headlights flashing, horn blaring, hellbent for whatever. Jeanie didn't even hesitate. She pulled out in full pursuit. She wasn't worried about staying in contact. The van couldn't go past seventy-five miles per hour, and her Honda could do over eighty.

The chase was short, sweet, and uneventful. The van drove straight on D321 to the Ile de la Chaussée in Bougival, about fifteen minutes from Louveciennes. It pulled off the bridge onto a side road and stopped in a driveway on Chemin de Halage, a small, unpaved road that circled the island. The property looked like some kind of an ancient industrial complex surrounded by big, leafy chestnut trees and a thick undergrowth of brambles, bushes, and weeds.

Jeanie didn't follow the van down the side road. She continued past and stopped on the bridge fifty yards down. The van was visible through the underbrush below the bridge, parked just in front of the complex. The cab light was on, and the driver had not yet exited. Outside of the occasional passing car on the highway, the whole area was deserted. She parked her bike and crept down the side road toward the van to get a better look.

All of a sudden, the van's door burst open and a tall, thin figure jumped out, gun at the ready. Jeanie froze behind the tree standing between her and the tall, thin figure silhouetted in the rays of the van's cab light. There was no way he could have heard or seen her. She held her position and waited.

It was a long wait. The tall, thin man pulled out a powerful flashlight and began to search the driveway and the area around the van. He extended his search to the buildings in the complex and then shined it into the underbrush. He was searching every bush, every flower, every tree.

The light swept toward the tree hiding Jeanie. It stopped. He advanced and let the light linger on the base of the trunk. Seconds ticked by. Silence. Tension. He inched closer. She could hear his heavy breathing. She prepared to pounce. Too late. The tree burst into life, an explosion of flapping wings and swishing branches.

Jeanie jumped and squelched a screech as the birds blasted by, inches from her head. She was only half as surprised as the tall, thin man, however. The surprise racket of the nesting birds he flushed out caused him to drop his flashlight. He was cursing out loud as he scrabbled around trying to recover it. When he finally found it, he returned to the van and extinguished the cab light. Then he headed on foot back up the driveway. At the Chemin de Halage, he turned right along the river.

Jeanie waited for ten Mississippis, then crept back through the underbrush to the Chemin. She was surging with adrenaline. There was no mistake. She had just seen the high priest of the Prophecy, the Priest of Priests, the Prophet's next in command, the priest who had prepared her for her consecration into the Prophet's personal harem. It was he who enforced the laws, determined the verdict, decided the sentence. It was he who chose the victims he delivered to Sammy, the Prophet's "purifier," the priest who delighted in inflicting pain and humiliation on his fellow believers, the priest who perished painfully and ignominiously in the ramshackle barn of a remote ranch in Wyoming. This was too good to be true.

The Priest of Priests followed the Chemin de Halage along the Seine until it ended about seventy-five yards down. He jumped onto a *péniche*, a river barge, docked at the roadside. There was no cover for Jeanie to get any closer to the barge without being discovered. She decided she could come back later to check it out. For the moment, the Priest of Priests was her priority.

Jeanie knew what she had to do. The Priest of Priests required a welcome befitting his esteemed reputation. She hurried back to the van to prepare her one-woman welcoming party. First, she fixed the silencer onto her Colt .38. Her backpack contained a six-pack of syringes. She took two and filled them with the Prophet's secret formula, then placed each one in the plastic case she used to transport them. Finally, she snuggled up to the passenger side of the van and waited for the Priest of Priests to return. She hoped it would be soon.

Her wish came true. A short fifteen minutes later, she heard footsteps in the driveway. It was the Priest of Priests. He wasn't alone.

The Priest of Priests had someone with him. This was something Jeanie had not anticipated. An extra adversary could be a problem. The guy was young, somewhere north of twenty-five, and athletic-looking. They were moving fast.

She held her position by the front wheel on the passenger side of the van. She cocked her Colt. The second man cut around the back of the van to access the shotgun seat. Jeanie popped him with two bullets to the brain before he turned the corner.

The Priest of Priests felt it before he saw it. His perceptive powers were legend in the annals of the Prophecy. He threw himself to the ground and drew his gun. Jeanie's position behind the front wheel hid her from the Priest of Priests, who was looking for a shot from under the van. She jumped onto the bumper just as a bullet tore through the wheel she had abandoned. She dove and rolled. Came up on her feet behind him. She fired once and took out the shoulder of the hand holding the gun. The second shot missed the other shoulder and blew out the back tire.

The Priest of Priests was down, but he was not out. He came up with a knife in his good hand and lunged forward. Jeanie wanted him alive. She dropped him with a shot to the knee, then kicked him in the head before he could begin to scream.

She had just finished taping his mouth and hands when he came to. There was fear in his gray eyes. There was also hate and resistance. Jeanie was in a hurry. The Priest of Priests' gun had no silencer. The shot he fired would inevitably attract attention in this island of silence and calm. She wanted to be long gone before that attention arrived.

She ripped off the tape. "What are you doing here?"

The Priest of Priests was not immediately forthcoming. Jeanie had no time for tough-guy games. She popped him in the other knee. He fainted. She taped his mouth again.

Meanwhile, she went into the back of the van and found the reason he was there. An unconscious young twenty-something female lay sprawled on the floor. Jeanie recognized her from the compound. She was obviously part of the next shipment of trafficked women. This was going to complicate her exit plans.

Back outside, the Priest of Priests was struggling to get his mouth free. Jeanie used the flashlight to get a good look at him. He was starting to go gray, and his hair was thinning. His eyebrows were dark and bushy, and at one time, he had probably been handsome. Handsome, but stern. Now his thin lips and long, gaunt face made him resemble a bitter, middle-aged man going to seed.

Jeanie went to her pocket and fished out one of her syringes. The Priest of Priests saw it, but it did not immediately register. It was only when Jeanie asked, "Remember this?" that he realized what was in store for him.

The hate and resistance in his eyes morphed into terror as Jeanie approached. When she injected him with the Prophet's poison, he began to writhe, quiver, shiver, and shake. She dosed it so he would not lose consciousness while he was in his death throes. The duct tape kept him silent.

She would have preferred to watch the whole show, but her time was running out. She had to clean up the crime scene and double-time it out of there. First, she collected all the spent cartridges. Next, she loaded the guy who came with the Priest of Priests into the back of the van. Getting the Priest of Priests himself into the back of the van was a little more difficult because of all his thrashing around, but she managed. By the time she got him in, he had run out of gas, so to speak, and only had a few more minutes of earth-time before his body gave out. Finally, she covered the bloodstained areas with some loose soil she dug up on the side of the driveway.

Before the van's two tires got destroyed, Jeanie had planned to drive it off to some secluded spot where it could be abandoned. That was no longer an option. She would have to leave it in the parking lot farther down toward the opposite end of Chemin de Halage. It was a dirt road, so the blown-out tires would not pose a problem to drive at least that far.

The unconscious female from the compound was another problem. She couldn't leave the girl anywhere near here. There was too much of a chance somebody from the barge would find her. Since it was the barge where the trafficked women were ostensibly being held, that would be a death sentence at worst, or a life of slavery at best.

Jeanie retrieved the keys from the Priest of Priests' pocket and cranked up the van. She backed out of the driveway and took Halage to the left. The van wobbled and clanked and dug up the roadway until the parking lot a hundred and fifty yards down the trail. She picked a spot at the far end of the lot, got out, locked the front and side doors to the van, then went back down the trail covering the tracks left by the wheels of the blown-out tires.

She returned to the van, opened the back door, and dragged out the unconscious girl. She used the Magic Marker she found in the van and wrote *Save my kidnapped friends* on the girl's shirt.

After locking the back door, she arranged the girl on the motorcycle and mounted behind her. She wound the duct tape around their torsos to hold the girl upright, then kick-started the Honda and drove off toward the bridge. She planned on dropping the girl off at the American Hospital in Neuilly.

The bike was stolen, and she had no papers. Her big worry was the cops would notice the illegal position of her passenger and stop her. That was exactly what happened.

Jeanie got as far as the Pont de Neuilly when a cop whistled her down. She blasted by and cut down toward the Parc de Bagatelle. She managed to cover only a few hundred yards before she heard the sirens go off. She could see the lights of two motorcycle cops in her rearview. She had no choice. She pulled off the road, ripped off the tape, laid down the bike with the girl still on it, and sprinted for the woods. The cops would take care of the girl.

38: The Mongoose and the Cobra

Jeanie had been out all day. Chuck had heard her leave just after he got into the office early in the morning. Since then, nothing. In his opinion, she shouldn't be out running around. Too dangerous. The French were after her. Benjamin was after her. Brandon was after her. Il Messia was after her. She was like a post office missing persons bulletin board.

It was getting close to midnight when Brad called. "Have you seen Jeanie?"

"No."

"I need to see her. Been calling, but there's no answer."

"I thought I heard her in there." Chuck stopped and listened. The sound was faint, but there was definitely somebody in there trying to be quiet. Jeanie was thoughtful like that. "Yeah, I hear her in there."

Brad tried the number again. No answer. He decided to go over and see for himself. He parked his bike on the Champs-Elysées. Took the Rue de Berri to the Rue de Ponthieu and pseudo-window-shopped down the street past the entrance to the building, checking for surveillance as far as the Rue de la Boétie. He was wary, but there was nothing suspicious. He backtracked and entered the building. Once in the foyer, he eschewed the elevator and walked up the six flights of stairs. It was quieter.

He stopped at the landing and listened. Silence. He knocked, one-two, one-two-three. Ten Mississippis later, there was no reply. He knocked again. No reply. He took out his key. If she was in there, she was going to be pissed if he barged in. But, as Evel Knievel once said, "It's better to be safe than sorry." Encouraged by those words of wisdom from the wise old man who had broken every bone in his body at least once, Brad stuck the key in the lock and turned it.

With his back flat against the wall, he pushed the door using his left hand. The door opened onto a short hallway about eight feet long. The bathroom was on the right. From his position on the landing, he could see the bathroom door was closed. He snuck a peek into the hallway, then dropped and rolled forward to the other side of the door. There was no movement. No sound. He snuck a second peek down the hallway, then entered in a crouch, his knife at the ready. He had his gun if he needed it but would only use it as a last resort.

At the door to the bathroom, he stopped, flattened his back against the wall, and pushed slowly on the door with his right hand. It swung open. From his position, he could see the toilet and the shower cabinet. Empty. The lavabo was behind the door. Through the crack in the doorjamb, he could see this part of the bathroom was empty as well. Complete silence. No movement. The faint odor of expensive aftershave was the only hint of an invasive presence. Jeanie did not use aftershave.

Brad kicked the door to the apartment closed and backed into the bathroom. From here, he could see about twenty-five percent of the main room. Empty. If anyone was in the studio, they would have to be somewhere to the right of the hallway. He stationed himself patiently in the bathroom doorway and tuned his senses to full alert.

There was no sound. It was the fragrance of the expensive aftershave that tipped him off. It was getting stronger. Conclusion: The invader in the studio was getting closer. Brad was effective in closed spaces, but he preferred to battle in open spaces where he had more room to move. It was time for him to flush out the invader.

He slipped to the other side of the hallway and hit the light switch. The sudden explosion of light surprised the invader and enabled Brad to enter the main room unimpeded. The stench of the aftershave was overwhelming.

The invader struck, faster than most eyes could see. Brad saw it but couldn't evade it. His shirt was shredded, and he had a superficial six-inch slash on his ribcage.

There, tightly coiled, knife at the fore, swaying rhythmically before him, stood the image of the man from Michaelangelo's *Last Supper*. He had a Jesus Christ mustache, a Jesus Christ beard, and a Jesus Christ hairdo.

This was Il Messia. He had come for Jeanie, and, to his credit, he was dressed for the occasion. He was sporting custom-made threads—a dark blue silk suit over a cream-colored silk chemise with an oversized Elvis collar open to the navel, highlighting an elliptical gold medallion hanging from a thick gold chain.

Now Brad understood what he was up against. Il Messia was a show-off. He was fast, very, very fast. Brad feinted to the left, to the right, back to the left.

Il Messia barely moved. He did not play defense. Only offense.

Il Messia struck, again, then again, strikes faster than most eyes could see.

Brad saw them, and hours of training in the dojo enabled him to evade them easily. Il Messia was a cobra. Cobras are fast and cobras are deadly. They don't bob. They don't weave. They don't run and they don't hide. Cobras coil, strike, and kill. It is almost always a winning strategy. Only the mongoose can conquer the cobra. The mongoose is not as deadly as the cobra, but it is just as fast, and it knows how to play defense as well as offense. Up to now, Il Messia had never met a mongoose. Brad was the first.

Il Messia struck again. Brad parried the right-handed thrust and stepped inside. He grabbed Il Messia's wrist with his right hand, rolled forward, and threw Il Messia over his right shoulder. Il Messia landed on the right side of his back.

Brad followed through and came down on top of him, still holding the wrist of the knife hand. Rather than wound, he went for the kill. With his left hand, he drove his blade into Il Messia's throat. It went straight up to the hilt, through his pallet, and into his brain.

39: Hand Off to the French

"Hi, Jeanie. Late date?"

It was 7 a.m. and Jeanie looked like she'd had a rough night. The adolescent look she had adopted when she set out the previous morning had disappeared. No more big red lips, dark eyes, and rosy cheeks. Only the cute little ponytail and bangs had survived, just barely. She was surprised to see Brad waiting there for her. She was even more surprised to see the cadaver wrapped in plastic lying in the middle of the room.

She glanced over at him. He was relaxing in the armchair. His left leg was crossed over his right knee, and he was puffing nonchalantly on a cigarette.

She squinted down and studied the head sticking out of the plastic wrapping. No doubt about it. Definitive identification. This was Il Messia, the guy who was supposed to be stalking her. How he'd wound up dead on the floor of her current domicile was the obvious next item on the agenda.

"Looks like we have a lot to talk about."

Brad filled her in on Il Messia's ill-fated visit. He described the confrontation and explained that after he took Il Messia down, he packed him in plastic and waited for her to come home. "Do you have any idea how he found out you were staying here?"

Jeanie took a long time reflecting on her comings and goings over the last few days. She shrugged and shook her head. "None at all. And I've been super careful."

"Maybe he just got lucky, or unlucky. I don't believe in that kind of luck, although only Chuck and I knew you were here. He must have picked you up somewhere. Where have you been?"

She decided to omit her intervention at the Studio Davout. She recounted her adventures with the Priest of Priests and detailed where she had left the van with the bodies. Her late arrival was due to the time hiding from the cops after she dropped the bike and sprinted into the woods.

They both agreed Chuck's studio was no longer an option. The sooner she got out of there, the better. She would have to go to the safe house in Levallois for the moment. Brad volunteered to arrange that while she cleaned up and got her things together.

The body was going to be a problem that would have to wait until later in the evening to be solved. Too much activity in the building during the day.

Twenty minutes later, Jeanie was packed and ready to go. She was decked out in her now-signature black outfit. Brad wondered how many sets of those she had. Couldn't be many. She only had two bags: the backpack she carried around with all her tools in it, and the big backpack with her clothes and personal belongings.

"Take the metro Etoile," he told her. "It's one change to the safe house at Levallois. Here are the keys."

"We have to get the info on the trafficked women to Gary."

"I've got a coffee date with him over by the embassy in thirty minutes. Let's go."

CAFÉ ON RUE DE RIVOLI

Gary was at a table for four at the back of the room. It was too early for the lunch crowd, so occupying a big table wouldn't be a problem.

Brad spotted him and sauntered over. "Hi, Gary."

"Hi, Brad. What's up?"

"I just left Jeanie at the safe house."

"I thought she was staying at Chuck's studio."

"Somehow, the bad guys found out she was staying there. I went to see Jeanie last night. Got attacked by the guy who calls himself Il Messia. Before you say anything, don't worry. The body's been taken care of. Everything's under control."

Gary leaned in and spoke softly. "You killed him?"

"Had no choice." This wasn't quite true, but was the best choice for the success of the ongoing operation as well as for Jeanie's safety.

"What about Jeanie?"

"She was out. Came in this morning. She found where they're keeping the trafficked women. Saved one and killed two of the traffickers. Had a close call with the cops, but managed to get away unseen."

"Jesus Christ! Three more COGs wiped out. Two others were assassinated at a Children of God recording session yesterday. That makes what? Five in one day. Five more rescuing Sally Ann. Plus the three overdoses before. The goddamn cult is getting wiped out."

"Couldn't happen to a nicer group of guys. They deal in drugs, prostitution, human trafficking, and terrorism, as well."

Gary scratched his nose and dipped a sugar cube. "Yeah, it looks like the terrorist attack is programmed for Sunday. Otherwise, why would the shepherds force the choir to include four men from outside the group for their Sunday television spot at the ORTF?"

"Could be the right time to shut this thing down. You should contact the frogs and let them take it from here."

"You're probably right." Gary got up and dropped ten francs on the table. "My treat. By the way, the reason I called the meeting is to tell you Sally Ann is all squared away. Tell Chuck her parents will be getting in touch soon."

US EMBASSY

Five minutes later, Gary was at his desk putting the finishing touches on his thoughts. All things considered, he had all the info he needed. He knew who the terrorists were and where they were hiding. He knew when and where they would attack. He knew who was directing the drug dealing, prostitution, and human trafficking, and where they were hiding as well as the time and place of the forthcoming delivery. He decided it was time to pull his team off the case and alert the French authorities.

He hit the interphone. "Marilyn, can you come in, please?"

Marilyn took her time. When she finally sauntered in, her left eyebrow was cocked and her upper lip curled in an expression somewhere between a snarl and a smirk. She should be neither snarling nor smirking, because her days with him at the embassy were numbered.

"Marilyn, I want you to set up a secure call with Langley for 3 p.m. sharp. It will be 9 a.m. there, and I want to get them first thing in the morning."

"Oh, sounds important." Her voice was the singsong high pitch used for small children. It was the same singsong high pitch that had always irritated him as a child and continued to irritate him as a grown man.

Gary looked her up and down for a long moment, his expression unchanged. "It is important. That will be all."

Marilyn raised her eyebrows and nodded her head. As she turned to leave, Gary saw it. She was smirking, and he had to find out why.

40: Winding Down

The sun was low in the sky. The rays flowed through the garage window and reflected off the dust particles swirling around Lazarus as he brushed off the wooden table. The effect illuminated him in a dynamic golden halo.

Michael was transfixed. He wondered if Lazarus created these illusions on purpose or if there was some supernatural force out there that produced them.

They always seemed to occur in times of crisis, and they always restored serenity no matter how chaotic the situation. Joseph referred to these illusions as "grace storms."

Lazarus folded his hands in front of him and bowed his head. Michael and Joseph did the same.

They lingered a long moment in deep meditation before Lazarus broke the spell. "Have you heard from Il Messia?"

"He called last evening and said he'd be back here with the woman before morning."

"It's past four in the afternoon and he still has not arrived. Did he say where he was?"

Michael gave Joseph a what-can-we-do look, then turned to

Lazarus. "Said he was on the Rue du Ponthieu near the Champs-Elysées."

"So what's taking him so long?"

Michael was sincerely puzzled. "Dunno. Haven't really thought about it."

Joseph was less objective. He slapped his hand on the table and sent a puff of dust swirling in the air. "Maybe he's playing around with his prey, or, better yet, maybe the prey took him down."

"No way." Lazarus was unambiguous. "Il Messia is the ultimate professional. He would never 'play around' with the prey. He is also virtually invulnerable in hand-to-hand combat. There's no way a mere female could take him down. If he's down, it took a whole gang, and we would have heard about it."

"Maybe it wasn't the female. Maybe it was somebody else. Yesterday, two of our best men were murdered in the men's room of a recording studio. We lost five men in the sneak attack on the compound, and before that, three of our men were stalked and overdosed, and two more were killed in the American girl's apartment. Now Il Messia is missing, and the Priest is missing along with the shepherd of the *péniche*."

Surprise gripped Lazarus's face. "What's this about the Priest?"

Mike and Joe exchanged knowing looks. Mike spoke first. "Last night, he made a delivery to the *péniche*. Since then, no one has seen him or the shepherd who met him at the *péniche*. The woman wasn't delivered, either. Somebody is stalking us, man. Takin' us out one by one."

Brad's image came immediately to Lazarus's mind. "Have you taken care of the American?"

"Everything is set up for tonight."

CHAMPS-ELYSÉES

Chuck grabbed the keys to his motor scooter and was headed for the door when the phone rang. It was his secretary. "Mr. Hall, there are three policemen here to see you."

Cursed his luck. "Okay, send 'em in."

In walked three uniformed national policemen—the cop named Chef who came by Brad's apartment the other night, flanked by two younger and thinner colleagues.

Chuck recognized him immediately. "Welcome, Chef, we meet again. To what do I owe the honor?"

Chef wasn't smiling, but he didn't seem angry, either. "It's a pleasure, Mr. Hall. I have some questions to ask you."

"Please have a seat. Coffee?"

Chef was about to decline when he caught the erstwhile expression of his subordinates and changed his mind. "Yes, thank you very much."

Chuck picked up the phone and asked his secretary for the coffees. He hung up, folded his hands, and waited.

Chef cleared his throat. "Last night, a young American girl was admitted to the American Hospital in Neuilly. She had been drugged and was incoherent. On her T-shirt, there was a message asking for help to save her friends who had been kidnapped. The hospital took the message seriously and contacted us. We took the message seriously, as well, and went to interview the girl. She told us she was a member of *Les Enfants de Dieu*. She told us she had been drugged and was going to be sold into slavery. She said she had been saved by somebody on a motorcycle. Her savior abandoned her when the police tried to flag the motorcycle down."

Chef paused and looked at Chuck. Chuck looked back and waited. Patience was his strong suit.

"Do you know anything about this?"

The secretary came in with the coffees. She made a big fuss over the two strapping subordinates, fixing them up with sugar and milk and chocolates. Chef noticed the secretary was pretty cute, and his men were loving the attention.

"So, Mr. Hall. Do you know anything about this?" he repeated.

"No, I don't, but I am interested in why you would even ask me."

"We contacted the embassy, and the embassy suggested we come by. They said you would likely end up with the case."

Chuck was pleased about that. "I'll have to thank them for their publicity. Unfortunately, no one has contacted me. If and when they do, I will contact you."

Chef stood up and extended his hand. Chuck took it, and they shook. Chef hesitated at the door. "You're a military man, aren't you?"

"Yeah, Vietnam. How about you?"

"Central African Republic. A bientôt."

Chuck watched from his window as the three cops piled into the dark blue Renault and drove away. He snatched the keys to his scooter and took off for Louveciennes. He wanted to get the latest info from the tapes.

41: Along Came Jones – Redux

Gary sat head in hands, hunched over the metal table in the glass bubble situated in the center of the embassy's security room. His phone call with Langley could only be described as catastrophic. His boss had been unequivocal. The Company was off the Children of God operation. After much bureaucratic wrangling, it had been decided that the Children of God dossier was a domestic affair in the sole remit of the FBI. Olivia Townsend Ritter-Jones would assume responsibility as of yesterday.

The decision had been taken yesterday, and he had only been informed about it today. That explained Marilyn's smirky attitude this morning. She had heard about it before he did. The chummy camaraderie between Olivia and Marilyn had not escaped Gary's sensitive political antennas, but he wrote it off to feminine bonding or something down that alley.

Of course, Gary protested vociferously, to no avail. It had been decided the Children of God operation was the direct extension of an ongoing FBI investigation of domestic terrorism in the United States. The same individuals who were masterminding the anticipated terrorist attacks in the US had infiltrated the Children of God in Paris.

Gary argued that the investigation was settled. His team had identified the terrorists and found their hideout. They knew when and where the attack would take place.

They had also uncovered a human trafficking network and knew where the victims were being sequestered. It was now just a question of turning the information over to the French and letting them take care of the rest. There was nothing more the US could do on its own.

The answer to all this was that anything going down in France would have serious repercussions on the US investigation. Olivia Townsend Ritter-Jones would be responsible for deciding when and how much the French should know.

Back in his office, Gary brewed a double Costa Rican arabica. He took four sugar cubes from the blue box and dumped two into the cup. The other two went onto the saucer he placed carefully on his desk. His mind was churning. His immediate problem was protecting his assets. Olivia would not hesitate to sacrifice them. That thought was punctuated with a coffee-dipped sugar cube he popped into his mouth.

His second problem was ensuring that the intelligence he had managed to produce was used judiciously—that is, to thwart the terrorist attack, save the trafficked women, and arrest the traffickers.

Gary was not convinced those were Olivia's priorities. That thought was punctuated with another coffee-dipped sugar cube he popped into his mouth.

His third problem was putting himself into an unassailable position if anything went wrong after Olivia took over.

He reached toward the saucer to punctuate this thought. No

more sugar cubes. He was about to get up and go after one when there was a knock at the door.

It was Marilyn. She was all smiles. "Brandon Butler to see you, Gary."

"Send him in."

Brandon straightened his silk sports coat, slicked back his hair, and strode into the room. Gary's eyes were blazing, and his jaw was set. His fists were balled up so tight they were stretching the freckles on the back of his hands. Brandon suspected this might be a bad time. "I can come back later."

"No, I just went ten rounds with Langley, but I've still got some gas in the tank. What can I do for you?"

"Actually, it's about Olivia."

Gary perked up. "How 'bout some coffee? Or are you still in denial?" Gary couldn't help needling him a little.

"No, no, coffee's fine. Coffee's fine. Olivia's a tough customer, *n'est-ce pas?*"

Gary brought him his coffee. "Have a seat and tell me how well you know her."

"I worked for her for a while in California on the narco-prostitution beat. She's a tough boss, but she works harder than anybody else. And she delivers results. She was the one who broke up the criminal network fronted by a religious cult called the Prophecy. Remember that a few years ago?"

"Yeah, it was a big deal. Didn't it end in a mass suicide?"

Brandon recoiled at the thought and shook his head. "It was horrible. Some of the disciples weren't ready for the ultimate sacrifice and refused to take the drugs. They were dragged onto the beach and hacked to death with knives and machetes. There was blood and body parts and pieces of flesh and bones strewn all over the place. When they finished off these 'heretics,' the perpetrators went into their cathedral and performed a ceremony where they overdosed on some kind of drug cocktail. Then they lit the house on fire."

"I thought you said Olivia broke up the network."

"Basically, she did, but there was a leak. Somebody tipped off the cult before the raid. The cops were bearing down. It looks like they decided to go out in a blaze of glory. There were no survivors."

"How do you know that?"

"Olivia had all the information. Everyone was accounted for."

Gary made a face. "Do you believe that?"

"I had my doubts, Gary. I voiced them. At the end of the day, she was the boss, and her view prevailed. That's when I moved on to another division."

Gary didn't react right away. He was processing this new information along with what he had learned in his meeting with Olivia. He took off his glasses and wiped down the lenses. Brushed some imaginary lint off his shoulder. Took a sip of his coffee. Replaced his glasses and looked Brandon straight in the eye. "So, why are you here?"

Brandon flinched. The question took him by surprise. "I wanted to know what Olivia had to say. It might have a bearing on my investigation. Don't forget, I'm responsible for the drug enforcement on this operation."

"You were. Past tense. Olivia has been named honcho of the operation. *As of yesterday.*"

Brandon's face fell. He looked down, but he wasn't surprised. The opposite would have surprised him. "What's your take on that?"

"My take is this smells, bad, like three-day-old fish and houseguests. Things have been moving fast, too fast for me to have kept you up to date in real time. Basically, outside of a few details, everything has been solved. We know who the terrorists are. We know where they hide out. We know when and where they plan to attack. Finally, we know where the drugs and trafficked women are being held and when they will be shipped. I had scheduled a meeting with my counterpart over at the DST, where I planned to turn everything over to him. Now is the time for the French to take over."

"Does Olivia agree?" Brandon already knew the answer, but he had to ask.

"No. She says she wants more information on the terrorists, their background, their funding, their contacts, etcetera, etcetera, etcetera. Delivery of the trafficked women is set for tomorrow evening. There's a load of drugs going out with them. The attack is set for Sunday afternoon. Olivia says she doesn't want to act until just before the attack. But by then, the women and drugs will be long gone. Olivia says this is no big deal. Collateral damage. She says the terrorists are our main concern."

"Fill me in on the drugs and the women. Where and when is delivery supposed to happen?"

"I wrote a report with everything in it. I'm going to ask you to sign a receipt for it. This will be partial cover for my 'A-double-S.' Olivia refused to sign a receipt for my report. This report includes my statement that Olivia refused this report, as well as my suggestion to alert the French."

Brandon froze and let his pen drop. "Does Olivia know about this?"

"No. But she will when you give her a copy of the report."

Brandon began to rock slowly back and forth, deep in thought. His hands were crossed over his chest, and he was biting his lower lip. "I can't sign this without Olivia's consent."

Gary's voice was soft but firm. "In that case, Brandon, this meeting is over."

Brandon closed his eyes, slicked back his hair, and softly massaged the bridge of his nose. "I have a right to all the information pertaining to this case."

"You'll have to go through Olivia if you want to take that route. Like I said, as of yesterday, Olivia is the honcho."

Brandon took his time weighing the pros and the cons. He made his decision. He needed the report more than he needed Olivia's approval. He picked up his pen and signed the receipt. His voice was soft. "When Olivia finds out, you will have made the worst enemy your long life has ever known."

Brandon left Gary and had his secretary photocopy the file. He then went straight to Olivia's office to deliver it.

"Thank you, Brandon." Olivia was distant, uninterested. "How is your investigation progressing? Have you located this Jean Jones?"

"No, she disappeared."

"Any other leads? Children of God? License plates, addresses, things like that? Good old tried-and-true FBI procedures? Remember the days? By the way, you'll be reporting to me for the foreseeable future."

He tried to show surprise and admiration. "That will be a welcome pleasure. Congratulations, Olivia." Her questions raised suspicions she was already privy to the info in the dossier as well as the info in the secret dossier Marilyn had stolen for him.

Olivia took the file and sent Brandon packing. No questions. No interest. Back in his office, Brandon was just settling in for a long session of strategic analysis when his fortunes changed for the better. He got the call from California he had been expecting. His former colleague had been able to dig up some information on the James MacDonald driving an E-Type Jaguar and living in

Hampstead, UK. This was information even the CIA could not get without a long, drawn-out legal process, and it was sensational.

This James MacDonald was a high-profile member of the US Marshals' Witness Protection Program. His real name was Randall Linder from San Francisco who also went by the name of "the Prophet." The information he had just gotten from Gary provided the address where Randall-James-Lazarus-the Prophet was living in France. Brandon was on the cusp of being able to right a few wrongs.

42: Captured

Brad parked his bike on the Rue Guynemer and headed for home on foot, a short seventy-five-yard walk. It was a security precaution. His building was line-of-sight, and he could check out the area for potential surprises on the way. He decided to stop off at the café Guynemer first. He had two hours to kill before he had to be at the Barbary.

He took a table on the Assas side of the terrace, sat back, and relaxed. His day had been pretty boring. After his workout at the Montagne, he went to stake out the terrorist hideout over in Courbevoie. He discovered the "hideout" was a euphemism for a sprawling two-story brick family home with a triple garage on a third of an acre of land. The garage was full with a Renault van, a Deux Chevaux, and a medium-sized Peugeot. The lawn was mowed, and the flowerbeds well-tended. The neighborhood itself was upper-middle-class suburban.

There was no vantage point from where he could spend time watching the property. He contented himself with four pass-bys and was lucky enough to eyeball three of the four terrorist suspects performing various tasks in the yard. They were similar in style and came in three sizes: large, medium, and small. The large dude looked like a friendly fellow with a happy-go-lucky bounce in his step. The small dude was intense and meticulous. It was the medium-sized dude who retained his attention. He was just as Chuck had described him, thin and sallow and scroungy, one of those supercilious, brooding, self-absorbed cool cats. Just like Chuck, Brad disliked him immediately.

The garçon came over. He was new and didn't recognize Brad. *"Bonsoir, monsieur."*

"Bonsoir. Un demi, Stella, s'il vous plait."

Brad went into his white leather pouch and came up with his Zippo and his Gitanes sans filtre. The terrace was half full, mostly with students from the uni. One table had three really cute French girls brushing back their bangs, chatting away, and having a great time. The table next to them had a couple of beefy, good-looking young dudes drinking beer and smoking Marlboros. The girls were obviously trying to attract the guys' attention, to no avail. Brad could not believe these dudes were not zooming in.

The waiter came with his beer. *"Voilà, monsieur. Autre chose?"*

"Non, merci. Je vous règle tout de suite." Brad paid and settled into his surroundings. After La Rotonde, this was his favorite café. The Jardin du Luxembourg was right across the street. It was only fifty or so yards from his apartment building, the waiters were friendly, and the atmosphere was carefree and gay with the youthfulness of the students from the uni.

It was getting dark, and the terrace crowd was thinning out. The three girls had long since departed, but the two beefy guys were still there. Brad checked his watch. 8 p.m. Time to get a move on. He gathered up his things and headed for home.

A quick backward glance as he was entering his building revealed the two beefy dudes from the café were ambling along behind him. Probably a coincidence, but he was still in Evel Knievel mode. Better to make sure.

The elevator was available. He reached in and hit the button for the fourth floor, stepped back out, and waited. The doors closed, and the elevator began its rise. He listened at the stairway. As the elevator passed by the second floor, Brad could make out the faint sounds of someone moving around. This was a problem. Of course, it could be someone he knew waiting for him. The two brawny dudes turning down the path to his building made that explanation unlikely.

It was time to make himself scarce. The stairway door to the underground parking was behind the elevator shaft. He slipped over, pulled out his keys, and unlocked the door as quietly as possible.

He heard the entry door to the building click open. Sounded like two sets of feet creeping up the stairs. There was some whispering, then footsteps coming down the stairs. He closed the door and hustled down into the garage. With any luck, the dudes who were stalking him would not be able to access the garage, and he would be in the clear. The problem was there were only three ways out of the garage: the stairway he had used, the elevator next to the stairway, and the car ramp. Even though all three access points were locked, if the dudes were determined enough, they could wait for him outside.

They were more than determined. The door to the car ramp clanged open. Four figures silhouetted in the light from the streetlamps were swaggering down the ramp. They had somehow captured the electronic signal from the car exit and come to hunt him down. At least two of them had guns. Bad luck his Beretta was hidden away in his apartment.

From Cassius Clay's battle with Sonny Liston, Brad had learned to float like a butterfly and sting like a bee. In other words, he would have to stay away from these dudes until he got close enough to take them down one by one with his bare hands and feet. That was going to be difficult in a two-level parking garage where hiding places were few and far between.

Besides the four in the garage, there were probably a couple more upside waiting for him as well. They separated, two on each side of the ramp leading down to level 2. Their progression from one row of parking places to the next was thorough and systematic. They looked inside and under every car. They inspected the inside of every unlocked covered space.

Brad made his way to the middle of the garage using the wide support columns as cover. His plan was to create a diversion at the back of the garage that would attract their attention and allow him to get behind them to the exit ramp. Once outside, he would deal with whoever was on guard out there. He figured there would be two of them at most.

He waited until they were two rows of parking places from his position behind a column. He took a metal ballpoint pen from his pouch and launched it diagonally toward the back of the garage. It ricocheted off the wall and clanged against the fender of a black Mercedes.

They halted. Looked to the sound. Looked to each other. After a series of hand signals, three of the four dudes converged slowly toward the source of the noise. The fourth guy hung back. He was between Brad and the exit. Brad would have to take him down to get to it.

Brad waited until the other three had gotten to the rear of the garage before he made his move. The guy blocking his path was one of the brawny dudes from the café. He was focused on his buddies in the back of the garage. Brad was fast. Brawny Dude was faster. He dodged right and used Brad's momentum to throw him against the hood of a Volkswagen. He followed with a front kick to the balls. Brad had just enough time to slip sideways and parry the blow with his hip.

Brawny Dude had to weigh at least two hundred and fifty pounds, but he had the speed of a welterweight. He followed up with a series of *mawashi geris*, perfectly executed, powerful round-house kicks. They lacked precision, but they were quick.

The first caught Brad on the shoulder. It knocked him off balance, and his shoulder went dead. Brad used the Cassius Clay butterfly head-fake to avoid the second. The third was aimed at Brad's head. Brad ducked under it and swept Brawny Dude's pivot foot. He went down.

Too late. Brawny Dude's buddies were coming to the rescue. Brad just had time to take the first one out with four body blows and an uppercut. The second stepped back and pointed his pistol. Brad didn't even think about it. There was no way he could cover the distance before the guy got off a shot, maybe even two.

Brad was putting up his hands when a blow to the kidneys knocked him to his knees. A blow to the back of the head put him on the ground. A kick to the groin curled him up. The boss dude stepped in. "Knock it off. We need him conscious." Brawny Dude's revenge would have to wait.

Brad was still groggy when they got him to his feet and duct-taped his hands. Boss Dude pulled out his walkie-talkie. "Mission accomplished. We're comin' out." The walkie-talkie crackled. Boss Dude repeated, "We're comin' out. Do you read me?" More crackling. "Goddamn worthless machine." He nodded at Brawny Dude. "Tiny, go see what's up."

After five minutes, Brawny Dude was still not back. Boss Dude looked worried. He tried the walkie-talkie a few more times with the same negative result as before. He made his decision. "We've gotta get outta here."

Suddenly, the exit door creaked and rolled open. They ducked back against the wall. A Citroën pulled in. Dude Number Two drew his pistol. Boss Dude waved him down. They waited.

The Citroën slowed at the ramp. Stopped. Motor died. Number Two took aim. Five long seconds. The motor turned over, and the Citroën drove down to level 2. They listened as the driver locked up his car and exited through the elevator.

"Okay, let's go." Boss Dude grabbed the lapels on Brad's leather jacket and got right into his face. "One false move, motherfucker, and I'll blow your balls off." Brad made it a point to remember that if he ever got the gun in *his* hand.

Boss Dude led the way up the exit ramp, his pistol discreetly arranged and ready to shoot. The other two bracketed Brad.

The entrance to the uni bordered the exit ramp to Brad's garage. At the sidewalk level, Boss Dude led the way toward the heavy shadows of the entrance to the uni located about ten yards off the street. He nodded toward the thin guy next to Brad. "Go get the car."

Brad was beginning to get his mojo back. It was time to figure out how he was going to ditch these guys. There were only two of them, but they both had pistols and knew how to use them.

Suddenly, Thin Guy was running toward them. His eyes were wide, and he was hyperventilating. "They're in the car! They're in the car!"

"Who's in the car, fuckbird, and where is the car?" Boss Dude was pissed off.

"Larry, Roy, and Tiny. They're in the car. They're dead."

Mississippi one, Mississippi two, Mississippi three. Boss Dude was struggling to process the news. "You sure?"

"They were bleedin' and they weren't breathin', man. We gotta get outta here."

A dull pop in the distance broke the silence. Boss Dude spun to the right, his arm spewing blood. Brad spun to the right and side-kicked the gun from the first dude's hand. A roundhouse to the left took down the second dude.

Boss Dude was holding his arm. Couldn't stop the blood. Made a run for the car. Dude One dove for his gun. Brad kicked it away. Dude One hesitated. Saw Boss Dude running for the car and took after him.

Dude Two struggled to his feet. Looked for his gun. Brad moved in for the kill, but his duct-taped hands slowed him down. Dude Two was able to turn tail and scurry off behind the other two. The three of them jumped into a dark van and tore off down the street. A motorcycle with a rider dressed in black pulled off the sidewalk and followed.

43: Aftermath

Michael's brows were knitted together. The man stretched out on the gurney before him was a trusted comrade-in-arms. "You saved your life with that tourniquet. We got the bleeding stopped. The bullet tore right through your arm, in one side and out the other. Blasted out an artery. David's a certified doctor. Says you'll be fine with a little rest and some antibiotics."

"How are the other guys?"

"They're all dead. Jesus Christ! It was a friggin' ambush."

Michael knitted his brows. "Tell me exactly what happened."

"Everything started as planned. We cornered the American when he came back to his apartment. Larry and Roy stood guard outside the building. Zeke and Pete staked out his apartment. Me and Tiny picked him up from the café. He spotted us. Tried to escape through the underground garage. Me, Zeke, Pete, and Tiny cornered him and captured him. He's a tough SOB. Knocked Tiny on his ass. Then, everything went to shit."

Michael rested his chin on his steepled fingers. "How, *exactly*, did everything go to shit?"

"Dunno. I walkie-talkied Larry and Roy a 'mission accomplished' and that we were on the way out. They didn't acknowledge. After three tries, I sent Tiny out to see what was goin' on. He didn't come back. When we left the garage, I sent Zeke to get the car. He came runnin' back. Said the other guys were in the car, dead. Then somebody opened fire on us. Hit me in the arm. The American ran away before anybody knew what was happenin'. We ran for the car and took off."

"The American *ran away*?" Michael was skeptical.

Boss Dude looked away. "Yeah, we were occupied with enemy fire. He's a speedy SOB." Michael moved closer to the gurney and bumped it. Boss Dude winced. "Shit, man, be careful."

"Sorry, sorry. Go on."

"Here's where it gets real scary. We got to the stoplight at the end of the street and were startin' to relax. I was in the back seat, Pete was drivin', and Zeke was ridin' shotgun. A motorcycle pulls up beside us, the rider looks in, pulls out a gun with a silencer, and pops Pete in the head. Two bullets. Pop! Pop! Zeke just sits there, lookin' at what was left of Pete's head. Two more bullets. Pop! Pop! And Zeke's head explodes. It was an execution. No other word for it. Cold-blooded execution."

"What'd you do?"

"Whaddya think I did? I played possum. After the motorcycle took off, I took Pete's place and drove here. Ever tried drivin' a stick shift with only one good arm?"

Michael ignored the question as rhetorical background noise. "So you think it was an ambush?"

"They were waitin' for us, man. Sucked us right in. Used the American for bait. We're bein' hunted down like animals. They got Toad and Angel over at that music studio. They got two of the new guys over at the American girl's apartment. They got Joseph's whole team when they raided us the other night. The Priest, the Italian guy, and the *péniche* guard have all disappeared. Before that, we had all those overdoses. With the five they got today makes twenty. Bad shit, man. Bad shit."

Michael didn't disagree, but he couldn't call this in over the phone. He'd have to go to Louveciennes to tell Lazarus. How could anyone have found out about the operation on the American? Only he, Lazarus, and Joseph knew what was going down. He knew he didn't betray the attack. That left either Lazarus or Joseph.

BARBARY COAST SALOON, MAY 10, 1974

"Night, Brad. Good show. I like the 'Bad Moon Risin' song."

"Thanks, Jacky." Brad was pleased; Jacky was stingy with his compliments. But Brad was in a hurry and didn't have time to hang around and shoot the breeze. Chuck was waiting for him over at La Rotonde with an urgent message.

From the entrance to the Barbary, the street was quiet and empty both ways. He spotted Doris on her corner, and she gave him the thumbs-up. The coast was clear. He headed straight for La Rotonde and found Chuck installed at his favorite terrace table with a big balloon glass filled to the brim with house red.

"Hi, Chuck. What's up?"

"Heard you had some uninvited visitors this afternoon."

"Yeah, very uninvited. How'd you hear about that?"

"From the bug. Wanted to warn you, but couldn't track you down. I was in Louveciennes and couldn't get back in time. Got a hold of Jeanie instead. She told me she was almost too late. By the time she got there, there were already two guys sittin' in a car stakin' out your place. She just had time to neutralize those two when a third guy came out of the garage and went over to their car. She neutralized him as well."

"When you say *neutralized*, you mean *killed?*"

"She didn't specify over the phone. She just said you came out of the garage with three other guys, and she created a diversion that made it possible for you to get away. Told me she made sure they couldn't go back after you."

"Good thing she was there. I was in big trouble. Since you got the info from the bug, I guess that confirms they're part of the army from the Children of God."

"No doubt about it. Not clear why they went after you, though. They didn't name you, but I knew it was you they were after."

"How so?"

"When they said, 'That pretentious pussy,' I knew it was you. Didn't even have to hear when they mentioned 'the American from the nightclub in Montparnasse.'"

"Your jokes are hilarious. You should go on the stage, the one leaving in fifteen minutes."

The garçon appeared with an ice-cold Stella, said hello, and disappeared. He could see they were in no mood to fool around.

Brad sipped at his beer, thinking it over. Chuck was uncharacteristically quiet as well. There was a nice breeze coming off Raspail, and the sky was clear. It would be at least another hour before the last show at the cinema next door let out, so, there were quite a few free tables on the terrace. The Dôme and the Coupole across the street were full, as usual.

Brad finished off his beer and put ten francs on the table. "My treat. Too dangerous for me to sit around out here. Can't go back to my place, either. I'll have to go over to Levallois with Jeanie."

Chuck smiled at that one. "Sounds like the only option. It's obvious a hotel room would be too costly." Chuck waited. Brad didn't react. "It also fits right in with the plan. Jeanie wants to meet us there ASAP."

LEVALLOIS, MAY 10, 1974

Chuck only stayed long enough for the exchange of information. He had to catch the last metro that left the station at thirty minutes past midnight.

As soon as he left, Jeanie took charge. It was obvious Brad was hurting from the beating he had taken. Her days as a high-level athlete had taught her a lot about injured bodies.

The head wound was only superficial. Probably just a glancing blow. Brad's abs were well able to resist the kick in the gut. It was the shot to the kidneys that had her worried.

She had Brad lie face down on the sofa to check it out. It looked bad, already going from dark red to dark blue. "You might have to go to the hospital."

"No way."

"If the kidney's damaged, you'll need professional help. Go urinate. If there's blood in the urine, we'll go down to the emergency room at the British Hospital down the street. If there's no blood, chances are the kidney's okay."

Brad made a weak protest, but his heart wasn't in it. She was right. He went and urinated. He came out with a big smile on his face. "We're good. No blood. Feelin' better already."

Jeanie patted the sofa cushion next to her. Brad sat down and took a long look at the woman sitting next to him. She was different tonight. In fact, she was different every time he saw her.

She still had the big brown eyes and the short turned-up nose that made her kind of cute. But now, her wavy auburn hair was a little shorter than it used to be, and she no longer parted it down the middle. Tonight, she had it pulled back in a perky ponytail. She had abandoned the long, formless shirts and skirts that concealed her beautiful body in favor of more feminine attire. The all-black sports outfit was the one he preferred. Tonight, she had exchanged it for a low-cut, knee-length, blue cotton print. For some reason, she looked even more desirable than she did in the black outfit.

It was difficult for Brad to associate this heavenly creature sitting next to him with the pitiless warrior of the Parisian sewers. It was also difficult for him to understand the tenderness he felt for her. Women warriors had never held any attraction for him. None at all! Yet here he was, sitting on a living room sofa like a clueless teenager overwhelmed by emotion.

Jeanie felt it, too. She laid her head on his shoulder. He took her hand and held it tightly. It was a beautiful moment packed with the excitement of magic, mystery, promise, and joy. Only once had he ever experienced this before—with Alice, the love of his life.

That was then. Alice was gone. This was now. Brad savored the moment. Head on shoulder, hand in hand, each with their own hopes and desires, the silence was intense with emotion. Neither dared move, afraid to break the spell. Finally, Brad brushed his lips across Jeanie's forehead. She turned to face him. They rose together and walked as one into the bedroom.

Brad was awake before the sun was up. He felt like a new man, ready to take on the world. It was surprising because they had made love and talked into the early hours of the morning. While he observed the sleeping beauty lying beside him, he gave himself a reality check.

It wasn't the usual morning-after-the-night-before. There was no overpowering desire to get away. Just the opposite. He wanted her to wake up so they could hang out some more.

They had done a lot of talking between their sessions of tender lovemaking. But Jeanie didn't behave like most of the other women he knew. She respected his privacy. None of this I-want-to-know-every-deep-secret-of-your-life stuff. She accepted and appreciated whatever he wanted to give.

He did the same. But Jeanie wanted Brad to know who she was, where she was coming from, and where she was going. It was a revelation that left him astonished. And afraid. For both of them.

44: Gary Throws Down the Gauntlet

Olivia Townsend Ritter-Jones stood up and stretched her six-foot frame to its full height. She arched her skinny, narrow shoulders and with both hands began to massage her big, bulky bottom. Her graying "pageboy" was in total disarray. The dark circles around her bloodshot eyes gave her long, thin face the rabid Rocky Raccoon look. Combined with tight, thin lips, cleft chin, and wicked nose, she resembled something like a movie monster in a comic horror film. She felt like a hangover on steroids.

She had just pulled an all-nighter. She had read all the files Gary had given her, all the files Brandon had given her, and all the files Marilyn had given her. Thank God for Marilyn! Along with what she already knew, it was obvious she would have to change her strategy. Things were getting out of hand, and it was time to cut her losses. It was also time to meet with Gary.

Gary didn't look much better than Olivia, but he had managed to get a few hours of shuteye. He figured the coffee in his hand, his first of the day, was the best thing that had happened to him in the last twenty-four hours. He glanced up, and there she was: Olivia Townsend Ritter-Jones, hovering in the doorway. He figured this was the worst thing that had happened to him this whole year.

"Gary, are you free for a few minutes?"

Gary wasn't free for even a second. The turmoil surrounding the French elections was overwhelming every aspect of his life. Since President Georges Pompidou passed away on April 2, he had not had one free day. He barely had time to eat. On top of all that, he now had to deal with the president's protégé and exceptionally irritating Olivia Townsend Ritter-Jones.

Gary took a long sip from his mug and rubbed his forehead. "Good morning, Olivia. It will have to be fast. I've got a full schedule. What can I do for you?"

Olivia barged in. Gary took no notice. No matter where she went, her peculiar form of physical coordination always made it seem as if she were "barging in."

She beelined for the coffee machine and poured herself a generous mugful of steaming hot, pure Costa Rican arabica, swigged back three greedy gulps, and refilled her mug. She smacked her lips and heaved herself into the visitors' chair. "I have made my decision. Contact your French counterpart and proceed to arrest the terrorist gang ASAP."

Gary squeezed his eyes shut and counted out ten Mississippis. When he opened them, she was still there. So, unfortunately, was he. "I thought you had decided to wait until the last minute before alerting the French."

"I had time to consider all the angles. We cannot take the chance that something goes wrong and the terrorists succeed in their attack or avoid capture. We must act immediately. The

Louveciennes address and the *péniche* must, of course, remain secret for the moment."

Gary had had time to consider all the angles, as well. Olivia was angling to take all the credit for foiling the terrorist attack in the first instance. In the second instance, she could claim credit for waiting if everything worked out. She could blame Gary if it didn't.

Gary leaned forward with his elbows on the table and rested his chin in his hands. "Why?"

"I have decided it's too early. I want to know more about what they're up to, who their contacts are. We can learn a lot more before we turn this over to the French."

"The *péniche* is scheduled to leave this evening. If it gets away, those women will be lost. Once the French intervene on the terrorists, the people in Louveciennes will waste no time in disappearing. We have nothing to gain by waiting. It's either all or nothing."

"My mind is made up, Gary. Contact the French immediately."

Gary rose slowly from his chair. He rested his hands on his hips and studied Olivia's features long and hard. Her chin jutted out, and her mouth was set in a thin, straight line. She was daring him to try and disagree. He turned his back to her and gazed out the window. Bright sun, blue sky, small, white cloud puffs, cars whizzing around the Place de la Concorde. The only thing different, the only thing new, was that Olivia was determined. Now Gary was, too.

"No can do, Olivia."

"*WHAT* do you mean, 'No can do?' "

"I mean that I cannot go to the French with this partial information. They'll find out I misled them, and our relationship will be compromised. If something goes wrong, they will blame us in general, and me in particular."

Olivia's face went red. Her eyes were on fire, the tight, thin lips twisted and snarling. "This is an order from the president."

"I doubt that. But if it is, you'll have to give me the proof. In writing. Otherwise, if you want to contact the French under those conditions, you'll have to do it yourself. Have a nice day." There it was. Gary had thrown down the gauntlet.

Then, something strange happened. There was no challenge. No threat. No disagreement whatsoever. Olivia relaxed and nodded her head as if she were relieved. She smiled. It was one of those condescending smiles he had been seeing a lot of lately; more like a smirk. "Thank you, Gary."

Olivia clomped out of the office. The "Thank you, Gary" triggered his alarm system.

45: The Leader of the Army for World Peace

Brandon stationed himself by the Children of God minibus parked by the side exit to the ORTF building. He wouldn't have long to wait. The rehearsal for tomorrow's show was scheduled to end in the next fifteen minutes. The parking lot was almost deserted, anyway, so he wasn't worried about attracting any undue attention. His two hired guns were waiting inside the building.

The choir came out right on time. Its eleven members were preceded by three bearded security escorts from the Children of God. Three more bearded escorts brought up the rear. His two sidekicks followed the group outside.

Brandon spotted Benjamin at the front of the group in deep discussion with the lead singer. Brandon had been in regular contact with Benjamin ever since he returned from London, but Benjamin was not at all forthcoming in their discussions. His ostensible motive for meeting Benjamin was to query him on drug use in the cult. Benjamin, however, recognized this as a not-so-clever pretext for something else and remained as evasive and aloof as possible. They both knew Brandon had no authority on French soil. Both also knew, however, that if push came to shove, it would not be difficult to get Benjamin back to the USA.

Brandon stepped from the shadow of the minibus and called to Benjamin. The three security men went on alert. They moved forward and fanned out. Their eyes darted right and left as they approached Brandon cautiously. Brandon flashed his embassy identity badge and slicked back his hair.

"Hi, Benjamin. The embassy sent me over to have a word with you." As he spoke, Brandon sized up the three security men. They were all over six feet tall and muscular. Their long hair was pulled back and attached in various versions of a ponytail. They were concentrated on him and forgot to watch their backs as Brandon's men slipped in behind them. It was obvious they were not professionals. Brandon figured their presence was more to ride herd on the choir than to protect it from external threats.

A Deux Chevaux with a group of teenagers drove by, honked and waved, and called out Zebulon's name. Another group of older men dressed in suits and ties leaving the building laughed as the teenagers drove away. Brandon waited.

Benjamin was whispering something to Zebulon and shaking his head up and down. Brandon noticed he was scrawnier than usual and more stooped over. Otherwise, he looked more or less the same, shaved head, thin lips, and pointed nose. It was the eyes that had changed. The dark sockets on either side of his nose were no longer blazing from deep within. They were dead. The ambition, greed, and malevolence were gone. Replaced by fear.

Brandon identified the smallest of the three security guards as the boss. He was alert and had spotted Brandon's colleagues on either side of the group. Their jackets were open, and the pistols they had removed from their shoulder holsters and stuffed into their belts were clearly visible. Bossman stepped aside as Benjamin came forward. "Hello, Brandon. I'm very busy now. We'll have to make an appointment for later."

Bossman noticed the deference and fear coming through Benjamin's voice. That and the two *pistoleros* were enough to make him back off. Brandon put his arm around Benjamin's shoulders and walked him to the side. "I want you to come with me."

Benjamin jerked up to his full height. "You know you can't make me do that."

Brandon didn't react. He smiled. Slicked back his hair. It was a beautiful smile, and it was sincere. "Benjamin, you are in no danger from me at the moment, and I need your help. I think you need my help, as well, and I think you know it."

"What do you mean?"

Brandon reached into his dark blazer and pulled out a black-and-white newspaper clipping with a photograph. He read the headline. *"The Leader of the Army for World Peace Wanted by the FBI."* Beads of perspiration formed on the top of Benjamin's shaved head. Brandon continued. "This picture looks a lot like you with hair. My understanding is that the man in this picture is in grave danger if he gets caught. If you are this man, I can help you."

Benjamin twisted right and left. His little legs were jiggling. He lowered his voice to a whisper. "They will never let me go."

"I think they will." Brandon put his arm around Benjamin's shoulders and ushered him back toward the group. He looked at Bossman. "You guys can carry on. Benjamin and I have some things to work out. I'll bring him back later."

Bossman had had time to evaluate the situation. He had five men with him. This Brandon fellow was a pretty-boy. He had only two men with him, and both of them had one arm in a sling. They did have pistols, but they would not dare to use them. It was a bluff. "Benjamin's not goin' anywhere." He moved toward Brandon and struck a defiant pose.

Brandon shook his head. "Don't underestimate my friends. They have diplomatic immunity. It wouldn't be the first time they were deported from a country. I really need to talk to Benjamin."

Bossman looked from Brandon to Benjamin. He had orders to bring everyone back to the compound, no exceptions. These orders, however, had not factored in three armed *pistoleros* more than ready to shoot. He would be in serious trouble if he didn't bring Benjamin back. On the other hand, if he didn't let Benjamin go, he might not bring anybody back, including himself. He made his decision. Benjamin had to go. He tapped him on the chest and squinted out his fiercest expression. "You better get your ass back to the compound. Fast." He turned toward the minibus and clambered on. Brandon and his men drove off with Benjamin.

46: The Succubus

L azarus had already packed up most of his nonessentials. By Sunday evening, it would be all over. By Monday afternoon, he would be long gone. Before then, he had one important meeting and a few loose ends to tie up.

The American was the first loose end. He had managed to thwart the kidnapping Lazarus had planned for him. No problem. He didn't seem to be an immediate threat. There would be time enough to come back for him later.

Il Messia was the greater problem. It had been two days, and still no sign of him. The two dead bodies in the American girl's apartment confirmed that any communication with Il Messia was most likely a thing of the past. This posed an important problem for delivery of the merchandise on the *péniche*. Lazarus had considered letting Thibault take care of it. He had to nix that idea. Thibault was just a snot-nosed preppy trading on his daddy's reputation. He would be no match for the kind of client he would be dealing with. Better to wait until after the fireworks tomorrow and let Michael and Joseph handle it.

Waiting was a risk. The disappearance of the Priest, the steward, and the woman suggested the *péniche* was already a liability. Lazarus had considered ditching the whole cargo and cutting his losses. He decided against that because the cargo represented over five million dollars, his total budget for the next year. Furthermore, since the disappearance, there had been no evidence of any other hostile activity anywhere in the area. Lazarus concluded that the *péniche* and its cargo were not under threat from the authorities. The disappearance was the work of the person or persons who were stalking him and his cult. If that were indeed the case, he might be able to use the *péniche* and its cargo as bait to turn the tables on the stalkers.

Lazarus turned to the papers spread out on the table. Everything seemed to be in order. The contract with Latorre Legal to negotiate the recording contract was signed and sealed. As the legal representative of *Les Enfants de Dieu*, Latorre Legal would not be able to represent the families of any disciples litigating against *Les Enfants de Dieu*.

The members of the choir for tomorrow's television show had been handpicked by Michael and Joseph. They were all true believers, all but Zebulon. There was no way to exclude Zebulon. He was the lead singer. In any case, once the shooting started, he would be the first to go down. It was important that everyone from the choir be eliminated to eliminate the organization, *Les Enfants de Dieu*, as a suspected conspirator. It would look like a rogue group led by Benjamin dedicated to freeing the world from capitalism and the hegemony of the USA.

Lazarus held up the photo of the full choir of thirty-one men and women. The eleven chosen for the show, including Zebulon, were all in the first row, which included twelve people.

He flashed on number twelve and looked again to make sure. His chest constricted. His mouth went dry. The twelfth person at the end was not part of the choir, but she was someone he knew well. She was the succubus, the female demon who destroyed the Prophecy.

The legend at the bottom of the photo said she was Jean Jones.

THE CHILDREN OF GOD COMPOUND, MAY 11, 1974

Bossman didn't wait for the minibus to park. He jumped off and raced for his office. Michael and Joseph intercepted him in the hallway. "We need to talk. It's urgent."

Bossman did not slow down. "It'll have to wait."

He tried to blow by them. Joseph grabbed his arm. "Now. Talk now."

Bossman whipped around and shook his arm free. He had been calling the shots at the compound ever since he arrived with the reinforcements. Neither Michael nor Joseph was happy with their newly subordinate positions. They were also unhappy Lazarus refused to provide an explanation as to why they had been demoted. "It's out of my hands" is all he would say. So the situation was already volatile. This could be the spark that made it explode.

Bossman was an experienced mercenary. He was aware of the danger and he decided to disarm it. He had three alternatives. The first was to kick their ass, something that might be easier said than done. They were both bigger and stronger than him, and they were both accomplished full-contact fighters. The second was to have his men subdue them. Although his team outnumbered their team, both teams would take heavy losses, and the compound would be destroyed. The third was to listen to what they had to say. He chose number three.

He stroked his blond beard and struggled to control the adrenaline pumping through his body. Joseph was ready to fight. He was caught off guard by Bossman's calm reply.

"What is so goddamn important?"

Joseph hesitated, and Michael stepped in. "Lazarus called. He has identified Jeanie Jones. She is the succubus."

It was Bossman's turn to be surprised. "You mean the one that got away from the Prophecy?"

"Yeah. That's the one."

"This is good news and explains a lot of things. Now that we know who she is, we can just take her down."

"Have to find her first."

"We can work that out after I make an urgent call. I think we have a major problem for tomorrow. I'll be right back."

Five minutes later, his door opened. He motioned to the two men. "Come on in. We have some changes to our plans."

THE EMBASSY'S SECURITY ROOM

Olivia was livid. Her face was red. Her eyes were blinking a mile a minute. Her mouth was moving faster than most men's minds. For the moment, her ire was focused on Brandon, but Gary was pleased she was not overtly excluding him from her verbal aggression. Like everything else about her, her voice was extremely annoying. The soundproofed acoustics of the security room did nothing to improve the abrasive cadence and pronunciation.

"Who gave you permission to intercept this 'Benjamin'? Nobody. That's who. Who is running this show? I am. That's who."

Brandon was unmoved. Gary observed his studied calm. He wore a tailored camel-hair sports coat over perfectly tailored gray worsted pants and soft brown leather loafers. His thick, black hair was slicked back, not a strand out of place. His serene, handsome face projected just enough sarcasm to taunt Olivia. His words hit the sweet spot that set off the fireworks. "I think you might be exaggerating your authority."

She wasn't hyperventilating, but her face was red and her fists were clenched. Her thin lips peeled back over her gums. "Exaggerating my authority? I represent the president, POTUS, the president of the United States. Who do you think you are? You are an insignificant little agent in a brand-new department."

Brandon folded his hands and chuckled. "A brand-new department that is entirely independent of any authority under your remit. Until you understand that, this meeting is going nowhere."

He looked at his sleeve and spent several long seconds removing an invisible piece of lint. He was giving Olivia a chance to object. When she didn't react, he continued.

"So let's move on to point number two. Benjamin has been a fountain of information with respect to the Children of God, drug dealing, prostitution, and the forthcoming terrorist attack. I think your remit is related to terrorism, Olivia, so this information should interest you."

Brandon stopped and waited. Slicked back his hair. He was going to make her ask. When she didn't ask, he continued.

"Benjamin has confirmed what we have already documented about the Children of God. They have been taken over by—"

"Cut the crap, Brandon, and give me the info on the terrorists," Olivia interrupted.

She was holding it in, but just barely. Gary was impressed by her willpower, and by Brandon's skill.

Brandon smiled. It was a beautiful show of straight, white teeth, with just enough condescension to make the point. Gary had to admire his style. He had Olivia on the ropes. He leaned back and struck a thoughtful pose. "Benjamin says his role in the terrorist attack is limited to being an intermediary. Somebody else is calling the shots. That somebody else is using him and the Children of God."

Olivia froze. Hesitated. Then puffed. "Nonsense. He's trying to save his own skin. Why would he agree to be the intermediary?"

"I asked him that. He answered that he's wanted in the US on a charge of terrorism. He says it's a charge trumped up by the FBI. The group who has taken over the Children of God in Paris threatened to out him if he didn't cooperate."

Olivia's eyes were wild. It was either anger or fear. Her thin lips curled up in an attempted sneer. "That's a ridiculous bunch of BS." She was not convincing.

"Be that as it may, we are going to have to decide what we want to do. Given the circumstances, I think we should contact the French and let them take down the whole operation—drugs, human trafficking, and terrorism."

Gary chirped in, "I have to agree. As I already explained to Olivia, it's all or nothing. We have all the info we need now. There's nothing to gain by waiting."

Olivia was adamant. She stuck out her chin and wagged her finger in Brandon's face. "I want these terrorists. All of them. I refuse to let anything endanger that. I will not agree to turn the terrorists over to the French until I am sure I have all the information. This meeting is over."

Gary was alarmed. Olivia's argument made no sense. The terrorists had all been identified. Delay would give them a chance to disappear. It would also give the gangbangers over at the Children of God time to complete the drug deal, ship out the trafficked women on the *péniche*, and get away. In other words, delay was the strategy for the good of the bad guys.

At the door, Olivia stopped. She turned slowly back toward the desk where Brandon and Gary remained seated. She cocked back her head, and this time the sneer was successful. "By the way, I have agreed to turn Bambi Cutts over to the French authorities and ask for her extradition."

When there was no reaction from either Brandon or Gary, Olivia continued.

"Bambi Cutts was a well-known pentathlete in the sixties. Some even favored her to win the 1968 Olympics." When there was still no reaction, she continued. "She was injured right before the games and dropped off the sporting world's radar. She appeared on the FBI's radar several months later as a major drug dealer. She had joined a hippie group for cover and used her contacts in the sporting world to develop a lucrative business supplying illegal drugs. She was known for her ruthless treatment of deadbeats. Nonpayment meant career-ending injury. When the FBI started to close in on her, she skipped out to a cult specializing in drugs and prostitution, where she was able to continue exploiting her knowledge of performance-enhancing drug concoctions."

Brandon and Gary looked quizzically at each other. They had no idea what Olivia was talking about. Gary was the first to speak. "We don't have anything on anybody like that or anybody with that name."

Olivia was enjoying this. She was back at the top of her game. The smile on her face was fierce. "I think you know Bambi Cutts as Jean Jones."

47: The Péniche Problem

Lazarus was alone in the house. Everyone else had packed up and left. He would be gone by Monday. Overall, his situation didn't look too bad. The house rental was in Michael's name. Michael and Joseph were the contacts for the Children of God. Joseph was the intermediary with the street gang. Benjamin was the contact for the terrorist gang. He, himself, had no official presence in France except as James MacDonald when he came through customs. The Children of God in Paris was under the control of his disciples. So if nothing else, he had successfully established a network for drugs and human trafficking with access to the Children of God's autonomous worldwide communication system complete with housing, transportation, and legal services.

With Benjamin under arrest, it looked like the terror attack on the ORTF was going down the tubes. No big loss. He would never have undertaken it in the first place if his FBI colleagues in the States hadn't insisted. It was a political thing, anyway, and would have minimal effect on his operations. Benjamin was the cutout, the only contact with the terrorists. No one else in his organization or the Children of God was involved. Nothing was in writing.

Instructions were delivered verbally through Joseph.

Lazarus *was* worried about the *péniche*. There was a five-million-dollar payload of women and drugs in there. Someone had already discovered it, but so far, it remained undisturbed. Lazarus reasoned it was the cult stalker, the succubus, who found out about it from the woman they took in the raid on the compound. She probably had it under surveillance hoping it would lead her to more victims. He had planned to use it as bait to attract her, but waiting until Monday to deliver the merchandise was too risky. If it were discovered by the French, the trafficked women would talk and lead the French directly to the Children of God. That would be the end of his network. He could save the drugs but would have to sacrifice the *péniche* and the rest of its cargo.

It had been several hours since Benjamin was taken. Lazarus had calculated the terrorist hideout would be raided and the terrorists arrested by now. His man watching the terrorist hideout reported the situation was still normal. There was no strange activity of any kind anywhere within a six-block radius. That meant one of two things: Either Benjamin was refusing to confess, or there was a trap being set and the terrorists were the bait.

Lazarus put zero money on Benjamin's willingness or ability to resist a professional interrogation. He was a worthless coward who only accepted the role of intermediary with the terrorists because he was blackmailed into it. That probably meant there was a trap. Not Lazarus's problem. Benjamin was out there on his own on this one.

The more he thought about it, the more it made sense for him to leave town tonight. He had been notified his political protection would not last another twenty-four hours. Once the *péniche* had been taken care of, his network would be protected. The shepherds he had put in place at the compound would keep the network going until things calmed down. Michael had informed him the six remaining members of the reinforcement team had vacated the compound. It was the right thing to do, but it irritated him they had done so on their own initiative and not waited for an order from him. That was something he would have to check up on.

There was nothing he could do about the terror attack. He'd just have to cut his losses on that one. It did gall him to abandon his revenge on the succubus and the American, but he was a devout believer in the old Seminole sayings, "Better safe than sorry" and "Better late than never." His wise conclusion was he would play it safe and get his revenge later.

He went into the kitchen and poured himself a glass of milk. Nothing like a glass of cold milk to calm a man's nerves and clear his mind. He checked on the dogs through the window. They were milling around getting anxious for their next meal. Those Doberman Pinschers were the best security investment he ever made. Nobody could get anywhere near the house without them knowing. He was going to miss them.

BOUGIVAL, MAY 11, 1974

It was nearly dark, but in the unlikely case there was some kind of surveillance on him, Brad had not turned on his headlight. To maintain as much stealth as possible, he slowed by downshifting before turning off the Pont du Maréchal-de-Lattre-de-Tassigny onto l'Ile de la Chaussée rather than using his brakes and flashing his lights. Jeanie was in the passenger seat with her arms around him. She was holding on a little tighter than necessary. Made him feel good. They were both dressed in black from head to toe. The only evidence of their presence was the soft purr of the vertical single 220cc engine. Unless someone was really concentrating, for all practical purposes, they were invisible. He turned left onto the

island and parked in the parking lot under the bridge. The psychedelic van was still there where Jeanie had left it two days before.
They dismounted and resisted the urge to go over and check it out.

Their plan was to circle around the back of the island and approach the *péniche* from the west. There was a wooded area nearby
where they could hide out and observe it. They would then have
to improvise, depending on what they observed. Their goal was to
save the five women prisoners on the *péniche* before they were delivered to the traffickers.

They left the parking lot and strolled hand in hand along the
back of the island, two lovers, two shadows. They got to their observation point without incident. The *péniche* was dark. It looked
deserted. For thirty long minutes, there was no movement on the
péniche or anywhere in the area. The moon would be coming up
pretty soon, and they would have to make their move before then.

It didn't look like the delivery would take place anytime soon,
either, but they wanted to be careful. They didn't know if the delivery would take place by river or by road. They checked both.
There was nothing in either direction on the river, and the road
was deserted.

They were on the move to the *péniche* when headlights flashed
on the offramp to the bridge. They stopped and melted back into
the underbrush. It was a large van. It hesitated at the intersection,
then turned onto Chemin de Halage and drove slowly toward the
péniche. It stopped under the bridge. The back doors slid open and
two dark, heavyset shadows emerged. They advanced cautiously
toward the *péniche*. The darkness hid their features, but not the automatic rifles cradled in their arms.

They stopped at the *péniche*, pulled out powerful flashlights, and
set about inspecting the premises. One shadow jumped onto the
péniche. The other flashed his light into the bushes and trees

bracketing the Chemin and moved forward. He got as far as the stand of trees and bushes where they were hiding.

Jeanie was ready to pounce. Brad figured their chances were slim and none against four professionals armed with automatic rifles. He squeezed her arm, but she didn't relax. Her pistol was already on target when the shadow came to a sudden stop. He raised his head. Sniffed the air. Looked toward the river. Turned back toward the underbrush. Flashed his light. Seconds ticked by. He whipped around and waved an all-clear to the van.

The two front doors opened, and two more shadows exited the van. The driver's shadow looked heavyset like the other two. The passenger shadow was smaller and thinner. It moved gracefully in a manner Brad recognized as feminine. She exchanged some words with the shadow who had inspected the *péniche*. The two of them then stepped on board and went inside. The other two positioned themselves to guard the entrance.

Jeanie squeezed Brad's arm and pointed to her watch. Five minutes had passed. Brad shrugged that he didn't know what was happening. It looked like the two people who had entered the *péniche* were inside doing the deal. If that were the case, when they came out, Brad and Jeanie would have to decide whether to stand down or risk a shootout that would end badly for all concerned, including the prisoners.

Jeanie signaled to Brad she wanted to go for it. Brad's experience told him their little peashooters would not be worthy adversaries for automatic rifles, even with the element of surprise. Jeanie stood and inched forward. Brad was about to move when the woman came out of the *péniche*, followed by the man. They jumped off the boat. The guards covered their retreat as they hustled back to the van, jumped in, and drove off.

Brad realized he was dripping with perspiration. Jeanie stood at the tree line until the car disappeared off the bridge. She put her finger to her lips and waved Brad forward. She reached into her knapsack and pulled out her flashlight. Brad followed suit. Jeanie was the first onto the *péniche*. She positioned herself on the right of the entrance. Brad followed and went to the left.

Jeanie kept her back to the wall. With her left hand, she shone the light into the entranceway. Her right hand held her gun. There was nothing. She stuck her head around the corner, then jerked back. Still nothing.

Brad took to the entrance and jumped down the stairs. He rolled when he hit the bottom, but had a bad landing and hurt his knee. There was still nothing. No reaction. He whispered, "I think this place is deserted."

"Yeah, but we still have to be careful. It smells like a men's locker room."

It took them five minutes to inspect all the rooms in the passageway. Empty. As they advanced, the smell got worse. Smelled like a homeless men's street village full of unwashed bodies. The last door had metal bars. The stench was overwhelming.

Something was moving. They jumped back and cut the lights. More movement and high squeaks. They shined their lights. It was rats; an army of them. They were having a feast on what was left of the kidnapped women.

They chased the rats away and had a look at the five bodies, five young women. Their throats had been slit. The bodies were not yet cold. So it must have happened sometime in the early evening right before they got there. Nothing more they could do here.

"Okay, Jeanie. We've got to hurry. Let's see what we can find. You take the cabin. I'll take the office. Be sure you have your gloves on. No fingerprints."

Jeanie bit back the tears in her eyes. "Okay, Sherlock."

The office had been cleaned out. Brad was about to leave when he noticed a small rectangular plastic pouch under the desk. It held five passports, the passports of the five young women. Must have dropped out in the rush to get away. He studied each one for a few short seconds, then went to see Jeanie in the cabin. "Find anything?"

"No, they cleaned everything out."

"Got your passport with you?"

"Yeah, why?"

"Let me see it." Jeanie extracted her passport from a pocket in her knapsack and handed it to Brad. He placed the passport on the table next to the passport of one of the girls. "Can you tell the difference?"

"She does look a lot like me, but she's no relation. I can assure you."

"Of course, you're a lot better looking." Brad was not above a little self-serving flattery. "But she does look a lot like you, enough that you could go through security control with no problem." Brad winked. "What do you think?"

"What are you suggesting?"

"Jeanie Jones is gonna be in a heap of trouble when this is all over. They'll eventually find out who Jeanie Jones really is, if they haven't already. We can kill her off, right here, right now, and nobody will be the wiser."

Jeanie fingered the young woman's passport. Noticed the name. "Barbara Croft. Barbie Croft for short. I like it. Same initials as my real name." She pocketed the passport and left Jean Jones dead on the table. Brad stuck it in the pack and replaced the pack back in the office where he found it.

48: The Coda

A heavy cloud of dissatisfaction hung over the two men gathered in the safe house. They sat there each one alone with his thoughts.

Brad broke the ice. "Did you stay with Jeanie until the hovercraft took off?" His voice had a worried edge to it.

"Yeah, she went through customs and controls without a hitch. The hovercraft for the UK was on time. I waited until it was out of sight before leaving. She was sad."

Brad snapped to attention. "Why do you say that?"

"She was talking about how much she loved Paris, all the experiences she had here."

"That's all? Nothing else?"

"Well, she also mentioned she might never see it again, and seeing as how you live here…"

Brad sat back, blew a series of perfect smoke rings, and watched them disintegrate. "Yeah, there's no way she can ever come back to France. Can't go back to the US, either. You know that Olivia woman outed her to the French. Told them she was wanted for drug dealing and murder in the US and gave them her real name."

"Bambi Cutts. Cool name! Cool broad! You know I saw her run once when I was on leave from Nam…"

Brad held up his hand. There was noise in the service stairway by the kitchen. Unusual. They were on the top floor. Brad went to the kitchen door. Five short taps and two longs. Brad opened the door. It was Gary. "Why are you slinkin' around the service stairway?"

"Six flights of stairs. Approximately one-hundred-twenty steps. I'm working off the extra pounds."

"It's the same distance on the main stairway, Einstein. Come on in."

Brad poured coffee all around and waited for Gary to perform his sugar cube ritual. Gary didn't oblige. Brad waited a respectable ten Mississippis, then popped the question. "No sugar today?"

Gary sat with his shoulders forward and squinted down at the coffee cup. Rubbed the handle absently between his thumb and forefinger. "Not today, and not until I lose ten pounds. I promised myself that when I got rid of Brandon Butler and Olivia Townsend Ritter-Jones, I'd go on a ten-pound diet. Brandon and Olivia left for London this afternoon."

"Olivia stole your thunder, huh?"

He was resigned. "Yeah, she's a master politician. She could spin a thick rope on a thin spindle. Took all the credit, which for us is not all bad. Keeps us dark. The Company knows the truth."

"How did that play out?"

"After you filled me in on the women's fate, I had someone call in anonymously complaining about a problem on the *péniche*. Then I contacted my French counterpart. It took him less than three hours in the middle of the night to mount an operation on the terrorist hideout over in Courbevoie. These guys are pros. Hit them at 6 a.m. while they were still in their pajamas, so to speak.

Bashed in the door and took the plotters down. They were gone before anybody in the neighborhood even knew they were there. The only thing they left behind was a team of forensics to gather evidence."

Chuck interrupted. "So how did Olivia get in on the deal?"

Gary chortled, picked up his spoon, and stirred his sugarless coffee. "She insisted on speaking with my counterpart. He was livid when he learned we had waited until the last possible moment to inform them of the attack. She took over the meeting, explained she was the president's personal representative in charge of the operation, and it was she who had decided on the timing. She took the blame, and that's how she stole the credit."

Brad scratched his cheek. He was itching to know what was happening with Jeanie. "What about Jeanie?"

"Olivia handled that as well. She had all the information on who Jeanie is and her background in the States—champion pentathlete turned hippie drug dealer on the run from the law. She was so anxious to share that information with the French authorities. I think she knew Jeanie was working for me and did it on purpose."

"How could she have known?"

"Marilyn. Marilyn was the FBI's mole, on their payroll."

"You sure?"

"Certain. I've had her under surveillance for a couple of weeks now. Caught her red-handed. She's on her way back to Langley, where she'll spend the next few weeks undergoing a thorough investigation. As they say in French, 'If you'll steal an egg, you'll steal a cow.' I know she stole information and gave it to Brandon. Who knows who else got information from her? Her family is French."

"How did she know who Jeanie was when you didn't even know?"

Gary stopped in mid-stir. He squeezed his eyes shut. "You're right. Marilyn couldn't have helped her on that. You don't think Jeanie was working for Olivia, and that's how Olivia knew, do you?"

"No way." Brad was adamant.

Chuck put his arm around Brad's shoulders and looked him in the eye. "Hey, buddy, I know you two were close, but we can't let emotion cloud our analysis. It's a possibility. Admit it."

"Not a possibility. Jeanie confided in me about her life in the States the night before she died. She escaped from a cult that was trying to traffic her specifically because she discovered the FBI was complicit in the cult's drug-dealing, prostitution, and human trafficking activities."

He called up Jeanie's words.

"Here is exactly what she said: 'I overheard the Prophet and a peculiar-looking middle-aged female FBI agent discussing the cult's income from prostitution, drug dealing, and human trafficking, its political cover, and which clients would have to be sacrificed to justify the protection it was getting from the FBI.' Here's my question. You don't think Olivia could be that FBI agent?"

Dead silence. Brains burning through the believability of this being true. Gary broke the silence. "Olivia *was* working in California for the FBI at that time. And she *is* peculiar looking. And she *has* behaved strangely since she got here. If it were true, she would definitely know Jeanie's real identity. Still, that's a big leap. She's the president's personal emissary, after all."

Brad pointed at Gary. "Remember when you told me 'wearing a monk's clothes doesn't make you a monk'? Olivia might not be the monk she wants us to believe she is. We have to follow this up if we want to get closure."

"Let it go, Brad. It's over. Jeanie's dead, and Olivia has gone on to bigger and better things." Gary took a sip of his sugarless coffee and made a face. "Man! That is nasty stuff. Anyway, the French cops went to the *péniche* and found the dead bodies along with the passports. The embassy is contacting next of kin. One of the consuls is handling the rest of the legal stuff. There was nothing else. The only lead the French have is the *péniche* belongs to a known mafioso, Thibault's daddy. This daddy's gonna have some explaining to do."

Brad was mulling it over. He started to dig. "Think there's any way to link him to the guys over at Louveciennes?"

"No. Those guys got away clean. The renter gave notice a month ago. He skipped town along with the other guys. Lazarus, Michael, and Joseph all got away scot-free."

"We've got the name and address in London."

"True, but that's a dead end. We ran a check on the guy. He's just an ordinary Joe working for a big finance company in the city. He's been there for a couple of years. No criminal history. I used that address to send Brandon on a wild goose chase."

"What about the car? The Jag."

"Stolen. Reported it months ago. We're gonna keep looking for these guys. Don't worry. They won't get away. The hard part's been done. We broke up their ring and foiled their attack. It's just a matter of time before we bring them in. The problem now is Benjamin."

"Benjamin was the brains behind the terrorists, wasn't he?"

"He says he wasn't. Claims he was only the intermediary and was blackmailed into doing that. He says this Joseph guy was the one giving him his orders. He's going to fight extradition. Says the FBI is behind the plot and they're out to get him."

Brad snickered. "As if he were that important!"

Gary rubbed his chin and took another sip from his cup. "It's not him. It's the organization he used to lead, the Army for World

Peace. Benjamin says it's a nonviolent movement whose goal is world peace, as the name implies. He says the FBI infiltrated it and tried to turn it into a vehicle for subversion and insurrection. When he refused to yield to these insurrectionists, the FBI put him under investigation and called him in for questioning. He skipped town and headed for France, where he joined up with the Children of God."

Brad thought that over, shook his head, and asked, "Why would the FBI do that?"

Chuck jumped in. "Yeah, why would they do that?"

They both stared at Gary. They were anxious for more. Gary was looking down. His brows were knitted. He was deep in thought. Finally, he broke the spell. "It sounds like a lot of self-serving BS. However, it is exactly the same story Olivia told me, minus the FBI acting as the catalysts for insurrection, of course. In any case, Benjamin is going to fight extradition, and that means more work for me."

Brad was really down. No matter how much lipstick they put on it, this caper still looked like a big, fat pig. Smelled like one, too. The women were slaughtered. The drugs were distributed. All the bad guys got away. Gary said they left no clues behind, so it was unlikely they would be brought to justice any time soon. That made Brad, Chuck, and maybe Jeanie vulnerable to retaliation. Brandon and Olivia Townsend Ritter-Jones got all the credit for shutting down the terrorists, the only positive aspect of the whole deal.

Gary looked at his watch. "I have to get moving. It's chaos over at the embassy. I'm just glad we got the terrorists and shut down the trafficking."

Brad zeroed in. "We didn't shut anything down. We just moved it out of Paris. The traffickers are still on the loose with all their knowledge and contacts."

"Yeah, that's the bad part. Later." Gary stepped out.

He had been gone for the better part of fifteen minutes, and they still sat in silence, trying to digest what Gary had to say. Finally, Brad clapped his hands. "I've still got a lot of questions, Chuck."

"Me too."

RUE D'ASSAS, MAY 14, 1974

The terrorists were under arrest, and the Children of God had been defanged, but Brad decided to err on the side of caution. He parked his bike on the Rue Guynemer and went the last hundred yards to his building on foot. The terrace of the Guynemar café on the corner was empty, so there was no surveillance there. Nothing on the street. It looked like the coast was clear.

It wasn't. In front of Brad's building sat Chef with his two wingmen in their dark blue Renault station wagon. Brad had expected Chef would come by to see him, just not so soon. "*Salut, Chef. Quoi de neuf?* (Hi, Chef. What's new?)"

Chef and his two wingmen clambered out of the car. Chef seemed younger than the last time he saw him. He was smiling. His big face was relaxed, but his square jaw gave him a determined look. He had let his hair grow, and it wasn't as gray as before. He had also lost weight. Brad had to admit he looked pretty good.

"Mr. James, I have been looking for you. Where have you been?"

"Out and about, Chef. Same old thing. Workin' out, recordin' songs, puttin' the moves on the girls. Things like that. How about you? You're lookin' good, like you're gettin' younger."

The two wingmen obviously enjoyed that one. They looked at each other and concentrated on stifling the smiles that were struggling to break through their somber, professional expressions.

Chef got a little red around the gills but pretended he didn't hear the compliment. "Mr. James, have you had any communication with Jean Jones lately?"

"No."

"How about the Children of God?"

"No. I've been pretty busy. New record comin' out. If you buy it, I'll sign it."

Chef blinked and stepped back. Brad saw he was offended. The French don't make jokes like that.

"Just kiddin', Chef. I've already reserved one just for you. You don't even have to pretend you like it. So, what about Jeanie and the Children of God?"

"*Du neuf* (new stuff). Mademoiselle Jones, a.k.a. Bambi Cutts, has been identified as deceased."

Brad opened his eyes wide and hung his head. He was hoping he looked both surprised and sad. "What happened? Who is Bambi Cutts?"

"Bambi Cutts is Jean Jones's real name. She is a US fugitive. We found her body on a barge along with four other bodies. Their throats had been slit. It looks like some kind of a trafficking deal gone bad. You, of course, wouldn't know anything about that, would you?"

"No, like I told you before, I'm not into drugs or the drug scene."

Chef stepped forward and studied Brad's face. His eyebrows were raised in his signature I-doubt-it expression. "Not drugs. Human trafficking. It looks like Mademoiselle Jones was part of the merchandise. From what I know, Mademoiselle Jones doesn't fit the victim profile."

Brad had no trouble agreeing with him on that one. She was anything but a victim. "You're right on that. I don't see her as a victim. Any idea on how she got on that barge?"

"We're working on it. I'm convinced there's something fishy going on, and I can't help but feel you're involved."

That kind of hurt Brad's feelings, insinuating he was a human trafficker. He had no trouble showing his indignation. He squinted deep into Chef's eyes. His lips were tight. There was a sharp edge to his voice. "For the last time, I don't fool around with human trafficking."

Chef was taken aback by the violence of Brad's reply. "Sorry, Mr. James. I did not mean to insinuate you are involved with human trafficking. My ears and eyes on the street suggest, however, you might be more involved with Mademoiselle Jones than you let on. She hasn't contacted you, has she?"

Coming from someone who had just announced Jeanie's death, that sounded like a trick question. Brad thought about it before he answered. "I thought you said she was dead."

"This is what we are led to believe. We have a good working relationship, you and me. Let's not spoil it. Promise me you will contact me if you hear anything, anything at all."

"No problem."

After Chef left, Brad was left with the solid impression this policeman might not be fooled by his passport switch.

49: One Last Time with Feeling

The American Express office was situated on the Rue de Scribe, just behind the Opéra building. For a small fee, American Express had a service where travelers could have their mail delivered there. Brad had anticipated he might end up under some kind of suspicion, and that was why he agreed with Jeanie to route any written communication through the American Express. As a further precaution, they established a simple code.

Chef's visit the other day made him glad he had taken the necessary precautions. Brad had no doubt any correspondence to his address on Rue d'Assas would be intercepted and scrutinized. So here he was at the American Express. The clerk handed him the postcard signed *Barbie*. He took it to the Café de la Paix across from the Opéra and sat down on the terrace to decipher it.

Jeanie had made it to London. She gave him the address to the room she was renting in a suburb called Colindale along with a telephone number. She wanted to know what was happening.

Brad took a big bite of his sandwich *saucisson sec, cornichon, beurre*—summer sausage, pickle, and butter—and a big slug of his ice-cold Stella. He wasn't ready to let go and admit defeat.

Although it looked like a dead end, there were still some loose ends. Why was Olivia so determined to delay alerting the French? How did she know Jeanie's true identity? How much of Benjamin's story was true?

Brad had one last card to play. He walked over to the post office and made a long-distance call to Colindale.

COLINDALE (LONDON), MAY 20, 1974

When he dismounted, Jeanie was waiting for him at the door. Her furnished room was the whole top floor of a detached house right off Aerodrome Road, not far from the Royal Air Force Museum. It had a spacious bathroom, a large sitting area with a small kitchen, and a sleeping area off to the side. The added attraction was the private entrance through the exterior stairway.

"Nice place you have here."

"I really like it, Brad. I think I'll be here for a while."

Brad wasn't surprised. With France and the US off the table as viable options in the short to medium term, London looked like a good alternative.

For the moment, Jeanie was mulling over Brad's summary of the situation in Paris. Valérie Giscard d'Estaing won the election with 50.81% of the vote. The status quo was intact. She still was upset the Prophet and his two sidekicks had managed to escape. "You know, Brad, it's a crime those cult creatures were allowed to escape. They must have had help."

"You're right on that. I think Gary feels the same way, even though he's playing it down."

Jeanie's face was set. This story wasn't over yet. "Thanks for coming over to help me find them. Why did you come by motorcycle? It must have been a long trip."

"It was, but that French cop is not convinced. He's still sniffing around. I didn't want to leave a paper trail by purchasing a train or plane ticket. We might also need a set of wheels. There would be a paper trail if we had to rent something."

Brad was dog-tired. It had been a long trip. It had also required some concentration to get used to driving on the wrong side of the road once he got to the UK. Thankfully, the weather was good for the whole trip except for a little spring shower while he was on the hovercraft. He'd had time to work out a plan. It was a long shot, but it was the last card they had to play.

Jeanie poured him another glass of wine and kissed him on the cheek. He knew she would not feel fully at peace as long as the Prophet was on the loose. It was a good time to tease her a little. "What am I supposed to call you now? Jeanie, Bambi, or Barbie?"

She feigned a pout. "I don't care what you call me. I just want you to treat me like you treated Jeanie in Paris."

They had a good, complicit laugh. Brad was feeling so comfortable, too comfortable. He knew it, but he didn't care. She knew it as well. She didn't care either. They would deal with "tomorrow and forever" when the time came.

Brad took a sip of his wine and a puff of his Gitane sans filtre. "We have a big day tomorrow." Jeanie nodded and smiled. "Let's hope it works out."

"Yeah, it's our last chance. I'll tell you my plan tomorrow."

HAMPSTEAD, MAY 21, 1974

They had agreed they would have to disguise themselves. If Brad's intuition was on the mark, they would be dealing with people who knew what they looked like, and it would be catastrophic if they were recognized.

Brad combed his hair straight back and put on his granny glasses. He traded his black leather jacket for a baggy tweed sports coat with patches on the elbows and his snakeskin *santiags* for a pair of brown, scuffed-up earth shoes. He was the spitting image of a dedicated educator and would fit right in with the Hampstead scene.

Jeanie went for the horror-film look. She put on a white makeup base, black mascara and eye shadow, bright-red lipstick, and combed her hair forward, letting it fall limply around her face onto her shoulders. She looked like a bloodthirsty vampire. Not necessarily the Hampstead scene, but unrecognizable as Jeanie Jones from Paris.

The plan was to check out the address in Hampstead where the E-Type Jag was registered. Although the car was reported as stolen, Brad had a feeling there was more to it than that. Gary had mentioned Brandon had been to London to check on the address. Brandon never mentioned what he discovered. Brad found that intriguing. He was also wondering why Brandon had traipsed off to London as soon as the terror plot was foiled.

They decided they would work separately, using a simple system of head and hand signs to coordinate their actions. Brad was hoping to find some link to the Hampstead address and the address in Louveciennes that would lead them to the Prophet and his men. Their morning objective was to reconnoiter the area and stake out the building. They agreed to meet for lunch in Golder's Green to share their information and make their plans for the afternoon.

Hampstead was a beautiful residential area brimming with boutiques, restaurants, cafés, and all sorts of shops. The information Gary had given him was that the E-Type Jag belonged to a James MacDonald, who lived in a third-floor apartment located on Greenhill in Hampstead. The apartment complex was a ten-minute walk down Hampstead High Street from the underground station.

Brad spent the morning wandering around the area. The

complex was spread over a whole city block between Prince Arthur Road and Vance Close. Across from Greenhill on Hampstead High Street, there were several cafés and restaurants that could serve as observation points. Brad liked the feel of Hampstead. He was satisfied with his morning reconnaissance.

Since it was a beautiful, sunny day, he decided to walk to Golder's Green rather than take the underground. It was a good decision because about halfway there, he ran across Jeanie, who had decided to walk as well. They found a nice Italian restaurant beside a big park and chose a table on the terrace.

Jeanie's vampire look was not unbecoming. Just the opposite! He repressed an overwhelming urge to give her a big hug and kiss. The current must have been strong. Jeanie felt it and shivered.

"Cold?"

"No, just an emotion jolt."

Brad liked that.

They began to compare notes and found they had both come to the same conclusion. The complex would be easy to watch, but because it was so large, there would be many people going in and out. In other words, they wouldn't have many chances to relax their vigilance. The underground parking posed the same problem, but it would be less of an effort to spot a yellow E-Type Jag. Brad decided he would go into the parking area later in the evening and see if the car they were looking for was in there. If he found it, that would be a big step in the right direction.

Countersurveillance was always a problem. Brad concluded that if the culprits were holed up in the complex, they would take some serious security measures. "Did you see anything suspicious?"

Jeanie's pained expression fed Brad's worries. "Not really sure. Of course, there were many people just wandering around and hanging out. Any of these could be potential adversaries. There's no way of knowing. Above and beyond this type of situation, however, I did notice two separate instances where I had a feeling. The first was when I came out of the underground. There was a mature man scrutinizing everyone leaving the station. When I say mature, I mean above forty-five. He was dressed in an ill-fitting suit and just seemed out of place. When I say scrutinizing, I mean he was studying everyone closely. I got halfway down the block and noticed that he was on the other side of the street, pretending not to notice me. I ran across him several times over the course of the morning.

"The second was when I was coming off Prince Arthur Road and preparing to cross Hampstead High Street. There was another guy who reminded me of the first guy staring at me. They didn't look anything alike. The first guy was kind of sloppy-looking, with a big belly and a light complexion. The second guy was dark and sleek. He was wearing sunglasses. He was somehow familiar to me, somewhere deep in my past. They both gave me the same feeling, like they were on the lookout for something."

"Yeah, I noticed the sleek guy with sunglasses as well. He might just be a hustler trying to identify a mark. If somebody's watching, there will probably be at least three of them and maybe more. We're going to have to be careful, especially when we leave the area, so that we don't bring them with us. We'll also have to stagger the times we watch. There's no way we can do an all-day, full-court press. Too obvious. Mornings and evenings to catch people going and coming for work are the best bet. We'll also have to choose our cafés carefully where we can fit in and not draw attention. We're the new kids on the block, and anyone who knows the neighborhood and has been watching will know it. We'll also need to establish a purpose for hanging around this particular neighborhood. There are several bookstores around. My 'educator' look should make it easy for me to frequent them for a few days. Maybe you can pretend you're looking for a job."

"Good idea. There are some jewelry stores and makeup boutiques. I'll go in and make some inquiries. Making myself part of the local fabric was one of my best tricks in my bounty hunter days."

"By the way, Chuck's coming in to help out. He's got a room booked for tonight in a hotel around the corner."

HAMPSTEAD, MAY 21, 1974

They met Chuck at the pub up on The Burroughs about a fifteen-minute walk from the Hendon underground station. His hair was longer now that he was the bona fide proprietor of his own detective agency. He was dressed in a dark three-piece suit with a silk tie and shined dress shoes.

Brad could tell he thought he looked pretty good. "You goin' to a wedding, or a wake?"

That really pleased Chuck. "Neither, but don't get too close to me. I don't want anybody to think I know you."

After they got through their male-bonding banter, Jeanie wanted to know the latest from Paris. Chuck confirmed what Brad had already related. A few women had lost their lives, the terror plot had been foiled, a few of the bad guys had gotten away, Benjamin was fighting extradition, and nobody was questioning Jeanie's death. The case was closed. Jeanie and Brad were the only ones who thought the address in Hampstead was relevant. Chef was the only one who was suspicious. He smelled a rat and had been by Chuck's office, nosing around.

With all the preliminaries out of the way, they got down to business. Chuck would be the point man on the operation. He would use his rank as a licensed private detective to make inquiries about an imagined missing person. If there was surveillance out there, they would go straight for him just like fleas go for the dog in the room. They would be easy to spot. Brad reminded them that surveillance was a good thing. If surveillance there was, it meant their prey was nearby.

The next day came and went. They were frustrated. They all had sensed surveillance, but none had positively made any particular surveillant. So either there was no surveillance or the surveillants were so good or numerous that they remained impossible to detect.

HAMPSTEAD, MAY 23, 1974

Brad snapped to attention. His guard-duty daydream was over. Jeanie was standing across the street, sending him the signal. He paid the bill and headed to the agreed rendezvous café two underground stops away. When he arrived, Jeanie was already there, and she was excited. She kissed him. It was spontaneous and affectionate. He held her close. He was churning with emotion.

Jeanie's eyes were open wide and glistening. Her voice was huskier than usual when she announced she had spotted Brandon Butler. He didn't think that Brandon Butler was the cause of her husky voice, but he was very surprised that Brandon Butler was back in the picture.

They took a table in the back corner of the café and settled in. Jeanie waited patiently as Brad lit up a Gauloise sans filtre, took a deep drag, and, deep in thought, blew out five perfect smoke rings. "Are you sure it was Brandon?"

"Positive. He has a face that's hard to forget, and a signature slick-back-the-hair move."

"Did you try to follow him?"

"No. He knows me. I think he's familiar with the area. Knew where he was going. No hesitation. He came out of the pharmacy up the street and headed for the taxi stand near the underground."

The waiter came over and stood expectantly by their table. Brad motioned to Jeanie. She ordered a white coffee. Brad did the same and asked for the telephone. The waiter indicated a big red telephone cabin on the street in front of the café.

"I'm going to call Chuck. He'll have to do the heavy surveillance lifting now. Brandon knows me, too." The coffees were on the table when he got back. "So, what do you make of Brandon's presence on the scene?"

"I think it means we're onto something. I don't know what, but we have to find out. I can't imagine Brandon being in bed with the Prophet."

Brad cocked an eye and sighed. "I don't know. He's a strange hombre. He's also from the FBI. They are…how can I put it? Gary says they have their own agenda. Chuck can find out where Brandon is staying."

*　　　　*　　　　*

Chuck was adamant. "If Brandon is coming around here, the most obvious conclusion is the bad guys are here, too. Brandon is staying at the Dorchester in the center of town. I'm not going to waste my time hanging around there on the off chance I can spot Brandon Butler wandering around. The action is here. We've got to go on the attack. You with me?"

Jeanie did not hesitate. "All the way."

Brad was more circumspect. He was thinking about Murphy and his law of the universal constant. "Agreed, but something tells me we should wait until we have more information."

50: Olivia's Farewell Gifts

The plan was for Chuck to call James MacDonald's apartment in order to find out who was living there. As far as he knew, he was unknown to anyone associated with the people who were living in the house in Louveciennes and would not be recognized. He would pretext getting the wrong floor and excuse himself. Depending on what he found out, they would then decide where to go from there. Just to make his story believable, he got the name of the person who lived in the apartment above James MacDonald.

Jeanie was on her way to the rendezvous point when she passed the world-renowned gourmet restaurant on Heath Street. She wasn't a big fan of gourmet restaurants in general, but this one exuded a welcoming atmosphere that attracted her attention every time she went by. This time was no different.

She looked in as usual, but this time she got the shock of her life. There, at the window table, sat the Prophet, and across from the Prophet sat the mysterious, peculiar-looking middle-aged woman from outside the Prophecy, the FBI woman who controlled the Prophet and his realm of prostitution and drugs. It was she who had forced the Prophet to condemn her to a death sentence in the Prophet's personal harem. The Prophet had resisted. She had insisted. The rest was history.

Jeanie crossed the street. Her emotions were raging. Her heart was pumping. Adrenaline was flowing. She was ready to explode. This was her chance, just like every competition she had entered, only this time it was life and death. She had to control it. She knew how to control it. She closed her eyes. Relaxed her muscles. Slowed her breathing. Concentrated her mind.

She was still wearing her vampire look, so she would be difficult to recognize. However, she knew implicitly she could not count too much on this. The Prophet possessed an uncanny sixth sense that made him totally unpredictable. Maybe he already sensed her presence. The woman would also be a troublesome target. She never went anywhere without at least two bodyguards. In fact, it was because of the bodyguards that Jeanie had been caught eavesdropping on the conversation between the woman and the Prophet, the conversation that had sealed her fate in the Prophecy.

Jeanie took a cautious look around. She saw nothing, but she knew they were there. She reached the obvious conclusion she would need help. She also knew this might be her only chance at the woman.

It was early in the evening, and Jeanie noticed they were just beginning their meal. This would give her time to go get Brad and Chuck. As she stepped out onto the sidewalk, she felt a hand on her shoulder. Her reaction was swift and violent. She lashed out and pivoted to the right. Anyone slower than Chuck would have been taking a ten-count.

"Cool your jets, Jeanie. It's me, Chuck."

"Why in heaven's name did you sneak up on me like that?"

"Didn't sneak up on you. I've been sheltering in this foot

passage for the last fifteen minutes, tryin' to stay out of sight. This Lazarus guy is in there with his date." He motioned toward the restaurant. "I was on my way to knock on his door when I saw him come marching out of his building. I followed him here."

"His date, as you call her, is the same person who caused me to be imprisoned by the Prophecy. Because of her, I came within an inch of being trafficked into the Prophet's prostitution system." When Chuck drew a blank, Jeanie explained. "She was the power behind the Prophecy and its activities. She is the Prophet's boss, the head of the operation."

Chuck guided Jeanie into the foot passage. "We won't draw any attention here. Anybody who comes by will think we're lovers. So let me get this straight. You are saying that woman in there is the head of a criminal organization involved in prostitution, human trafficking, and drug dealing?"

"That is exactly what I'm saying. I will never forget her. I overheard her giving the Prophet detailed instructions on how the business was to be run—who was to be paid off, how much, and when—names, numbers, and dates. I got caught, and she condemned me to what was the equivalent of a death sentence in the Prophecy's whorehouse."

Chuck rubbed his chin and sighed. "Jeanie, that woman in there is Olivia Townsend Ritter-Jones. She is the White House liaison with the FBI, the president of the United States' personal choice and personal emissary to France. Gary pointed her out to me at an embassy cocktail party. She's one of the most influential people in the entire United States of America."

HAMPSTEAD, MAY 23, 1974

Lazarus had been enjoying the meal and the conversation. "I only regret we lost the *péniche* and the women."

Olivia beamed a satisfied smile and nodded modestly. "Me too, but I couldn't delay the operation any longer. It was an insignificant loss. Everything else worked like a charm. We foiled the terrorist plot we masterminded and got credit for that. Benjamin's role confirmed our arguments that his Army for World Peace was a terrorist organization. Gave us the green light to arrest all the members and shut down the terrorist plot we planned for them. We got credit for that, as well. Our budget and remit are being expanded. Our Paris operation is in place and will only be delayed for a few months."

Olivia stayed seated as Lazarus stood to leave. "Goodbye, Olivia."

"Goodbye, Randall. We'll be in touch."

She insisted on calling him Randall. He preferred being called the Prophet but was satisfied with Lazarus. Randall just didn't rock with the power and charisma he was convinced he emanated. Lazarus knew it was just one of the numerous mind games she played to maintain a psychological edge over her underlings.

There had been a game change, though. He wasn't an underling anymore. She knew it but wasn't ready to admit it. That Brandon from the DEA had her by the balls. He had sniffed out her dark side and connected the dots, from the Prophecy to the Prophecy's demise, to Witness Protection, to the Children of God, to the terrorists.

She had everything to lose. She was the one who had set him up in the US Marshals' Witness Protection Program. As a confirmed member of this program, his own involvement in the Prophecy was officially recorded as approved undercover work. He was safe on that score. He himself was only vulnerable for what had gone on in Paris. Fortunately for him, he had no obvious link to Paris. Everything was handled by third parties. No one but that clown, Thibault, even knew he was in Paris, and Thibault had no idea who he was.

Olivia was sucking up to him. He could feel it. She would be dead meat if anything went wrong and he testified against her. All her admonitions about them being in this together were just more mind games. Olivia had indirectly accepted her inferior position when she accepted his proposal to change the cut from a 50/50 split to a 75/25 split in his favor. It was easier than he had imagined. She accepted it right off the bat.

Randall-Lazarus-the Prophet could honestly say that for the first time in a long time, he was at peace with himself and the world. His operation in Paris with the Children of God was intact and ready to resume once things calmed down. Meanwhile, his digs here in Hampstead were top-of-the-line.

The walk from the restaurant was over. He was already home. One of Olivia's men opened the door for him. She was really pouring it on, having her two best men take him home. She had Michael and Joseph running an errand for her in London. He liked his new-found position of power. Over the next few days, he would push it a little to see how far he could go.

Lazarus thanked his escorts and entered his building. They followed him in. "It's okay, guys. Thanks again."

The sleek-looking bodyguard launched a big smile. His teeth were long and white, like they were painted. "Hey, Randall, our orders are to make sure you're safe and sound in your apartment."

"Okay, suit yourself. The elevator's out of order."

"We could use the exercise."

Lazarus hated walking up the stairs. His short, bowed legs made it difficult for him to climb. He was out of breath by the time they got to his apartment. His escorts were breathing heavily as well.

Lazarus was on a high. Didn't want the evening to end. "How

about a nightcap?"

Sleekman was all in. "Can't say no to that."

In they went. Lazarus went straight to the bar and poured three generous bourbons. "As the Brits say, cheers."

"Cheers."

Lazarus turned to the bar for another round. Sleekman drew his syringe and plunged it into Lazarus's neck. Lazarus turned. His face was twisted. His eyes were blazing. He knew what was happening. He grunted, grabbed Sleekman by the shoulders, and headbutted him.

Sleekman didn't fall. He just stumbled around like a mindless chicken, holding his face in his hands.

His companion was already on the move. Lazarus met him in the middle of the room. He used the prodigious power of his upper body to wrestle the man to the floor. He locked his arm around the man's throat and began to squeeze. The man twisted and writhed. He clutched at Lazarus's eyes. He kicked and he scratched. Weaker and weaker, but still he held on.

Lazarus knew he had to hurry. His resistance to the drug cocktail was limited, a matter of minutes before he passed out. His life depended on killing these two men before then.

Sleekman recovered from the headbutt. His vision was blurred. His nose was bleeding and smashed against his cheek. He managed to stay on his feet and grab the second syringe. His partner was barely moving by the time he administered Lazarus his second dose. The second dose concluded the affair. Lazarus relaxed his grip and collapsed in the throes of unbearable suffering.

Sleekman slumped onto the couch. "The guy's an animal."

It took his sidekick a long time to answer. "Yeah. Let's make sure he's a dead one."

DORCHESTER HOTEL, MAY 23, 1974

Brandon had several reasons to celebrate. His conversation with Olivia had been less disagreeable than he had imagined. In fact, she had offered no substantial resistance to anything he proposed. First of all, she agreed he would be credited with uncovering the crucial information that enabled the French authorities to thwart the terrorist attack. Secondly, she would have his work record with the FBI amended to show he had been instrumental in exposing the Prophecy and its activities. Thirdly, and most importantly, he would be named Olivia Townsend Ritter-Jones's personal consultant at the White House. It didn't get any better than that.

He leaned back in his chair and signaled the waiter. Another scotch on the rocks was in order. By the time he finished, his appetizer would arrive. He loved the Vesper Bar at the Dorchester Hotel, its illustrious history, its lively reputation—London's ultimate destination for cocktail sipping, celebrating, and dealmaking. He was on top of the world.

He was still aglow as he left the Vesper Bar for his room on the third floor. Two nice-looking young men held the elevator for him. He nodded his thanks and pushed the button for the third floor. At the third floor, he exited along with the two nice-looking young men. His balance was suffering from the scotch and brandy portion of his personal celebration.

One of the young men steadied him. "Let me help you."

"Thanks, thanks, I'm fine."

Brandon opened the door to his room and turned to bid farewell to his young friends. One of them took his right arm, the other took the left. They ushered him into the room.

"No, no, I'm fine. Thank you very much. No problem."

The dark-haired man retrieved a syringe from his vest pocket. Suddenly, Brandon understood. He whirled around and caught the blond-haired man with a vicious elbow to the head.

Blondie was dazed. Brandon grabbed the dark-haired man's wrist, twisted it, and used his forward movement to drive the syringe into the man's abdomen and hit the plunger. Darkie dropped to the floor, writhing in pain.

Brandon rolled right to dodge Blondie's wild roundhouse. Too little, too late. The alcohol had slowed him down. He took the blow to the side of the head. Blondie followed with a direct to the chest that knocked him back and took his breath away. Blondie finished him off with a kick to the testicles.

Brandon was down and out. Blondie went to his sidekick's vest pocket and extracted another syringe. His sidekick was no longer writhing. He wasn't breathing, either. Brandon was just coming to when Darkie plunged the needle into his neck. Brandon began moaning, groaning, and writhing around. It took a couple of minutes, which seemed like an eternity to Blondie. Finally, Brandon ceased moaning, groaning, and writhing around. He also stopped breathing.

Blondie went to his sidekick and patted his face. "Joseph. Joseph. It's me, Michael. Wake up, wake up."

There was no reaction. Joseph was dead. Michael started to cry.

51: Michael's Last Act

Chuck saw Lazarus stand and say goodbye to Olivia. At the door, he was greeted by two men. One was overweight and sloppy-looking. The other was sleek and slim. Jeanie whispered that these were two of the men she had fingered as surveillants in the area. Chuck put his finger to his lips and maneuvered Jeanie further back into the footpath. "I'll take these three guys. You stay here and keep an eye on Townsend Ritter-Jones. Brad should be here any minute now."

Chuck was barely out of sight when Brad came up the footpath. Jeanie had heard him park his Indian Arrow and was waiting for him. "Lazarus just left with those two guys we spotted watching the area. Chuck followed them."

Before Brad could answer, Jeanie pointed to the taxi that had just pulled up across the street. They exchanged surprised looks when they saw it was Michael exiting the cab and heading for the restaurant. He went straight to the table where Olivia sat sipping champagne from a crystal flute. Several minutes of intense conversation followed. Michael was ostensibly upset. His head jerked to the cadence of the points he was making.

Olivia listened attentively, interrupting only occasionally to ask a question. Her long, thin face framed by the graying, ear-length pageboy showed sincere concern.

When Michael finished, her tight, thin lips peeled back into a soft smile. She patted Michael's hand. Michael rose, said goodbye, and left.

Michael crossed the street. Instead of heading toward the underground, he went straight for the footpath. Brad was taken by surprise and had no time to slip away. Michael gave no sign he recognized Brad. Then, as he passed by, he struck out violently with a right hand aimed at Brad's solar plexus. His forward momentum and two hundred and twenty pounds of muscle packed his punch with bone-breaking power.

Brad twisted away. Too slow. Not enough. The punch rammed into his ribcage. Doubled him over. Gasping for breath, he rolled to the right. Michael followed through. Lost Brad in the darkness. Brad took advantage. Front-flipped to his feet. Almost lost it. The pain was excruciating. He was mobile. But just barely.

He had to stay on his feet. He could not let Michael take him to the ground. Michael's athleticism and fifty-pound weight advantage would be impossible to overcome.

Michael bull-charged. Brad danced away. Landed a left-right combo to the head as Michael passed by.

Michael charged again. Brad dodged. Connected with a roundhouse to Michael's ear. Ducked out of range.

Michael slowed his game. Positioned himself in a boxer's crouch. Feinted right. Feinted left. Shuffled forward. Jab. Jab. Right-footed roundhouse. Left-footed roundhouse.

Brad retreated out of range. Saw Michael hesitate. Shot forward. A long front kick to the solar plexus took Michael down.

Brad went for the kill. Tripped on a tree root. Fell to a knee.

Michael pulled him to the ground and began to punch him violently around the head.

Brad managed to avoid or soften most of the punches, but he was losing his strength. Michael had him pinned in one of those wrestler body locks that are all but impossible to escape. Brad risked it all, took a punch, and went for Michael's eyes. His thumb penetrated and ripped. Michael screamed. Brad slipped free. Michael was blind, swinging at sounds. Brad downed him with a side kick. Stomped his shoulder. Took him out with a kick to the head.

Jeanie was there, syringe in hand. Brad shook his head and held out his hand. "Give it to me."

Michael struggled to a sitting position. Brad planted the syringe deep into his neck, returned it to Jeanie. Suddenly, Michael leaned forward, his face contorted in a hideous mask of hatred and malevolence. He fell to the side, jerking and groaning, spittle frothing from his lips. Jeanie stood above him, empty syringe in her left hand and, in the darkness of the footpath, what looked like a satisfied smile on her lips.

Brad took Jeanie into his arms. She leaned into him and she was, in fact, smiling. He wanted to smile, but his ribs were hurting too bad.

They stayed that way for a long time. They would have stayed longer, but Sleekman and Sloppyman showed up at the restaurant. They spent a few minutes in animated conversation with Olivia, then picked up their belongings and left. A short time later, Olivia left the restaurant and got into the car waiting out in front. Jeanie and Brad headed for his Indian Arrow.

52: Closure

HAMPSTEAD, MAY 23, 1974

The waiter informed Olivia her car was ready. It was about time. She had been waiting for the better part of an hour. Michael was the first to report. She was sorry to hear they had lost Joseph, but at the end of the day, Michael could do the job alone from now on. Her sleek, white-toothed bodyguard was the second to report. Randall had put up a fight, as she knew he would and as her bodyguard's nose confirmed, but he was gone. She would miss him. They went back a long time. There was no other way. He had left her no choice. She could see he was becoming too independent. Too independent meant too dangerous.

Olivia leaned back in the car seat and, for the first time in many months, heaved a sincere, satisfied sigh of relief.

She had managed to establish the foundation for her drug/prostitution/trafficking business in Europe. She had thwarted a terrorist plot in France and demolished a terrorist organization in the US. Who really cared they were her own creations? She would get all the glory for foiling them.

As an extra feature of her success, she had also managed to eliminate the only persons who could incriminate her.

She decided to soak up as much publicity as she could in London and Paris before she returned to Washington.

DORCHESTER HOTEL, MAY 23, 1974

Olivia was at the Dorchester reception desk with Sleekman. Sloppyman was nowhere to be seen. Jeanie and Brad observed them from the area near the elevators. Following them to the hotel had been a cakewalk. Slow-moving traffic, plenty of stoplights. They never got closer than three cars behind.

Brad was hesitant to go after Olivia in the Dorchester Hotel. It was arguably the swankiest hotel in town with lots of security. When Jeanie explained to Brad who Olivia really was, he had to admit this might be their only chance. Jeanie had a right to confront the person responsible for her persecution and loss of identity.

Sleekman accompanied Olivia to the elevators. Jeanie and Brad followed them in. Olivia had a slight reaction when Jeanie entered the elevator cabin, but it was more quizzical than anything. She was probably wondering what this vampire woman was doing at the Dorchester. Brad, on the other hand, was looking pretty good for somebody with sore ribs and a bruised face who only an hour earlier had been rolling around the ground on a footpath in Hampstead. It all went with his educator look.

He smiled at the couple. "Good evening."

That's when the situation got complicated. Sleekman asked which floor they wanted. Jeanie improvised. Said they were going to the fourth floor. Sleekman hit the button for the fourth floor, then pushed the button for the sixth floor.

The doors were closing when a young lady broke the circuit and entered. Pretty face, blue eyes, wrinkled white cotton print, dumpy shoes, and an English accent. "Fourth floor, please."

Bad luck!

The elevator was out as a confrontation point. They wouldn't be able to do anything with this young English woman as a witness.

At the fourth floor, they exited along with the English woman and rushed to the stairway. They had to get up to the sixth floor before Olivia got into her room. At the worst, they had to see which room she went into. Otherwise, she would be out of reach, definitively.

The corridor to the sixth floor was deserted when they arrived. Brad's heart fell. Jeanie held up her hand.

Voices. They followed the voices to a side corridor. As they turned the corner, they saw it was the short hallway to a single room. The two groups spotted each other simultaneously.

Sleekman went for his gun. Brad went for Sleekman. Jeanie went for Olivia.

Sleekman was not fast enough. Brad slammed his head into the wall, kneed him in the testicles, and karate-chopped him to the back of his neck. He folded and fell to the floor. Brad kicked him in the head. He was down and out.

Jeanie was having more trouble than expected with Olivia. Olivia was a big woman, and she knew she was fighting for her life. She tried to scream, but Jeanie elbowed her in the throat. That ended her resistance.

TRJ was struggling to breathe. Jeanie grabbed the key and opened the door to a huge suite. It took only seconds to drag the bodies inside and duct tape them up. Sleekman was coming to. Brad grabbed his head for a lethal twist. "No witnesses."

Jeanie looked at Brad and put her finger to her lips. "Shhh. I've got a better idea." From her backpack, she extracted a syringe and a small bottle of a clear liquid. She filled the syringe with a full dose of the liquid and held it for Brad to see. "This is the Prophet's personal poison. I think our friend here has been using it in the service of our other strange-looking friend here." She pointed to Olivia, who was still coming to terms with a damaged windpipe.

Sleekman knew what was coming. His eyes were darting back and forth from Jeanie to Olivia. Jeanie contemplated the man. His mojo-sleek was deserting him—two-day-old beard going gray, dark circles of perspiration under the armpits of his soiled jacket, broken nose.

He began to mumble. Attempted to move. Jeanie reached down and planted the needle deep into his neck. A short hesitation. He began to shudder. Then he quivered, shivered, and started to shake. He was writhing in pain. He tried to scream. The duct tape kept him silent. It lasted a long time. Jeanie had measured the dose so he would not lose consciousness while he was in his death throes.

Brad was starting to feel uncomfortable. He and his sweetheart had just impassively rubbed out a helpless adversary. Jeanie sensed his weakness. "He was this woman's enforcer. Tortured and killed many. His reputation was legendary in the Prophecy. No witnesses. Same as always."

"No problem. I was just thinkin' that maybe we let him off too easily." Jeanie turned to Olivia. Brad stopped her. "Hold it. Don't shoot her in the neck. Make it look like a suicide/murder. Olivia kills him, then takes her own life. It's poetic."

Jeanie rubbed her eyes and studied the bottle of liquid. Brad checked his watch.

"We've gotta get a move on," he said.

Jeanie nodded, held up the bottle of liquid, and carefully loaded the syringe.

Olivia was hysterical, but too weak to move. She tried to scream, but her voice had still not recovered from Jeanie's elbow to the throat. She twisted and turned. Jeanie effortlessly immobilized her and gave her the shot of her life—not in the neck, but in the thigh.

She was convulsing on the couch as Jeanie and Brad carefully wiped down everything they had touched. Brad used a handkerchief to place the bottle and syringe in Olivia's hands. He ripped the tape off the bodies and stuffed it in Jeanie's backpack. They left the room and softly closed the door.

They exited the hotel separately. Jeanie took the stairs to the fourth floor and called the elevator. Brad took the stairs to the third floor, waited a few minutes, and called the elevator.

Out on the street, Brad hustled over to his bike. He took a slow drive down to the intersection, where he picked up Jeanie waiting on the corner. As they pulled away from the curb, the calm was shattered by sirens, searchlights, and cop cars careening down the street. They were just in the nick of time.

Back in Colindale, Brad packed up his gear. He would go first to tell Chuck how the evening had turned out. Then he would head back to France. It would be too dangerous to hang around. By now, the cops would have descriptions of everyone who could possibly have been involved in the Dorchester crime scene. Someone might also have noticed his Indian Arrow. Although he had disguised his license plate by changing a three to an eight and an eight to a three, that would probably not throw the limeys off for long. His main hope was for the crime scene to speak for itself and limit the investigation to the two occupants of the room.

Jeanie would stay long enough to cancel her room rental and then go on to somewhere far from London. Their *au revoirs* were heartfelt. At this moment, they could not imagine what the future held in store for them. In the short term, they would have to remain apart. Jeanie teared up. She said she would always remember the time they had together. Brad said it was the best time of his life. Their last kiss was a chaste affair, soft and sincere with all the passion and feeling stored within their hearts for the future. Then, Brad was off.

53: The Final Scoop

Brad and Chuck were anxious to get the meeting started. They had been waiting for days to find out how the story had played out. Chuck couldn't hold it back. "Okay, Gary, what's the scoop?"

Gary went straight for the coffee pot, poured a generous amount of the steaming liquid into his mug, and stirred before taking a sip. No sugar. His face was rested, no more dark circles under his eyes, and he was smiling.

"We've pieced everything together as much as we could," Gary said, "and here's what we think happened. The Prophecy was created by a San Francisco boy named Randall Linder, who renamed himself the Prophet. It was a politically protected cult that engaged in high-end prostitution and drug dealing. The so-called 'harem' was the whorehouse. The prostitutes were conscripted from the Prophecy's disciples."

Gary stopped and looked at his hands like he was thinking about making a momentous decision.

"The clientèle was handpicked. Each client was a confirmed member of the 'deep state,' including members and supporters of both parties. The criteria were that you had to be rich enough, powerful enough, and compromised enough. Everything was top secret. None of the women who entered the harem left it alive. So there was no problem of leaks from that side.

"The FBI under Olivia Townsend Ritter-Jones was charged with monitoring the client side of the operation and providing cover from the local authorities. Internally, the FBI contingent justified their involvement as undercover activities organized to penetrate the drug gangs and human traffickers. In fact, their job was to keep an eye on each client and make them aware they were being monitored by the FBI. From time to time, the FBI would make a drug bust to justify the existence of their involvement with the Prophecy and its activities."

Chuck was listening intently, but Brad already knew all this. His attention was distracted by two fat pigeons strutting around on the windowsill. Gary paid no attention.

"The secrecy of the operation was ultimately compromised by the clients. Even though precautions above and beyond FBI blackmail were taken. For example, every client was photographed while they philandered at the harem. At the end of the day, people just cannot keep their mouths shut. A little too much to drink, a tip for a favored friend or client, a matrimonial confession, no matter what it is, the word gets out. The Prophecy was already a subject of interest by the local authorities and in danger of losing its political protection when Jeanie made her escape.

"Jeanie's escape was important for two reasons. First of all, because she could testify to the Prophecy's illicit activities, and secondly, because she could identify Olivia Townsend Ritter-Jones as the 'capo' of the whole operation. They did everything they could to find her. Pulled out all the stops using all the levers at the disposal of the FBI. Finally, when it became clear they weren't going to catch her anytime soon, they decided it was in their best interest to terminate the Prophecy."

Gary was on a roll.

"It was an ingenious scheme. First, all the members of the Prophecy's hierarchy were entered into the US Marshals' Witness Protection Program and given new identities. Then they proceeded with a mass, drug-induced suicide for the other members. Those who weren't ready to commit suicide were slaughtered with knives and machetes. Finally, they burned the place down.

"Olivia Townsend Ritter-Jones was in charge of the investigation into the affair. She saw to it that the members of the Prophecy's hierarchy were certified as deceased. Since they were in the Witness Protection Program, their 'death' effectively made them newborn young adults with a past as white as the driven snow. There was only one loose end. One member of Ritter-Jones's team saw through the cock-and-bull story Ritter-Jones was promoting to her superiors and voiced his concerns. This member was Brandon Butler. Ritter-Jones put an end to Butler's objections by transferring him out of her team. That move also put an end to Butler's career at the FBI. I'll come back to Butler in a moment.

"Out of an 'abundance of caution,' as the bureaucratic argument to justify any and all self-serving decisions goes, the Witness Protected members of the Prophecy's former hierarchy were sent to Europe, where there was only a very small chance they would be recognized. In fact, they were sent to Europe to reproduce the same type of operation they had with the Prophecy. The Prophet was one of them. His Witness Protection name was James Mac-Donald. He's the guy who was living in the apartment on Greenhill in Hampstead. He is also the one who called himself Lazarus, drove an E-Type Jag, and lived in Louveciennes."

Brad started paying attention. This was starting to get

interesting. Gary rambled on.

"Language, legal, and cultural obstacles made it difficult to create a new 'Prophecy' from zero, so Randall/James/The Prophet/Lazarus got the idea of taking over a going concern and transforming it. That's where the Children of God comes in.

"Meanwhile, back in the States, Olivia Townsend Ritter-Jones and her FBI group needed a big success to justify their continued existence and budget. They decided domestic terrorism would be the most effective. Unfortunately, there were no new known active domestic terrorist groups around. No problem! They decided to create one."

Chuck was incredulous. "You mean the FBI created a terrorist group just to increase their budget?"

"To increase their budget and to justify their existence. Their unit was a costly affair, and outside of the small drug busts I mentioned before, they did not have much to show for it. Anyway, the Army for World Peace was their vehicle. Its avowed aim was just what the name implied: world peace. It was a motley crew of tree-hugging, pot-smoking, Jesus-loving, peace-and-love social misfits. Their meetings were an excuse to complain about the world, feel morally superior, do some drugs, and possibly hook up with a member of the opposite sex. Irritating organisms they were, but they were farther from terrorism than Hitler was from a Nobel Peace Prize.

"The FBI decided to change that. They infiltrated the movement. They brought money and organization and ideas. The ideas involved armed revolution of one form or another. Benjamin, his real name, was the head of the Army for World Peace. Of course, he opposed violence of any kind. He argued, logically, that violence was contrary to peace."

Chuck chirped in, "That Benjamin was a real shitbird."

"Yeah, by now, the infiltrated FBI agents were so numerous in 'the army' that they began to dominate the discussions and the votes. Decisions were made for a series of violent attacks on various and sundry US military installations. The problem was that the only volunteers participating in the attacks were the infiltrated FBI agents. To convince Benjamin to cooperate and get the other members to participate in the attacks, the FBI trumped up some charges against him and called him in for questioning. He could see the writing on the wall and skipped out of town and out of the country. He landed at the Children of God in Paris. Unfortunately for him, the Prophet—for now, let's simplify everything and call him the Prophet—found out who he was and transmitted the info to his accomplices back in California.

"This led to a new, more ingenious plan. The Prophet, now known as Lazarus, had his men infiltrate the Children of God in Paris and seize power. He then elevated Benjamin to the leadership of the Paris compound of the Children of God. The drug business had put Lazarus in contact with a group of terrorists anxious to change the world. Following orders from Olivia Townsend Ritter-Jones and the FBI, the Prophet/Lazarus, used Benjamin's status as a fugitive from the US to blackmail him into negotiating a deal with the terrorists to undertake an attack on the French state during the election period. Benjamin's fugitive status gave him credibility with the terrorists. The Children of God would finance the operation, and the terrorists would supply the manpower.

"Now, wait till you hear this. The plan was for the FBI to provide the critical information to foil the plot at the last minute and arrest the terrorists. The Bureau would be heralded as the saviors of French democracy. The investigation would reveal Benjamin was the only member of the Children of God involved in the plot. So the Children of God would remain a going concern controlled by Lazarus still dealing in drugs, prostitution, and human trafficking. Benjamin would be condemned as a violent terrorist. The FBI would use this as proof the schemes dreamed up by the infiltrated FBI agents in the Army for World Peace in the US were credible threats. The FBI would then obtain the required warrants, swoop in, and arrest all the members of the Army for World Peace. It would be a bonanza for the FBI and Ritter-Jones's group. They would reap the rewards of a spectacular double success, the foiled attack in France and the foiled attack in the US, and they would still have their lucrative vice business on the side. As you know, it worked."

Chuck's mouth was agape and his eyes were open wide. "That is more Machiavellian than Machiavelli himself. What kind of a twisted mind could cook up something like that? Who would even want to?"

Gary brushed off the questions. "Now back to Butler. With his career in the FBI destroyed, Butler joined the DEA and ended up in France. There's nothing official about how he ended up here just when Olivia Townsend Ritter-Jones and her flunkies were preparing their new scheme, but we think it was not accidental. He had suspicions, proof, and a bone to pick with Townsend Ritter-Jones. As the new agency on the block, the DEA needed credibility. What a coup it would be for the DEA to catch the FBI red-handed under the nose of the CIA!"

Gary spread his arms toward Brad and Chuck.

"Unfortunately for Butler and his great expectations, he ran into a CIA brick wall in Paris, thanks to you guys. Thanks to Marilyn, as well. Marilyn was Townsend Ritter-Jones's mole here in the embassy. She was keeping Olivia Townsend Ritter-Jones up to date on everything she could find out. I already told you I had been suspicious of Marilyn and her loyalty for a long time.

Consequently, I kept anything important secret from her and fed her as much disinformation as possible. It looks like Marilyn fell head over heels for Butler and, thinking she was helping him, actually was feeding him the same disinformation I was letting her feed Townsend Ritter-Jones. FYI, Marilyn is back in the US in the process of being prosecuted.

"Butler did finally catch a break, though. The address in Hampstead that nobody thought was important turned out to be the fatal flaw in Townsend Ritter-Jones's scheme. I found it so unimportant that I used it to throw Butler off the trail. Butler took the bait and used his contacts with some buddies in the US Marshals to expose Townsend Ritter-Jones's use of the Witness Protection Program to cover her tracks.

"Rather than use the information to bring Olivia Townsend Ritter-Jones and her FBI gang to justice, it looks like he used it to blackmail her. In the dated report he left, he details everything. But then he says if this report is being read by anyone, it means he has been assassinated. He names Olivia Townsend Ritter-Jones as the assassin. We interpreted that to mean if his blackmail did not work out, his revenge would be this report."

Brad relaxed and lit up another Gitane. He had a good idea of where this was going. So did Chuck. Gary rattled on.

"Here's how everything turned out. Lazarus was found in the Hampstead apartment, dead from an overdose. Brandon and the man known to us as Joseph were found in Brandon's room at the Dorchester Hotel, dead from an overdose. Olivia Townsend Ritter-Jones and an American known to us as an enforcer for the Mafia were found dead in Olivia Townsend Ritter-Jones's Dorchester Hotel room, dead from an overdose. Michael Bishop, the man known to us as the renter of the house in Louveciennes, was found on a footpath in Hampstead, dead from an overdose."

Chuck interrupted. "When did all these deaths occur?"

"They all occurred on the same day: May 23. We don't know the exact chronology, just that the Brits discovered the bodies in Olivia Townsend Ritter-Jones's hotel room after they were called to the Dorchester to investigate the bodies found in Brandon's room. Room service stumbled on the bodies when they came up to deliver something Brandon had ordered before he left the Vesper Bar."

Brad breathed a sigh of relief on that piece of information. He had been worried the cops he saw when leaving the Dorchester were called because of what he and Jeanie had done in Townsend Ritter-Jones's room. Made it less likely he and Jeanie could be fingered by anybody. To reassure himself about the Hampstead high jinks, he had to ask, "What about Lazarus's apartment and Michael Bishop?"

"Bishop's body was discovered by a jogger early on the morning of the 24th. After I found out about Brandon, Olivia Townsend Ritter-Jones, and the others, I put two and two together and sent somebody around to the apartment in Hampstead the next day."

Brad stubbed out his Gitane in the ashtray and brushed an imaginary fleck of tobacco off his bottom lip. He knew about some of the deaths but was curious about the others. "Who was doing all this killing?"

"We don't really know. Our best guess is that it was the 'cult stalker,' the same person who was systematically rubbing out the former members of the Prophecy in Paris. Same modus operandi, a violent drug cocktail. There were signs of a struggle in all the deaths."

Brad was dubious. "Sounds like a lot of activity for one single person in one single day."

"Yeah, it does. Maybe it was more than one cult stalker. Maybe there were a couple of them. I suspected Jeanie for a while."

Brad kept sipping his coffee and didn't react. That was coming from left field. Was Gary trying to ambush him? He realized it was just a fishing technique when Gary continued.

"That French cop you call Chef has contacted me twice over the last week about Jeanie. He's a crafty old fox. Smells a rat. I told him she was deceased, the body repatriated to the family in the US. Be careful of him. I think he might suspect something. He still wants to keep in contact with you. And, oh yeah, where were you last week? I tried to get in touch as well."

Brad knew Gary would be suspicious, but there was no way he could let Gary know what had gone down in London. Gary would have to report it, and he, Jeanie, and Chuck would be prosecuted. There was no way even Gary could save them. Knowing this, Brad had already prepared the answer to this question. "Had a gig at a private party in Millau." Time to change the subject. "So, what's gonna happen with all this, Gary?"

"Benjamin's still claiming political asylum, but has agreed to turn state's evidence. His testimony, Brandon's testimony and documentary proof, your pictures and recordings, along with other evidence coming out in the wash, have triggered a massive investigation of the FBI's activities in California. Some of the suspects implicated in the affair have already come to the table. Looks like they are going to clean house. At the least, the foot soldiers will get slaughtered. We doubt the higher-ups will be held accountable. At the end of the day, Olivia Townsend Ritter-Jones and Lazarus/the Prophet are already dead, anyway."

Brad couldn't argue with that. Quite a story! It wasn't pretty, but it had a happy ending. Except for one thing.

THE AMERICAN EXPRESS

The American Express was crowded. This was tourist season, and the backpackers were like locusts on a wheat field.

Brad waited patiently for his turn. A snappy young Frenchman with a clipped British accent asked for his passport. Verified the match. Went into pigeonhole "J" and came back with a postcard in different shades of green.

Brad scooped it up and slipped off to the side.

The one line on the card made him the happiest man in the world.

Ireland is beautiful. You will love it. Love, B.

The following is an excerpt from *Agents Scorned*, the sequel to *Cult Stalker* by Ephraim Clark, also available from Glass Spider Publishing.

Prologue

PARIS, JULY 3, 1974

Mario Yrigoyen fingers the smooth vanilla folders containing photos and certified copies of documents filed with the legal authorities on the island of Jersey. This folder is his last chance. It is all that is standing between him and a painful death.

His mouth is dry. His stomach is churning. His shirt is soaking wet from the sweat dripping from his armpits. He wonders if anyone notices. Looks around.

The Rincon Argentino Café is half empty. It's the only place in Paris that serves genuine Argentine *mate*. Two gangbangers slouched over a *vino tinto* in the corner are giving him the evil eye. His bodyguards know these guys. They've been hanging around Mario's apartment building for the last week. They're biding their time, waiting for the order to make their move.

The waiter arrives with a pot of hot water and a silver encrusted, wooden gourd. Mario lifts the calabash to his nostrils and breathes in the heady aroma of *mate* mixed with honey and ginger.

The gangbangers push back their chairs and get to their feet. Mario tenses. The four bodyguards stand. The gangbangers smirk out some kind of a taunt and swagger out onto the street. The bodyguards sit down and start to argue.

It's not a false alert. It's a message. Makes his decision so much easier. Mario has always known that once he makes his move, he might actually find himself closer to a premature death than he was before. The message the gangbangers are delivering has made it crystal clear. He cannot get any closer to death than he is now.

Mario reaches into his briefcase and extracts a small metal cylinder—a *bombilla*. It serves as a straw and a filter. Tipping the calabash forward, he creates a well in the *mate* and inserts the *bombilla*. Normally, the *mate* would be shared around in a kind of social ceremony. That won't happen today. Today, Mario is all alone.

He reexamines the photos and documents in the folders as he sips. They contain the details of secret, private bank accounts held on the island of Jersey by influential bureaucrats and politicians in South America and the United States.

His attention focuses on Bellweather, SA, a company domiciled in Jersey with a capital of one thousand bearer shares with a face value of one U.S. dollar each. It has an account containing over one hundred million U.S. dollars. This investment fund is the default account for José Lopez Rega's "golden parachute."

Mario knows Jersey well. It is a bailiwick of the British crown, a free-wheeling offshore financial center offering a rare combination of political stability, legal security, and personal anonymity on a conveniently located island right off the coast of Normandy.

Mario had anticipated his own impending downfall. Perón was old and ill. His days were numbered. As Perón's right-hand-man, Mario was top-dog in the ruling hierarchy. He represented Perón's authority and wielded his power accordingly, often to the detriment of Rega's personal agenda. There was no doubt in his mind. Perón's death would extinguish Mario's power base. Rega, Isabel's right-hand-man, would become the new, uncontested top-dog. In the context of the Argentine dog-eat-dog political arena, Mario's position of power would be a thing of the past and he would become the main course of Rega's next meal. It's not personal. Rega doesn't do "personal." It's all about power.

Mario doesn't do "personal" either. It's all about saving his skin. He neglected to deliver the Bellweather shares to Rega. Without those shares, Rega can't access the money. Mario smiles as he sips. So far, Rega doesn't seem to have realized this.

He savors the last few drops of his *mate*. He catches his reflection in the mirror and smooths back his dark hair. His mind is made up. It's time to act. Rega has almost finished consolidating his power in Buenos Aires. His next move will be to purge the embassies. Mario knows he's dude number one on that list. He's also dude number one on the list of the foreign bureaucrats and politicians he's dealt with through their accounts in Jersey. Out of power and on the run, he knows too much and threatens their anonymity.

He's already contacted the Americans with the information that should take him off their target list. Now his immediate concern is the neutralization of the very real, mortal threat of Rega's vengeance. His program to prolong his biological life beyond his impending political death is simple, but therein lies its ultimate strength. He will inform Rega he is holding the bearer shares in escrow. He shivers with satisfaction knowing that Rega's fury will be boundless when he realizes that access to his one hundred million U.S. dollars is contingent on Mario Yrigoyen's continued good health.

In a burst of perverse pleasure, Mario imagines José Lopez Rega, impotent and livid, stomping around, cursing and swearing, pounding his frustration on the table. The image dies quickly. He knows his life will be hanging by a fragile thread, a wager on Rega's greed, the wager that one hundred million dollars in the Bellweather investment account will be enough for Rega to keep him alive. Then only the one thousand bearer shares will remain standing between him and oblivion.

He signals the waiter. His bodyguards are still arguing. The old bodyguard *jefe*—chief—bangs his fist on the table, and two of them slink outside with the gangbangers.

That's it. Half of his protection team just defected to the enemy. The other half is conflicted, watching him, searching for signs of weakness. *Jefe*'s been around the block a few times in his forty-year career. He's wondering if it's time to change sides.

Mario feels the panic. His heart is pounding. His hands are trembling. His breath is coming in short gasps. He calls up his willpower. Takes a deep breath. Doesn't let himself hyperventilate. All his instincts are telling him to run for his life. His brain tells him this is not the time to surrender to his instincts. He *is* going to run for his life, but first, he has to make sure he has a good head start.

He signals his two remaining bodyguards to sit tight. He goes to the bar and asks for the telephone and a long-distance line. He makes one call—to Rega. Leaves a message. Hangs up the phone. Closes his eyes. He's relieved. The game is on. Rega has been notified.

Mario heads for the men's room. It has a window that opens onto a courtyard with access to a building on another street. He takes a leak, washes his hands, and slicks back his hair.

Someone starts pounding on the door. He jumps from the window into the courtyard and starts to run.

Chapter 1

Greta Papachristou was the bereaved widow of the late Georges Papachristou, vice president of the Crédit Lyonnais and undercover CIA agent. She was a handsome woman, mid-fifties, a perfectly coiffed brunette greying at the temples. Her eyes were swollen and her nose was red. She had been crying.

Brad felt slightly embarrassed to be there under the circumstances. Her husband had just been buried after committing suicide. The suicide was as unpredictable as the way he did it. He threw himself from the penthouse terrace at a cocktail party organized by the Argentine embassy. Landed on his face eight stories down.

Brad was there representing Latorre Legal on behalf of the embassy. Charles "Chuck" Hall, the managing director of Latorre Legal, had just arrived and was doing the talking. Brad took advantage to explore the premises.

Security was heavy. Too heavy as far as he was concerned. There were two men stationed at the entrance to the apartment, two more in the living room, and two on the terrace. Brad wondered who had hired them. They were aggressive and arrogant. Rubbed him the wrong way. They behaved more like they owned the place. Greta Papachristou kept casting furtive glances in the direction of the head honcho every time she spoke.

Brad sidled over for a closer look. The crack of a slap and a hail of piercing screams from the main hallway stopped him in his tracks. The biggest guard, the one with the scarred face and flat nose, was dragging a little kid six or seven years old by the arm.

"How you get in here, *cabronito* (little bastard)?" The accent was Spanish. The vocabulary was South American.

"*Mon grand-père, mon grand-père* (my grandfather, my grandfather)!" The little kid was terrified, and he was hurting.

The big guard drew back for another slap. Brad grabbed his arm and threw him against the wall. "Leave the kid alone."

The kid scampered away. The guard went for his baton. Brad went for the guard.

The head honcho grabbed the guard. Pointed to the kid. "Who is this?" The accent was Spanish.

Greta Papachristou cuddled the boy. "He is our concierge's grandson. He's looking for his grandfather."

"Shouldn't be here. How did he get in?"

"Through the service stairway, probably."

Head honcho glared at Brad. Stabbed the air with his fat forefinger. "*Never, ever* interfere with my men, *gringo*."

Brad was pumping adrenaline. He bit it back and smiled. Softspoken. Looked him in the eye—cocked and ready. "Your men should watch the stairway, not bully little kids." It was a challenge. Dead silence—Mississippi one, Mississippi two, Mississippi three.

Head honcho blinked. He turned to his men in the hallway. "*La pinche escalera de servicio, cabrones. Que pasa?* (The goddamn service stairway, shitheads. What's going on?)"

Greta Papachristou smiled at Brad. She took the boy's hand and led him out to the landing. "Your grandfather is downstairs." Back in the room, she seemed relieved and took up her conversation with Chuck as if nothing had happened.

Brad ignored the menacing looks from the bodyguards and continued his search of the living room. Photos galore. Georges with athletes. Georges with starlets. Georges with celebrities. Mostly Georges with politicians.

Georges had a picture with every politician Brad had ever seen or heard of. He seemed to have been especially friendly with Juan Perón and a tall, balding gentleman with thick, shaggy eyebrows and a crooked, slapstick smile. In fact, they looked like a trio. There they were, in picture after picture, the three of them together, dining, drinking, laughing, singing. Brad wondered where Greta was when all the photos were taken. She was not in any of them.

Chuck was closing down the visit. "Mrs. Papachristou, it was a pleasure to meet you. If I can do anything, anything at all, please do contact me."

Greta Papachristou was expressionless. She was running on autopilot. "Thank you so much for coming by, and thank my friends at the embassy for sending you."

Brad said his goodbyes and they were out of there. Out on the street, Brad was uncharacteristically melancholy. "It's really sad. She's all alone. Her only family is her son and his family. They live a busy life on the corporate fast track in New York. They won't have much time for her. Her friends are all spouses of her husband's colleagues and clients. With him gone, it won't be long before they drift away. She's a looker, and three will be a crowd as far as the wives of any of their acquaintances are concerned. She's gonna be a lonely little lady."

"Yep. She was devoted to her husband. She told me she can't

understand why he would take his own life. Doesn't believe he did. She's in shock. She even seemed afraid. That's about it. How about you? What's your take?"

"Same conclusion as you. One thing did grab me. There was no physical evidence of her existence in the apartment. The apartment was decorated like a man cave. You know, the whole room was crammed with photos of her husband at work and at play. She's not even in one single photo."

Chuck nodded. "Yeah, she said she spent a lot of time in London."

"Those gangbangers she hired as bodyguards are another big question mark. They behaved like they own the place."

"Yeah. I don't think she approves of them. It looked like she was hoping you'd clean that guy's clock."

"Chickenshit bully, beating up on a little kid."

Chuck's pink Thunderbird parked on the street was drawing a group of admirers. One of them yelled, "*Super caisse* (super wheels)."

Chuck grinned like a goose. *"Merci beaucoup."*

Chuck was romantically attached to his set of wheels. Only twenty thousand 1957 T-Birds were ever made, and only ten were pink. He got it for a song from an embassy hotshot who fell in love, got married, and needed a bigger, cheaper car. It was a definite attention-getter.

Brad's warning broke the spell. "Somebody's in the car."

"Shit. I forgot to lock it."

Chuck slipped to the left onto the street. Brad stayed to the right on the sidewalk. Cautious approach. The admirers felt the tension and began melting away.

Brad could make out the head and shoulders of a man through the tinted window. It was a casually dressed, elderly man with a full head of silver hair. He was sitting in the passenger seat staring off into space.

Brad came level with the door. Jerked it open. Chuck jerked open the driver's door. The man paid no attention as he climbed out of the car. He shook Brad's hand, said, *"Au revoir,"* and wandered off down the street. Brad watched him till he turned the corner. Chuck hadn't moved. He was still holding the door handle.

They were both puzzled. Checked out the car. Nothing damaged. Nothing out of place. Just a brown A4 envelope on the floorboard, and it was filled with pictures.

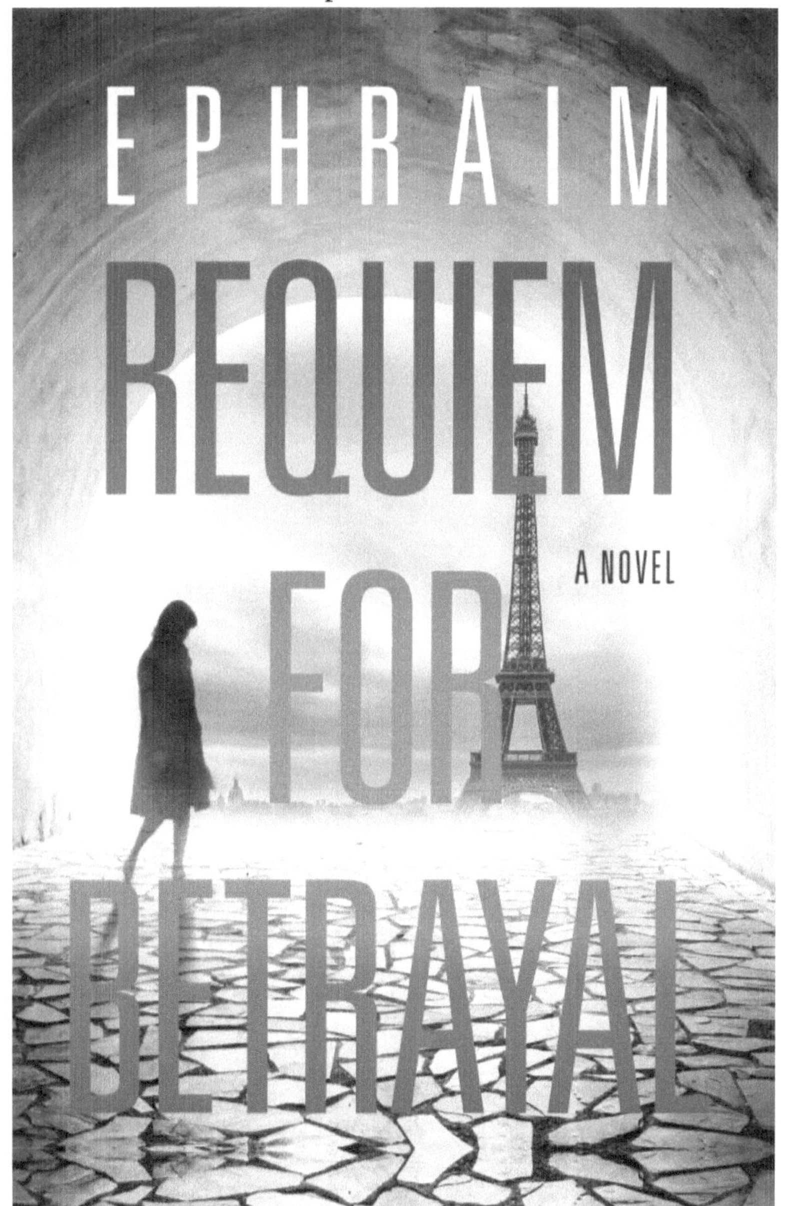
EPHRAIM
REQUIEM
FOR
BETRAYAL
A NOVEL